Also by Mia Sheridan

AVAILABLE FROM BLOOM BOOKS

Travis

Kyland

Stinger

Grayson's Vow

Becoming Calder

Finding Eden

Falling for Gage

Unwanted

MIA SHERIDAN

Bloom books

Published by Bloom Books, an imprint of Sourcebooks
P.O. Box 4410, Naperville, Illinois 60567-4410
(630) 961-3900
sourcebooks.com

Originally self-published in 2019 by Mia Sheridan.

Printed and bound in Canada.
MBP 10 9 8 7 6 5 4 3 2 1

To those of you who have been saved by books, in big ways and in small.

PROLOGUE

Will you die today? Maybe tomorrow?

The question wove through Jak's mind, deep and slow, like he was hearing it from under a deep pool of water. *Will you die today?* The echo of the words the man had yelled seconds ago made a trickle of fear move down Jak's spine, but everything was…dreamy, not…real. He couldn't see. He could hardly hear. His head felt foggy and…strange.

Am I dreaming?

Was he trapped inside a nightmare? Would Baka shake him awake any minute, telling him to keep it quiet with her sharp voice and soft eyes? The last thing he remembered was falling asleep in his own bed and then…*this.*

He wrapped his arms around himself, his teeth making clicking sounds as they chattered together.

No, not a dream. Dreams are never this cold.

All of a sudden, something was pulled from his face, and he let out a short yell as he realized something had been covering his head. He blinked into the darkness, starlight catching his gaze, flecks of light in a dark-blue sky. The circle moon shined yellow, big and round and bright.

He turned his head around, his breath coming from his lips in clouds of white. *Snow.* Snow everywhere. Trees. And—he cried out, tripping back from the edge of what he now saw was a cliff right in front of him. His backside hit the snow, his bare hands sinking into the freezing powder almost up to his elbows.

His heartbeat went fast, the fog in his head moving away as fear raced through his body.

"Get up."

Jak's head turned, and he stared at a tall man behind him, his face hidden in the shadows of his hooded coat. "Get up," he repeated, only now it was a low growl. Jak pulled himself to his feet as fast as he could, catching movement to his left. Now that his eyes could see in the darkness, he noticed that there were three other boys standing at the edge of the cliff, only a few steps from each other. Two dark-haired boys, one small with eyes too big for his face, filled with confusion and fear, one tall and skinny, and a blond boy, who was shaking even worse than Jak was.

Why? Who? What is this? Where's Baka?

"Will you die today?" the man repeated from behind them. "Maybe tomorrow? Next week? Many years from now a lauded warrior? *Celebrated?*" Jak didn't know all those words, didn't know what the man was talking about, and when he started to turn his head, the man stopped him with a mean-sounding "face forward." His shivering got *more*, he was so scared, and he could barely stand up, his thoughts rolling all over each other, but slowly, too slowly. He couldn't think. *Why is my head all funny?*

"You will die. Or you will survive. But that is up to you.

2

It will all depend on your will to live." The man suddenly placed his gloved hands on the side of the blond's head and leaned in close, the darkest of the shadows. "Do you have a will to survive? To fight for your life? Tooth and nail? Heart and soul?"

The blond nodded his head in a jerky way. "Y-yes," he said, but tears were sliding down his cheeks, and a sob came after the word. Jak's hands fisted. He was scared, so scared, but he wanted to *do* something. Make this *stop*. He looked at the big-eyed boy next to him, and that boy was staring at Jak's clenched fists. He looked up, meeting Jak's eyes for a second before looking away.

The bad man let go of the crying blond's face. "Good." Jak heard snow crunching under the man's feet as he stepped farther back behind them. "Now, in a minute, I'll tell you what is happening. After that, the only rule is to survive." He paused. "Survive or die."

What does he mean? What's going to happen? A sudden cloud of white filled the air in front of Jak's face as he let out a fear-filled breath. The blond sobbed again, and the dark-haired boy with the big eyes tilted on his feet, his hand going into the pocket of his coat. Jak looked away quickly, so he wouldn't bring the man's eyes to whatever the small boy to his left was reaching for.

He felt a tap on his hand, and the boy slipped something hard and cold into his palm. Jak took it, dropping it into his pocket fast. His heart was thumping so hard it felt like it might jump right from his chest, but that feeling of being underwater stayed. His mind grabbed for something to hold his thoughts still.

I can't think. I can't think. Why can't I think? His baka had told him he was a "smart monkey too big for little britches,"

3

and she had said it with a frown on her face but in the way that made him think she was happy with him anyway. But he didn't feel smart now. He felt…scared out of his mind.

Jak gave a quick look over the cliff and saw that even though it wasn't a straight drop, it was far down to the bottom. Really, really far down. He didn't know how to describe it in numbers, but he was smart enough to know that if he jumped to get away, he would die. *The only rule is to survive. Or die.*

Why? Why why why? This can't be real. This can't be real.

A cracking sound exploded around them, making Jak cry out in shock and terror. But before he could question where the noise was coming from, he felt a gust of cold air, and then the ground started to move. *Slide.* The snow went out from under his feet, and he slid forward, grabbing at the empty air for something to hold on to. But there was nothing.

He heard the bad man yell something, and then he yelled too, along with the screams of the other boys as they all slid over the edge in an explosion of white powder.

His thoughts were still slow. *Everything* was slow…but then he was *awake* suddenly. He could hear every fast beat of his heart. He could feel the stinging of the wind as it hit his face, and he could smell something *green* that he couldn't name any better than that.

Someone grabbed his hand. The small boy next to him. Their eyes met for one quick second, the dark-haired boy's gaze filled with the same fear that must be in his own. With a grunt of strength, he turned his body as the world dropped out from under them, putting his hand on the other boy's wrist and holding on tight so they were falling together.

They whirled and tumbled and hit something solid—a

4

piece of ground—with a loud grunt and a short scream. Pain exploded through Jak's body. He felt the other boy's hold loosen, so he gripped harder, and they kept going down, down, still holding on to each other.

Tumble, roll, fall, hit. *Pain.*

So *fast.* They were flying so fast. He couldn't catch hold of anything, his empty hand reaching, grabbing, slipping.

Smack. They both yelled as they landed on a small ledge, immediately flipping off, their empty hands shooting out and catching hold of the edge.

Do you have a will to survive?

Yes!

We can do this. We can do this.

They stared, tears streaking down the smaller boy's cheeks, their breath coming out in sharp pants. The other two boys raced past them, their screams echoing into the dark nothingness below.

Jak's lungs hurt with every breath, and his body screamed in pain. Terror grabbed him. All his feelings were suddenly *real. He* felt real, not underwater anymore, not half-asleep, and it was an awful, terrifying wake-up.

Still gripping the other boy's hand, he raised them both, grabbing the side of the ledge so they were each holding on with both hands. In a quick glance, he saw that the ledge was too small for two boys, but there was a skinny tree root next to it that looked like it might lead to stronger ground. A chance. A small, small chance.

From the low light of the moon, Jak saw that the boy's large eyes were starting to close, blood streamed from his nose, his face was bruised and bloody, and his head was rolling on his neck like he might fall asleep. His arms were shaking, his fingertips dark with holding on. *Oh God.*

Don't use the Lord's name in vain. Where you hear that expression? That fat, stinky mailman?

His baka's voice in his head gave him a small burst of strength, and he gripped tighter, knowing he could pull himself up if he tried. The ledge, though, was only big enough for one. The boy's half-closed eyes met his, his mouth opening a little, blood trailing.

He was about to let go.

If Jak was going to pull himself up on the ledge and slither along the root like a snake, the way he did in the backyard at home where he was king of the forest—the woods area that he played in most of the day because his baka believed that children shouldn't be *bothering, always bothering*—he'd have to do it now. Or…he could save the other boy and take his own chances with the fall.

These thoughts streaked through his brain quickly, and all at once, his body got a message he didn't know he'd sent as he moved his hands over and grabbed the other boy around his waist just as his hands slipped and he cried out.

"Climb up me," he grunted, using the last of his strength to keep them both from falling. "Now!" he ordered. With a sharp cry, the boy, much lighter than Jak, grabbed at the ledge again, putting a foot on Jak's shoulder as Jak removed one hand and used it to push the boy up onto that tiny piece of solid ground.

Jak's other hand slipped. "Live!" Jak shouted, demanding it with the last breath in his lungs as he rushed toward the unknown below.

CHAPTER ONE

Present Day

Deputy Paul Brighton gripped the steering wheel of his patrol car. *Christ*, his hands were still shaking. He turned on the wipers as snow flew at the windshield, creating a field of whirling white. He squinted, barely able to see the road in front of him. "Just what I need," he muttered, trying to slow his racing heart. He'd never *seen* a crime scene like that, though there'd been a similar one in town just the week before. What kind of psycho went around committing murders with a bow and arrows? He'd heard about the first one—all the gory details, as a matter of fact—but the sheriff had answered that call, and now Deputy Brighton knew that hearing about something and seeing it up close and personal were two very different experiences. The picture of the victim from the scene he'd just left appeared in his mind, and he grimaced. The victim had been—*fuck*—he'd been nailed to the wall by an arrow, for Christ's sake, his blood spreading across the floor like—

Deputy Brighton slammed on his brakes and turned sharply as a man, larger than life, rose up out of nowhere, looming in front of his windshield. His tires slid on the icy ground, and for a moment he thought he'd lose control of the vehicle. But he managed to hold on, correcting his slide, and the SUV skidded to a shuddery halt on the side of the road. Deputy Brighton's breath came sharply. *Who the fuck was that?* He'd looked like a goddamned…*caveman.* He shook his head to attempt to set things straight in his brain.

He quickly opened the door, the ding ringing out into the silent, snowy landscape, the only other sound the low hum of the engine. Deputy Brighton took cover on the side of the vehicle, removing his gun from the holster for the first time in his career.

"Show your hands!" he called into the frigid onslaught, using his forearm to shield his eyes as he looked cautiously over the hood. He saw the man's shape first—huge, muscular. "Show your hands!" he said again, his voice wavering.

The man stepped forward, his hands raised, details coming into focus. His legs were clad in denim, but the rest of him was covered entirely in…animal fur from his boots to his jacket to the hat on his head, pulled low so his eyes were partially covered. *Who the hell is he?* What *the hell is he?* "Get down on your knees!" he yelled.

The man paused as though considering but then did as he was told, his hands still raised. Deputy Brighton saw that his eyes had narrowed. Snow clung to his dark-bearded jaw, and thick, unruly hair grazed his chin. The man watched him, waiting, his gaze moving between the gun and his face. *He's a savage.* The thought ran through Deputy Brighton's mind, the gun shaking in his grip as he stepped from the cover of the car. When he moved forward, he noticed the final detail about the man.

He had a bow and arrows slung over his shoulder.

CHAPTER TWO

"Harper, there you are." Keri Simpkins slid a pencil behind her ear as she stood from her desk, walking quickly to Harper, who was hanging her parka on a hook by the door. "Did you hear the news?"

"News?" Harper rubbed her hands together, attempting to warm them as Keri glanced behind her toward the back of the small county jail.

Keri bobbed her head. "Mm-hmm. That murder the town's been buzzing about? There's been another one. And"—she lowered her voice—"they have a suspect."

Harper's heart constricted. "*Another* murder?" She frowned, the surprise of the news prickling her skin. *Here? In Helena Springs?* And a suspect?

"Mm-hmm. And get this, the suspect is some kind of wild man."

"Wild man? What do you mean, *wild man*?" And why in the world had *she* been summoned to the station?

Keri glanced toward the back again, and when she

spoke, her voice was rushed. "Like the guy's never lived in civilization before. Like a…like a caveman. Wait until you see—" Keri's words cut off abruptly as footsteps sounded, and a second after that, Dwayne Walbeck, Helena Springs's sheriff, emerged from around the corner, tipping his chin as he spotted Harper.

"Harper. Thanks for coming."

"No problem, Dwayne." Harper glanced at Keri quickly, but she had already turned away toward her desk. *Wild man?* Harper turned her attention back to Dwayne. "What's going on?"

Dwayne looked to where Keri had taken a seat at her reception desk, her head tilted in a way that let Harper know she was hanging on every word. Despite Harper's current confusion—and the trickle of dread moving down her spine knowing that something awful had happened to someone in her small town—a smile teased at her lips. Keri was as sweet as she was nosy, and everyone in a twenty-mile radius knew exactly where to go if they wanted to find out the latest gossip. It was a wonder Dwayne kept her around. Although normally, her loose lips weren't too much of an issue—generally, the most newsworthy thing coming out of the station was an occasional drunk and disorderly.

"Keri, hold my calls, will you?" Dwayne shot over his shoulder.

"No problem, Dwayne," she sang.

Dwayne placed his hand on Harper's shoulder as he led her to the back of the station where his office was located, along with two holding cells and a small interview room that mostly served as a break area for Dwayne, Keri, and the two deputies, Paul Brighton and Roger Green.

"Dwayne, what in the world is going on?" Harper asked

once they'd entered the interview/break room and he'd closed the door.

Dwayne picked up a remote and turned on a monitor hanging on the wall to Harper's left. She turned toward the screen. It showed one of the two holding cells, and a man was sitting on the bench attached to the wall, staring straight ahead.

Harper tilted her head, moving closer, her gaze zeroing in on the man. He was wearing regular blue jeans, stretched taut over muscular thighs, but his jacket was anything but usual. Was it made of...animal fur? Patched together in a way that made it look hand...sewn. She couldn't make out the details of the jacket's specific construction from the picture on the screen, so she didn't even know if that was the right word. In any case, his boots—*footwear*—were made of the same pieced-together animal skins and went halfway up his calves. He suddenly looked up, his eyes moving directly to the screen as though he knew she was there—or at least knew a camera watched him—and Harper took a step back like he really could see her and she should be embarrassed for staring at him the way she was.

"Recognize him?"

She shook her head, taking in his face still aimed directly at her. Straight brown hair framed it, choppy in a way that made her think he'd cut it with some sort of dull cutting tool. His jaw was shadowed by facial hair somewhere between heavy stubble and a short beard, and despite his overall unusual appearance, she could see that he was handsome, albeit in a way that made her wonder if he bathed.

And if so, where? In an icy stream? The picture her mind conjured wasn't unpleasant, and ashamed of herself, she pushed the image aside.

"You sure you never ran across that guy either on a guided tour or when you were out by yourself?"

No, I'd remember him. Harper shook her head again.

"He might've been wearing something less conspicuous. Especially if it was summer."

Like what? A loincloth? Somehow, she didn't think that would be any less conspicuous. "I'm sure. Who is he, Dwayne?"

Dwayne blew out a breath, shutting off the monitor. Harper felt a momentary twinge of loss that was totally bizarre. But truthfully, she wanted to study the man. She wanted to be left alone in this room and watch him on that camera for a little while just to see what he would do. *As if he's some kind of alien life and not a human being? What's wrong with you, Harper?*

"Says his name is Lucas. That's it. No last name. Just Lucas."

"I don't get it."

Dwayne rubbed at his eye, and Harper suddenly realized how tired he looked. "I don't either yet." He leaned on the edge of the table. "I suppose Keri mentioned there's been another murder?"

"Yeah. Can you tell me who?" She'd kept her mind from drifting to the question that made her stomach clench because she knew that whoever it was, she'd probably either know them or know them *well*. With a population of two thousand residents, Helena Springs was too small for that not to be the case.

"A man by the name of Isaac Driscoll, who lived in a cabin about twenty miles south of town."

She let out a slow breath. She didn't know that name. But...*south?* There was *nothing* south except plains, mountains, rivers, and valleys, miles and miles of unforgiving wilderness. Snow- and ice-covered unforgiving wilderness at the moment. Nothing particularly habitable...or so she'd thought.

Dwayne continued. "The victim was somehow able to reach his cell phone and dial 9-1-1. He didn't speak, but a cell tower helped pinpoint his location, and he died before Paul could get there. The old cell tower used to get us to within a thousand feet, but the new system gets us to within thirty. Nice piece of technology. Anyway, Paul thought it was probably the usual, a lost hiker or something of that nature." The lines around his eyes tightened for a moment. He looked concerned that those words would hit her in a personal way, and he was right.

But she shook off the feeling and focused on the situation at hand. *A hiker?* Anyone hiking out in that direction this time of year would have to have a few screws loose. Or...be very lost. The memory rose again, and with more effort, she mentally pushed it aside as Dwayne continued.

"When Paul got out to the remote area where the ping had come from, he spotted a cabin in the distance."

"Oh." She was surprised there was road access out that far or even flat land by which to travel.

"Luckily, there was a small break in the weather, so Paul could get out there because the snow really started coming down before he had even left the crime scene." Dwayne riffled through a folder on the table and pulled out what looked to be a photo printed from the internet. He handed it to Harper. "This is the victim. Ever see him on one of your tours?"

Harper studied him. He was a nondescript older man. Sixties. Gray, balding hair, glasses. Short beard. A thick neck leading her to believe he was stocky. Harper handed the photo back to Dwayne. "Not that I can remember."

Dwayne placed the picture back in the folder, and Harper glanced at the blank screen. "What does he have to do with all of this?"

Dwayne sighed again. "Suppose you heard about the murder weapon used on the woman staying at the Larkspur."

A statement, not a question, but Harper nodded. "I did." She didn't need to mention that Keri had confided to her—and half the town—that the woman had been shot with a bow and arrow at the one establishment in town that was available for out-of-town guests.

Harper grimaced internally at the picture that still formed in her mind when she thought of the unknown woman she'd heard about a week earlier, an arrow shot so powerfully that it had come out of the other side of her body and still had enough force to lodge in the wood of the wall.

"The weapon used in that crime is the same type of weapon used in Isaac Driscoll's murder."

"Oh," she breathed.

"Yeah. Unusual to say the least. Not too many people use them in general, and especially not to commit murder. Much less *two.*" Dwayne glanced at the blank screen the same way Harper had. "Paul had just left the scene and almost ran that guy over on his way out. Acted like he'd never seen a truck before—which, come to find out, maybe he hasn't. Anyway, Paul was already shaken having just discovered a macabre crime scene, and here this guy comes, right across his path, carrying a bow and arrows on his back."

Harper widened her eyes. "Carrying—You think he's the murderer?"

"He says he's not, and there's no evidence at this point to

15

say he is except the bow and arrows. Though the one he was carrying has arrows different in appearance than the ones used in the two crimes. And there are spots for each arrow in the case he was carrying and none were missing. We took it into evidence. But add in the fact that he knows how to use one *and* that he lives in the vicinity of Isaac Driscoll, and he's at least a person of interest."

Harper stared at the sheriff for a moment. "They *both* live out there?"

"Appears so. Says he lives ten thousand, five hundred seventy-three steps from Driscoll, in the direction of the three mountain peaks."

"Huh?"

"I know. That's how he described the distance between their residences. Strange."

To say the least. She led guided tours into that wilderness—nature lovers, campers, hunters. But she couldn't imagine living there permanently—in every season. It would be... practically impossible to survive, at least without a whole hell of a lot of gear.

"Did they know each other?"

"Lucas says he traded things with Driscoll, who made trips into town. Fish Lucas caught for clothing items, etcetera. He said other than that they didn't have much of a relationship—he didn't consider the man a friend. Just someone he did business with."

Business. "Fish he caught? So...that man in there has *never* been to town?"

"That's what he says."

"So he couldn't have killed the woman at the bed-and-breakfast."

Dwayne shrugged. "We're going on his word alone right

16

now because it's all we have. We won't have forensics back for a little while, but so far, nothing places him there. We really have nothing to hold him on."

Harper went back over Dwayne's words. *Never been to town? Never been out of that wilderness?* How was that possible? Her questions were endless. But that wasn't why Dwayne had asked her there. He wanted information from her, not the other way around. "I don't typically take tours south, and hunting is better east of the river. But in any case, I've never run across either one of them that I can remember. And I've never come across a dwelling of any sort. I'm as surprised as you are." Twenty miles made a hell of a difference as far as terrain, but it wasn't so far that someone couldn't live a more comfortable life in a populated town and still enjoy the wilderness for all it offered. She didn't get it.

Dwayne stood up from the table, gesturing to a small fridge near the door that she assumed held drinks. She shook her head, and he removed a water bottle, uncapping it and taking a long sip before saying, "We called in the Missoula crime lab to process the scene, but we've had to call in the Montana Department of Justice to investigate. We're simply not equipped to deal with a crime like this. The agent they sent is at the first crime scene at the Larkspur, but he should be back shortly to ask Lucas a few more questions. And"— he paused, creasing his brow as if he was worried about what her reaction would be to his next words—"I'm hoping you're okay that I've offered up your services. We could use your help."

CHAPTER THREE

Agent Mark Gallagher stood still, taking in the room as a whole, memorizing the layout, waiting for anything that immediately seemed out of place to catch his attention. Nothing did except the large dark stain on the carpet. But he'd expected that. The woman who'd died here had not experienced a peaceful death.

No, there had been fear and suffering and finally death, though a quiet one, as the arrow that had been driven through her throat had cut off her air and the scream he was sure had been trapped within. He'd seen the crime scene photos. The woman was wearing nothing but a T-shirt and white cotton underwear—presumably what she'd worn to sleep in—and her eyes were open in horror. Judging by the thrown-back covers, she'd been halfway between the bed and the window—she'd attempted to run but hadn't gotten very far.

Of course, she hadn't had much of a chance. Killing with a bow and arrow didn't require close proximity. That was kind of the point, wasn't it? The killer hadn't had to move much farther than the doorway, where he'd entered by picking the flimsy lock while the woman slept.

Mark opened a dresser drawer. Nothing. She had a duffel bag holding several items of clothing, and there was toothpaste on the sink, but it appeared she hadn't intended on a long trip. Or the woman didn't own much.

There was a stack of books on the nightstand, and Mark picked up the one on top. *The Giver*. He placed it aside and looked at the next three: *Ender's Game*, *The Maze Runner*, and *The Lightning Thief*. Mark's brows lowered. He didn't know anything about the victim, but the titles seemed like odd choices for an adult woman the ME had estimated to be in her mid- to late thirties. Mark recognized them as books geared toward young adults.

Mark spotted something on the spine of *The Giver*, and upon closer inspection, it appeared that a sticker had been there but had been peeled off recently. Some of the remaining glue was still sticky. A price tag? Although…the books on the nightstand were well used. Maybe they'd come from a used bookstore. He inspected the other books and found visible traces of glue and small pieces of yellow sticker on the spines of those ones as well. *Huh.* So they'd probably all come from the same place. Somewhere in town that might remember this woman? He opened the book covers one by one and saw that the first page of each one had been torn out. *Weird.* They could very well be books the woman had owned for years, old favorites she'd brought along to reread. Still…they felt out of place, and that nagged at him. He snapped a couple of quick pictures of the pile of books on the nightstand.

"Sir? Agent Gallagher?" The woman standing in the

doorway wringing a dish towel in her hands was small and thin, in her late sixties he estimated, with a blond bob that ended at her jaw. She was wearing an apron, a smear of something bright red on the skirt. In the midst of a bloody crime scene, the vision was decidedly unsettling.

He smiled. "Mrs. Wilcox?"

The woman he knew to be the owner of the Larkspur Bed & Breakfast/Restaurant nodded, glancing nervously around the room and then taking a step back. He led her into the hallway and closed the door behind him. "Terrible what happened here."

She bobbed her head, swallowing, her hands still wringing the towel. "Oh, I can hardly sleep for thinking about it. Right under my own roof too." She grimaced. "Do they know anything about that poor woman yet?"

"Not yet, ma'am. I was wondering if you could tell me anything about her that might have stood out to you?"

She looked to the side and frowned in concentration. "Mostly the fact that she was staying here at all. We don't get many guests in the winter. We only have the three rooms. The restaurant is our main business through all the seasons, but especially the cold ones. We get the occasional person passing through town who needs a place to stay for the night or someone visiting relatives who wants a space of their own, but it's rare. So I was surprised when she rang the bell last Wednesday and said she wanted to rent a room for the week."

He jotted that down in the notebook he kept in his jacket pocket. *A week.*

"She didn't mention she was visiting anyone then?"

"No, and I asked. 'What brings you to Helena Springs?' I'd said. She got this faraway look on her face and then told me she was here to try to right a wrong. Well, I didn't know exactly what to say to that, but she changed the subject anyway, asking about the restaurant hours."

Here to right a wrong. Mark wrote that down as well, tapping the pen on the pad for a second before he asked, "She paid in cash?"

"She did. I asked for ID, of course, per protocol, but she told me her wallet had been stolen recently, so she didn't have any. Well, not having ID made me hesitate to rent the room to her, but she was paying up front, and it was so very cold out. It wouldn't have been Christian of me to send her back out into that weather with nowhere else to stay in town."

"Of course. I understand." Mark gave Mrs. Wilcox a pleasant smile, which she returned, her shoulders dropping as if she was worried he'd disapprove of her lack of following protocol. "Did you happen to see if someone dropped her off?" There hadn't been a vehicle left in the parking lot, which meant the woman had either walked or been driven by someone else.

"No. I didn't even hear her come in. I was watching a show when I heard the bell ring at the front desk. Took me completely by surprise," Mrs. Wilcox said.

"What can you tell me about that night?"

Mrs. Wilcox had ceased wringing the towel, but at the reference to *that night*, she started up again. Mark wondered if it would tear in half. "I heard yelling," she whispered, glancing back down the hall over Mark's shoulder as if someone might suddenly appear and overhear her say something she shouldn't. "I couldn't hear everything, but I did hear him yell, 'How could you? How could you? You ruined everything.'"

"And it was definitely a man's voice?"

"Oh yes. No mistaking that. I thought about coming up here. Guests aren't allowed to have other people stay in their room without paying for double occupancy, you know? And there was the fighting... That was concerning. But then the yelling stopped, and I decided to address it in the morning." She frowned, shaking her head. "I did the wrong thing, didn't I?"

"No, ma'am. It's understandable. There's no way you could have known it was anything more than a couple's spat."

"Nothing like this has ever happened in Helena Springs." Her hands stopped working the towel as she leaned forward. "There have been accidents where people lost their lives. The Ward family comes to mind, of course." She pursed her lips and shook her head. "That poor girl, Harper, losing both her parents that way. Well," she said, drawing her shoulders back and seeming to catch herself talking of things she hadn't been asked about. Mark was used to that, though. It was a thing people did—they looked to fill the silence, so he made sure to leave plenty of it available. Because often, that uninhibited chatter contained useful information. Having worked the job for almost thirty years, he'd learned to wait, listen, and store information away, just in case.

He handed Mrs. Wilcox his card. "If you think of anything else, anything at all—no detail is too small—give me a call."

She took his card, slipping it into the pocket of her apron and nodding. "I absolutely will." She began to turn. "I'd better get back to those pies. I bake when I'm nervous. It helps—" She waved her hand around. "Anyway, Agent Gallagher, I'll call if I think of anything."

He tipped his head. "Thank you, ma'am."

She gave him a nervous smile and then turned, heading back toward the stairs to the kitchen where he could smell the sweet and tart aroma of cherry pie baking.

Laurie used to make cherry pie—the crust woven together like a basket so the little spaces in between bubbled red and gooey when the pie was hot. That smell made him yearn, made the empty spots inside him throb with the reminder of what had been. He shook it off, concentrating on things he'd jotted in his notebook, turning his mind back to the two murdered people deserving of justice.

He needed to get to that second scene. He wanted to look at it as soon as possible after examining the first—see if something about them seemed familiar in a way he might not recognize if the timing was further apart. Tomorrow morning wouldn't be good enough. He'd told Laurie he'd be home for dinner, but she'd understand that with a new job, he had to give it his all. Not that he'd do less regardless. It wasn't in his nature to half-ass anything, never had been. Although he wondered distantly if he was doing everything he could where his marriage was concerned. He pushed those thoughts aside for the moment. That would take time. *He hoped. God, he hoped.*

It felt like he'd been hoping for a long time. Too long maybe.

As he walked to his truck, snow was falling again, the icy air burning his skin. The sky was gray and low, as though at any moment it might descend lower and crush everyone beneath it. It made him feel depressed and claustrophobic. Jesus, how did these people survive months and months of this? He guessed he'd know soon enough, but he already missed the endless blue California sky.

The sheriff had told him he had a local girl in mind

who knew the terrain well. Good, because he'd need her. His knowledge about *wilderness* could fill a shot glass. And him trekking around alone in the snow sounded extremely unpleasant and mostly pointless.

After he'd slid inside his SUV, turned the ignition, and started blasting the heat, he checked the name he'd jotted in his notebook. Harper Ward. *I thought so.* It was the same girl Mrs. Wilcox had mentioned. *That poor girl, Harper, losing both her parents that way.* The sheriff had told him her father had been the previous sheriff in Helena Springs, and a guilty look had flashed in the man's eyes that Mark didn't have enough information to understand. He wondered what it meant and figured he could find out easily enough if he wanted to—there was always someone—or twenty someones—willing to talk about their neighbors in a small town. But he'd rather keep his focus on what was important to his case and solve this crime—*crimes*—before anyone else in this small town got hurt.

Or killed.

CHAPTER FOUR

Jak's teeth were chattering so hard he thought they might crack. He pulled his legs closer to his chest, wrapping his arms around them, trying to curl into every tiny bit of heat his body was making.

He knew he had to move. He *had* to get dry. He had to... Tears filled his eyes and then moved down his cheeks, freezing over his icy skin. He wiped at them, making himself sit up. *Live!* he'd told the dark-haired boy as he'd flung him up on that small ledge. He'd *demanded* it because only *one* of them could have that ledge—that *chance*—and if the boy he gave it to died anyway, then it was *wasted*.

I should have taken it for myself.

But even though the thought flashed in his mind, it didn't feel true. He'd somehow survived the fall by grabbing another piece of branch sticking from the side of the slope. There hadn't been a ledge or anything for him to climb onto, and he'd quickly lost his hold. But that branch had been closer to the ground, and when he'd landed in a deep pile of snow, it hadn't been with as much speed, though it had still knocked the wind from his lungs anyway, and he'd had to fight his way out of the icy hole his fall had made.

One of the other boys had been lying nearby, both legs twisted in different directions, and Jak had rushed to him, shaking and panting as he turned the boy over. But he could see right away that he was dead. His face was bloody and beaten, his gaze forever staring at the stars above. Jak had cried out, jumped back, and rushed as fast as he could to get away. Away, away.

Because he didn't know how long he had before someone came after him.

He'd made it to a group of trees close by, out of breath, soaking wet, his shoulder hurting badly, and he was so scared that whoever the man had been at the top of that cliff was on his way down to *find* him.

Did he know that Jak had lived? That the dark-haired boy might have too? And what happened to the blond one? Jak hadn't seen any trace of him at the bottom of that cliff, but he must be dead too. Buried under snow, his limbs twisted grossly like the other dead boy's.

Help me, someone. Anyone. Please, he begged in the quiet of his mind. But no one was listening, except the silent moon hanging in the nighttime sky.

Jak tripped through the forest, his shivering getting *more,* his eyes starting to blur around the edges. The strength he'd felt had drained out from him, making his muscles feel loose and filled with water. He ran anyway, stumbling, on and on until his legs had no feeling. Heat filled his bones, moving up, shooting flames through his chest. He was suddenly burning hot. *Too* hot. And thirsty. He bent down and scooped up some snow, bringing it to his mouth and eating it as he moved deeper into the darkness.

So hot. So hot. The world started to tilt. He took off his jacket, dropping it in the snow and moving forward. He tripped over something under the snow he couldn't see, picking himself up and falling forward. *I will not die, I will not die.* But his thoughts felt slow again, the same way they had at the top of that cliff. At the thought of that terrifying fall—that man with the loud, deep voice—he pushed forward again, his strength getting less. *So hot, so hotsohotsohot.* With the last of his strength, he pulled off his jeans and his sweatshirt, leaving them in the snow.

His head swam, and he tripped, falling to the ground with a crunch of ice and cry of pain, sharp needles sticking into every part of his naked skin. He reached a hand forward and felt nothing. He tumbled into it, rolling, falling, somewhere small and dark and soft where the cold and the wind couldn't find him.

Will you die today?

No, he tried to yell. *Live!* But the words died on his lips as the world around him disappeared.

CHAPTER FIVE

Offered up her services? Which ones exactly? "Dwayne, what do I have to offer in a murder investigation?"

"No one's asking you to be a police officer. Although I'm sure some of it is in your blood." He gave her an affectionate smile. "What we really need is someone who knows the area very well and owns a four-wheel-drive vehicle. That's you. You'll meet the agent who's been sent in. Nice guy, it seems. New at the department and get this—a native Californian. The guy showed up wearing so much winter gear, he was walking like the Michelin Man and asked me how to deice his windshield." Dwayne laughed, and Harper smiled at the image of the unknown agent. "He's over at the Larkspur now, but he'll be back soon, and he'll let you know what he needs."

A knock at the door interrupted them, and without waiting for an answer, Keri stuck her head in. "Dwayne, line one for you. Bob Elders from Missoula."

Dwayne's lips thinned. "Thanks, Keri." He looked at

Harper. "I gotta take this. Do you mind waiting in here for the agent? Mark Gallagher's his name."

Harper gave a distracted nod as Dwayne left the room. She hadn't decided if she would help out on this case. Something about it felt...risky in some personal way. She was sure it had to do with the fact that her dad had worked in this very building for so many years. She could practically *feel* him there, smell the aftershave he'd worn, hear his laugh...

Suddenly weary, she sat in one of the chairs at the table, glancing at the dark screen. Her attention was pulled by the thought of the man sitting alone in the cell, and she was grateful for the shift in focus. The soft sound of her fingers drumming on the table filled the room as she wondered what he was doing right then. Still sitting there? *What else would he be doing, Harper?* Was Dwayne right when he said the man hadn't seen a car before? Curiosity needled her, the fact that he might be a killer—one who had a penchant for nailing his victims to walls with sharpened arrows—not enough to douse that particular sensation. *Apparently.*

She drummed at the table for a few minutes longer and then fiddled with her hands, bit at her lip, looked over at the door, and hesitated only another moment before she stood quickly and walked to the monitor. It came on with a click, the view of the small cell where the man still sat blinking to life. He was in the exact same position as before. In fact, it appeared as though he hadn't moved a muscle.

For a solid minute, Harper simply watched him as he sat on the bench in the other room, still and unmoving. Through the anonymity of the screen, she allowed her eyes to roam freely over him—from his unruly hair down to his strange footwear. He was lean but muscular. Solid. He'd have the strength to shoot an arrow straight through a body. He was big. And strong. And wild looking.

Caveman, indeed.

She could see this man fighting wildebeest. And winning.

Who are *you?*

Her eyes moved to his hands, resting on his thighs. They were large, and even through the monitor she could see they had numerous scars. He had the hands of a...warrior, scarred and supremely masculine, and Harper wanted to study them, as though they were a work of art. They were... brutally beautiful in a way she'd never seen before. And she couldn't help wondering what he'd done with those hands to cause so many injuries.

A tremor went through her, not born entirely of fear. But she sucked in a surprised breath when he suddenly turned his face to the camera like he'd done before, his eyes seeming to study hers. She felt her face flush as she looked away and then almost laughed at herself. He couldn't see her. Couldn't see *anyone*—he was simply looking up at the blinking eye of a camera. She stepped closer, studying his expression. There was something in his eyes...bitterness, if she wasn't mistaken. But...why? If he didn't know what a vehicle was, how in the world would this man know that the flashing red light he could see would enable someone else to watch him? And even if he did, why would it cause that fiery intensity on his face? She tilted her head, studying him intently. He stared back as though he could feel her on the other side of the camera. Silly, of course. She knew that, and yet the feeling persisted. His eyes were piercing as he stared at the piece of equipment high up on the wall in the room he occupied, and...there was no mistaking the sharp intelligence in his gaze. Caveman maybe. But no brainless Neanderthal.

Thoughts were whizzing through his brain. She could *see* it. *Perplexity. Confusion. Anger.* So many emotions.

He looked away, facing forward again—expression suddenly blank—as if he'd heard her thought and refused to accept that she could see what he hid. Or tried to. It didn't stop her though. She leaned closer. From this angle, she could see a scar arcing down the side of his face under his right cheekbone. It was slight and mostly faded, but it called attention to the sharp lines of his bone structure. And... yes, his expression was blank now, but there was a war being waged behind his eyes. She recognized it as someone who had perfected the art of stoicism. *Don't react. Don't let them see your fear. Don't let them know you care.*

Harper felt a surprising jolt of empathy but then chastised herself internally. She was creating a narrative about the man based on her *own* experience, not his. She really knew nothing about him. Although...if he was only a "person of interest," as Dwayne had said, was it ethical to keep him sitting in that cell? If all he'd done was have the bad timing of stumbling in front of a police vehicle and they weren't charging him with anything, he had the right to leave. Would he know it? Had they even told him that?

The door opened, startling her from her voyeurism and the questions running rampant through her mind. She blushed again, turning off the monitor, but not before Dwayne and the older man entering the room had seen what she was doing.

The man who must be the agent extended his hand, and Harper took it as Dwayne came to stand next to them.

"Mark Gallagher, this is Harper Ward. Mark, Harper knows why you're here. Harper is our local wilderness guide slash psychologist."

Harper let go of Mark Gallagher's hand and gave Dwayne an exasperated look. "The first is true. But, Dwayne, I'm not a psychologist, and you know it." She gave him another stern look, but he didn't look the least bit contrite. She breathed out a sigh and gave Mark Gallagher a small, embarrassed smile. "I work part-time at a group home."

"And you're taking some classes in Missoula, aren't you?" Dwayne asked.

"I haven't signed up for those yet," Harper said, feeling like a complete loser. The accomplishments Dwayne had obviously listed under her name were dwindling by the moment.

Dwayne winked at her. "Well, closest we got. And it's mostly your knowledge of the area that Mark needs. And that truck you have. Now, I've got to make a couple of calls, but you and Mark chat, and then you can let him know if you're available."

"Okay."

The sheriff left the room, and Mark Gallagher nodded to the table, where they both took a seat across from each other.

The agent took a notebook and a pen from his coat pocket and began flipping through it while Harper took that moment to study him. He was older, probably in his fifties, but he was still fit and very much an attractive man with a full head of salt-and-pepper hair, trimmed short, and a sort of…capability about him. A competence few men carried. He was the type of man who would always take charge during an emergency situation, and he'd remain calm while doing so. He was the type of man you'd naturally turn to if you were having a problem. He seemed like…like her dad had been. She recognized that quality in him because she'd experienced it in her father. And because of that, her comfort level increased immediately.

"Dwayne tells me your father was the sheriff here before him."

For a moment Harper simply stared at him, the question taking her by surprise after she'd just literally been thinking about her dad. She gave herself an internal shake and cleared her throat. "Yes. He…he was. For a short time."

"I'm sorry for your loss."

Harper's eyes darted away. She wasn't used to speaking about her parents and especially not with strangers. "Thank you. It was a long time ago."

"Time can be relative."

When she returned her eyes to him, he looked down at his notebook, tapping the pen on the cover.

"Dwayne also says you grew up in this area and that you know every nook and cranny of the surrounding wilderness."

Harper blew out a breath. Dwayne apparently had said quite a bit. "I did grow up here. I moved to Missoula when I was seven but spent summers here when I was in high school and then moved back four years ago. Since then, I've spent practically every day in the wilderness, nine months out of the year. I'm very familiar with the area. But there's no way any one person could know every inch of the wilderness surrounding Helena Springs. It's vast, and it's extremely harsh in winter—deadly even." Unexpectedly, her breath hitched. *Deadly even*. Yes, she should know. She'd lost both her parents in that unforgiving terrain. She shook off the emotion, surprised that it'd gripped her so suddenly. *Time can be relative*. Yes, and who knew that better than she did? She still grappled with their loss well over a decade later. But she rarely lost control of her emotions, and especially not in front of a perfect stranger. She cleared her throat, annoyed with herself. "But I'm very familiar with quite a bit of it, depending on what you're looking for and where you're looking."

Agent Gallagher leaned back in his chair. "That might be the difficult part. We're not quite sure what we're looking for, other than someone adept with a bow and arrow. Although there were some unusual things found at the second crime scene that might prove helpful. I'm assuming Dwayne filled you in on the basics about the two crimes?"

Harper nodded. "Yes. I've got the basics."

Agent Gallagher leaned forward, clasping his hands together. "Good. Mostly, I need someone who can get me out there, and you seem to be just that person." Before she could reply, he went on. "You'd be paid as a consultant to the case. Reimbursed for your mileage and any other expenses."

Harper bit at her lip. She could use the money. She could *always* use the money. Still, she'd never imagined she would be a consultant to anyone, much less someone trying to solve two grisly crimes. "How long do you think you'll be here?" She had no idea how crime solving worked despite the fact that her father had made his livelihood in the field. But she'd been so young when he died. And anyway, then, or now, crimes simply didn't occur in Helena Springs. In fact, the last time she could remember a crime that had been remotely similar to this one was when Lyle Fredericks beat his wife half to death and then used his shotgun on himself. His wife, Samantha, had survived, but she'd left town to live with her cousin—and to escape being "the woman whose husband almost beat her to death before committing suicide." Labels were difficult to get away from in a small town.

Of course, what had happened to her parents, what had

happened to *her,* had been an accident, not a crime. Still, she'd heard the whispers, knew the labels she wore.

That poor thing.

Orphan.

"Depends. Might be three days, might be three months. There's no way to say at this point in the investigation. I'm here to do my very best to find justice for the two victims. Or, at least, answers." He studied her for a moment in a way that made her feel slightly itchy. "If you agree to help, you'll need to keep any information quiet. Like I said, I'll need your help canvassing some of the area, and I may have a question or two pertaining to the case, and so you'll be privy to things I'd prefer aren't discussed openly."

Harper nodded. "Of course. I understand. I'm a vault."

Agent Gallagher chuckled. "Okay, good. Then what do you say?"

What do you say? Why did she have this feeling in her gut that getting involved—even as a glorified chauffeur—was going to matter in some way she couldn't possibly know right then? The picture of the man with the fiery eyes sitting one room over flashed in her mind, as did the terrain she'd be driving this stranger in front of her into. This man who seemed capable, yes, but was used to sunny skies and sandy beaches, not frigid canyons and frozen rivers.

She wasn't out there as much herself during the cold season. For one, there were fewer clients who wanted to venture into the wild tundra to freeze their asses off, and two, it would be foolish to carry on her personal search during the snowy months when what she was looking for would be piled under a mound of icy white. She paused for another brief second, resolve filling her. "I'll do it."

Agent Gallagher's lips tipped. "Great. Can you start

now? I need to get out to that second crime scene, Harper. If I may call you Harper?"

"Yes, of course."

"I need to take a few minutes to ask the man in the next room some questions. I'll be quick. I imagine he's ready to get home."

She nodded, and Agent Gallagher left the room, headed toward the "wild man." *No, Lucas. His name is Lucas. And his home is in the middle of nowhere.*

CHAPTER SIX

Unhappy smells. Old sweat, tears, fear. The stink of human urine. And over that, something sharp and strong that Lucas could not name. Unnatural.

He hadn't been paying enough attention, his thoughts flying like the whipping snowflakes all around him. And then there had been the truck where a truck had never been before. The big machine that roared and rumbled and left deep tracks in the snow. But he hadn't run. Hadn't fought. Because he'd *wanted* to see the man who drove it. Up close. Wanted to know if he might be a friend or if he was an enemy.

Were there really still enemies? Or had *Driscoll* been the only enemy? He still didn't know. He was trying to figure it out.

The man in the truck had steered off the road when he saw Lucas and then taken out his gun and pointed it at him. His hand had been shaking, and Lucas had smelled his fear, knew he could overtake the man, steal his gun if he wanted, but he didn't. The man had asked him to come into town and answer questions. Lucas didn't want to answer any of his questions. He could have darted away like a fox. Too quick to catch. But he had needed to *know* more about what was *out there.*

So he'd let the man drive him into town, and the man had put him *here,* in the cell that unhappy people had sat in before him. Sweating. Crying. *Peeing on the floor? Why?* He couldn't make sense of that. Even animals peed far away from where they slept.

Driscoll had talked about a cell. With bars. A cage. This must be what he meant. But the men who told him to sit there had also said he could go home after they asked him questions. But maybe they were lying.

He looked at the camera in the corner. He knew what a camera was. The redheaded woman had told him what to look for, and he'd *remembered.* Remembered from the long-ago world, the one he'd lived in. *Before.* The life where there had been cameras and cars and food in cans and boxes, even bottles of sweet orange-colored drinks with little bubbles that'd popped on his tongue.

Some of it he could remember the names for, some of it he could not. The tastes though…the tastes had already left his memory.

He looked up, and a red light on the camera flashed. On. Off. On. Off. Like the slow blink of a red-eyed owl. They were watching him. Taking pictures. *Why?*

If they didn't have guns, he could fight them all. He was bigger, stronger than both men, the one who had driven him there in the truck and the other one who asked him questions and then put him in the cage.

That man was in the room next door, he could smell him,

his scent both strange and familiar. Like pine trees only…too much. Too…*everything*. The smell made Lucas picture pine trees as tall as the sky and as wide as a mountain. Bright, blinding green with pine cones huge like boulders. Lucas wasn't sure what to think about that. His smell was just *very*.

But suddenly, underneath that, there was something else. He leaned his head back, closing his eyes and trying to pick up the scent beneath the other one. It was faint, very faint but he caught it and held on. A faraway wildflower field after a rainstorm. Clean. Earthy.

A woman.

Her smell…soothed him.

Confused him.

Her scent made the whispers stir up inside. They weren't whispers, that was the wrong word, but the only one he knew to use. The feelings he got when everything else disappeared, except for his instincts. They were always quiet, but sometimes he understood them, and sometimes he did not.

He pulled in another breath. The scent of her was new and old, something that was not known and already a part of him. Deep down. Deep, deep down. Something came alive like a spark, rising up to greet its match, a singing in his blood that was like the wind that showed up on a cold winter morning telling the forest that springtime was in the close faraway.

Startled, he opened his eyes, letting the feeling settle, until his breath evened again.

Now there was another man in the room next to the cage Lucas was in. Lucas could smell him through the thing high on the wall that blew air out of it. Hot. Cold, he thought. Both. What was the name of that thing? He couldn't remember. But the scents of the men were stronger than the lighter scent of the woman, and he lost his grasp on it. She faded away.

After a time, he smelled the man getting closer and was unsurprised when he showed up, using a key in the door with bars and sliding it open, coming into the cage with a smile.

"Thanks for waiting for me," the man said. He had hair the color of the big rocks that sat on the river's edge—light gray and dark silver all speckled together. "If you'll follow me this way, we can talk."

Lucas followed the man, turning his head to see the woman. But the door of the room she was in was closed. The man brought Lucas to another room with a table and two chairs. "Please sit," the man said, and when Lucas did, the man sat too. "My name is Mark Gallagher. I'm an agent with the Montana Department of Justice." He smiled again. *His eyes are nice,* Lucas thought. But he didn't trust himself to see niceness. Or meanness. Lucas knew well that people lied and pretended. "I know you've been Mirandized and that the sheriff already asked you some questions, but I have a few more if you don't mind."

Lucas nodded slowly, not wanting to answer questions but understanding that they weren't asking, they were telling.

"Good. Will you tell me again how you knew the victim, Isaac Driscoll?"

"He traded things with me. Things I needed but couldn't get."

"Okay. And why couldn't you get the things you needed?"

He didn't tell the man why. He wasn't sure he should. Didn't know who to trust and who not to trust. Not yet. "I didn't want to leave the forest. I wanted to stay there. And I…didn't have a car."

"I see. Okay." But he could tell by the man's face that he didn't see. Did he know Lucas was lying?

"Is there anything else you can tell me about your relationship? Anything you knew about him that we should know?"

"No." He tried not to picture the blood when he answered, the puddle that had grown and grown moving across the floor.

"Okay. And you live in a house on Isaac Driscoll's property?"

"Yes."

"And you traded things with him in exchange for rent?"

Rent? Lucas wasn't sure what that meant, but he knew the man—the agent—expected it was true, so he answered, "Yes."

"So, in essence, you depended on Isaac Driscoll to obtain things not available to you?"

There were too many words in that sentence he didn't understand, but he nodded anyway. "Yes."

"Did you like Isaac Driscoll?"

"I don't know. I just traded with him."

The agent waited for a second before talking. "Okay. Have you seen anyone unusual in, er, your area of the woods, so to speak, recently?"

Don't tell anyone about me.

"No."

"Okay." He gave Lucas a long look, and Lucas stared back. "Have you ever been to town before, Lucas?"

"No." That was almost the truth. He'd been to town once, but only walked a few steps into it. He didn't want to tell the agent about that. His muscles still got achy and tight when he thought about it.

"How did you come to live way out there?"

"I… My…parents couldn't care for me. Driscoll let me stay on his land."

The agent stared at him, but his face didn't say anything. "So you've been living out there how long?"

"Fifteen winters." *So many. So much cold. So much hunger. So much loneliness.*

The agent was looking at him in that funny way. Lucas didn't know what he was thinking. "Alone? All of them?"

"Yes."

The agent was quiet for a minute. "All right, Lucas, thank you for your time. We'll be out to talk to you if we have more questions. And, of course, to return your property once it's been tested."

Lucas had no idea what they were testing *for*, but he nodded. *I want to go home.* But even as he thought it, his heart dropped. Because the forest was no longer the place that made sense. Everything was different now.

CHAPTER SEVEN

Agent Gallagher opened the door and smiled. "Ready to go if you are."

She nodded, getting up from the chair where she'd been sitting as she'd resisted turning on the monitor again, and followed the agent out of the room. She stopped in her tracks when she saw the man—Lucas—being led out of the holding cell by Dwayne. "Sorry for the holdup," Dwayne was saying. "Thanks for answering our questions. You're free to go."

Dwayne turned, and Lucas followed, swiping a magazine out of the holder on the wall outside the restroom door as they walked by and quickly sliding it under his coat. Harper blinked. Had he just *stolen* a magazine right behind the sheriff's back?

Dwayne stepped aside, and Lucas looked up and met Harper's eyes. For a frozen second, their gazes locked, and Harper felt trapped in his stare. Spellbound. She wanted to shake her head in amazement at seeing him in the flesh. As though he might have only existed inside that screen in the room she'd just exited and the reality of his three-dimensional presence in front of her was almost... shocking.

And, God, the way he was looking at *her*—the animosity she'd seen when he'd stared up at the camera gone, replaced only by...deep curiosity and that same keen intelligence. She'd never felt so completely captured in someone's gaze. She swallowed. He was *big*. Bigger than he'd appeared on the small screen. At least six four and muscular. Completely overwhelming.

"Harper is going to give me a ride to Driscoll's," Agent Gallagher said as Dwayne approached them, Lucas trailing. The agent's words—thankfully—snapped her from her trance before the older men noticed.

Dwayne looked pleased, shooting Harper a smile. "Excellent. Glad it worked out."

Lucas stopped a few steps behind Dwayne, his gaze not having left Harper. He stared, his eyes moving over her like he was trying to figure something out. She stared back, and after a beat, Lucas looked away, his gaze roving the room, stopping quickly on this or that and then moving on to something else. He was cataloguing as though he had just landed on some alien planet. Or stepped out of a time machine. *Maybe he did*. Maybe he'd recently come from the Cretaceous period and was experiencing civilization for the first time. Then again, the Levi's he was wearing sort of disproved that theory.

"I'm going home now," Lucas murmured, and even in that low tone, his voice was surprisingly smooth and expectedly deep. He looked at Harper again, and she saw that his eyes were blue with gold surrounding the irises. *Sunset eyes,* she thought. They were especially extraordinary in the otherwise rough-hewn lines of his face.

He turned toward the door, and Agent Gallagher stepped forward, halting him. "Deputy Brighton will give you a ride. It's a long walk, and we've inconvenienced you."

Lucas glanced out the window where large snowflakes were drifting past the glass, the sun already low in the sky. He paused for a second and then said simply, "Thank you." He looked back at Harper again, and she switched from one foot to the other.

For a moment there she had wondered if they'd ask her to drive Lucas home too since he lived near Driscoll. Maybe the men were being cautious with her safety, or maybe they had another reason pertaining to protocol that called for Paul to transport him. *Whatever* the reason, she felt relieved and also slightly...disappointed. "Harper Ward," she said, thrusting her hand in front of her.

"Harper Ward," Lucas repeated, his gaze held steady on her face. He dropped his eyes, staring at her outreached palm for a moment before raising his own hand and wrapping it around hers. His hand was large and warm and calloused, and the feel of it made her breath catch, part thrill, part fear. He was all man, every bit of him, and never in her life had she felt another person's presence so keenly. Never had she been stared at with so much *intensity*. It unsettled her. It intrigued her.

Mostly it unsettled her.

Maybe.

Deputy Brighton appeared from the front of the office, glancing at Lucas. "All ready?" he asked. But he looked like the one who was unsure. Lucas nodded, and they all left the station together, a blast of icy snow hitting them in the face, causing Agent Gallagher to draw back and raise his hood. "Damn that's cold."

"Welcome to winter in Montana."

Agent Gallagher gave Harper a rueful smile, squinting against the flurry. "Is this a welcome or a warning?"

Despite the heightened awareness of Lucas trudging next to her, she managed a laugh. "Maybe a little bit of both."

Harper glanced at Lucas and saw that he was looking around, his gaze moving from the lawn and garden shop across the street—closed for the season—to the distance where a few homes could be seen among the bare trees, smoke spiraling lazily from the chimneys. He looked her way, and, for a fleeting moment, she swore she saw grief on his face. *But why?* She shook it off, focusing on her boots stepping through the snow in the parking lot. She had to stop trying to read that man. He sent her mind spinning.

And he might be dangerous.

Even Deputy Brighton was glancing at him suspiciously like he'd been assigned to transport a wild animal. But what? Was Lucas supposed to walk twenty miles home in a snowstorm just because he'd had the bad luck to walk in front of a sheriff's vehicle and knew the murder victim? Okay, there were the bow and arrow too—but they were *different*, and didn't it stand to reason that if one person hunted that way, others did as well?

She had no idea why she was trying to justify anything on his behalf.

They got to her truck next to Deputy Brighton's SUV, the words *Helena Springs Sheriff Department* plastered across the side, and Harper turned at the same time Lucas did.

Like a few minutes before in the station, Lucas's eyes locked on Harper's. "Goodbye." Lucas's coat had opened slightly in the wind, and Harper noticed a dark shirt beneath it that looked to be regular cotton. A T-shirt? Something Driscoll had given him for some fish or berries or who the hell knew what else? What had he had to trade in order to stay on Driscoll's property? A shiver went down her spine.

"Goodbye," she murmured.

As he shifted to turn away, something around Lucas's neck fell forward onto the dark material of his shirt, pulling Harper's gaze to it. A round silver locket on a leather string. Strange jewelry for a man. Something about it…something about it… Harper realized she was holding her breath as she leaned forward, her hand beginning to extend unconsciously to pick that locket up in her fingers, get a better look at it—

Lucas turned and opened the back door of the deputy's vehicle, closing it between them. Their eyes caught one last time through the glass, and then the SUV pulled away, disappearing into the falling snow.

CHAPTER EIGHT

A burst of light. Jak flinched, reaching back for the darkness. He floated for a minute, two, but cold was pricking at his skin. Hurt. Yes, he was achy, cold…but not as cold as he'd been…before. He smelled earth…dirt and leaves and something he couldn't name. It smelled sort of like urine, and he wondered if he'd wet himself.

His thoughts tumbled, his mind trying to grab a memory. Something wiggled against his foot, and he pulled his knee to his chest, whimpering. He felt another movement near his shoulder, and his eyes flew open. Memories of the man and the cliff and…and…he couldn't remember more than that, but that made him move, clawing his way toward the circle of light above him. He came out of the hole he'd been in, rolling to the frozen ground, a cry of fear and confusion bursting from his cracked lips.

He put his arm over his eyes, waiting for them to stop blinking, and then slowly lowered it. Woods. And snow. *Sunshine.* The sound of dripping water all around him. At first, he thought it was rain, but no, it was melting snow. He closed his eyes and opened his mouth, the sweet taste of fresh water dripping from the bare tree branches above and catching on his tongue. *Relief. Relief.*

Looking down, he saw that his body was black and blue with bruises and he was only wearing his underwear. Somewhere in the back of his mind, he remembered stripping his wet clothes off. He'd been hot. Burning hot and then…he'd fallen. He looked quickly behind him and saw that the place he'd climbed from was a den. There were moving things around him, *on* him, whimpering and *warm*. On a rush of breath, Jak dropped to his knees and peeked back inside to where his almost-naked body had lay through the deep, dark night. There were six wolf pups, four sleeping, two staring up at him. He blinked, and they blinked back.

He saw the outline of where his body had been curled next to the pups. He'd fallen into their den, and they'd kept him warm when he would have frozen to death. "Hi," he croaked, tears springing to his eyes. He was scared, hurting, and still cold. Shaking. He was only in his underpants, his bare feet in the snow, but all of a sudden, he didn't feel so alone, and the feeling made a lump of thankfulness block his throat.

The two pups who were awake were still staring up at him, and when he reached down slowly, carefully, to pet one of them, he shrunk back in fear. Jak saw that their ribs were showing, and his heart squeezed tight.

They were starving. They'd been abandoned by their mother.

Just like me.

But they had no baka to take care of them.

49

He reached into the den, touching one of the pup's heads softly and petting him as he whispered the words his baka had said to him when he had trouble sleeping. "It's okay. You will be okay. You will survive. You are strong boy."

When he reached his hand over to rub one of the sleeping pups' bellies, he pulled back quickly. The pup was cool under his touch. The other four pups weren't sleeping. They had died. To be sure, Jak touched them one by one, all of them cool though not cold. Not yet. Not like the alley cat he'd found dead by the building behind his baka's apartment before screaming for her to come help it.

She'd come running, but there was no help for that cat. It was gone to cat heaven, she'd said, and it was not coming back. Just like these pups. But these pups were different. They'd saved his life before they'd lost their own.

"Thank you," he choked, touching the heads of each small wolf.

His feet were starting to tingle with cold, and he stood, shaking the snow off and turning toward the woods where sunlight lit the spaces between the tall green trees. He spotted a piece of gray cloth and walked to it, his limbs burning with soreness, especially his arms. But other than that, he seemed to be okay. No broken bones, he didn't think. He stepped on the rocks and bare spots of grass where some snow had melted until he came to the piece of cloth.

His sweatshirt. And it was in the grass in a circle of sunlight, so it was only a little wet. Shivering, he grabbed his jeans and his coat, which were both close by, his coat hung over a rock like it'd been set there to dry. He put the coat on quickly, sighing at the warmth that hugged him. His jeans were a little wet too, but he put those on anyway and stuffed the bottom of his pullover sweatshirt in his pocket. He'd find a spot of sunlight to set that and his pants on until they were all dry. He had to hunt a few minutes longer for his boots, but he finally found those too, both wet, but he'd have to wear them for now.

Jak had gone to bed in his blue PJs. He wondered who had dressed him in warm clothes. Who had known he'd be out in the cold and snow?

He stood in a patch of light for a few minutes, his face raised to the sun as it warmed his skin. He pictured the pups, two of them still alive in their den as they waited for their mother, who must have died.

He stood unmoving. He didn't know anything about wolves, but he'd read a book about dogs once, though he couldn't tell anyone that. His baka had made him promise he would never ever talk about the reading or the books or the numbers or any of that. It had to be a secret, she'd said. He must never tell anyone or very bad things would happen.

He couldn't leave the two living wolf pups alone out there. His baka would send someone for him soon. Would she even know where to start looking for him? He didn't know how he had gotten there to that unknown place. He didn't know who the bad man was who told him it might be the night he died. The man, who was the reason those other boys went over the edge of the cliff. Yes, the ice had broken, had made the snow slide, but they wouldn't have been there except for the man. But he didn't want to think about that now because it made him want to cry and he knew this wasn't the time to cry. He had to be brave. For himself and now for those two little wolves who were all alone, except for him.

He went back to the den and picked up the two pups, checking to make double sure the other ones were dead.

They were even colder now, and their bodies felt sort of stiff. He knew they had gone to wolf heaven.

He picked up the two live wolves, their ribs sharp on his hands, and he carried them out of the woods and into the bright light of an open field. "It's okay. You are strong boys," he whispered to them both, even though he had no idea if they were boys or girls. When he sat down on a rock in the sunshine to warm them, he realized that one of the pups had died like his brothers and sisters, and he let out a shaky breath, holding back a sob and placing the wolf's body down on the grass next to where they sat.

Everyone was dying. The boy with the twisted body had been dead. The one he'd pushed up onto the ledge was probably dead, just like the blond boy, who must be buried under snow. Dead. Now five wolf pups had died, and the last one would probably die soon too, his body getting cold and stiff. And then Jak would die.

The skinny little wolf looked up at him, his eyes tired and sad like he could hear Jak's thoughts. "I think it's hopeless," he whispered to the wolf.

The wolf stared up at him, his small pink tongue darting out to lick Jak's hand. He was hungry, just like Jak. They both needed to eat, the pup more than Jak, he could tell. *But how do I keep you alive? What do I feed you?*

Jak bent down and scooped up some water from a puddle on the ground where some snow had melted. He held it up to the wolf's mouth, and the wolf stuck his tongue out, lapping at the water like he hadn't had a thing to drink forever, his eyes not leaving Jak's face.

"That's better, right?" Jak asked. He kept on feeding the wolf water until he seemed to have had enough.

They both sat there for a long time, Jak's clothes drying,

his soreness getting better, and the wolf's fur growing warm under the pale-yellow winter sun. There was a spiderweb stretched between two dead plants sticking out of the snow. It sparkled, moving slowly in the cold breeze. It reminded him of his baka's lace. His chest hurt.

He petted the tiny wolf. "I'm going to call you Pup," Jak whispered, afraid each time he reached over to touch him that he would find him cold as well. Stiff. Gone to heaven, a place someone never came back from even if they wanted to.

And then Jak would be alone again. Lost and alone.

Suddenly in the distance, a helicopter moved across the sky. Jak sucked in a breath, jumping to his feet and waving his arms in the air. "Here!" he called. "I'm here!" He jumped up and down, yelling, running back and forth, until his voice was gone and his muscles were screaming with hurt again. The helicopter circled and circled but was too far away to see him. After what seemed like hours, it turned and disappeared out of sight.

Jak picked up a rock and threw it at the empty sky, crying out, his voice nothing more than a broken croak of sound. He returned to the rock where he'd been sitting when he spotted the helicopter and sat on it. Pup looked up at him sleepily and then lowered his head once more, closing his eyes. Were the helicopters looking for Jak? Had his baka sent them to find him in the middle of this wilderness? They'd be back then. They *had* to come back.

The sky turned orange and then a swirly purple, and then the sun hid behind a mountain. Jak was so tired. His hunger grew and grew, and he didn't know what to do. The night got colder, and Jak started to shiver. He realized he needed to find a place for Pup and him to sleep where they could keep each other warm.

And if no one found him by morning, if the helicopters *didn't* come back, he'd have to try to find something for them to eat. Pup let out a tiny whimper sound and curled into Jak's thigh like he agreed with the thought.

"I won't let you down, Pup," Jak said, and it felt good. But it felt bad that he had no idea how to start or what to do. Jak put his hands in his pockets, lowering his head against the cold, almost-night air and startling when he touched something solid and smooth in his pocket.

The thing the dark-haired boy had passed to him before they'd fallen.

He pulled it from his pocket and looked at it. It was shiny, and he ran his thumb over it.

A pocketknife.

Jak's heart jumped. *Live!* he'd told the other boy, and maybe...maybe this had been that other boy's way of telling Jak to do the same.

CHAPTER NINE

The cabin was small, dim, and somewhat shabby, with dirty wood-planked floors and a few pieces of worn, mismatched furniture. Definitely not the rustic getaway Mark had pictured when he'd learned that Isaac Driscoll had taken early retirement and moved out there immediately afterward. Mark flipped the overhead light switch and then stood just beyond the doorway and gave the room a once-over before stepping inside, Harper entering behind him.

She pulled her jacket around herself and moved to the right of the door as she put her hands in her pockets. "Is it okay that I'm in here?" she asked, her breath emerging as white vapor in the chilled room. "I could wait in the truck—"

"It's fine. The crime scene techs have already completed their work. And I might have a question or two." He smiled back at her. "This isn't exactly what I'm used to, location wise. You might see something I don't. If some item or another seems strange or out of place, don't hesitate to mention it."

He walked to the table next to the kitchen area—really just a counter and sink with a two-burner hotplate and a mini fridge. Just like at the first crime scene, there was fingerprint dust everywhere.

"I hear you're from California."

"Born and raised," Mark answered.

"What brought you to Montana?"

"Just looking for a change. My wife's sister lives in Butte, and when I saw the opening at the Montana Department of Justice, I applied." He looked back at her, and she was watching him with a small skeptical look on her face that told him she knew he was leaving something out. He almost smiled at the way it was so obvious when her wheels were turning. He'd only known her for an hour, but he could already tell she questioned a lot and didn't quite know if it was insight or her brain running wild. He could relate. That inquisitiveness had turned out to be a good quality for him as far as the job he did. He hoped she'd figure out where to apply it as well instead of allowing it to run amok. She was young. Very young. She had time.

Then again, his daughter had been young too, and she hadn't had nearly enough time. Not nearly enough. He shut those thoughts down, picking up a notebook on top of a short stack of other notebooks in various colors on the table and leafing through it. It appeared to be a field journal of some sort with observations about possums and…he turned the page…deer…wolves. Different sections were labeled with chapter headings as though he was outlining a book. Mark flipped through the rest of the notebook quickly and then checked briefly inside the others. Why had Isaac Driscoll taken special interest in those three specific animals and no others?

He gave the cabin another once-over. Was *that* the reason the guy had been out here? To write a nature book? "Harper, you're a wildlife expert of sorts," he said, and she opened her mouth as if to disagree with the statement, but he went on before she could. "If you were going to observe animals and, say, write a book on their behaviors, would you want to live among them?"

"I mean…yeah, maybe. But I can't think of any animal that hasn't already been highly observed in its natural habitat, especially around here…a hundred books written, etcetera. It wouldn't be new material."

"That's what I was thinking too," he murmured, slipping the notebooks into a folded paper evidence bag he removed from his pocket. The techs hadn't deemed them important, but something told Mark he might want to look through them later.

"Unless," she said, stepping into the room, "the animal or animals were being observed under very specific circumstances that were different in some way." She pulled her bottom lip between her teeth in thought for a moment. "Like if the data being recorded was about how an animal would react to something it hadn't previously been exposed to? Like what they do in labs."

"Yes. Only Isaac Driscoll was a researcher with a doctorate at Rayform Laboratories. He took early retirement sixteen years ago and moved here. He left the lab for the wilderness." Albeit not the kind of lab that studied animals, from what Mark gathered.

"I don't know what to make of that. Unless he was just observing animals for his own interest," Harper offered.

Could be. The real question was, why would living alone in the wilderness observing possums get you murdered? And in such a violent fashion? He needed to see the spot where Driscoll had been killed. "I'll be right back," he said to Harper before walking toward the room where the murder had occurred.

The technicians had taken some of Isaac Driscoll's blood for processing, but the majority was still there on the wall and floor—a large, dark, congealed puddle.

He wondered if the victim had a next of kin—he was still waiting for that information—and, if he did, if they'd even want this dingy cabin in the middle of nowhere where their relative had been killed. Would they want the property? And if so, what would happen to Lucas with no last name? He sighed, staring at the large, dark stain. What the hell had happened here?

It hadn't been a quick death—again, the arrow had been shot with enough force to pin the victim to the wall so he was rendered helpless. His blood had drained from his body. The same as the Jane Doe in town, though this shot had hit the victim in the chest and he'd remained conscious long enough to reach his phone and dial 9-1-1. Maybe it had been in his pocket? Accessible enough so he could reach it even in the throes of death.

There was malice in both cases—hatred even. Neither was a random crime, though the arrows found in each body were slightly different in appearance. Whether that meant there were two killers or whether a singular killer had simply used different arrows, he didn't know. The crimes were too similar not to be related though. But how? Why? That was the most important thing to figure out really. Find out *why* and he should find out *who*.

And whoever had shot the victims certainly knew their way around a bow and arrows. He would double-check with an authority on the weapon, but from his own educated guess, both were kill shots, carried out expertly and swiftly. *Powerfully.* How strong would someone have to be to shoot through a human body? He'd have to look into that. What he did know was that neither victim had been shot by a novice.

Mark took one last look around the sparsely furnished room: a bed, stripped now of bedding, and a dresser. Hanging above the dresser was the only piece of art Mark had seen in the house. He moved closer, studying it. It was a depiction of an old-fashioned battle. Men with shields and arrows stood facing another group with the same weaponry across a great divide. He wasn't a big history buff and didn't recognize the uniforms, if they could be called that, many of the soldiers bare-chested and wearing what appeared to be short skirt-type bottoms. Was it a historical Roman battle? Mark took a picture of it with his cell phone so he could look it up later.

He opened the top drawer and found it full of boxes of matches, lined up in two rows. The rest of the drawers held a few random clothing items, folded haphazardly. Mark closed the drawers, left the room, and returned to where Harper waited for him.

The rest of the information he needed would come from the crime lab. He hoped to God there was something for him to work from—a lead of some sort. He knew the department had thrown him this case because no one else had the desire to trek through the frigid wilderness in the middle of winter. And he didn't either, but he was going to do his damnedest to work this case well. To settle into this job and this new life he and Laurie were trying to accept. *Mostly separately.*

Harper was standing by the door where she'd first walked in, her hands in her pockets again as if ready to leave as soon as possible. He didn't blame her. There was something... depressing about this place. And not only that a murder had been committed there—though that would increase the dismal factor anywhere. No, the whole place felt oppressive and dark. He had the urge to fling open the door and escape outside, which was saying something since *outside* was a virtual icebox.

"Ready?" she asked.

"Yup. I want to ask you about something that was found here, but I can do that in the truck. The crime lab was supposed to email it to me after it was processed, so I'll have to make sure it's there first."

She seemed even more eager to get out of the gloomy cabin, taking two quick steps to the door and pushing it open with perhaps more strength than necessary. It banged against the side of the porch, and she glanced back with a sheepish look on her face but didn't slow her descent down the two rickety steps. Mark closed the door behind them and took a deep breath. The cold air filled his lungs, and it felt good—cleansing. *Vital.*

As they trudged to her truck, Harper glanced toward the three mountain peaks to the south and then back at him. "Agent Gallagher, what do you think about Lucas? Living out here alone on Driscoll's property? Trading with him? It's odd, right?"

Mark nodded. He planned to be the one to talk to Lucas if any evidence arose that involved him, and even if it didn't, he'd make a point to return his bow and arrows and get a better feel for the man. "I'm going to look into his situation. I'm confused by it too." Lucas hadn't been very forthcoming at the station, and whether that was because he was hiding something or that he simply didn't have the answers to many of the questions he and Dwayne had asked, Mark didn't know. Hell, Lucas didn't even seem to be certain about how old he was or his age when he'd come to live on Driscoll's property. Fifteen winters, he'd said, the look in his eyes so bleak, Mark had cringed inside. And it'd been a damn long time since someone had said something that made him cringe. If Mark had to guess, he'd say the man was about Harper's age—young, early twenties probably, and very sheltered, though obviously toughened too. Mark stared at the frozen landscape, the mountainous terrain blocking the last of the dying sun. *You'd have to be tough, living out here.* And maybe "tough" didn't even begin to cover it.

He wondered how Lucas factored into this whole thing—or if he did at all. He'd made it sound as if his relationship with Driscoll was extremely limited and that he only saw him a few times a year, if that. The quiet, watchful man was difficult to read, but Mark sensed he was holding something back.

Harper seemed troubled as she started up the truck and turned the heat up to high. The snow flurries had died down, but it was still below zero according to the temperature gauge that had been hanging on the house next to what had been Isaac Driscoll's door. Why the hell would anyone want to live out here? This sort of cold was miserable. Biting and painful.

Mark swiped his phone, relieved to see he had service. He pulled up his email and was glad that the message he'd been expecting was in his inbox. He clicked on the attached PDF, and a scan of the "map" that had been in Isaac Driscoll's bedside table filled the small screen. He handed it to Harper, and she stared at it for a minute before looking at Mark questioningly. "Is it a map?"

"Seems to be. Only I don't know what it's of. And what these"—he used his index finger to point to two red boxes containing X's and an empty black box—"might indicate, if anything."

Harper turned the phone so it was horizontal, enlarging the picture and zooming in on the X's and then back out again. She studied it for another few minutes. "This squiggly line might indicate water? There's a river in that direction." She pointed off behind Driscoll's cabin. "Or maybe it's a trail?" She shrugged. "But there are a hundred trails in this wilderness. There's really nothing here that speaks of any landmark I'd recognize."

"I figured. What about when the snow melts?"

She thought about it. "If we used his house as a start-ing point, we could hike out around the area, look for something that might provide some information about what he was marking." She gestured her head toward the phone. "It looks old though with all those creases and the ink faded the way it is. He might have been marking the location of water or something he found necessary when he first moved out here? Maybe even a location where he was observing the animals you mentioned."

She looked back to the phone. "Obedient?" she read, the one word printed at the bottom of the piece of paper. "What does that mean?"

"I don't know yet."

Harper looked at it for another moment and then handed the phone back.

Mark put it in his pocket, and Harper backed out of the turn-in, heading onto the snow-covered back road they'd used to get to the cabin. She was right, of course. The "map" was most likely related to whatever animal observation Driscoll was doing here in the boondocks. But something in his gut told him he needed to locate those X's and find out exactly why Isaac Driscoll had considered them important. Looking at how aged the piece of paper was, it seemed he'd kept it beside his bed for many years. *But why?*

CHAPTER TEN

The snow crunched softly under Pup's paws as he ran to Jak and dropped the stick at his feet. Jak knelt down and took the stick, running his hand along Pup's thick fur, warm from the early winter sunshine. "Good boy," he said. "But there's no time for fetch today." He looked at the gray sky, squinting against the brightness for a minute before looking back at Pup. "We need to get ready for winter." His chest got achy at the thought of what was soon to come.

Cold.

Hunger.

Misery.

Jak hadn't expected the snow yet. He'd tried to keep track of the months as they'd passed, tried to remember the order they went in and how many days were in each one since the helicopters had disappeared, but he didn't know if he had it right. Either that, or the snow had come early this year. He'd traveled to the place where he thought the helicopters had flown, but it had taken him almost eight days to get there in the snow and ice, and once he believed he was in the place where they'd flown above—it was hard to tell—there had been no sign of them at all. It was like he'd made them up. He'd found a covered place and stayed in that valley with Pup for a while, but it was rocky and cold, had barely any cover and not close to enough food. So finally, he'd traveled back to the place he'd started out—the place where there were trees and caves and rabbits that came out of their burrows to hop through the snow.

He was glad he did because the helicopters never came back.

Fear buzzed inside him, the memory of the two terrible winters before and how he'd felt sure he was going to die so many times. But he and Pup had kept each other warm enough to stay alive, and the pocketknife had given them both a way to eat. Rabbits and field mice mostly, squirrels sometimes, the meat still warm and bloody. It'd gotten easier, second nature since that first kill, the one that had made Jak vomit in the snow, hot tears running down his cheeks as he'd gagged. And then he'd found that when he washed the meat in the river, the blood would draw the fish, and he could grab them with his bare hands.

Jak thought fish were better than mice. Pup liked both the same.

Pup hunted for them most of the time now that he was big and strong and could smell things Jak could not. Sometimes Pup even brought back a deer and once a big thing he didn't know the name for with antlers twice as wide as Jak could stretch his arms. That meat had lasted for a while, but then worms and bugs started crawling in it, so Jak left it for them to finish. He wondered if the other three boys who had gone over the cliff with him had been eaten by worms and bugs too but made himself think of something different.

Jak watched which berries the birds liked and picked those for himself, and he ate the same wild mushrooms that the rabbits and squirrels chewed on. He figured if the animals ate them, they were safe for him too. When the water was cold, he scooped handfuls of orange fish eggs from the river, the taste rich and salty.

He wanted to try to find his way out of the wilderness and back home, but each day was filled with feeding his hungry belly and making sure he had a safe place to sleep out of the wind. And he was worried that if he moved too far from where he was, his baka would never find him.

But in the last few days, he and Pup had traveled farther than they ever had before, over many smaller mountains and across a deep river that had almost swept Pup away before he'd grabbed the loose skin at the back of his neck and pulled them both up and over the bank. There was one more cliff in front of them, and he wanted to stand on top of it and see if he could spot anything other than more trees and valleys and mountain ranges and wild rivers swirling with foamy white. Maybe he'd see other people, a town, and know which direction to head in.

A few fat snowflakes landed on his face, and he stood, looking at his too-short pants. His clothes barely fit him anymore, and his toes were curled uncomfortably at the end of his broken boots. He wondered what he would do if he hadn't found his way out of there or if his baka still hadn't found him by the time he outgrew them all the way. Thoughts of his baka still caused a twist of sadness, but when he tried to remember exactly what she looked like, her face was fading. And he couldn't hear her voice in his head anymore the way he had at first, when he'd sworn she was scolding him for thinking about giving up or when he needed to do something he didn't want to do like skin a rabbit or eat its raw, warm meat. "Do it anyway," she would have said. "You strong boy."

Jak couldn't remember the last time he'd cried. Crying didn't help anything, didn't make surviving easier. His tears froze on his face, making him even colder than he'd been before, making him sleepy and useless.

Pup stopped walking beside him, lowering his head and growling softly the way he did when there was another animal close by. Jak stopped, listening for the crunch of tiny feet or the flutter of wings, but he didn't hear anything. "There's nothing there, Pup." But a shiver went down Jak's spine, and he thought about turning back the way they'd come. He knew the land behind them, knew it well, knew every berry bush and rock cave, every wading pool and open meadow. But this…this was a strange place, new and different, and even Pup seemed to think they were in the middle of a mistake.

Something moved in the grass to Jak's left, and he startled, but Pup took off after whatever it was, and Jak sighed with relief. *Bring us back something good for lunch, Pup*, he thought hopefully, his stomach growling. He'd already eaten the pocketful of berries he'd brought with them, and his body was telling him—loudly—it wanted more.

It *always* wanted more.

There was a thin patch of trees in front of him, light spreading through from the other side, and he hoped there was a wide-open space that got enough sun that he could warm himself for a few minutes while he waited for Pup.

But when he stepped through the brush, he came up short, his mouth falling open.

A house? A house!

And there was smoke coming from the chimney. Jak ran to it, almost slipping in his hurry to get there. He was safe! He wanted to yell with joy, his chest suddenly too full to breathe. A person! Someone to help him!

He banged on the door, a small cry of relief falling from his lips. *Rescued. I'm going to be rescued.* His thoughts were already tumbling all over themselves—a river of happiness flowing quickly over uneven stones, bouncing, splashing—about the stories he'd tell about how he'd survived, about how—

The door opened, and a man stood there, staring down at him. He gave Jak a strange kind of smile, but Jak was too relieved to care about that. "You found it. Then it's yours. You've earned it."

Jak shook his head. He didn't know what the man meant. He had to make him understand so he'd call his baka and Jak could go home. "Hi, Mister, I'm lost." He swallowed, trying hard to slow his words, to think of the right ones to use. *Something bad happened to me. Someone tried to kill me.*

"Come in," the man said, standing back and holding the door open. "You're cold, and it's warm in here."

Jak stepped through the door into the warm room, another sob of relief clawing up his throat. He swallowed it down, doing his best to stay calm so he could explain to the man what had happened to him. To the other three boys who must be skeletons under the snow by now. Their families needed to know. Jak could tell them.

"What's your name?" the man asked.

"Jak. I need to—"

"She named you Jak? All right then." *All right then?* And…she? Jak was suddenly confused, scared. He took a step back.

68

"Do you know my baka?"

The man paused. "No. By she, I meant your mother. Sorry for my assumption."

Jak frowned, looking closer at the man. He felt scared again. What if…what if he'd walked into the house of the man who'd tried to kill him? He backed up another step. But…no. This man didn't look familiar, and he was a lot shorter than that other man. And his voice didn't sound the same at all. *Will you die today?* Another shiver moved through Jak. No, he'd never forget that voice, not until the day he died. It was deep and dark, the voice of the monster who haunted Jak's nightmares.

"I want to go home. Can you help me?" Jak asked, his voice shaky, the collection of tears he hadn't shed in so long suddenly filling his throat.

The man stroked his brown-and-gray beard for a few seconds. "There's a war. They're killing the children."

Surprise made Jak's mouth drop open. He swallowed and nodded his head. "Yes. Yes. They tried to kill me." He didn't know who *they* were, but the man had to be talking about the same people. *Will you die today?* The words rang through his mind, the memory as fresh as though they'd just been said.

The man nodded. "Then you're lucky. You must be very strong to have survived something like that."

"I—" Jak didn't know what to say. A war? People killing children? His mind grabbed for understanding. "Who are they?"

"The enemy. Outside these woods is very dangerous. Just try to survive as best you can until this war is over." The man walked past Jak, moving toward the door.

Jak spun around. "Wait. Mister. Can you help me?"

The man turned back. "This place is yours. It's well hidden from the road. You can live here."

"But...but who...who does it belong to?"

"It's on my property." He looked around the room, glanced at the empty cots against the wall. "It was going to be a camp for children, but the foundation constructing it lost funding, so it came with the land."

Jak looked around, desperate. *Foundation? Funding?* Jak didn't know what those words meant. He was happy to have shelter, a wood stove that was warming the room, but the man before him had just caused his world to crash for the second time in his short life. "When will the war end? I need to get home to my baka."

The man's lips pressed together. "Everywhere has been evacuated. Your baka is gone now. You must survive on your own."

Gone? No. His insides fell, and he swallowed.

"I saw helicopters once," he said, trying to hold on to his hope. "I think they were there to rescue me."

The man narrowed his eyes and tilted his head. "Enemy helicopters. They were looking for you, but not for rescue. If you see a plane or a helicopter again or hear a vehicle, stay out of sight, you hear? The police are on the enemy's side too. Don't trust anyone. If you need something, my house is that way." The man pointed to the far wall of the cabin. "I know someone, and I have a vehicle. I'm able to go into town sometimes and get supplies. It's very, very dangerous, but with the help of my friend, it's possible."

"How far is town?" Jak asked. *How far is the enemy? Where am I?*

"Very far. You're safe if you stay here in these woods. I

have to go now." With that, the man turned and walked out of the cabin, closing the door behind him.

Jak stood in the middle of the room, his brain cloudy with confusion and shock, his legs not wanting to work. When he finally pulled himself from the fog he was in, he rushed to the door, throwing it open and looking out into the fast-falling snow.

The man was gone.

Jak heard a yip and saw Pup running toward him, the limp body of a rabbit hanging from his mouth. He opened the door wider so Pup could come inside. He dropped the dead rabbit on the wood floor as Jak closed the door, leaning against it as he looked around his new home. He could sleep here and not have to look for a cold cave. It was warm and dry and yet…his heart felt empty.

He remembered the TV Baka always had on. *News,* she called it. All about war and fire. Sometimes it made Baka's eyes get shiny and her mouth turn down. She said it was far away, that war, but it must have come closer. All the way to his baka. And to him.

Your baka is gone now. You must survive on your own.

Survive.

On his own.

Again.

CHAPTER ELEVEN

Harper sat up abruptly, a scream on her lips, the sheets tangled around her legs. *The dream. It's the dream again.* She was in the car with her parents. They were chatting in the front. She watched the woods go by, her eyes beginning to shut, and then as suddenly as that, she was falling, falling, her stomach dropping into her feet as vomit rose to her lips. *Cold. So miserably cold. Water dripping down her face. Or was it blood?* She ran a hand over her sweat-drenched hair, and for a moment it seemed that the dream had followed her from sleep to wakefulness. But no, it was just the clamminess of fear. She smoothed the tangles back, swallowing down the sob that was clawing at her throat.

Somehow, she had known she'd have the dream when she went to bed the night before. It always occurred when she was mentally exhausted or emotionally distressed, and going from the Driscoll murder scene two days before to the group home yesterday, where she'd had a night shift, was obviously the catalyst.

She took several deep breaths, attempting to calm herself as she glanced at the clock. 4:13 p.m. She'd managed six hours of sleep, at least.

The hardwood floor was cold beneath her feet as she padded to the bathroom, brushing her teeth and rinsing her face with cold water and then patting it dry with the towel hung on a hook by the sink. She took a few seconds to look at herself in the mirror, her chest still rising and falling too quickly with her increased heart rate.

Her brown hair lay matted around her face in sweaty tangles, any rat's dream home, and there were dark smudges under her brown eyes, which were already too big in her face, making her look like a tired owl. *Lovely.* No amount of concealer would be enough today.

Coffee beckoned. A shower—and some cucumber slices on her eyes?—could wait. As she stood at her kitchen sink, the delicious scent of dark roast beginning to fill the room and clear her foggy brain, she stared out the window, going over everything that had happened two days before. She still couldn't believe she'd been asked to help out with a murder investigation. Or more specifically, she'd been asked to drive an investigator around and guide him through some wilderness areas. But he'd asked her opinion on a few aspects of the case that he didn't necessarily have to, and he'd listened to what she'd said and appreciated her input, and it'd made her feel…useful. *Good.*

She wondered if he'd share the things he ended up uncovering about Lucas, if there was anything to uncover at all. Which there had to be. *Right?* The picture of Lucas in the holding cell and then the way his eyes had caught hers right before he'd gotten into Deputy Brighton's SUV ran through her mind.

The machine beeped, and she poured herself a cup of coffee, added a splash of milk, and took a grateful sip as her mind moved again to the strange yet intriguing man. And that locket around his neck. *Had* she seen it before?

Her memories of her parents were clouded. She'd been so young when they'd died—only seven years old. But standing in her kitchen, the last of the afternoon sunlight streaming through the window, as she sipped the life-giving brew, that darn necklace was niggling at her mind again. Or at least something very much like it. Her mother had had something similar with…hearts maybe? Three hearts… The words were tickling at the edges of her mind. Something… entwined. She released a whoosh of breath, massaging her left temple. It was there but too far away to grasp, skating just outside her memory, taunting her.

What if… She placed her empty mug in the sink and returned to her living/bedroom area, removing the box from the top of her closet shelf and sitting on the bed to open it. Her parents' belongings—furniture and household items—had been put into a storage locker, which had gone delinquent thanks to an irresponsible "advocate" with a too-big case load, and subsequently been auctioned off. But Harper had a few photo albums and keepsakes that she'd been allowed to collect before being placed in her first foster home. Inside the box were not only photos but a few cards, memories that she hadn't looked through in a long time. She put the cards aside, not daring to peek inside. Today, seeing her parents' handwriting felt like too much, and she couldn't do it, not after the dream that had left her feeling so raw. What was it about someone's handwriting that brought them back to life with a single glance? A blessing. And a curse.

She flipped through the two photo albums, one of her parents' wedding and another of her as a baby and toddler. She didn't find anything in either one, and so she put those aside, pulling out the loose photos and putting them into a pile. She began going through them one by one, interested only in the ones of her mother. There weren't many. Most of the photos her parents had had were presumably in a digital format somewhere that she had no way to access.

She didn't linger on their smiling faces, not today, attempting to keep her emotions as objective as possible. She would put her roaming thoughts to rest and let them go. Let her questions go. Let *him* go. Him...and the way he'd made her feel, feelings she didn't dare dwell on too specifically. Him and his wild clothes and haunted eyes, the man who lived alone in the woods and had looked around at the town like he'd never seen civilization before.

No, it was impossible really. The more she thought about it, the crazier it seemed. That man had nothing to do with her or her parents. She was grasping at straws. Her memory was faulty, full of holes and—

Three hearts entwined...

She sucked in a breath and dropped all but one photo, bringing it closer to see the locket hanging at the base of her mother's throat.

Three hearts entwined in the middle.

It looked exactly like the one Lucas had been wearing.

———

Dusk was already falling by the time Harper pulled herself together, showered, and threw on clothes. She'd skipped the cucumbers and the concealer, more pressing things on her mind than her dark, overtired eyes.

She pulled on her winter gear, including her waterproof snow boots. She might have to hike a bit in the snow, and she wanted to be prepared. Large flakes were falling steadily by the time she pulled off onto the road leading to Isaac Driscoll's empty cabin. Isaac Driscoll's empty, *blood-stained* cabin, Harper reminded herself. A shiver moved through her, and for the first time since she'd spotted the necklace in the photo of her dead mother, she second-guessed her decision to drive out there and confront Lucas.

She glanced at the rifle in the back seat behind her, the weapon she carried when she took hunters out in the wild and what she'd placed in her truck before leaving. Instead of bringing her comfort, it only brought further uncertainty.

This is crazy. Temporary insanity.

She knew how to hunt and was a good shot, but she'd never been especially keen to do it. It always left her feeling kind of…sad. Her heart always ached when she saw the dead animal she'd killed staring unseeing at her with big, startled eyes. She never told anyone that—the quality wasn't exactly a selling point for people looking for a competent guide to take them on their wilderness expeditions, but…she could admit it to herself.

The land south of Driscoll's cabin was mostly flat, and she turned her truck in the direction of the three peaked mountains, the four-wheel drive making it easy to roll over the snow-covered ground. She drove around trees, her tires bumping over rocks and small hills that leveled out again.

How far had he said he lived from Driscoll? Ten thousand something steps? She removed her phone from her pocket, but there was no service. *Darn.* Agent Gallagher had been able to pull up an email though, and Dwayne had mentioned that Driscoll made a 9-1-1 call. Reception was probably spotty as it often was in the wilderness. She was pretty sure there was an old logging road with a dead end somewhere in the direction she was traveling. That open area where the trees had been removed might provide some service. But for now, Google wouldn't be any help.

She thought she remembered that it took the average person about fifteen minutes to walk a mile. How many steps would you walk in fifteen minutes? About…two thousand? Maybe? If so, that meant…Lucas lived approximately five miles from Driscoll.

If her math was right, which was iffy at best. Also, she was headed from Driscoll's toward the peaked mountains Lucas had mentioned to Dwayne, but there was no telling if his house was mostly a straight shot or if he'd turned in a different direction at some point. She might drive her truck right into a lake.

I should turn back.

This was totally stupid anyway. *Irrational,* actually. It was just…it was just that she'd spent so many lonely years looking for her parents. She'd gone out over and over, day after day, from the break of dawn until night fell, and had never come back with a thing. And then that necklace. And she *had* to know. Right then.

I can't wait another second.

Her breath hitched when she spotted smoke rising into the deepening night sky, her heart lurching. She pressed her foot to the accelerator, and the truck jerked forward, snow spraying to either side. *It's his cabin,* she thought, her nerves zinging. *It has to be.*

Anticipation trumped her caution, and she pressed on the accelerator, driving through the small copse of trees in front of what she could now see was a log structure, not large but larger than Driscoll's place. *Huh*. If Driscoll had two places on his property, why would he choose the smaller of the two?

She stopped in front of it, grabbed her rifle, and hopped out. Before she could talk herself out of it, she climbed the three steps to Lucas's front door and rapped twice, her breath labored even though she hadn't exerted herself with the short walk.

The door swung open, and he was standing there, bigger and more imposing than she remembered him, wearing jeans and a long-sleeved T-shirt. She stepped back, and he did too. She met his eyes, the shock on his face clear.

Harper cleared her throat, propping the gun on the small porch. His eyes followed it, and then he looked back to her. "Where did you get that locket?" she blurted.

He stared at her for a long moment and then tilted his head, his dark brows dipping.

"Tell me."

He looked behind her to where her truck was parked and then slowly back to her as if trying to understand the situation. His head turned toward the small grouping of trees, and he muttered something under his breath before stepping forward, directly into her.

Harper sucked in a breath, a small sound of surprised fear rising to her throat as he took her forearms in his hands, moved her aside easily, and walked past her. She whipped around to see him hop down the steps and prowl toward the trees.

What...

She watched him for a moment, immobile with surprise. He crouched down and started moving the snow with his arm, speaking words she was now too far away to hear.

She moved slowly down the steps, walking toward him, uncertain and completely baffled.

As the crunch of her footsteps sounded in the snow, he looked over his shoulder and then back at whatever he was doing, continuing to clear something. She leaned forward and pulled in a startled breath when she saw four sets of eyes peering back at her, shiny in the dim light, but not so dim that she couldn't see what they were. Foxes. Babies. She took in her own tire tracks right next to the den and clenched her eyes shut for a moment. She'd driven her truck right over a den of baby foxes. "I didn't know they were there."

He stood, turning toward her. She couldn't read the expression on his face, and they stood looking at each other for an awkward moment.

"God, I'm so stupid. I bring people out to the wilderness for my *job*, and I should know better."

He stared at her again, an infinitesimal narrowing of his eyes. But he didn't contradict her.

"Your feet are bare," she finally said. Stupidly. "They must be cold," she added. Even more stupidly. *Which, at this point, should be my middle name,* she thought with an internal grimace. She pressed her lips together, embarrassed and uneasy.

He simply stared at her for a moment and then turned toward his house.

She glanced at the fox den, and with the snow cleared, she could see it was only four baby foxes, no mother. She must be out hunting. They were still covered in the snow her reckless driving had caused to cave in on them, and they had to be cold. A tremor of guilt went through her. Concern for the helpless things.

Lucas had cared about them too. He'd run out there to make sure they weren't suffocating to death.

"Will they be okay?" she called, knowing it was better not to touch them, knowing it would risk their mother smelling a predator and abandoning the den. Still...to leave them that way, cold and wet and alone...

He slowed and turned his head slightly. "They will be or they won't. Better to let their mother do the job now. If she's still alive."

If. She knew he was right. Still she hesitated, watching as he climbed his short set of steps. He was going to go back inside his house. "Wait," she called. It only took her a few seconds to jog back to his house and climb the steps to the porch where he had turned and was watching her, that same thin-lipped expression on his face. He looked more... normal now without the layer of animal skins. Just a large, muscular man with several visible scars, longish hair, and a short beard. Not a caveman...no...more of a mountain man or...a guy who'd been out living off the land for several months.

An extremely good-looking mountain man who exuded testosterone and danger. And if she was so unsettled, why was she noticing the former? *Because it can't be ignored, that's all,* she told herself. His good looks *startled* her in their intensity. It wouldn't make her any less cautious of him. Maybe he was like one of those wildcats she'd spotted a few times. Sleek and beautiful to look at but wild and dangerous. Brutal even.

Although he didn't seem brutal. Just wary...and curious. Intelligent and uncertain.

He gave the rifle she'd left propped on the porch a casual glance. "I'm sorry. I was careless and rude. I...I thought I recognized the locket hanging around your neck. It looks familiar, and I... I was wondering if I could see it, just for a moment. I'll give it back. I just…may I look at it? Um, Lucas. Oh, and in case you don't remember my name, I'm Harper."

She'd stumbled over her words and felt breathless, a lump rising in her chest for reasons she wasn't sure she could explain. She could hardly believe she was out there, standing in the snow with this man. Couldn't believe she'd acted so rashly. Foolishly, maybe. But she couldn't manage to be sorry for it or wish she'd considered it more carefully. "Please," she whispered.

His light eyes seemed to soften minutely, though he was still regarding her as though she were an anomaly he couldn't understand.

Their gazes held as he pulled the leather string from the collar of his shirt, and her gaze shot to his large, scarred hand, watched as it pulled the string so the locket appeared. Her breath hitched, and she stepped forward, her trembling fingers reaching for the small, round piece of silver, hesitating midway, the fear inside her suddenly growing. *What if… What if…*

She was standing on a precipice. The next several seconds might change *everything*. With a rushed exhale, she extended her arm and grasped the locket, her hand touching his as she took another step toward Lucas. They were toe to toe. She tipped her chin, looking up at him, and he stared down at her, their breath mingling, the weight of the moment seeming to have fallen over both of them. She saw his nostrils flare and knew he'd just inhaled deeply. Was he inhaling *her*? His head dipped minutely, so minutely she wouldn't have noticed if she hadn't been so close, and then the same drawing in of breath. Yes, he was taking in her scent. And something about the flickering expression on his face told her he'd enjoyed the experience. It made her stomach clench in a foreign way, and she was so overwhelmed with fear and emotion and confusion, she thought she might faint.

She didn't *know* this version of herself. She always held it together. Always. And yet all she wanted to do was fall into his chest and ask him to hold her for a moment while she gathered herself to look at that locket.

Wildcat, Harper, she reminded herself, taking a small step back.

Time slowed, and with effort, she moved her gaze from his, her eyes going to the locket that was engraved with three linked hearts.

Always together, never apart.

She let out a small sob as she reached up with her other hand, using her thumbnail to open the small disk, her hands shaking so badly, it almost slipped from her grasp. But it didn't. It fell open to reveal a miniature photo of three people, their arms encircling each other, the joy in their smiling faces clear.

She remembered that joy, felt it cascade over her like a ray of warm summer sun.

The photo was of her father.

Her mother.

And herself.

CHAPTER TWELVE

"Agent Gallagher?" The tall, sixtyish man in the khakis and button-down blue shirt extended his hand, giving Mark an easy smile as they shook. "I'm Dr. Swift. What is it I can do for you?"

They were standing in an open reception area, hallways on two sides where a small group stood chatting. "I have some questions about someone who used to work here. Isaac Driscoll? Is there somewhere more private we can speak?" Mark was eager to talk to this man and to sit down in a place where he could make better note of his reactions—the man who had once worked closely with Isaac Driscoll.

"Isaac? Uh…I haven't heard his name mentioned in years." Dr. Swift appeared flustered for a brief moment. "But yes, of course. Please follow me."

Dr. Swift led him to a room down the hall with a white-board on one wall and, across from that, a long one-way mirror. It appeared that this was some sort of interview room, and when he asked, Dr. Swift said, "Yes. Project researchers use this room to observe subjects answering questions or relating to each other, reacting to things, etcetera, depending on the study."

"Ah," Mark said. He'd taken classes in social science when he was in school—which was a *long* time ago now—but was interested to hear exactly what was involved in the study aspect.

There was a large table in the center of the room with a pile of small white notebooks off to the side. "Is this okay?" Dr. Swift asked, pulling a chair out from the table and indicating one across from it.

"This is great, thanks," Mark answered, taking the seat across from the doctor.

Dr. Swift looked at him expectantly, lacing his fingers together on the table. He was a large man, and his shirt stretched tight over his wide shoulders, a button sitting on his stomach looking dangerously close to popping. "Isaac Driscoll retired...let's see"—he looked upward, obviously doing the math—"in two thousand two or three?"

Mark nodded. "Yes, I know it's been a while."

"What is this about, Agent? Is Isaac in some kind of trouble?"

"Yes, I'm sorry to be the bearer of bad news, but Isaac Driscoll was found dead two days ago."

Dr. Swift stared at him for a few moments, seemingly frozen with surprise. Finally, he blew out a long breath. "*Found* dead... How?"

"Murdered."

Dr. Swift's eyes widened. "Murdered? Isaac? How? Why?"

"We're still investigating the crime. I don't have many answers yet. I'm hoping you can shed some light on a few things."

Dr. Swift blew out another breath, running his hand through his black-and-gray-speckled hair, dramatic streaks of silver at his temples. "I can try. It's been a long time since I even talked to the man."

"What exactly did he do here at Rayform? His job title is listed as social researcher."

Dr. Swift nodded. "His job entailed collecting, analyzing, and interpreting data. The government was, and is, particularly interested in findings that might help change social policies or affect current ones. The applications are dependent on the purpose of the study."

"And are most of the studies conducted here funded by the government?"

"Most, yes, though some of the studies are funded by research grants or fellowships."

"Can you give me an example of a specific study Isaac worked on? I'm trying to get a better picture of who he was and why someone would want to harm him."

Dr. Swift looked off to the side in thought for a moment before answering. "I think the study he completed just before he retired was about poverty and criminal behavior, something along those lines. I don't remember the specifics, but I could probably look it up and email it to you."

"That'd be great. Thanks." Mark slid a business card across the table, and Dr. Swift took it, putting it in the breast pocket of his shirt. "What can you tell me about Dr. Driscoll on a personal level?"

"Overall he was a nice guy. He could be intense. A little...awkward at times maybe." He smiled. "What can I say? He was a researcher. We're not often known for our bubbly personalities." He frowned. "God, I can't believe... can't believe he's dead. Murdered." He looked back at Mark.

"You don't think his death had anything to do with his work here, do you?"

"It's doubtful since he retired so long ago, but I'm still trying to see the big picture. Dr. Driscoll bought several thousand acres of land about twenty miles outside the nearest populated area. Do you have any idea why he would retire and move out to the middle of nowhere?"

Dr. Swift looked surprised for a moment and then thoughtful. He sighed. "From what I remember, Isaac grew increasingly pessimistic about people in general…society as a whole." He pressed his lips together for a moment. "I do remember him saying several times that he was ready to be done with people entirely, that animals behaved more rationally and in a way that would preserve their species as a whole rather than destroying it." Dr. Swift chuckled, though there wasn't much humor in it. "I thought he was mostly joking or just…venting. Although I have to say, I didn't completely disagree with the sentiment. It's easy to become cynical after studying societal downfalls year after year. Sometimes it feels like things never change."

Mark offered a wry smile. He didn't completely disagree with the sentiment either. He'd seen things in his line of work that made the idea of abandoning people entirely and living with wild animals sound appealing. People were hateful and cruel, vicious and underhanded. But…but they were also capable of selflessness and acts of deep love and grace. Mark had to remind himself of that often. And the fact was, people needed other people in order to hold on to their own humanity. He didn't need to be a social scientist to know that.

"So you think Isaac Driscoll may have bought land far away from society because the work he did caused him to disdain people in general?"

Dr. Swift released a long breath and rubbed at his eye with one finger. "I can't speak to his exact motives. Like I said, it's been a long time since I've spoken with him. But… it doesn't sound improbable to me."

Mark nodded, reaching into his pocket and bringing out the small notebook. Inside, he'd placed a printout of a still frame of Lucas as he'd waited in the holding cell a couple of days before. He unfolded the printout and handed it to Dr. Swift. "Do you recognize this man?"

Dr. Swift regarded the picture for several moments before shaking his head. "No. Who is he?"

"A man currently living on Driscoll's property. He says Driscoll allowed him to stay there after his parents abandoned him."

Dr. Swift sighed again. "That sounds like Isaac."

"How do you mean?"

"Isaac did a lot of volunteer work for social services programs. We did many studies on the foster care system— still do—and it was one of the areas of research that particularly bothered Isaac."

Mark nodded. "Understandable." The worse cases he'd worked on had involved kids. He could never desensitize himself to the idea of a child suffering in any way. And as far as Mark was concerned, if he ever did, that was the moment he'd know it was time to turn in his badge.

"What's interesting is that he allowed this man"—he pointed to the photo of Lucas still on the table—"to stay on his property when he was only a child but never alerted any authorities that he'd been abandoned."

Dr. Swift stared down at the photo of Lucas for a moment before meeting Mark's eyes. "Maybe to Isaac, the foster care system was a fate worse than living alone in the wilderness."

"Do you think it's possible he was really that far gone?"

Dr. Swift shrugged. "I'm only speculating."

Mark nodded, pulling another picture out of his notebook. "What about this woman? Have you seen her before?"

Dr. Swift looked at the photo of the woman who'd been found dead in the bed-and-breakfast, and his brow furrowed. Finally, he shook his head. "Not that I can recall."

Mark took the pictures from him, refolding them and returning both to his notebook before reaching across the table to shake Dr. Swift's hand. "Thank you for your time. Please, if you think of anything else that might shed light on this crime, give me a call. And my email address is on that card too if you'd be so kind as to forward me the results of the last study Driscoll was working on."

"Absolutely."

Mark turned to leave when he spotted a picture hung on the wall to the left of the door. He moved closer, studying it.

"The Battle of Thermopylae," Dr. Swift said, coming up beside him and looking at the picture.

Mark glanced at him. "This same picture is hung in Isaac Driscoll's house."

Dr. Swift looked at him, a small smile on his lips. "In fact, Isaac is the one who hung this here so many years ago." His smile grew. "Government buildings rarely invest in decorating, I'm afraid." He looked back at the picture as Mark removed his notebook and jotted down the battle the doctor had just named, spelling it to the best of his ability. He'd google it later. "Talk about a study in courage against overwhelming odds. *And* teamwork. The Spartans took the cake."

"Is that what Driscoll liked so much about them?" He

must have admired that to hang the same picture at work and in his home. A rendering of what he wished society *was* despite what he considered daily proof that it was not? That it was worth the fight even if the odds were against you?

"Probably. They were a fascinating culture."

Mark gave the picture one last glance. "Thank you again, Doctor."

"You're welcome," Dr. Swift said, his eyes remaining on the battle in front of him.

He didn't look away as Mark turned and left the room.

CHAPTER THIRTEEN

Harper let go of the locket, and it dropped onto Lucas's shirt. Her heart was racing. Her skin felt prickly, and she was having trouble swallowing as shock waves rolled through her. "How?" she croaked. "Where?" She shook her head, attempting to clear the ringing that had started sounding in her ears the moment she'd seen the picture inside. It *was* her mother's locket, the one she'd been wearing when she died.

Dizziness rolled through her, and her teeth began chattering. Lucas turned and opened the door to his house, stepping inside and then looking back at her questioningly. She noticed his feet were still bare, and despite her own state of shock, she grimaced. *They must be freezing.* She followed him inside and closed the door but didn't move into the room. She leaned her rifle on the wall next to where she stood. "Please tell me," she said, and this time her voice sounded steadier, though her heart was beating wildly.

"I found this necklace in a car at the bottom of a canyon. It had a different chain then, but it broke." Her eyes roved over his face, his expression so intensely serious, she couldn't move her eyes away. He glanced downward to where the locket lay on his chest. "Do you...know these people?" He seemed to be holding his breath as he stared at her, his fingers finding the locket and rubbing it between them as if he'd made the same movement a hundred times before and did it now out of habit.

"Yes. They're my family," she whispered. "The baby, it's me."

He opened his mouth, closed it, and then finally said, "You." He stared at her again, his fingers grasping the locket as he looked at it and then at her as though trying to merge the tiny picture of the baby inside with the grown woman standing before him.

"We were in a car wreck when I was very young. I somehow wandered away from the crash and was found, but they never were."

His eyes roamed her face for a moment, something softening in his gaze. Understanding. "I can take you to them if you want."

Harper reached back, holding on to the doorframe so she wouldn't fall over. God, she couldn't believe it. *The car. The car. He found the car.* Her parents' final resting place, the thing she'd been searching relentlessly for since she was old enough to go out in this wilderness alone. She nodded, tears burning at the backs of her eyes. But she refused to let them fall, didn't want to share her grief with this man, this stranger. Truth be told, she didn't want to share her grief with anyone. She wondered if she even knew how.

"When?" she asked. "How long ago did you find it?"

"Five winters ago." He flinched very subtly and cleared his throat. "Five years ago," he amended as though he realized he'd answered incorrectly the second it'd rolled off his tongue. Only... *God, if I lived out here, I'd probably calculate time by how many winters I survived too.* But she couldn't think about that right then, not with the knowledge that her parents' car was so close and this man could take her to it. To *them.*

"Can you take me there now?"

Lucas glanced out the window. "No, it's too late. I can take you there in the morning. It's dark and icy now, and we'll have to climb down."

Climb down?

She started to argue, to beg him to reconsider, but she knew he was right. Night had fallen, the temperature had dropped, and going out now would be foolish when simply waiting until daybreak lowered any risks significantly. She'd waited this long. She could wait one more night.

"Can I ask you why you wear it?"

He glanced at the necklace on his dark shirt and then reached up and untied it, walking to where she stood, stopping when he was several feet away. He extended his hand and held it out to her, and she took it from him, clasping it in her fist. "It's yours," he said. He hadn't answered her question, but there was a lump in her throat now, so instead of repeating it, she simply nodded and tied it around her own neck. As his gaze lingered on it, there was such unmistakable sadness in his eyes. He'd just given up something of great value to him, she realized. Handing it over to her had cost him. Not a monetary cost, but something more important to him. *Emotional connection?* Whatever the answer to that question, he'd given it to her anyway.

"Thank you," she whispered, laying her hand over it. The small piece of metal was still warm from his body. "How'd you find it? What were you doing?"

Something skated over his expression, but he quickly schooled it. "Just saw it one day. The sun shined on the metal, and it called to me." He looked briefly confused like maybe he hadn't said what he wanted to say. She understood him though. The glinting metal had caught his attention.

"I see," she said, to reassure him she did. She sighed. "Well, I'm glad. I mean, it's very fortunate that I met you and...well..." He'd been wearing a picture of her around his neck for the past five years. It made her feel... She didn't know how it made her feel, but the feeling wasn't negative. It was as though he'd been protecting her family for her. *Always together, never apart.*

He regarded her for another moment and then turned, walking to the wood stove and feeding it a few logs. It was then that she finally took in the room. There were four metal beds lined up on the wall to her right, though three of the beds were barren of mattresses or blankets. The fourth was obviously the one Lucas slept on, a dark-gray wool blanket pulled to the top of the mattress and a single pillow. They reminded Harper of beds she'd seen in prison movies, and she frowned.

"Do other people live here?" she asked, nodding to the beds.

He looked at the empty cots from where he was squatting in front of the fire, poking the logs inside with a long stick. "This was going to be a summer camp cabin, but... someone ran out of money. Or something like that. It was empty when Driscoll came to this land. That's what he told me anyway. It's all I know."

Harper tilted her head. He'd phrased it strangely. "Do you think he was lying?"

Lucas came to his full height, the door of the stove swinging shut with a dull click. "I don't know."

Harper opened her mouth to ask him another question, but she wasn't sure what. It was just…the way he'd said *that's what he told me anyway* and the tone in his voice when he'd said it made her think he questioned Driscoll's truthfulness in general. And it made her curious. *You're not an investigator, Harper. Stop acting like one.*

"Okay, well, I'll just"—she pulled the door open, the arctic air causing an immediate shiver—"be back in the morning. How early?"

"First sunlight."

First sunlight. "Okay." She grabbed her rifle and turned back once more before pulling the door to close it behind her. "I'll bring coffee."

His brows lowered, and she suddenly felt stupid. "Do you drink coffee?"

"Sure."

"All right." She stepped onto the porch and shut the door, closing her eyes momentarily, feeling like an idiot. But he was going to take her to the place where her parents still rested, the site of that long-ago crash that had stolen the life she was supposed to live. Nerves tingled underneath her skin, and she inhaled a big breath of cold air as she climbed into her truck and turned the ignition. *Nothing.* She tried again, and still nothing. "Shit," she groaned, looking up and realizing that in her haste to confront Lucas, she'd not only almost killed a litter of foxes, but she also must have left her truck door slightly ajar, leaving the interior light on. Her battery was old and needed to be replaced, but she'd been putting it off because she couldn't really afford a new one. And now it was dead. *Nice work, Harper.*

Shit. Shit. Shit.

She sat there for a minute, considering her options. She needed a jump start. But it was too late and the weather too bad to call anyone now. She had planned on being back at Lucas's place at first light anyway, so…she'd just sleep in her truck. She was familiar with "roughing it." It was practically in her job description.

She'd need a blanket though, something other than only her coat to ward off the worst of the night chill. She sighed, resigning herself to knocking on Lucas's door again.

She trudged through the snow and back up his steps, and before she could knock, he was opening the door, obviously having seen her coming from the front window. "Hi." She attempted a smile but knew it fell flat. She gestured back toward her truck. "Dead battery. No big deal, but do you have an extra blanket I can borrow?"

He glanced to the truck behind her and then to her. "You're going to sleep out there?"

"In the truck, yes. It'll be fine. I'm used to sleeping sitting up anyway…" Her words faded away. She hadn't meant to say that. She cleared her throat. He regarded her again for a moment in the way that made her feel totally conspicuous when, in actuality, he was the one who was strange.

Right?

He turned, walking slowly to the bed with the mattress on it, grabbing the blanket he obviously used and carrying it back to where she stood. He held it out to her. "Oh…no, I couldn't take your only blanket."

His brow dipped, and he regarded her. "Why?"

"Why? Um, well…you'll be cold."

"I'm fine. I have a fire."

She still felt a little guilty, but not guilty enough to freeze to death in her truck in the middle of the woods. "Right. Okay, then. Thank you. I'll see you at sunrise." She jogged down the steps and back to her truck, where she brought the blanket around her shoulders and body. It smelled like him. Like—she leaned her head forward and inhaled the edge of the thick, scratchy material—mountain air and male skin? No, that sounded like a bad deodorant commercial. She inhaled again, more deeply this time. It was...*nice,* and it caused little flutters in her stomach. It wasn't soapy or piney or any of those descriptors she'd usually use for the way a man smelled. It *was* clean, and she was glad because she'd initially questioned his hygiene—which in hindsight might have been rude, even if it was only in her own mind—but his scent was clean in a natural way. Like he bathed in a stream and dried his body in the sun and—

Oh God, shut up, *Harper.* She dropped the blanket from her nose and leaned her head back against the seat. *No wonder I don't sleep. My damn brain will not turn off.*

Also, she was freezing. She tightened the blanket around her, her teeth beginning to chatter. The tip of her nose felt like an ice cube. Her mind turned again to the tiny foxes in the den she'd run over, and her heart stuttered as she thought about how cold they must be, their helpless little bodies covered in snow, ice matted in their fur. Had their mother returned?

Harper got out of her truck and trudged back to the den at the base of a massive pine tree. She turned on the light on her phone and angled it away so it wasn't shining directly in the den but she could still see the small creatures inside.

A quiet growl sounded from within, and Harper took a step back but leaned her head farther forward. Inside the den, the mother lay nursing her babies, snarling softly, a warning not to come any closer. "I won't," she whispered. "You're safe." She took one last moment to gaze at them, dry and cozy, and then switched off the light, moving away.

Harper couldn't help the tears that began streaming down her face. She wasn't sure why the emotion had overcome her so swiftly, but it had, and now she stood there, crying softly in the snow, the dark night engulfing her.

She felt so intensely...*alone.*

"You can sleep inside if you want."

She whirled toward his voice, turning on her light again. He squinted, so she lowered it, swiping at the tears on her cheeks, embarrassed to have been caught crying over a fox den. Embarrassed to have been caught crying at all. How had he snuck up on her like that anyway?

"She came back," Harper said quietly. She inclined her head toward the den. "The mother."

He paused for a moment. "Good."

She shivered again, and he nodded toward her truck. "Bring your gun and sleep inside." And with that, he turned, heading back to his house but leaving the door open. It looked warm in there—warm and lit by candlelight. Cozy.

She grabbed the blanket from the truck, pressing her lips together as she considered the rifle. It felt rude to take it inside when he was offering her a warm place to sleep, even though he didn't have to. But... Well, he *was* still a stranger *and* a wildcat *and* a person of interest in a murder investigation. Not to mention, lots of bad things in this world had happened to girls because they were worried about appearing rude. She grabbed the weapon and walked up his steps and through his door, closing it behind her.

"Thank you. I, um... You won't even know I'm here."

He looked confused. "I'll know you're here."

"I just mean I won't be any bother." She considered the three empty beds, but none of them had mattresses, and sleeping on bare metal springs didn't seem comfortable at all, and so she sat on the floor, leaning against the wall and laying her gun on the floor next to her. She wrapped herself in the blanket again and let out a pretend yawn so he'd know she was all taken care of. "This is very nice of you," she said. "If I can repay your kindness in some way, let me know."

She swore she saw his lips tilt slightly, but then he turned away, lying on his own bed, his back to her. "If you could try not to shoot me in my sleep, that would be good," he said without turning, and she swore she heard a smile in his voice. *Was he joking with her?* The idea shocked her, but it also caused a burst of pleasure too.

"I promise I won't," she said, and she could hear the smile in her own voice before she realized there was one on her lips.

His shoulder moved slightly, but he didn't answer, and after a moment she closed her eyes, reveling in the warmth enveloping her, her shivering ceasing completely.

She was comfortable, but she knew she wouldn't sleep. Harper had trouble sleeping in general, much less sitting against a stranger's wall with said stranger sleeping twenty feet from her. Yet, despite the cabin and its lack of refinement, she felt comfortable. Was it the fire? The man? The deep, enfolding silence of the forest surrounding them? Or was it that she felt peace? *Always together, never apart.*

No, she wouldn't sleep, but thank God she was warm. Content. And there were only a handful of hours until dawn.

CHAPTER FOURTEEN

Ribbons of powder. Puffs of wind. Both dancing across the frosty field. Jak stepped through it, moving around the buried rocks and hidden holes he knew by memory.

Driscoll's house came into view, smoke trailing from the chimney, and Jak picked up his pace, moving quickly through the falling snow. He didn't like visiting Driscoll. He did it as little as possible, but there were some things he didn't want to do without, now that winter had arrived.

Especially matches.

He could cook now but chose not to. When he did that, he couldn't taste the life in it anymore. He remembered his baka had talked about vitamins and minerals, and maybe those were the same thing. Now that words were hardly ever in his mouth, Jak had learned that pictures in his head explained things better. He saw vitamins and minerals like tiny grains of life that flowed through the living being, and when you ate them, you could taste all the things that animal had experienced. Its life flowed into you and, in that way, never really stopped living. Life went on and on and on. Never stopping.

But he didn't want to go back to a winter without the warmth of fire, even though he now had a roof over his head, a blanket, and Pup's body heat. Warmth was worth the walk—and worth a few minutes with Driscoll. Jak didn't like him though. He got a cold, sweaty feeling whenever he was around him. He hated how Driscoll's eyes got all squirrelly and the way he watched Jak's every move. Jak had learned to tell when there was a predator nearby, not just by the snapping of a twig under its step or the stink of its fur as it drew close. He knew from the whispery feeling inside and the way the small hairs on the back of his neck stood up when something dangerous was stalking him.

He got that feeling when he was around Driscoll.

The man had never done anything other than trade supplies with him, and yet…that feeling stayed. Jak figured that whatever Driscoll did in town to get supplies, it was probably sneaky and full of lies.

But Jak wasn't going to think too hard about that. His baka once explained that people did what they had to do to survive during wars. And he needed matches. That was all.

Jak had let Pup out of the house at first sunlight, and he still hadn't been back when Jak left, so he was alone on this trip. He wanted it that way, though, and always went alone to Driscoll's. Pup was loyal and faithful to him, and he didn't fear him in the least, but Jak had no idea what he'd do if he saw a stranger. Especially one who put off the stink of a predator the way Driscoll did.

The few times that Jak heard a car on the road in the

near faraway or what might be people walking in the wilderness around him, he turned in the other direction and moved away, quiet as a wolf. Quiet as Pup. He figured doing that had taught Pup to fear humans other than Jak. And besides that, he didn't know how Driscoll would act if he saw a giant wolf approaching him, whether he looked nice or not.

Driscoll opened the door before Jak had even knocked, like he'd been watching for him, which made those tiny hairs stand up on Jak's neck.

"Jak. How are you? Come in. Get warm."

Jak went inside the small room, thinking as he always did how much he wanted to leave, just as he was getting there.

He reached in the bag he'd made by stitching together two rabbit skins with long pieces of thick grass. It wasn't very strong and couldn't hold anything too heavy, but it worked for his needs, and it'd kept him busy for three full days. Jak pulled out the fish packed in snow and wrapped in another skin. He'd caught the fish that morning by banging a rock through the ice and dangling small pieces of rabbit meat into the hole. It'd taken him all morning, but he'd caught four. Two to trade, one for himself, and one for Pup.

When he looked up, Driscoll's squirrelly eyes were moving between the fish and the bag, a smile turning his thick lips up. "You've been working hard. Figuring out how to survive with what's available to you."

"What other choice do we have?" he asked. "Until the war's over."

"Yes. What are you looking to trade for?"

"Matches."

"Ah." He sighed. "Matches are a precious commodity."

Precious commodity. His mind whirred, working quickly through the meaning of those words. He remembered *precious. Important.* Matches were an important *thing*? A commodity was a thing. *An important thing.*

Yes, yes, they were. Jak knew that better than anyone. What was more precious than life-giving heat? "I can bring you more fish. How many?"

Driscoll ran his fingers down the sides of his mouth and over his beard, eyeing Jak in a way that made his muscles tense. "Bring me a pair of boots. These ones I'm wearing are old and worn, and I could use something warmer and lined with fur."

Boots? He looked down at the boots he'd made for himself using pieces of his old shoes, skins, and fur, stitched and wrapped together with long blades of grass. They did the job and kept his feet warm, but they were hardly something to trade. He looked at Driscoll's boots. They looked fine to him. Jak wished he had boots like those instead of the ones he'd made using whatever he could find—boots that fell apart so often he was always fixing something on them or leaving one behind as he took a step in the deep piles of snow.

"If you bring me a pair of boots that I approve of, I'll give you two boxes of matches."

Jak's heart picked up speed. *Two boxes.* That would get him through the winter and into spring. He'd come up with better ways to make boots. His mind started buzzing like cricket song, thinking about all the items that might work better than the ones he was using. He had the pocketknife that he used to make small holes, but using grass as thread wasn't the best. It dried out and broke. He was always having to fix pieces that came apart. "Okay," he said, before he could talk himself out of it. The worst that could happen was that Driscoll didn't like his work and didn't give him the matches.

Driscoll looked pleased. "Good boy. Come with me and I'll get you five matches for the fish."

Jak paused before following Driscoll into the room next to the main one that he figured was where he slept. He stayed in the doorway as Driscoll walked to a dresser, opened the top drawer, and counted out five matches. He tried to block the drawer with his body, but when he moved just a little bit, Jak was able to see that there were two rows of large matchboxes inside. He had enough matches for ten winters. Jak tried not to feel angry. They were Driscoll's matches, and Jak was lucky the man was trading with him for five.

He moved his gaze from the closing drawer to the picture above the dresser. It was a drawing of men fighting, and Jak stared at it for a minute. He'd played war with his toy soldiers when he lived with Baka, but the men in the picture were dressed in weird clothes, nothing like the military gear his action figures had worn.

"The Battle of Thermopylae," Driscoll said, stopping beside him in the doorway and looking back at the picture. "One of the most famous battles of all time. The Spartans held Thermopylae against invaders, a mountain pass of extreme strategic importance, for three days with a mere three hundred men."

Driscoll had just said several words Jak didn't know. He'd like to go over them—*collect them*—but he also wanted to leave. "The Spartans?" Jak glanced at Driscoll, and his eyes were shiny like he might be about to cry. But happy tears. Maybe he liked fighting. Maybe he liked *war*. Maybe he *liked* living this way. Maybe that's why Jak felt so funny around him all the time. Jak backed up two steps, putting more space between them.

Driscoll didn't seem to notice as he nodded his head up and down, up and down. "The greatest warriors of all time," he said. "They were *bred* for battle. Tested to know they were men who would *never* give up despite the most dire odds. It's said that the only time a Spartan soldier got a break from training was during a war." Driscoll laughed, and Jak gave a tight smile, though he didn't really understand the joke.

"But, see, *survival* is the greatest training of all. It's that inexplicable something that makes a man *keep going* despite the obstacles before him, despite miserable conditions or impossible feats. *That's* the thing that makes the most fearsome of all warriors. Any strong, dexterous man can learn to wield a weapon, but it's an extraordinary soldier who never gives up. *Ever.*"

Jak backed up a few more steps into the main room, and Driscoll followed him, his eyes still shiny. "We must study history to forge the future. Ancient people understood war so much better than we do today. They...they..." His hands flew around for a few seconds like he was trying to grab the right words from the air. His eyes met Jak's. "They understood that sacrifices must always be made for the common good of society. They knew that without sacrifice, humanity would fall to selfishness, greed, and ruin. One is never as important as all. That's what's brought us to this point, you see?"

No, Jak didn't see. Not at all. But he nodded to make it seem as if he got what Driscoll was going on about. He thought it must be about the war. Driscoll knew much more about what was happening in town, in the United States, in... That's all Jak knew of the world, other than it was round and people talked in different languages if you traveled far enough to find them.

"People are so *bad,* Jak. So bad and selfish and immoral. They don't *learn.* They never learn, and we all pay for their mistakes."

Jak stared at him. Was that true? Were people bad? Some were, he knew that. People had taken his baka away. Tried to kill him. Made it so he had to live in the faraway woods by himself. But some were good, weren't they? His baka had been good. She'd tried to pretend she didn't like him all the time, but he could tell she did anyway. She'd cared for him and taught him things and looked proud when he did a good job at something or another. She'd given him books and words and numbers and orange drinks with fizzy bubbles. But now he was confused and wanted to *go.* "Okay. I'll be back then with the boots."

Driscoll blinked, and then his eyes moved over Jak's head, his brow scrunching. "What?" He gave his head a shake. "Yes. Boots. Right. Yes, bring me a pair of boots. And I'll give you a box of matches."

"Two boxes," Jak corrected. "You said you'd give me two boxes."

Driscoll waved his hand as though there was no difference between one or two. But he couldn't mean *that.* The difference between plenty of matches and not enough was life...or death. "Two boxes. Yes, fine."

Jak nodded, already turning toward the door. "Bye," he said as he slipped outside into the snow. He turned his face, small bullets of icy hail hitting his cheek. A whipping wind had picked up. He should ask Driscoll if he could stay for a while instead of making the walk home. His face already hurt, and his boots were coming loose; he could feel it with each step. He didn't want to let Driscoll know that though or he might back out of their trade. And anyway, even as the thought of staying drifted through his mind, the whispery feelings were telling him to go, and he was moving away from the house. Away from Driscoll and his wild eyes. Away from the man who made him feel like prey, even though he didn't know why.

CHAPTER FIFTEEN

The girl named Harper was snoring. Loudly.

Lucas watched her where she was sitting on his floor, her head leaned forward and her mouth wide open. He took the moment to stare at her without her knowing, to let his eyes travel freely.

It's *you,* he thought. It felt like a bee was trapped in his chest.

She was the baby in the photo he'd worn around his neck for so long. Was that why the low-down whispers stirred whenever she was around? Why he felt like he *knew* her? He reached for the necklace out of habit, his hand falling away. Empty. Still staring. *She* was the small smiling girl with the pink bow in her brown curls.

How could it be? It shocked him. Although so much shocked him. Why wouldn't it? A jolt of unhappiness went through him, but he pushed it down. *For now.* While she was there. The girl made him jumpy. Or…no, not jumpy. It was the opposite. *What is the opposite of jumpy?* She made him *still*. Like he wanted to stop and wait and watch until he could understand her.

Still wasn't the right word either, and he thought about that for a minute as he put his jacket on, trying to be loud so she would wake. She let out another snore, which *almost* made him smile, except he was too tense to smile.

He turned away for a minute but couldn't help turning back. He wanted to look at her. *She's beautiful.* But could he trust her? He rubbed his head. The woman with red hair, who had taken her clothes off for him and kissed his mouth, had been beautiful too. Not as beautiful as the girl drooling in her sleep on his floor but still beautiful. But anyway, they were different, right? He *knew* this woman. Didn't he? He sort of felt like he did.

A piece of her dark hair fell over her face. The color of chestnuts in the sunshine. Deep, shiny brown. His hand itched to push it back, to run his fingers through it and find out if it was as silky as it looked. To touch. To smell. Her eyes were closed now, but he could picture them open and staring at him like she didn't know what he might do next.

What did she think? What did she see when she looked at him? An animal or a man? Something to fear? Yes, he knew that answer, or she wouldn't have brought a gun with her.

Silently he moved closer. Silent as a wolf. Trying to catch her scent from where he stood. There. He closed his eyes, drawing it in, holding it. It was earthier this morning, like he'd taken an entire flower and crushed it in his hands and then brought it to his nose, all the parts of it blending together. Sweet and not sweet. He didn't have the words for her scent, only pictures. Feelings. Low-down whispers. But it moved him. It made his body react, made him want her.

He peered closer, studying. Learning. Her mouth was wide, the top lip thinner than the bottom, and when her lips were parted—like right then—he could see her two top teeth. Pearly, smooth.

When he'd first seen her, he'd thought she looked like a fawn—fresh and young, her large brown eyes blinking at him with curiosity. He'd never seen anything prettier. Not even the almost-night when the colors of the bleeding sun filled the sky and came down to kiss the earth.

She moved in her sleep, and he took a quick, silent step back, but still she did not wake. *He* had hardly slept at all, so aware of her under his roof that he couldn't get his mind to quiet. Maybe she wasn't as scared of him as he thought if she was able to sleep that way. She let out another grumbly snore and tipped forward. His lips did turn up then, into an actual smile that felt strange on his lips. He reached up to feel it, his fingers running over the curved shape of his mouth.

He hadn't wanted her to stay there. He'd wanted her to leave so he could stop questioning everything, feeling things he didn't know what to do about. He needed time to think, to figure out what he was going to do now that Driscoll was dead and his tie to the outside world was gone. He had to figure out what he was going to do about a lot of things, and he had no idea where to start.

He remembered the night before when he'd looked out his window and had seen her crying near the den of baby foxes. At first, he'd thought it was because their mother hadn't returned, but when he understood that it was because their mother was *there*, keeping them warm and dry and fed, he felt something twist in his chest that he'd never felt before.

She'd lost her mother too. He knew that now.

It's *you*, he thought again. *You*.

He watched her for another minute, trying to figure the best way to wake her up since noise wasn't working. Should he shake her awake? Or would she shoot him with that gun of hers? She could try. But he could overpower her in a second—weapon or no weapon—and if she didn't know that, she should. At the picture that formed in his mind—his body coming over hers as she looked up at him with her round, brown, deer-like eyes—his skin flushed, and he felt dizzy.

Be still.

Wait.

She confused him the way all people did, but even... more. He didn't understand the way she talked or the expressions that changed from one moment to the next and without any warning. He didn't know how she laughed so easily one minute and then tears filled her eyes the next. He couldn't follow what she was saying half the time because she jumped between topics so quickly and for no reason that he could understand.

He *knew* her...sort of, but...she was a mystery.

Did other women act that way? Or was it only her? He didn't know. But he knew one thing: he liked the way she looked.

He liked her face and body. Her hair. He liked the way she moved and the way she smelled—especially that. Deep and rich and sweet. Something he wanted to bury his nose in, letting it overpower his brain. It spoke to him.

He wondered what she'd taste like, and it caused his muscles to tense so he was both uncomfortable and not. He'd seen a few other females when he'd gone into town—and he'd seen a lot of the woman with the red hair—but the

110

minute he laid his eyes on Harper, he felt *different*. Like a fire had lit inside him, the blue part of the flame licking at his bones and making them melt to liquid.

The feeling was so strong that if the rules of nature were the rules of humans, he would have claimed her right that minute, fought a battle against other males for her. And won. Whatever he needed to do so he could call her his. *She's the one I choose,* he wanted to tell all the other males. *That one.* But he knew there was far more to it than that. His instincts, though—the ones that had been sharpened so he was more animal than man—were strong and needy. Because his instincts had meant his survival. And to push them aside felt like a kind of giving up he was not used to or ready for.

He had no idea what the rules of town life were, no idea how to live by them or if he even wanted to. That was the thing about nature—there were…patterns. He wondered if people had patterns too and thought they probably did not.

At least the girl didn't seem to. *Harper.*

He wondered what other people would say if they knew what he was thinking about her. That he wanted to mate with her. Not just once, but over and over again until he was full and satisfied like the days when he stole a hive from the bees and stuffed himself with golden honey, his lips sweet and his fingers sticky.

Would they call him a beast?

Or did other men have these same feelings? Did *other* men, ones who'd lived in *civilization,* picture mating with the woman they wanted to claim? Bright, clear pictures that filled their minds and tightened their bodies? Was that *normal*?

He couldn't make himself care.

Those feelings were part of the deep-down whispers.

111

The scents that moved from her to him and back again. And his thoughts were his own. They belonged to him. They were the only thing that hadn't been stolen.

He coughed loudly, and her big eyes opened slowly. She blinked for a minute and then sat straight up, moving her hair out of her face and wiping the trail of drool on her bottom lip. "Oh, I must have…just…dozed off for a second." Her eyes darted away like she knew she was lying. That need to smile came again, and as she started to stand, he turned away, grabbing his bag.

"Is there, ah, somewhere I can clean up?" she asked.

He turned back to where she stood, moving from one foot to the other. "There's a shower out back. And whatever else you might need."

"Out back?" She glanced out the window and then met his eyes again, telling him with her expression that he was definitely not giving her what she "might need."

He felt ashamed. Heat moved up his neck, but he nodded. "There's a bucket hanging on the water pump." He knew she was used to inside bathrooms. He'd been used to that once too. In the long-ago time. Now he could barely remember what hot water felt like. He wished he could give her hot water.

Her eyes widened, but she set her shoulders straight. "Then I'll just…freshen up…out back." Her cheeks turned light pink, and it made his stomach muscles jump. She gave him one last big-eyed look and then turned, grabbing her gun and rushing out the front door.

He watched her close the door behind her and collected the small bag he'd packed, and then he left his house too.

She walked from around the corner a few minutes later, her hair stuck up on top of her head. She looked pretty in the morning light, wrinkled and fresh at the same time, and his blood started doing strange things inside his veins again, rushing quickly and then slowing, making his brain feel sleepy. He turned his back on her and started walking. She could follow or not. He heard her truck door opening and closing and then her quick footsteps.

She looked at the knife strapped to his hip. "Expecting trouble?"

"No," he said quietly. "Expecting dinner. If I'm going to be out today, I want to bring back something to eat."

"Oh. Right. Yes, of course," she said. "So you'll just use that to…" She paused for a long time before finally saying, "Get dinner."

He squinted ahead and then glanced down at her. Her expression made it look like she had a small, pointy rock in her shoe, and it made him feel like maybe he did too. She didn't like him, thought he was different…strange. He didn't like it. But it wasn't her fault. He *was* different and strange, and the loneliness opened inside him, widening like a black hole.

Yes, he was different, but that wasn't the worst of it.

They came out of the trees on the far side of his house, and the open field stretched before them, the sky glowing shiny silver and copper gold. The sight of the early morning sky calmed him, and he was able to move his mind away from the emptiness that would forever be a part of who he was. He could hate it if he wanted—and he did—but he could not change it.

"Thank you, by the way. I'm sure you have other things you could be doing. Especially considering the weather. I really do appreciate it."

Harper's words snapped Lucas from his thoughts, and he

nodded. He didn't have much else he needed to do. He had a supply of food for winter that he could use if he needed to. He'd learned how important that was to survival many winters ago, and now he knew what to do long before the first snowflake fell. Now all there was to do was wait and worry about his future. He could do that as well out here as he could sitting in front of his fire alone. Although he would be out of matches soon, and he hadn't worked out how he was going to deal with that.

The way you did before you had them.

He could go to Driscoll's house and steal matches if he wanted. But he didn't. He didn't want to ever go in that cabin again, not even for a box of matches.

"How far is it to the car?" she asked, coming up beside him. He suddenly noticed she didn't have her gun with her—that must have been what she was putting away when he'd heard her truck door opening and closing—and he wondered what it was that made her decide to leave it behind. Had she decided she wasn't afraid of him anymore? Or that it would be too hard to travel while carrying a big gun? It didn't matter, he told himself. He wouldn't think about the way the thought of her trusting him—the girl whose picture he'd worn around his neck for years, the girl who'd been *with* him during so many times of struggle and pain and loneliness—made him feel...good.

He realized she was glancing up at him and remembered she'd asked him a question. *How far to the location?* He didn't know how to describe *near* and *far,* and he knew by the look the sheriff man had given him the day before that he'd done it wrong when he'd told him how many steps were between Driscoll's and his cabin. "Not long now," he finally settled on.

They came over a hill, and a valley stretched before them. In the summertime, it was filled with flowers—red and purple and yellow, all melting together and sending the breeze back with their sweetness.

They walked in silence for a little while, just the sounds of their footsteps filling the air around them. It was cold, but not as cold as the day before, and the sun had broken through the clouds so it was warm on his back. Harper picked up a long stick and stopped to break a piece of it off, coming up beside him again and using it to tell the places that were safe to step and the ones that were not. He'd done that once, before he'd memorized every hole and rock of the land around him. "I know every step of this ground," he told her. "Just follow me."

She paused but then tossed the stick to the side. More trust. He picked up his speed, and she did too, keeping up with him even though his legs were much longer. "You bring people out here for your…job?" He wanted to know about her—he couldn't help it—and he also wanted to know about the world, about the ways people lived, the things they did. He wanted to know if any of it would be familiar to him anymore or if he was too different now to live among others.

He wanted to know whether he even *wanted* that.

"Oh. You remember that. Yes. Mostly in the spring, summertime, and fall. I take people out to hunt or to camp or just to hike for the day. There are fewer customers during the cold months, but I do take some ice fishers out, skiers, things of that nature. But I save my money so I'm fine working less in the winter. Eventually, I'll take some classes. But…oh, you didn't ask about that. So, yes, I bring people out here for my job. To, um, enjoy the soul-filling beauty of nature," she finished, a tilt to her lips. There was a word for that kind of lip tilt... What was it? Some kind of smile that was... She was trying to be funny in a sort of way. Was that right?

She talked a lot and moved from one subject to the next. Keeping up with her was hard. He had to go back over what she'd said in his mind in order to understand what to respond to.

"You don't believe the beauty of nature fills a person's soul?" he finally asked.

She gave him a surprised look. "Oh. I mean, no. I mean, yes, I do. It just sounded like a cheesy thing to say. But...being in the wilderness, it's brought me peace on occasion when I needed it." She stepped over a rock sticking out of the snow. "What about you? Does the beauty of nature fill your soul?" She smiled at him—so pretty—and all thoughts left his head. He looked away so he could think again.

He thought about the things he loved best about nature, about *home*...the long days of summer when his belly was full of fresh fish and sweet berries and his skin was warm. The way the fireflies flashed in the wavy blue of not-yet night, the way the wolves sang love songs to their mates, their voices rising high and clear to the full yellow moon, so beautiful the whole forest stopped to listen. The way the gophers laughed with their big-toothed grins as they made trouble and played tricks on each other, and the way the birds greeted the morning light, glad and thankful for another day.

But he also thought of the cold that stabbed his bones, the loneliness that felt like a dark pit of sadness yawning wide, the wild pigs with their crazy eyes and blood-chilling shrieks, and the terrible pain of being hunger-sick. "Fill?" he finally said, his voice low and quiet. "No. But it's saved me. And…punished me. If there are things that might fill my soul, I haven't found them yet."

Yet. A hopeful word, he thought. And it surprised him to know he still had some. Even a little.

She was silent for a long while, and when he glanced at her, she was staring at him with the strangest look on her face. A new and different one he couldn't put a word to. He'd said too much…in a way others did not. Maybe. But she didn't look upset with him, just…surprised and… something else that he also didn't have a word to describe. He looked away, pretending to think about which direction to go in, even though he knew exactly where to go.

"Well, I…hope you find it. The thing that fills your soul."

Or maybe most of my soul is dead. He didn't say that, though. It was the thing he wondered about in his most private self. The thing he was afraid of. Another part that had been stolen from him that he could never get back.

"Anyway," she went on, after he'd stayed silent, "you're right. Nature can be beautiful but cruel. I know that too."

He thought maybe she did. "You look for the car then? Is that why you come here? Is that why you do your job?" *I would,* he thought. *If my family was out here somewhere—dead or alive—I'd look for them too.*

She stopped, and so did he, turning to her. Her eyes were wide, and her mouth was twisted in a weird shape. She looked off to the side and then back at him. "Mostly," she said, very softly, a quick stop in the middle of the word that made it sound like she had something in her throat. He thought he saw tears in her eyes, and the speed of his heartbeat picked up. *Don't cry. Don't look sad.*

"I never really…I guess I never really admitted that to

117

myself, but…*yes*. I've been looking for the wreck since I was old enough to come here on my own. The job is just…a way to make money at the same time so I can still eat." She paused. "I've needed to move on, to figure out what to do with my life, but I'm…stuck." She laughed softly, but it didn't sound like a regular laugh. It sounded more *sad* than anything else.

He watched her pretty face and exhaled slowly. He could suddenly understand this woman in a small way, and it made him feel…human. Like a man. "I know what it's like to be lost," he said. It was the thing that made him different from all the animals. The reason this place would never really be his home the way it was to them.

She met his eyes, and it felt like sunlight filled the space between them. Invisible but bright and warm and real. The whispers grew so they were almost…singing inside him. He'd never felt that before. He didn't know what to think, but he liked it. He liked *her*.

Leaves crackled around them, and a hawk spotted a mouse below him and called out his attack, dipping low and then streaking back into the sky. The hawk cried out again, different hawk words this time. Anger. His lunch had gotten away. "How old were you when you came to live here alone, Lucas?" she asked.

He stared at her, his instinct to ignore the question, lie maybe. Protect himself. He knew now that was because he had been taught to do that, using fear and lies. Did it *matter* if he answered her? Before he could think any more about it, he said, "Almost eight, I think."

Her mouth fell open. "Almost eight? That's not possible. Lucas, that's…that's illegal. It's abandonment. Someone needs to answer for that."

"It's too late now. It won't change anything." *I'm guilty too.*

She looked like she was thinking about that and then shook her head. "I guess not, but it just seems…wrong not to do anything at all. Even if you're not going to involve the law…you should…"

"What? What should I do? What would you do?"

She glanced at him, biting at her lip. Finally, she sighed. "Well, you could curse God, I guess. That's usually my best solution. Do it really loudly and with great outrage." She shot him a quick smile that was also somehow sad.

He turned her words over in his head, figuring out the ones he didn't know, his mind working quickly.

Great outrage. *Rage. Anger.* Big anger. Very angry.

He squinted off into the place where the earth and the sky met. "Does it work?"

"Not generally. All it does is make me feel really small and useless."

"An ant, cursing God from the summit of a blade of grass," he quoted from memory, the words rolling off his tongue before he could stop them. He bit down, grimacing as he drew a small amount of blood.

She shot him a surprised smile that turned into a chuckle. "Basically." She was quiet for a moment. "What will you do? Now that Driscoll is gone? I understand you used to trade with him?"

"Yes. But not much in the last few…years. I don't need Driscoll to survive. I'll miss the things he got for me, but I survived for winters…years, without him. I can do it again if I have to."

She didn't say anything, and when he gave her a quick look, he saw that her brows were close together, and she was

119

biting at her lip again the way she seemed to do right before she began asking lots of questions all in a row.

"What happened to your parents?" he asked, trying to move her thoughts from him to anything else. "How did the wreck happen?"

Her chest went up and down as she took in a big breath. "I was young like you, too, when my whole world ended." She smiled, but it was quickly gone. "Or at least, that's how it felt." He again felt understanding. The way she'd said her *whole world ended*; that's exactly what he thought had happened to him once, twice. The whole world had ended.

There's a war.

"We were on our way back from dinner in Missoula. I fell asleep." She shook her head. "I don't *know* what happened. That's one of the worst parts about it. I remember the crash, I think, very vaguely. I remember falling. I remember being wet and freezing. It was winter. But then the next thing I remember is waking up in the hospital. I've tried to piece it all together, but there are just…hazy flashes that I can't put into context."

I can't put into context…*context. Understanding? I can't… can't make fit? Come together. Yes. Like a puzzle.* That's what she meant. *Context.* He stored the word away. A new one among so many new ones in the last few days. "How were you found but not the car?"

"Lost hikers found me."

"Out here?" He'd never seen anyone. He'd thought he'd heard people a few times. But that had meant danger to him, so he'd hidden until he was sure he was safe.

They're killing the children.

She shot him a glance. "Yes. They were out snow hiking, looking for caves friends had told them about. Two college

120

guys. It was suggested they might have gotten lost because they had smoked a copious amount of marijuana. Apparently, they reeked of it, but no one was very concerned about that, considering the circumstances. It's surprising they got us back to town at all."

That was a lot of words he didn't know. He only understood half a language, he realized. Maybe less. His head ached.

"Anyway, they left a statement but didn't know where they'd found me or any other details. The authorities in the area formed a search party, mostly based on the roads my dad would have likely been driving, but without any landmarks, they didn't really know where to specifically direct it. I was in the hospital for a long time, and when I woke up, I could barely remember anything."

"You were lucky" was all he had to say to that long string of words.

She squinted into the faraway for a minute. "I guess I was."

Lucas stopped, and so did Harper. He dug in his bag, bringing out a piece of wrapped fish and handing it to her. "Hungry?"

She took it, though she looked unsure. "Starving. What is it?"

"Smoked red-throat fish." He only ate smoked fish in the winter because he'd found that that made it last longer and he could store it. He liked fresh, raw fish better, but he'd brought the smoked kind because he thought Harper might like that kind more.

She gave him a strange look but unwrapped it and broke off a piece, putting it in her mouth and chewing. Her eyes widened, and she chewed some more, talking around the food. "This is good."

He smiled, pride filling his chest. He liked the sight of her eating the food he'd caught, cleaned, and smoked. He liked the look of the pleasure in her eyes and the way the oil from the food made her lips look shiny. He thought about licking her lips, tasting the oily salt on her skin.

He thought about hunting and fishing for her, bringing her things to eat, and keeping her warm and safe. He thought about her looking to him to do those things. He liked the picture in his mind, but it confused him. She couldn't live there.

"Ready?" he asked, dropping the rest of the wrapped food into his bag and turning away from her. She said something around another bite, and he heard her footsteps behind him.

As they moved, he took some fish out and ate it quickly, watching the sky as it changed from lonesome gray to blue, the fiery sun burning away the morning clouds, the mist in the treetops fading. Dripping sounds were all around them, the snow turning to water that would freeze again tonight, making silvery waterfalls of every size and shape and long, sharp icicles.

"Trout," she said.

"What?"

"The speckled fish with a red stripe on their throats. They're called trout."

"Trout," he said and then repeated it so he'd remember. When he looked at her, her eyes were soft like the sky. "Thank you." She nodded, a look on her face he didn't know what to call.

They walked for a while longer, Harper falling behind as the ground got rougher.

"It's there," he said when the canyon came into view.

Harper joined him, looking down into the snow-filled canyon. "How in the world are we supposed to get down there?"

Lucas looked at her. "Climb. If you want to get down there, you'll have to follow me."

She paused for only a moment and then nodded.

Lucas placed his bag on the ground and walked to the place where a tree grew from the side of the cliff, its root buried deep inside the rock. He grabbed hold of it and swung down easily, a move he'd done many times, in every season. He went down the sloped rock, finding the places his foot could rest and leaving room for Harper to follow him. When he tipped his head to see her, she looked nervous, but she followed behind him, doing the same thing he'd just done.

He moved slowly, far more slowly than he would have if he'd been on his own, but...he thought she did well. Like a baby racoon following its mother up a tree for the first time. Slow. Careful. But natural.

With each movement, her breath came faster like she might be having trouble catching it. But she hadn't gotten breathless once during the walk, and he wondered about it but didn't ask. Her parents were at the bottom, and he thought that was probably the reason why she couldn't catch her breath.

His feet touched the ground first, cracking through the icy-topped snow and meeting the frozen ground below. It was colder down there—darker—hidden from the sun, and her breath made tiny clouds as she stepped down to meet him. The world around them shushed.

Their eyes met, and Harper seemed different...scared or *heavier* or...something, her eyes jumping all over the area behind him. He moved toward where he knew the vehicle was. He brushed some snow aside, showing naked branches that covered the blue of the car with leaves during the other three seasons.

A bit of the blue paint was showing, light hitting the metal and shining off it. Harper took off one of her gloves and reached out slowly, touching it like she didn't believe it was real. She pulled her hand back, and Lucas cleared some more branches, using his arm to brush the snow from the cracked and dirty car.

The skeletons were the same as when he'd first found them—one turned toward the back seat, and the other bent forward. His heart felt heavy. These people belonged to her.

Everything grew silent around them, even the birds had stopped their morning chitter-chatter. But suddenly Harper fell forward, her sob shattering the air. She grabbed at him, and Lucas caught her. He startled and then stilled, taking her in his arms and pulling her against his chest as she cried, her sadness bouncing off the walls of the canyon and disappearing into the forest high above.

CHAPTER SIXTEEN

Harper rubbed at her eyes, still swollen and itchy days after finding her parents. Of course, she'd cried herself to sleep the night before, the vision of their skeletons filling her mind's eye and piercing her heart. Now she felt so incredibly drained. The door opened, and Agent Gallagher entered the room and placed a paper cup in front of her, reaching into his pocket and taking out several packets of creamer and sugar. He placed those along with a stirrer next to the cup. "I figured you could use some."

Harper wrapped her hands around the hot cup, the pleasure of the heat causing her shoulders to relax at least infinitesimally. "Thank you. I appreciate it."

It had taken a couple of days to organize the extraction, but the car, confirmed to have belonged to Harper's parents, had been hauled from the bottom of the canyon hours before and transported to Missoula. A team of investigators would attempt to determine whether the vehicle had failed in some way and that was what caused the accident.

Her parents' remains had been transferred to the medical examiner in Missoula, though Harper didn't think—based on what she'd seen—there was anything to examine except bones. She shivered at the memory of what was left of the two people she'd loved most in the world.

She appreciated the effort that had been expended and the care with which she knew her parents' remains would be treated. Of course, her father had been a well-respected sheriff and community member, and she knew the town as a whole would want to put him to rest properly.

As for Harper, she still wasn't sure how she felt. She'd expected to feel relieved, and she did, but she'd also expected to feel some sense of closure, some sense that she could finally begin her life. She felt neither of those things, but they had only been found forty-eight hours ago. Only forty-eight hours since Lucas had held her in that dim, cold canyon. Only forty-eight hours since they'd trekked the long, mostly quiet walk back to Driscoll's, where she'd phoned Agent Gallagher. It would take time, she figured. A week…maybe two, until she'd be able to finally put the tragedy behind her and accept that they'd never return.

I'm alone in this world.

It wasn't that she'd dreamed or hoped they were coming back. She hadn't fooled herself into believing they weren't actually dead and gone. It was just…not having proof of their deaths—of the fact that she hadn't simply *imagined* the accident, the cold, the falling, that had taken them from her—had kept her from being able to move forward emotionally.

Saying the words to Lucas a couple of days before, admitting she was *stuck,* was an important revelation for her. The hunt for her parents' wreckage had kept her from moving forward. All these years, it'd kept her trapped in a way—emotionally immobile. Looking into his eyes, answering his perceptive question honestly, it had suddenly become crystal clear. Now, though, she'd *found* her family. She didn't have to remain lost in time. Now…now she could figure out what she wanted to do with the rest of her life. She'd *want* to, she was sure of it. Just…not that day.

"I wish you would have told me before you went to Lucas's place. I would have come with you."

She snapped back to the present, considering what Agent Gallagher had said as he'd taken a seat across from her.

"I'm sorry. I thought about calling you, but…I thought I was being crazy. That locket… It'd been so long since I'd seen it. I thought maybe I was imagining things."

Agent Gallagher regarded her for a moment. "So Lucas found your parents' wreck at some point and took the necklace from there?"

Harper nodded. "He said he found it years ago."

"Did he say why he wore it?"

"I didn't ask. I figured it was just something interesting to him. I don't know." Maybe he liked the picture of a family inside it. Something he didn't have. She thought about the way he'd held her as she'd cried, gently but stiffly, as though he didn't know exactly how to hold another person. She wondered if anyone had ever held him, and her heart ached when she thought the answer was probably no. Or at least… not for a very long time.

"The car was found about nine miles from Lucas's house. And nowhere near the highway between Missoula and Helena Springs. Can you think of a reason your parents might have turned off the highway onto dirt back roads? Why they would have been so far from the highway?"

Harper shook her head slowly. "No. My dad had driven from Missoula to Helena Springs hundreds of times. He knew the route like the back of his hand." Harper searched her mind for anything about that ride home, anything that might shed light on this new information. But as always, when it came to the accident, there was nothing. Nothing except the feeling of the car falling and then the bone-shattering landing at the bottom of the canyon. Then...darkness. "It makes sense why the search party didn't find the car," she murmured aloud. They'd looked for it for weeks before giving up. No wonder her own search had never yielded results. She'd been looking miles and miles from where the accident had actually happened. She'd been—

"Do you have any memory of climbing out of that canyon?"

Harper frowned. "Not...really." Brief flashes maybe. *Her hands reaching, gripping. Then...nothing.* "And that's the weird part," she continued. "After surviving a near-fatal accident in freezing weather, I have no idea how I made it out of that hole. I *must* have climbed, but..." Her frown deepened. "Maybe the adrenaline...I don't know. I was in a coma for weeks afterward, and my memory is just so—" She massaged her temples as though she could fix her brain that way, help it recapture those lost hours.

"Maybe it's better that you don't," Agent Gallagher said softly. He tilted his head. "Is it possible you were thrown from the car, Harper? Before it went over the edge of that canyon?"

"Yes. I guess. I would have been wearing my seat belt, of course. But it could have malfunctioned? Maybe they'll find something in Missoula." She shook her head. "I just can't remember. But I was bruised and battered and had broken bones and internal injuries. I've just always assumed my injuries came from *inside* the car. But I guess if I was thrown from it before it rolled into that canyon, I might have sustained those injuries then." *Might have managed to get up and walk…to wander to where the hikers found me.*

Agent Gallagher nodded. "I think it's more probable." Her fall had been *from* the car, then, rather than in it. Which must have meant she'd known it was going to crash—or one of her parents did and had warned her… She massaged her temples again. She'd never have the answers to those questions. There was no way to ever know the exact sequence of events.

She'd been found hours later, wandering in the snow, soaking wet and on the verge of hypothermia. Thank God the lost hikers had found her and had the wherewithal to get her dry and back to civilization quickly enough that she didn't freeze to death. Weeks later, she'd woken up to a new world—one she hadn't recognized—and she'd been trying to navigate it ever since.

"Harper," Agent Gallagher began, stopping and seeming to consider his words. "I know what it's like to have the rug ripped out from under you. I can't imagine it happening when you were only a child, with limited coping skills."

She looked at him, took in the set of his mouth, the way his gaze was filled with empathy. Understanding. He did know. She wondered what proverbial rug had been ripped from beneath his feet. Wondered if there *were* coping skills for the loss of your entire world, whether you were seven or seventy. "Thank you," she said, and she meant it.

"Can I ask who raised you after you lost your parents?"

"I was put in the foster care system." She looked down, picking at her nails for a moment. "My dad was quite a bit older than my mom, and by the time of the accident, my paternal grandparents lived in an assisted living facility. They've since passed. My mother was estranged from her family, so I never knew them. They didn't step forward to claim me when she died." Harper paused. "My mom had a brother, but he wasn't willing or able to take me in. So…" There was a lot hanging on that little two-letter word, but she didn't want to get into the six moves, the bouncing from one foster home to another, the loneliness, the fear, the way the door had creaked open some nights in that first house, the way she'd pretended to be asleep and prayed to God he'd leave. The way she'd withdrawn completely and struggled to communicate for several years. The way no one took the time or made the effort to break through her walls and bond with her. The way it was books, not people, that had finally allowed her to step outside her own mind enough to process her grief and come out of her shell. No, there was too much there she didn't want to go into, much less ponder. Especially then.

"There was no one in town who could take you in?"

Harper shook her head, and Agent Gallagher paused for several beats. "That's…unfortunate."

She fingered the locket now hanging around her own neck, visualizing the picture inside, the happy family that had once been hers. "Yes, it's just the way it was." She couldn't stay in this funk. "Thank you for organizing my battery being jumped, too, by the way. I hope my going to ask Lucas about the necklace didn't…impede your investigation in some way."

"No, no. My investigation is a separate matter. It was a good hunch on your part, and I'm glad he was able and willing to help you." He smiled kindly. "What's your impression of Lucas now that you've spent more time with him?"

Harper met his eyes, considering his question. Lucas. Confusing. Reserved. Silent. Resilient. *Safe.* "I never felt threatened by him. In fact, he seems…well, caring. He was concerned about the baby foxes I practically ran over." She glanced at Agent Gallagher, the embarrassment over her careless behavior sweeping through her again. "Accidentally. And…he never came across as threatening. I was prepared had that not been the case," she added, wanting to grimace at what she must have looked like to Lucas, showing up on his doorstep practically holding a rifle on him and demanding answers. "His language is… simple, I suppose, but he's obviously intelligent. He seems confused by certain terms…he gets this look on his face… but he doesn't admit when he doesn't know a word. You can literally *see* him working it out. It's… Anyway, he's wary but funny sometimes. I mean, on purpose. And… why are you looking at me that way?"

Agent Gallagher smiled. "You like him."

Harper laughed. "Like him? No. I mean, sure. He's… interesting." She felt her cheeks heat and wanted to bring her hands to them but resisted.

Agent Gallagher's smile faded, and a look of concern came into his eyes. *Fatherly.* It made Harper's chest squeeze. "Just be cautious. We really don't know anything about him yet. And at this point, he's our only person of interest in this murder investigation."

"I will. I mean, I have no reason to interact with him anymore anyway."

"It seems serendipitous that you were called in to help on the Driscoll case and that a person brought in to answer questions ended up being able to help solve the mystery of where your parents' car has been all these years."

"I didn't think law enforcement agents typically believed in serendipity," she said, giving Agent Gallagher her first genuine smile since sobbing her heart out in that canyon.

Agent Gallagher chuckled. "We don't, as a general rule. It's our job to find explanations that go beyond fate." His smile grew. "But in this case, it seems like it's purely a stroke of luck."

Stroke of luck. Hadn't Lucas said something similar when she'd told him about being found by the lost hikers? She'd always considered herself *unlucky*. Perhaps one of the unluckiest people she knew. But maybe she'd been looking at it from the wrong angle. Yes, it had been a terrible tragedy that her parents had been taken from her when she'd been so young—a tragedy that had shaped her life in innumerable negative ways. But…but she'd also experienced incredible strokes of…yes, *luck*. And maybe she could learn to find the positive in her life now, too, if she looked hard enough.

"I know it's been a long, hard few days, but can I ask a quick question about something related to the crime at the Larkspur?"

Harper rubbed at her eye, happy to turn her mind to something else for a few minutes. "Yes, of course."

Agent Gallagher took out a photo from his notebook and handed it to her. It was a pile of books on what looked to be a bedside table. "You can see the titles on the spines. They're all young adult books. What I'm wondering about are the stickers that were obviously peeled off. They were still sticky in some spots, as though it'd been done recently."

Harper brought the picture closer, her gaze moving to

the places on the spines that looked as though stickers had been scraped off with someone's fingernail.

"I thought they might be from a used bookstore in town or something like that, but there isn't one in Helena Springs. I thought about the library, but the Helena Springs library uses white stickers for the book's location."

"Yes," Harper agreed. "So does the Missoula library. But the library in Missoula also uses yellow stickers on some of its books," Harper said. "I was there recently. That could be a portion of the yellow sticker. The bottom one tells the location of the book, and the top one tells how many days it's available to check out." Harper handed the picture back.

Agent Gallagher frowned. "I wonder why someone would peel stickers off books she'd borrowed."

Harper shrugged. "Maybe she wasn't planning on taking them back."

"Yeah. Maybe. Thanks, Harper, that's helpful. I'll give you a lift home," he said, standing. "You must be exhausted." He turned, meeting her eyes, that same empathy she'd seen a few moments before back in his gaze. "I hope being able to bury your parents, to have a place to visit them, will help you find some closure."

"I hope so too," she said quietly. "I hope so too." Because she'd always yearned for a place to take her grief and loss. A place to say goodbye.

CHAPTER SEVENTEEN

Jak hadn't eaten in three days. His belly ached, gnawed at itself, hunger making him feel weak, sleepy. But he couldn't sleep, not if he wanted to live. *Live!* Pup had gone out over and over during the long hours, but even he, a natural hunter, hadn't had any luck. The weather was miserable outside, the animals hidden away in their dens, covered by snow or blocked by ice. Many of them would die there before the winter was over. He wondered if he'd die too.

Jak's heart seemed to slow, like it was getting ready to stop. *Thump, thump.* Maybe it would. And who would care? No one. No one would even know.

He had had enough food to last him through four days of the storm that was still blowing, but no more.

Jak had tried to catch a fish but couldn't break through the thick ice even after hammering at it with a sharp rock for hours. He'd waited by the water, hoping a deer would come out for a drink, but the cold grew so painful Pup had started whining, a low sound of hurting that Jak understood even better than his fur-covered friend. He'd had no choice but to go back inside, starving and empty-handed.

"We've gotta try again, Pup," he said, and the animal raised his head, looking at Jak for a minute and then lowering his head again as if to say, *No way.*

"We have to," Jak argued. "The longer we stay in here, the weaker we'll get." Sometimes Jak wondered if it was a meanness to keep Pup inside with him, wondered if his wolf instincts would get...less if he didn't always have to use them. Pup was supposed to have a pack, a family of wolves that could help each other survive. Instead, Pup only had Jak, but Jak still needed him to help catch food, and mostly...*mostly,* he needed his friendship. Pup was his only friend in the whole world, and he knew he wouldn't want to live through the war for this long without him. Jak might want to give up, but because of Pup, he never would. Pup had saved his life that awful, terrifying night and many times since then, and now Jak would keep Pup safe and fed or die trying.

Jak put on his warmest clothes, animal skins he'd stitched together and a few items he'd traded with Driscoll for. He would have suffered through the walk to Driscoll's place if he had something to trade for food, but not only did he not have anything he could give up, but Driscoll had told him that was one item he could not get. There wasn't a lot of food in town, and even Driscoll had trouble getting enough to feed himself. Jak wondered if the war went on for many more winters and food grew less and less, if townspeople would start coming to hunt animals and gather the other food the forest could give.

Even now, when he thought of the war and the people Driscoll had told him were killing the children, that deep voice repeated in his head: *Survival is your only goal.*

A small tremble that had nothing to do with the storm raced through Jak as he stepped outside, squinting away from the stinging cold that burned his skin.

He gripped the pocketknife in his fur-wrapped hands, ready and willing to kill any small animal or bird he saw. The forest was still, though—quiet—even the winter birds too cold to sing.

Jak stopped at the top of a small hill, Pup a few steps behind, and saw what looked like a deer lying in the middle of an open area.

Jak's eyes widened, and for a minute, he simply stared. Had the animal frozen to death right where it was? But no...he could see its blood soaking into the snow. He moved toward it. Had another animal killed it and then left it there uneaten? Why would it when food was so hard to get?

Jak's stomach panged with hunger, and he sped up his steps. He didn't *care* why the animal was lying there. He only cared that it *was* and that it would take away the splitting pains screaming through his stomach.

"Get away from my food," he heard, and he lowered to a crouch, whirling toward the voice, raising his pocket-knife toward the threat. Pup let out a low growl, crouching down as well to attack. It was another boy like him, his blond hair past his shoulders, in a fighting stand, his left arm held out and something shiny in his hand. For a minute, Jak was shocked quiet, and then his heart started booming in his chest, pounding in his head. They stared at each other, the other boy's eyes shiny and...crazy, his face twisted into hatred. *Violence.* He came at Jak, his left leg dragging behind him. There was something wrong with it.

Jak raised his hands quickly, trying to let the boy know

he was not a threat. His stomach cramped in pain again. "Did you kill this deer?" he asked, his voice shaky.

"Get away," the boy barked, moving forward, swiping what Jak could now see was a hunting knife at him.

Jak jumped back, missing the blade. Pup snarled, moving forward. "Pup, no," he said loudly, not knowing whether Pup would listen. He needed to do something. And fast. "Whoa. Wait, wait. Listen to me. We can share it. We're both hungry, and there's enough for two. More than enough." He thought about offering his cabin, the blanket, somewhere to dry off and get warm, but he didn't know who this boy was—he might be on the enemy's side—and he wasn't sure it was safe to offer him anything at all. He looked crazy, and Jak wasn't sure his words were being heard.

But either way, he was not going to let him take all the meat on the ground between them. He could die if he did that. Pup could die too.

"We'll split it," Jak said again, louder, trying to make eye contact. But the boy's eyes stayed on the meat, a look so hurting in his gaze that Jak felt it all the way to his own aching belly. "I'll help you skin it and carve up the meat. Doing all that is long, hard work. I'll do most of it," he offered. "We can join together." He searched for the right words, words to make the boy *hear* him, agree, but the boy looked uncaring about what he was saying. "What's your name?" he asked, trying from a different side. "I'm Jak, I—"

The boy moved forward again very quickly, swiping the knife, and Jak leaned back, the blade just missing him. Pup jumped forward, and the boy let out a growl of his own, swinging the blade through the air, back, forth, back, forth. One of his swings caught Pup on the leg, and Pup squealed in pain, blood spurting onto the white ground as he limped back, still growling but not moving toward the still-swinging boy again.

"Stay back, Pup!" Jak yelled, holding his own pocket-knife toward the boy, trying one more time to talk him out of what he was doing. "I know you're hungry. I'm hungry too. I'm not trying to take your meat. I just want to split it. We can both eat. We can work together—"

The boy let out a screaming war cry and threw himself at Jak, and red-hot pain sliced down Jak's cheek. Jak cried out, jumping back again and bringing his hand to his sting-ing face. His fur-glove-covered hand came away matted and dark with blood. Anger and fear mixed inside Jak as he gave up the idea of talking instead of fighting. This boy had left him no choice but to defend his own life. The next swipe might be across his throat. The boy in front of him was fighting to kill.

The two of them circled each other, their breaths coming out in small white clouds of air. They were close enough now that any knife swipe could be deadly. Something hot spiked through Jak, his heart like thunder in his ears. *Maybe if I can knock the knife away from him, I can—*

The other boy attacked, his body hitting Jak with a loud *oof,* and they both went down to the ground, the crunching sound of the snow top breaking below them. They each yelled and then they were rolling, grunting, as Pup growled and yapped in the background, far away, or so it seemed to Jak. He could only hear his own pounding heart and the sharp gasps of breath as the two fought to hold on, fought to be the first to use his weapon.

They rolled again and Pup's growly bark got closer, the smell of him strong in Jak's nose. "Stay back!" he yelled at Pup, rolling again, juggling with his knife, trying with everything he had to rip the other boy's knife away from him. But his short call to Pup had given the boy the upper hand, and he went back and swung down, catching Jak on the arm with his blade before Jak could roll away.

Jak yelped from burning pain and terror, throwing his body forward and stabbing his knife into the boy. Directly into his heart.

Everything stopped. The boy froze in his movement, his eyes widening and then dropping. Blood fell from the side of his mouth, dripping down his chin and onto the ripped-up, too-small coat he wore.

Jak grabbed the boy. *What did I do? He can't die. Not with a single stab. No!* The boy's eyes met his, the crazy fog in them clearing away. Their gazes locked together, breath mixing, though the boy's breaths were getting weaker, farther from each other. Jak's heart sputtered when—for a lightning flash—the other boy looked…happy. He smiled before his body sagged, and both of them fell to the snow.

Jak sobbed, scooting out from under the dead boy, the boy's body dropping to the ground. Jak pulled himself to his feet, shaky, standing over the body, shock making the world seem too bright, unreal. A dream. A nightmare. He'd killed a person. He felt something warm on his cheeks and realized he was crying. He brushed at the wetness before the tears mixed with blood could freeze.

He stared at the boy, his eyes moving over his ripped clothes, down to his twisted leg, and blackened foot, bare now that the handmade shoe had come off during their battle. Jak closed his eyes for a second, his heart squeezing.

I would have shared with you, he whispered brokenly inside himself.

Jak stared at the boy's face, which no longer looked

crazy, death making him look younger. And with a jolt, he recognized him. He was the blond boy who had gone over the cliff with him that night. He'd been living out here all this time too.

And whatever he'd gone through, it had driven him out of his mind.

No! Had he passed him in the woods once or twice, hiding from the sound of footsteps because he'd thought they might belong to an enemy? The thought was too terrible for Jak to think about.

Instead, he turned toward Pup, who was now lying in the snow, a large spot of blood next to his hurt leg. His heart, which had slowed, began racing again. Jak had to get him home and treat his injury if he could. Jak picked up the boy's sharp, curved knife, put it in the waistband of his pants, and then went fast to Pup, picking the large animal up and hefting him over his shoulder.

Jak walked back to the dead boy, wiping the tears that were again sliding down his cheeks, trying to come up with words to say over the boy's body. His baka had said prayers, but he didn't remember any of the words she'd whispered as she'd held the beads in her hands.

Pup moaned softly, and Jak moved him a little, trying to be careful of his injury. "Star light, star bright," Jak finally said, the words coming quickly, knowing the rhyme wasn't a prayer but having nothing else to offer. "First star I see tonight. I wish I may, I wish I might, have this wish I wish tonight." And then he closed his eyes and wished that the boy was now running through fields of flowers under the warm heavenly sunshine. That he was healed, whole, and no longer hungry.

The ground was too frozen for Jak to bury him, so he

left the boy's body where it was. The boy didn't need it anymore anyway, and the forest did. Other hungry creatures would feed on it and live to see another day.

Like Jak.

Although he could feel that a part of him had died along with the boy left lying dead in the snow.

With Pup over one shoulder, he grabbed the leg of the deer, pulling it along behind them, beginning the journey back home. Anger and hopelessness roared through him. Anger built as he walked through the cold. He raised his face and yelled into the stone-colored sky, tears blinding him again. It was all their fault! The men who took him and the other boy. The men who tried to kill children. The men who turned a little boy into a crazed animal, wishing he was dead.

The men who made me a murderer.

CHAPTER EIGHTEEN

Harper sat on her bed, her feet curled beneath her, staring unseeing at the white wall across from her. The tea she'd brewed had grown cold, and she set the mug down on the bedside table, sighing. She didn't even like tea. But it always seemed like something that should accompany moments of introspection and deep serenity.

Too bad she hadn't gotten very far with the former and had failed completely to achieve the latter.

She picked up the remote, clicking on the television and turning it to a news program. The weatherman pointed to a screen as his voice droned on. More snow. More cold. Shocking.

She thought about Lucas out there in the middle of nowhere, snow piled up to the windows of his small cabin as he sat inside alone. Was he lonely? He had to be, didn't he? He was a human being with absolutely no one in his life. Harper was lonely too, she could admit that. But at least she had friends and community, books, a cell phone, a television to dispel the silence when she needed the illusion of company.

Was that why he'd taken the magazine? To have something to *do* on those lonely nights in the middle of the woods? She shivered despite being warm and cozy, curled up in a blanket on her bed. Just the thought of the deep isolation he must feel terrified her.

Because she understood it.

Not on the level he must—how could she? But she couldn't remember a time when she hadn't suffered loneliness, the sense that she was adrift, always trying desperately to catch hold of something—anything—that would anchor her. Forever attempting unsuccessfully to recapture what had been ripped from her so suddenly and inexplicably. *Comfort. Home. Love.* Now…she'd found the car, would be able to bury her parents, and yet she still felt as empty as ever. As lost as ever. As alone. Because what she'd really been attempting to reclaim would not be found in the places she searched.

Did he share the same feelings of loneliness? He'd been abandoned too. Left to fend for himself in ways she probably couldn't even fathom.

And forget the loneliness—though that in itself seemed, well, catastrophic—how was he going to survive with no way to hunt since his bow and arrows had been taken by the sheriff? She thought back to the hunting knife he'd had strapped to his thigh, the one he'd told her he was going to use to obtain *dinner.* She'd been struck dumb at the time, and even now, she was disconcerted. What was he going to do? Pounce on an animal and then cut its throat, skin it, debone it, and… She pulled the blanket tighter around herself, realizing she was grimacing, and allowed her muscles to relax. She was no stranger to hunting, but no one she knew wanted to involve themselves in an up-close kill like the one a hunting knife would insist upon.

Come to think of it, what was he going to do now that he had no good hunting weapon *and* no contact to the outside world since Isaac Driscoll had been killed? He'd told her he had survived before Driscoll and he'd survive now. And that might be true. But what if he *did* need something? What if he became injured or ill? He may have been isolated before, but now…now he was completely cut off.

What should I do?

Well, you could curse God, I guess. That's usually my best solution. Do it really loudly and with great outrage.

Does it work?

Not generally. All it does is make me feel really small and useless.

An ant, cursing God from the summit of a blade of grass.

Why did those words sound so *familiar*? And why did they seem…more sophisticated than she'd expect from a man who spoke little and had no access to books?

And yet he'd been quoting someone. Or…something. *That* was why. A book or a poem. She was sure of it. She *knew* those words somehow. And right after he'd said them, he'd looked as though he wished he hadn't. He'd quickly changed the subject.

Harper stood, the blanket dropping to the bed. She grabbed her laptop and sat back down, logging in and opening her internet browser, typing the words into the search bar. "I knew it," she muttered, her heart thrumming. It was one of the more obscure quotes from *The Count of Monte Cristo*.

Her caveman had quoted Alexandre Dumas.

Her caveman? Not exactly. But…

The caveman had quoted Alexandre Dumas.

She stared at the computer for a moment before closing her eyes. A vague picture of her mother flitted through her mind. Harper was sitting on a bench with her father, and her mother was walking toward them, smiling. Her father said something that made her mother laugh, and she put the turquoise backpack down next to where they sat and kissed him before taking Harper into her arms and asking what they'd brought for lunch.

That turquoise backpack. She'd used it to carry her class notes. Her father had laughingly told her it made her look like one of the high school girls instead of a teacher. An English teacher, who always included her favorite novel as required class reading: *The Count of Monte Cristo.*

A distant ringing broke through her trance, and she sat upright, her head turning toward the sound. Her cell phone. She stood, feeling somewhat off balance, and hurried to her purse where she'd left it hanging by the door. When she answered, she was slightly breathless.

"Harper, hi. It's Mark Gallagher."

"Oh, hi," she said, walking back to her bed and sitting. "How are you?"

"I'm fine. Listen, I'm hoping you can help me with something else." She heard a noise in the background that sounded like paper rustling and the phone shifting on Agent Gallagher's ear.

"Yeah, of course. Did you find anything out about those books and the Missoula library?"

"I'm actually going there shortly. I was looking through the entries in Driscoll's journal, and some don't make a lot of sense to me."

"How so?"

"Well, for instance, this one: *This morning I spotted the white-tailed deer eating raw fish at the river. Seems he is a natural survivor in that he will eat what is necessary to live, whether distasteful or no.*"

Harper frowned. "A deer eating fish?"

"That's what I'm confused about. I did a simple Google search, and I couldn't find anything that said deer eat fish."

"No, they're herbivores," she said, as confused as Agent Gallagher.

"What about in extreme cases like…famine or an extra-long winter, something of that nature?"

Harper chewed at her lip for a moment. "An animal will eat anything if it's starving, but how in the world would a deer catch a fish?"

"Maybe it was already dead, lying on the riverbank?"

"That'd have to be the case, I guess."

"So, if a deer were starving and it found a dead fish on the riverbank, it might eat it."

"Animals will do what they have to do to survive. Yes. But in general, no, deer don't eat fish."

"Okay, I wanted to double-check with you. I'm still making my way through this thing, but it's…odd. It almost appears as if Driscoll was watching one specific possum, one specific deer, and one specific wolf."

"Why would he do that? And how would he know it was the same one?"

"I have no idea. If anything comes to you, will you let me know?"

"Of course."

"Thanks, Harper."

"You're welcome. Any news yet?" she asked, knowing she didn't have to specify what she was asking about.

"Not yet. They're a little bit backed up, but I'm hoping for something by tomorrow morning. Then they'll be able to release the remains so you can make arrangements."

Harper was quiet for a moment as she digested that. It was what she'd hoped for, for so long—the ability to lay her parents to rest—but the impending reality caused a lump to form in her throat. She needed to start thinking about burial or cremation and how she'd pay for whichever she chose. She needed to begin making calls and arrangements, but all she wanted to do was stay buried under a blanket on her bed, drinking tea she didn't like.

"Harper? You there?"

"Yes, sorry. Um, I was also wondering if anything was found in the car or in the trunk? Specifically, a turquoise backpack? It was my mother's, and she always threw it in her trunk after classes were out." They'd taken her mother's SUV that night because the roads were icy and her mother's vehicle had brand-new tires. Harper remembered that because she liked riding in the take-home sheriff's car her dad drove and had complained that they weren't in it that evening. The last car ride she'd ever take with her parents and she'd whined and sulked about everything that evening. She remembered *that*. To her great regret and shame.

"No. There was nothing in the trunk except a disintegrated blanket."

Harper frowned. It was possible her mother had left her backpack somewhere else, but that damn quote kept pricking at her mind.

"Okay, thanks. Agent Gallagher, can I ask if there's an update on the forensics on that bow and the arrows taken from Lucas? If you can't tell me, I understand—"

"Traces of blood were found on all the arrows that

147

belong to him, but it's all animal blood. No human matter at all. And none of his DNA is on either arrow used in the murders."

Harper let out a slow breath. She felt a little odd about the sudden rush of relief, but she couldn't deny it. Something inside her was rooting for him. Not only that, but she couldn't see him as a murderer. He'd practically pushed her out of the way to provide assistance to a den of baby foxes, for God's sake. She'd never once felt afraid, and he hadn't taken advantage of her even though she'd slept so hard under his roof that she barely knew her own name when she'd woken up. Oh, and there had been drool... *Please, God, don't let him have seen the drool.*

"There also doesn't appear to be any of Lucas's DNA at the bed-and-breakfast crime scene either. A few prints at Driscoll's belong to him, but that was expected since he'd been there over the years. None were found in the bedroom where the murder occurred."

Harper released another slow breath. "So he's no longer a person of interest?"

"I wouldn't exactly say that. But...we have nothing to tie him to either crime at this point."

"Have you found out anything about his background?"

"No, but I have to be honest, I don't have anything to go on. Lucas doesn't appear to *want* to find out anything about his background, and solving the murders has to be my first priority. I'm going to dig more once I have the chance, but for now, finding out about Driscoll's background comes first."

Harper had stood as he'd answered her question, and now she paced once in front of her bed. "The thing is," she said, turning and pacing in the other direction, "I've been wondering what Lucas is doing on his own now that Driscoll is dead and he doesn't have any access to the outside world."

"That's not entirely true. He has legs. He could walk to town if he chose to. Hell, he could move if he chose to. In fact, if Driscoll didn't have a will that left that house to Lucas, then he might be forced to do so."

"Walk to town? In the snow and ice?" Harper asked, the barest bit of outrage seeping into her tone.

"I have a feeling Lucas is used to the snow and ice."

She couldn't disagree with that. "Okay, but there's no way he can have any money. He traded with Driscoll using fish and animal skins. What if I at least took him some provisions until he gets his bow and arrows back and…and… things are clearer as far as his living situation?"

"Harper…listen, I'm not your father"—there was a strange catch in his voice and a slight pause before he cleared his throat and continued—"but you don't know Lucas. And to go out to his house alone doesn't seem like the wisest choice for a woman on her own. I understand why you did it once, but maybe repeating it should be avoided."

Harper stopped pacing, sitting back down on the bed. "Okay."

"Why do I sense that your *okay* doesn't mean what I think it means?"

Despite herself, Harper blew out a small laugh. "I appreciate you keeping me updated on the case. Any idea when you might want to look for those map markers?"

"The sooner the better, but the weather forecast doesn't look promising. They're saying a storm's moving in."

"Just let me know then, okay?"

"I will. And, Harper, please take my words under advisement."

"I will. I promise."

They said goodbye, and Harper hung up, tossing her phone next to her on the bed. *They're saying a storm's moving in…*

She did take Agent Gallagher's words under advisement. She respected him. She *liked* him. She appreciated that he'd shared information he didn't have to with her and that he cared about helping her with her situation too—a situation that wasn't even part of the reason he was in Helena Springs. He obviously cared about her safety, and after a lifetime of not having a father figure, his concern was a balm to her soul. But…but…he hadn't spent a night and a day with Lucas. He hadn't had time to develop a sense of the man's…goodness.

She wished she could call Lucas and thank him for what he'd done for her—not only led her to her parents' car but helped her find the closure she'd been searching for since that snowy night when she was a child. She wished she could call and ask him if he needed anything now that he was totally alone—a ride to town, some food or water…matches… She wished she had some way to repay the favor he'd done for her, but she couldn't ask him without going in person.

Harper glanced outside her window at the darkening clouds. *I understand why you did it once, but maybe repeating it should be avoided.* She understood Mark's logic, but she needed to answer her heart's call. If she was going to gather some items and make the drive to Lucas's, she didn't have a lot of time to stand around waffling.

She hesitated only another moment before grabbing her coat, hat, and gloves; pulling on her boots; and heading for the door.

CHAPTER NINETEEN

Morning sun touched Jak's naked shoulders. Warm. Soft. Good. An invisible hand tossed glitter all over the surface of the river. Jak laughed as Pup splashed through the water, his tongue hanging out and making it look like he was grinning. He came to Jak, his limp less now. He had gotten better from his injury, but it had taken the whole winter, and the limp still stayed. Pup would never be the hunter he was before. Jak was responsible for him now. That was okay. Pup had taken care of him for a time, but now it was Jak's turn and he was up to the job. "I won't let you down, boy," he told Pup, as much as himself. Saying it aloud, saying it so another pair of ears heard too, felt like the most important promise of all, one he would never break.

Pup was his best friend. And best friends kept promises to each other. That was all.

Pup let out a chuff noise, and Jak smiled, knowing that Pup had understood him and knew he was not alone out there, even if he didn't have a *true* pack. "I'm your pack and you're mine," Jak said, scooping up a handful of water and throwing it at Pup. Pup shook off the water, throwing droplets right back, and Jak laughed as he turned his head away.

It was a good day. The sun was warm. Spring was waking up the earth. He had enough food, and soon the forest would give him more. And he had a friend he loved. War fighting might be going on somewhere in the near faraway, but there, for that moment, he was safe.

He looked to where the mountains became the sky, a shiver rolling through him. Winter always waited. It might seem far away for now, but it would be back before he was ready. It would come back to steal his hope—of survival, of rescue, of having a family or people to love him.

Maybe no one could ever love him now anyway. Not after the things he'd done.

The rushing sound of the water brought him from his dark thoughts, and he tried his best to shake off the feeling of...aloneness. His sad feelings inside were all different, though he didn't have names for all of them. But the word that seemed to fit each one was *alone*.

He reached down and brought a handful of water to his chest, using his hand to wash under his arms and then along his shoulders. It felt good to be clean, good to feel the cold drops sliding down his skin, reminding him he was alive. Not like the boy he'd killed and left lying in the snow.

Thinking about that boy still caused a dark hole to open in the pit of his stomach, something that felt like it would always be empty. Hollow. Sometimes when he thought about that boy, he remembered the picture he'd seen in Isaac Driscoll's house, the one of the men fighting the bloody battle with spears and arrows. He wondered if pits opened inside them each time they took a life and thought that if they did, those men must feel like walking darkness.

At the first thaw, Jak had gone back for the blond boy's bones, planning to bury them on the hillside where an old bent tree grew with a hundred million wildflowers all around that, from the close faraway, looked like rainbows touched the earth. There was a lake at the bottom of the hill where pairs of white swans—mates for life—floated, even in the winter when the water was icy and mostly frozen. He'd thought about it and decided that if someone was going to bury him, that's the place he would hope they'd pick. But the blond boy's bones had been gone, carried off by animals, scattered through the wilderness.

He dreamed of him sometimes, his bodiless head talking to him from the ground, asking Jak to give back the rest of him. He woke up screaming, Pup whining next to him.

Jak picked up a stick and tossed it to Pup, who splashed through the water, taking the piece of wood in his mouth and bringing it back to Jak. He did this a few more times as Jak kept washing his body, looking with interest at all the places hair was sprouting, prickly like the late summer grass. His skin was rough and scarred, and he could feel the way his muscles had grown as he ran his hands over his bare skin. He'd grown so much taller since last winter that his pants were now way too short and his shirt had ripped across his shoulders. He'd have to see what Driscoll would take for a few new pieces of clothing, though summer was coming and new clothes could wait. He would rip the too-small pants into shorts and go shirtless for a while. He never looked forward to seeing Driscoll, so he'd live with what he had and hand-make anything he could.

How old am I now? Time was a cloudy, wavy line he

couldn't quite hold on to. He had no idea if it was Monday or Sunday, February or March. Only the winters stood out to him—those dark, miserably cold days, when even the sun left early. Even though he had shelter now and warmth when he could get matches from Driscoll, he still had to go outside to find food, and he and Pup were still alone when the wind screamed and howled and the roof shook and it felt like the world was ending.

Sixteen, he thought, counting in his mind. *I think I'm sixteen.* He'd lived alone for ten winters.

Jak started making his way to the shore, whistling for Pup, who hadn't come back with the stick Jak had tossed into the trees a while ago. Damn wolf had probably seen a squirrel and gone after it. Well, good for him if there were still a few things he wasn't too limpy to hunt.

Jak used his shirt to towel off, shaking his shoulder-length hair like Pup did, water drops flying out around him. The back of his neck tickled, and he raised his head, squinting into the forest. He felt…watched. He sensed it sometimes, like today. The tiny hairs on the back of his neck would stand up, and he'd feel *sure* someone was looking at him through the trees.

He whistled again, that feeling of being watched staying with him. Jak had learned to trust his instincts, to count on them for his survival, so he did not brush away the feeling. He wondered if the enemy sent spies into the forest to see who lived there and find out why. Or maybe others—like the blond boy—were living close by and watched Jak to find out if he was good or bad.

Jak pulled on his jeans, running his hand over the pocket to feel the hard bump of the pocketknife there, and then grabbed the knife that had belonged to the blond boy, tying

154

it to his waistband with an old piece of cloth from clothes he'd gotten too big for. He tossed the damp shirt over his shoulder and headed for the woods to find Pup.

It got cooler as soon as he stepped into the trees, splinters of light coming through the gaps at the tops of the old giants of the forest. He talked to them sometimes when Pup was out hunting or when Jak had left him sleeping in front of the fire. Sometimes he got so lonely—*needed* another person so much—that he pretended the trees were wise old men who had answers to his millions of questions, and if he just listened hard enough, they'd whisper what they knew. The way they whispered to each other deep under the ground.

The same, only different, as the whispers inside him.

Maybe he shouldn't hope the trees would share their whispers. Maybe if they did, he'd know he'd started to lose his mind.

Maybe the forest made everyone who lived there go crazy finally because Driscoll didn't seem right in the head either.

"Pup," he called, pushing a branch aside. *Where is he?*

Jak stilled when he heard what he thought was a whimper, turning toward the sound and moving faster through the shrubs just sprouting pale green leaves. That's when he saw him, lying on the forest floor in a pool of spreading blood.

"Pup!" he yelled, running to him and falling to his knees at his side. There was a long wooden arrow sticking from Pup's neck, blood flowing from the wound. Jak's heart pounded with fear and sickness. "It's okay, boy. It's okay," he choked as he pulled on the arrow and Pup made an awful, high-pitched screaming noise and more blood poured from the wound. Jak let out a sob, not knowing what to do. He put his hands around the arrow, trying so hard to stop the

155

rushing blood. He met Pup's half-closed gaze, and the wolf held eye contact for a few moments, his tongue poking out to lick Jak's wrist, his blood pumping between Jak's fingers.

Jak sobbed again as Pup's body went still, the blood slowing into a trickle. Tears flowed down Jak's cheeks as he took his hands from around the arrow and picked up Pup's large body, rocking the giant animal in his arms. *My friend. My friend. My friend.* He cried, his sobs mixing with the wind as it blew through the branches of the trees who stood on, watching, whispering to each other, but only ever that.

"I thought he was wild. I didn't know."

Jak whipped his head around, and Driscoll was standing close by, a bow in his hand, arrows strapped to his waist. Jak's gaze moved slowly from Driscoll's face to the weapon he held and back again. The man had killed Pup. Rage, hotter than the sun, went through Jak, and slowly, he lowered Pup's body to the ground, coming to his full height, the feel of Pup's blood warm on his bare chest. He lowered his head and growled, low in his throat.

Driscoll's eyes went wide as he looked at him, and though he looked scared, there was something else shining from his eyes. That look that had shined from Baka's eyes when Jak did something good. That weird excitement that had been on his face when he was showing Jak the picture in his bedroom.

"I'm going to kill you," Jak growled. Meaning it. He was going to tear his throat out.

Driscoll nodded, backing away as he raised his hand. Jak went forward, sadness and anger making him feel dizzy like the forest had started to spin around him. No, he wouldn't tear his throat out. He was going to grab the bow and arrows from Driscoll before he could raise one and bury one of

156

those arrows in *his* neck. His heart. Jak's back teeth scraped against each other.

"I understand how you feel, but listen. Listen," Driscoll said, his voice shaking. "I can get you one of these if you want." He held up the bow and nodded down to the arrows at his side.

Driscoll raised his hand again. "If you harm me, they'll come looking. My friend in town will know something's wrong if I don't show up for supplies. And they'll come out here and find you. Do you want that?"

They're killing the children.

Only Jak wasn't a child anymore.

But he wasn't yet a man either.

He stopped, that old terror swimming in his veins, mixing with the horrible swirling sadness of Pup dead behind him. He all of a sudden felt so tired he wanted to drop to his knees. He ached inside. "I can get you one of these," Driscoll repeated again. "Pig meat is going for lots of money in town. If you can kill one, I'll bring you your own bow and arrows." When Jak stayed silent, Driscoll added, "I'll throw in another box of matches too."

Jak looked back at Pup's body, his heart crying out with loss. What good would it do to kill Driscoll now? It wouldn't bring Pup back…and the bow and arrows would help him survive, especially now that Pup was gone. The hurt inside swelled. He hung his head. *A pig.* One of those wild hogs with the razor-sharp tusks. He avoided those pigs like they were the devil's children. Even Pup—

"I'll do it," he said, turning away from Driscoll to gather Pup's body. He'd bury him by the river where he'd once buried the small bodies of Pup's brothers and sisters, those loved creatures who had once saved his life. And he'd say

157

goodbye to his Pup and wonder how he would walk each day even more alone than he'd already felt. Pup had saved *more* than just his life…he'd given him a reason to live.

Once Driscoll was long gone, Jak sank to his knees next to Pup, twisting his fingers in his friend's fur, raising his head and howling his sadness into the empty sky.

CHAPTER TWENTY

Tiny ice crystals. Sparkling. Glittering on the glass in the last light of the ending day. Lucas threw another log on the fire, holding his hands before it for a minute, thankful for the wonder of warmth. Sometimes, still, the flames felt...holy to him, like the first time he'd felt them after living through so many miserable winter days and nights with nothing but cold. Ice. Suffering. Aloneness.

A rumble made him pause, tilting his head as he listened. A vehicle? Shock and fear rolled through him. He walked quickly to the front window, his eyes widening when he saw that same large truck Harper drove, moving slowly—carefully—through the woods toward his house.

He watched as it came to a stop, and a minute later, Harper climbed down, a heavy-looking bag over her shoulder, walking to the place where the fox den was and staring down into it. When she turned toward his house, she had a smile on her face.

He stepped back quickly, making his body still as he

heard her climbing his steps. He shouldn't answer. *Why is she here? What does she want?* She knocked at his door, and he stayed still, trying not to answer, but in the end, a different part of him won out. The part that had come alive at the sight of her face, seeing that she'd come back. The part of him that knew she was *his,* even if he'd lived a life that could not make it be true.

When he opened the door, she smiled at him, moving from one foot to the other.

He waited for her to tell him why she was there, not knowing what to say. *Hi? Hello? Why are you here? What do you want?* He thought those questions might sound like he didn't want her there, and maybe he didn't—*shouldn't*—even though he knew he did.

"I've been advised not to do this," she finally said.

Advised. I've been…told. Someone told her not to do this. He frowned. "Do what?"

She looked away and then back. "Um, come out here." Her cheeks turned light pink like flowers had suddenly blossomed under her skin, and she moved the bag from one shoulder to the other.

He leaned against the doorway, and her eyes moved to his arms as he crossed them over his chest. His arms were bare, and he thought she must be looking at the scars that crisscrossed his skin here and there. Everywhere. It made him feel…naked even though it was only his arms. Those scars told too many awful stories about the way he'd lived. Stories he didn't want told. *Ever.* "Why didn't you listen?"

"Oppositional defiant disorder?" She let out a small, uncomfortable laugh.

Those were three words he didn't know and nothing to go along with them that would help him figure them out. Lucas tilted his head. "I don't know what that is," he admitted.

She smiled. "In my case, it just means I'm pigheaded."

He squinted at her. There it was again, three minutes into a conversation with her and he was already mostly lost. A gust of wind blew hard, and she held the bag tighter to her, moving her shoulders in and making her head go lower against the cold. "Come in," he said. "It's cold."

She looked thankful, not scared like she had the last time and she stepped inside. "No gun this time?" he asked as he closed the door and walked back toward the fire, looking inside the small glass window to make sure there was enough wood. Wanting to keep her warm.

"No. I'm...I'm sorry about that. I just—"

"I don't blame you. You don't know me. It was smart."

He turned toward her, and for a moment, time seemed to stretch out, long and thin. Breakable. Like a blade of grass pulled too tight. She moved in place again. "Anyway, I came to say thank you for what you did." She looked to the side for a minute like she was trying to find words written on his wall. "You helped me with something that was very, very important to me, and I'm grateful."

He looked down, wanting to tell her something, but not knowing if it was right to say. Not knowing the rules about things like that.

"What is it?" she asked, like she could read his face, knew his thoughts. It surprised him that he liked the idea of that.

"I wanted you to know that...I visited them. I...talked to them too. They weren't alone." He couldn't look at her. His face burned. But when he finally did, there were tears in her eyes, and she looked like he'd made her happy.

161

"Thank you," she whispered. "Those words feel too small. I… You've given me a gift. The gift of peace."

Lucas lifted his head, smiling. He'd given her a gift, and it had pleased her. "I'm glad it…helped you. To find them."

She let out a breath. "Yes, um." Her voice stumbled, and she cleared her throat, nodding her head to the bag on her shoulder. "Anyway, I also brought you this. A gesture of gratitude."

"What is it?"

She took the bag off her shoulder, moving past him to set it on the table by the back window, and then she turned to him. He took the few steps so he was standing beside her, waiting. She shot him a smile before opening the bag and pulling a few items out. Cans. She held them up to him one at a time. "Chicken noodle soup and pears." She set them on the table and then pulled out a few more items, listing them as she did. "Baked beans with ham, oh." She pulled out another item and held it up to him like it was the best of all. "Peanut butter," she said, her voice lowered to a whisper.

"I remember peanut butter," he murmured.

"Oh. You do? Did you like it?"

"Yes, I liked it."

Her face lit up so brightly that Lucas blinked. Each time she smiled at him, he felt good in a way he couldn't describe. *Like I'm a man. She makes me feel like a man.* She took off the top and peeled back some silver paper showing the smooth food he hadn't had since he was a little boy. He leaned forward, sniffing at it before dipping a finger in, pulling it out, and sticking it in his mouth.

Oh, God. Good. His eyes wanted to roll to the back of his head, but he kept them glued to Harper's, surprised by her eyes getting bigger as she watched him lick the peanut butter from his finger. The way she was watching him… *Oh no,* he was doing something wrong, acting…wrong. He dropped his hand to his side. Ashamed.

"Good?" Harper asked, and her voice sounded different than it had, deeper and a little slower. She reached into the bag, pulling something else from it. "Crackers," she said, the word rushed as she threw the box to the table. "And a few other things. Food. I brought you food because I was worried you might have a hard time getting out to hunt without your bow and arrows. And there's a storm coming too, in case you didn't know."

"Thank you. I have what I need. You didn't have to worry." He said it, but he didn't say that her worrying about him felt good because it meant someone remembered he was alive. It did him no good, but maybe he was still part human. And that mattered to him.

She tilted her head and looked long at him for a minute, her eyes moving from his eyes to his lips, staying there for a second and then moving over his jaw. It made him want to run a hand over his short beard to make sure he didn't have some peanut butter sticking to it. But he stayed still and let her study him. She seemed to like what she saw, and he was curious, wanted to know her thoughts, but had no idea how to ask.

What do I look like to you? I was human once, but now I'm part animal. Which one do you see? And why aren't you afraid?

He'd crawled.

He'd cried.

He'd eaten mud and bugs and dead grass when he was so starved he thought he'd die.

He'd begged.

He'd *killed*.

Could she tell? Could she see in his eyes how *low* he'd gone to survive? *To live?*

"I'm glad you have what you need," she finally said, turning her head and looking at the food on his table. "I'll leave this stuff anyway." She looked up at him. "Is there anything that you do need? Matches? Or…" Her white teeth caught her bottom lip and slid over it, and it made his body tighten with want, his muscles filled with that heat that made him want to *move*. Toward her. "I don't know." She shrugged, letting out a small laugh.

He tried his best to ignore his body. "I do need matches, but I don't have anything to trade." He frowned. "And I know that's not how things work in—"

"Oh, you don't need to pay me in any way. I told you, you've already given me a gift. Let me repay *you* for your help. Your time."

He watched her, not liking the idea of that, but not able to say why. He had always worked for the things he got. He didn't know how to take without paying. The way she was looking at him, though, with that *something* lighting her eyes and her lips pressed together like she wouldn't breathe until he said yes. And he *wanted* to say yes, not only for the matches, but because he wanted her to come back. "Okay."

She grinned, letting out that breath he knew she had been holding. "Great. What other foods do you like?"

He stared. He couldn't remember. His baka had cooked for him. Meats and vegetables wrapped up in something he couldn't remember the name of anymore. "Orange drink with bubbles," he said, feeling shy, thinking he was probably saying it wrong.

But her eyes lit up. "Orange Crush. Yes, that is good. I'll bring you some. What about bread? Do you like bread?" She

164

smiled happily again, and his stomach flipped, all thoughts of food disappearing. But she was looking at him waiting, so he closed his eyes, trying to remember bread. *Bread*. Yes, he'd liked that. It was soft, and he'd eaten it with peanut butter. "Yes."

"Okay, great. I'll bring you Orange Crush and bread and…oh, I'll surprise you. How's that?"

Lucas gave her a small not-knowing nod. She said the word *surprise* with a smile, but he didn't like surprises. To him, surprises were not good. Surprises came out of the clear-blue sky and knocked your head for a loop. But she was still smiling, so he'd trust that her surprise really did only mean food, nothing else.

Harper looked at the cans. "I can heat this up for us if you don't mind sharing?"

He nodded quickly, and she smiled again, using the little ring on the can to pull the top open. He had one pot that he got for her, and she started heating the chicken noodle soup on the top of his wood stove. Lucas watched her as she moved, his eyes moving from the curve of her backside as she bent over to the female shape of her legs under her jeans, the straight line of her back. He loved the look of her, loved seeing all the ways a woman's body was so different from his own. He wanted to see her naked, undress all the secrets hidden under her clothes, wanted to know what a woman's skin felt like against his own. His male parts throbbed, and he turned away from her, pretending to be busy moving the cans uselessly to the other side of the table.

He wanted her to leave, and he wanted her to stay, but he didn't know what he should feel. She *wanted* to share food with him. She'd liked his smoked fish too. And because the woman standing at his stove was heating soup for them to share, he felt confusion, but the one thing he *didn't* feel was alone.

165

CHAPTER TWENTY-ONE

The Missoula Main Library was a relatively nondescript brick building, located in downtown Missoula. Mark asked for directions from the man at the circulation desk and then made his way to the area where young adult books were kept. He took a moment to peruse the shelves, noting the white stickers at the bottom of the spines indicating the author and location and the yellow sticker near the middle with a large number on it, indicating how long the book was available for loan. *Harper was right.*

There was a woman standing in front of a library cart nearby, reshelving books, and Mark headed in her direction. As he approached, she looked up, removing her glasses and dropping them so they hung on the chain around her neck. "Hello."

"Hello, ma'am, Agent Gallagher with the Montana Department of Justice." He opened his wallet and showed her his badge, which she glanced at quickly, her eyes widening. "I'm hoping you can assist me."

"Oh. I can try. What is it I might help you with?"

Mark pulled out his cell phone and showed her the photos he'd taken of the books that had been on the night-stand at the Larkspur. "Is there anything you can tell me about these titles and whether they might have come from this library?"

She studied the photos, swiping between the one of the covers and the one of the spines. She looked up at Mark and handed him his cell phone back. "Yes, they did. I helped the woman pick these out myself after she asked for my help. Then instead of checking them out, she stole them."

Mark reached in his pocket, bringing out his notebook and the picture of the woman inside that the morgue had forwarded him. "Is this her?"

The librarian peered down at it. "Yes." She raised her gaze to Mark's, her eyes wide. "Is she *dead*?" she whispered. She brought her hand to her stomach, appearing ill.

"I'm sorry to say she is. Any information you can give me on her demeanor or something she said that seemed off to you would be very helpful."

The woman bobbed her head. "Um, yes, well, she asked me if I would help her choose some books for a young man. I asked for a specific age or reading level, and she seemed not to know how to answer that, and so I chose a few of our most popular titles for mid- to young teens. She seemed appreciative, but then I noticed later that the books were missing. I just got this weird feeling, you know, so I checked the computer and found that they'd never been checked out. Are you able to tell me what happened to her, Agent?"

"Unfortunately, she was murdered."

"Oh. Oh, that's terrible. My goodness…" She trailed off, and Mark nodded.

167

"Is there anything else at all you can tell me about her?"

"Oh, um… Oh yes, one thing. She used the computer right over there." She pointed to a couple of monitors. "She was sitting at the computer, actually, right before she asked me for help, so that's why I noticed. She stood up from the monitor and came toward me where I was reshelving books."

"Does the library have security cameras?"

"No, no cameras."

Mark nodded. "Okay. Would the history still be on that computer?"

"If she was using the internet, I think so. Or at least we don't delete the history regularly. That was, what…two weeks ago?"

"Yes, about that."

The woman came out from behind the desk, and Mark followed her to the computer monitor, where she sat down and logged in, bringing up the internet and then going to the browser history. "Let's see," she said softly, "that would have been Monday…no, Tuesday." She smiled up at Mark. "I'd come back from lunch with my sister earlier, and we always do Taco Tuesday down the street." She turned back to the monitor. "Okay, hmm…there wasn't a lot of activity on this computer, but visits to pages don't have time stamps. However, it looks as though all these entries are related to ancient China…probably a research paper of some sort…and then there's a visit to the contact page of Fairbanks Lumber Company and then…to the contact page of the CEO of the company, Halston Fairbanks."

"Could you print the entire history out?"

"I can take a screen shot and print it for you."

"That would be very helpful, ma'am."

Ten minutes later, Mark exited the building, the printout

in his hand. Had the woman killed at the Larkspur looked up the contact information for Halston Fairbanks, a local lumber company CEO? And if so, why? Moreover, why had she stolen books from the library that looked to be for a young man? He had nothing to go on regarding the stolen books, but he'd contact Halston Fairbanks and hope to God the man was able to provide some information that would move this case forward.

CHAPTER TWENTY-TWO

Jak sat up sleepily, blinking around the dark room, the objects he knew well coming into focus as sleep cleared. There was a sound outside, one he didn't recognize as part of the forest, a strange noise that must have pulled him from his dreams.

He reached for Pup, deep sadness squeezing him when he realized he wasn't there. He'd never be there again.

His feet hit the cold floor, and he stood, rushing to the back window and looking out into the snowy, moonlit woods. A bright light suddenly blinded him, and he startled, turning his head and using his arm to shield his eyes. He crouched, his palms hitting the wood hard and making him grunt with the pain.

For a minute, he hid beneath the window, his heart beating loudly in his ears, his mind spinning. *What is that light? What do I do?*

Had the enemy come for him?

Would they break down his door? Overpower him? Hurt him? Kill him?

Will you die today?

No!

Jak gathered his bravery and raised his head, peeking over the sill as the light went out. There was a person—a woman, he thought—standing outside the window, some sort of light in her hand.

Jak watched, wide-eyed and tensed with fear, as she walked to the window next to the one he was hiding below and peered through that one. She knocked on the glass, and though it was soft, it seemed to ring through the silent woods, the drumbeat of his heart following, loud and pounding in his head.

The woman stepped back and stood in the moonlight, looking at his house, seeming as scared as him. Jak leaned closer, trying to get a better look at her. No weapon, just a big bag hung over her shoulder. She looked one way, then the other, then behind her, before coming back to the window he was crouched below and knocking softly at that one again.

He turned, pressing his back to the wall as the soft tapping continued. For several minutes, he simply sat there, waiting to see if the woman would go away. But instead, she knocked again, this time calling out softly yet loud enough to be heard through the window. "Please let me in."

She sounded scared. *What if she needs help? What if she's lost and alone like the blond boy?*

He sat there for another few seconds, nervous, unsure, before finally standing, and looking at her through the glass. She stared back, raising her hand. "What do you want?" he called.

She stepped forward, letting out a sob and then putting her palms on the glass. "It's you." There was a small thump sound as she let her head fall forward so it was against the glass. "Please let me in. It's so cold out here, and I just want... I just want to talk to you. Please."

He paused for another second but finally reached out, lifting the window slowly. "Who are you?"

The woman smiled, tears shining in her eyes as she moved from one foot back to the other. She itched at her neck, sniffled, and then wiped her nose with her sleeve. She looked behind her and then climbed through the window, even though he hadn't invited her inside. "Do you live here alone?"

Jak figured she was worried there was someone else inside who might hurt her. "Yes. Don't worry. It's just me."

She let out her breath. "I left the car way up on the road and walked here. I came to the back of the house in case the front is being watched."

Watched? No one was watching him. Was this woman acting this way because of the war?

Jak stepped back, and she shut the window quickly, turning toward him, her eyes moving from his hair to his feet. She smiled again as she met his eyes. She was pretty, with long, black hair and smooth, tan skin, but her eyes had red around them, and she kept itching and moving like there was something wrong with her.

"Look at you," she said, her eyes wet, teary. "You're so handsome. I hoped you'd look like him, and you do."

Jak frowned, confused and still nervous. "Who are you?" he asked again. "What do you want?"

She stepped closer, and he stepped back, keeping his space though he was larger and stronger than the small woman in front of him. She reached her hand out, trying to touch his face, and he moved back. Away. A tear fell from her eye, and she dropped her hand. "I'm your mother."

172

Shock made him go still. "My mother? How... I don't have a mother."

She stepped closer again, and this time he didn't step back. His *mother*?

"Of course you have a mother." She made a jerky move again, scratched at her neck, and then shook her head like she was trying to clear it. "It's me. I knew, God, I knew I shouldn't have given you to him. But I didn't have a choice—" Her face screwed up, and she started to cry but then stopped herself. "I thought you'd be better off with him. And he's taking care of you, I see that." She looked around at the cabin. "You're safe, right? Warm?"

Jak nodded slowly. "I'm warm. But no one's taking care of me." He took care of himself.

The woman—his mother?—tilted her head, jerking and scratching at her neck again. His eyes moved to the place she'd scratched, and he saw that she'd opened a sore and that a trail of blood was moving slowly down the side of her neck. "But he gave you this house, made sure you had a safe, warm place to live."

"Driscoll? Yes, he gave me this house... How do you know Driscoll?"

"It's a stroke of luck that I found you. I saw Driscoll in town, and I followed him but lost his car. I thought I was lost, but then I saw your house. It's like God led me here, you know?" She sniffled, wiping at her nose with her sleeve again. "I know it's not right, him keeping you out here. And I'm going to fix that. I'm going to get clean, I promise, and I'm going to find a place. A nice little house with sunflowers in the garden. Do you like sunflowers?"

Sunflowers? "But there's a war out there. Don't you know that?"

173

She stared at him for a second before nodding, her head jerking up and down and her eyes filling with tears again. "I know. God, I know. No one can be trusted. The whole world's on fire. It's always on fire."

"Yes. You shouldn't go back out there."

She smiled weakly. "I'm a survivor. I'll be okay."

He stared at her, trying to understand this confusing visit. Could it be true that she was his mother and she'd given him to Driscoll so he'd be safe from the war? But what about his baka? He felt his brow pinch together as he tried to make sense of it all. Of the ways he might have been passed around from person to person so he'd be kept safe. *Is it possible?*

And if it was…he had family. He had a mother. He stepped forward, gripping her arm. "Let me come with you. I can protect you. I can find food for us and…and make warm clothes to wear."

She smiled again, another tear slipping down her cheek. "Sweet boy." She sighed and then shook her head slowly. Sadly. "No. I can't take you with me yet. Soon, I promise. I'll be back for you. But," she said, her voice cheering in a way that sounded like a lie, "I did bring you something." She stepped away, bringing her bag from her shoulder and setting it on the floor. She knelt down and dug inside, bringing out a couple of books.

She stood, handing the books to him. He took them, reading the titles: *The True Story of the Three Little Pigs* and *Goodnight Moon*.

"I was told they're the most popular books for kids." She frowned. "I know they're for younger kids, but…I wasn't sure so…"

He looked at her blankly. His baka had told him he must never ever tell anyone she'd taught him to read. His baka had

174

told him it would be very dangerous. But this woman was his mother, or so she said. He didn't have to tell her he could read, but he didn't have to lie and say he couldn't either. "Thank you," he finally said, but he couldn't help adding, "When you come back, will you bring me more?" *Not baby books,* he wanted to say but didn't. He didn't want her to take back the ones in his hands. He held them tighter.

"Of course. Yes." She smiled and stepped away before picking up her bag again, and moving toward the back window. "I'll be back. I will." She smiled again, bigger this time, but there was hurt in her face, and her body was even more jerky than it'd been. "I just need to get well, and then I'll be back. Until then, you take care of yourself, okay?"

Jak nodded, and she opened his window and began climbing back through, out into the snowy night. "Wait," he called, and she turned. "What's your name?"

"My name's Emily." She turned back toward him. "But you can't mention me. Don't tell anyone I've been here, okay?"

Jak nodded. But he didn't understand. Who was he going to tell? And he didn't get why everyone always wanted him to keep their secrets. He didn't know who was protecting him or who the bad men were. He was all twisted inside and had no idea who to trust or if he should trust anyone at all.

She turned away again, starting to duck out the window but then paused. "What does he call you?" she asked over her shoulder.

He knew she was talking about Driscoll, but Driscoll didn't call him anything at all. And he didn't know if there was any point in saying anything about his baka, wherever she might be now. Why did Driscoll and his mother not know what the other called him? *Who am I?* he wondered. "Jak," he said.

She nodded, still turned away from him. "Jak's a good name. I called you Lucas." She sounded very sad. "I know that's not your name, but when I was carrying you, that's what I called you. I'm sorry that in the end, I never even gave you that." She ducked out the window then, landing in the snow with a soft crunch.

He watched as she turned on her light and walked into the woods, the light fading in the darkness, along with the woman who'd called herself his mother but had left him alone again.

Jak read the books, three times each, memorizing the words, and then got back under the blanket on his bed and lay staring at the ceiling. But the books didn't make sense. Wolves were good, not bad. Pup had been his best friend. Wolves had families and mates that they stayed with for life. They sang love songs to the moon and rolled on their backs in happiness at the smell of the rain. It was wild pigs who were mean and bad and greedy for their mushrooms. They liked the smell of blood and laughed at things no one else could see. He shivered when he thought of them, and the memory of Driscoll's words came back. *Pig meat is going for lots of money in town. If you can kill one, I'll bring you your own bow and arrows.* He hadn't found any pig yet, not that he had looked very hard. He couldn't seem to make himself want to do much of anything the last few months. He missed Pup. He hated the loud and empty quiet.

The other book, the one with the little boy and the red balloon, just made him more sad. The old lady in the chair made him think of his baka, made him know there was no one sitting in a chair in his room, or anywhere else, watching over him. No one to make him food or make sure he was warm and happy. The person who called herself his mother had left him that story and then walked away from him. He had a feeling she wouldn't be back. Just like when she must have given him away to his baka. But why? When? He didn't understand anything about who he was.

It was a long time before he slept again that night, and when he did, pictures of an unknown enemy with a face in shadow and dark eyes filled with meanness haunted his nightmares.

CHAPTER TWENTY-THREE

Harper stirred the soup with one of the plastic spoons she'd thrown in the bag with the canned items she'd brought to Lucas. A quick glance at the things on the table told her he had one of everything: a pot, a bowl, a spoon, and a fork. Things he'd traded Driscoll for? *What did the fork cost him?* How much did a pot go for? If it was a kindness Driscoll had been doing for him, why didn't it feel that way to Harper?

Something was way off about this whole situation, and she hoped Agent Gallagher would find out what it was, though he wasn't under any obligation to share it with her. But she could be a... She searched her mind for the most fitting description... Friend? Contact? Yes, *contact* at least. She could be a contact to this man who had few options for obtaining needed items after the way he'd lived his life thus far. So why didn't that word...satisfy her?

As she stirred, she thought back to his expression as he'd licked the peanut butter off his finger, and a shiver went through her just as it had at the time. She was attracted to him, not only because of his looks but for the way his gaze sharpened with intelligence when he was curious about something, for that shy expression when he was worried he was saying the wrong thing or using the wrong word, for the way his voice sounded and the way his body moved. He appealed to her in a deeply sexual way no man ever had, and it scared her, but it also came with an edge of excitement.

Maybe the rules and social structures she'd grown up with didn't apply here. Maybe it was easier to acknowledge your base instincts in a place with no grocery stores or electricity, nothing to keep you warm except the heat of a flame and another's body. He was a caveman of sorts, but maybe they *all* were if put in the right environment and forced to live on instinct and prowess alone.

She snuck a glance at him. She knew he was attracted to her too. She saw the way he watched her, the way his smile was innocent but the heat in his eyes primal, the way he studied her body when he thought she couldn't see. She'd learned to watch men for unwelcomed interest, for a warning of impending danger, a red, flashing caution sign that told her to run and hide.

And yet she didn't want to run from him.

And that should scare her too. But it didn't.

The soup was bubbling, and so she dished it into his one bowl and his one mug, setting each on the table and sitting on the tree trunks that acted as stools. Had Lucas made them? No, how could he? He didn't seem to have tools. Did he? She didn't want to ask and make him feel like everything in his world was weird and questionable, but it felt like there were a hundred small things she wanted to know. How had he gotten by without everyday items she took for granted?

Did he really hunt with nothing more than a knife and his bare hands?

How had he made the boots and jacket he wore? The ones that were so carefully stitched together with…what?

Was he lonely?

Scared sometimes?

He had to be. He was human after all.

She smiled at him as she took a spoonful of the soup, watching as he did the same. That look of pleasure came over his expression, and her stomach muscles quivered. "What do you think?"

He scooped another bite into his mouth, slurping loudly. "Salty. Good."

Harper hadn't ever heard anyone seem to enjoy chicken noodle soup from a can quite as much as Lucas, and it made her grin, taking pleasure in his pleasure. Although she made note that he was pushing all the squares of chicken meat to the corner of his bowl.

They ate in silence for a moment before she finally got the nerve to ask him one of her gazillion questions. "Lucas, can I ask you something?" He scooped more soup into his mouth and met her eyes, wariness in his expression, though he nodded. "Why did you take that magazine from the sheriff's office?" She put her hand up, rushing on, "It doesn't matter. I won't say anything. I mean, it's not that anyone would care anyway, but I'm…curious."

He put his spoon down, and it appeared he was considering whether to answer her. Or maybe he was surprised she'd seen him take it. Finally, he said, "Just to look at the… pictures."

"The pictures? Oh. So…you… Can you read?" She hadn't considered that, but…if he'd been abandoned at a young age, maybe he'd never been taught to read at all. Maybe he'd never attended school. "Don't be embarrassed," she said when he didn't immediately answer. "You can learn. I could teach you if you want." She liked the idea. Bent over a book with Lucas, their heads close together...

But he had narrowed his eyes and looked to be on guard, and she suddenly regretted ruining what had been an easy camaraderie for a few minutes there. "I read some." The words came out spaced strangely, as though he was reluctant to release each one.

She bobbed her head. "Oh."

"I don't know about the world. I thought the magazine might help me understand."

Harper released a breath. "That's understandable." She tilted her head. "What did the magazine tell you?"

He gave her sort of a bewildered smile and raised his eyebrows as he brushed a hand through his thick, choppy hair. He'd cut it himself. Without a mirror. The thought combined with the boyish expression on his masculine face made her heart jump. "That there's a lot of food out there. Almost every page was a picture selling something to eat."

She smiled. She could only imagine what he thought when he'd experienced only a diet of meat and fish and whatever he could forage. "Is there something new you want to try?"

He looked unsure. "I don't know. Pizza maybe. The people eating it looked happy."

The way he mispronounced it with a soft i, his expression so serious, made Harper laugh. "Then I'll bring you a pizza too," she said, pronouncing the word properly. "Add it to my shopping list."

181

Lucas regarded her for a moment, tilting his head in that questioning way of his. "Why are you coming out here, Harper? Is it because you're helping the police?"

"No, I don't work for them or anything. I have my own business, like I told you, taking nature lovers out. I'm helping the agent get around in these backwoods and answering questions that arise. Honestly, Lucas, you'd probably be better than me at helping Agent Gallagher figure out who killed Isaac Driscoll."

He looked behind her, out the window on the far wall. "I don't care who killed Isaac Driscoll." He met her eyes, and something burned in them. *Hatred*.

Harper was taken aback. "I thought you said you barely knew him."

"I didn't." The fire in his eyes dulled and then went out, leaving what looked like hopelessness behind.

"I don't understand."

Lucas looked at her. "He was a cheat and a liar. My life is harder now that he's gone, but I won't miss him."

Oh. Harper wondered if he'd hinted at that to Agent Gallagher or if he was confessing that to her because he'd come to trust her a little. "If you have information that might lead to—"

"I don't," he said. It was clear he was done discussing Driscoll.

"If it turns out you're not allowed to stay on this land, where will you live?"

He shrugged, though he really couldn't be that unconcerned about the potential of being homeless. "I'll survive."

What did that mean, though, when it came to lodging? *Survival* alone sounded like a dismal goal. He couldn't be planning to simply find a…cave or something. *Could he?* She couldn't let that happen.

Harper felt on edge. She still sensed this man's goodness, and spending more time with him had only made that feeling grow, but there was no denying there were secrets in his eyes. And she would not let some sexual tension get in the way of her asking the questions she felt required answers if she was really going to be a…contact. She bit nervously at the inside of her cheek for a moment as she watched him stare into space, his mind obviously somewhere else. "For all evils there are two remedies—time and silence."

His gaze shot to hers, eyes flaring with recognition as his body stilled. As quick as that, his expression shuttered dispassionately. But she'd seen it. He hadn't been quick enough to hide from her.

"Lucas, you read more than *some*. You read as well as anyone." Why had he lied about that? He was eying her warily now as though waiting for her to pounce. "I just quoted Alexandre Dumas. But I think you know that." She paused for a heartbeat, two. "Do you have the backpack, Lucas? It was my mother's."

He remained still for another few seconds, and then he blew out a breath, seeming to come to some internal conclusion. He stood and walked to a place near the front corner of the cabin, kneeling and lifting a board from the floor. Harper watched, confused, as he lifted something from it, the turquoise color causing her to put her hands over her mouth. *I was right.* She'd remembered correctly. She stood quickly and then knelt next to him, taking the backpack and hugging it to her chest. "Thank you," she whispered. *Another piece of my mother.*

But as he stared at the backpack, there was a look of

acute loss in his eyes…as though it'd been as precious to him as it was to her. "It was your mother's. You should have it," he said, as though convincing himself. "I'm sorry I didn't give it to you when I gave you the necklace."

She took in his expression, feeling as though her intention was to *give* to him, yet she was somehow always *taking* instead. She slowly opened the backpack, removing a few loose papers and a stack of spiral-bound notebooks. Tears filled her eyes as she leafed through the notebook on top, her mother's handwriting immediately familiar even though it'd been so long since she'd seen it.

As she took a moment to look through the pages, she noticed they were wrinkled and dog-eared as though they'd been read over and over and over. Some sentences were faded as though a finger had gone over them repetitively, underlining, memorizing maybe. In many places, there were identical lines written under her mother's words, as though someone had sought to recreate the writing or perhaps practice his own. There were drawings in the margins too, renderings of trees, leaves, a wolf, and other forest animals all connected, swirled together so that you had to look closely to single out the individual elements. As Harper looked through, she saw that the practice lines of text went from boyish to more polished and the doodled artwork got better too, crisper and more realistic. He was no Picasso, but there was a loveliness in the simplicity of his artwork. And she knew what she was seeing: Lucas growing up right there on the pages. Her chest felt tight.

Near the end, there were questions written in his handwriting. He had gone over and over her mother's notes and questions and realizations about life and love, friendship, vengeance, forgiveness, and all the themes Harper knew were in her mother's favorite literary work.

When she looked up at him and met his eyes, he was blushing, an acute look of shame in his expression. "Sorry," he said, his tone remorseful, glancing at the place where he'd drawn a wolf howling at the moon.

"It's okay. Lucas, I...I love them." She tilted her head. "Was the book in here too?" she asked, peering into the empty backpack, seeing only a few pens that looked as though they'd been used until the ink ran out.

"No book. Just her notes and pens."

Harper raised her eyes to Lucas again, who knelt watching her go through the pages, what had surely been a form of human connection when he was so very alone. The thing books—*emotions she could relate to in other people's stories*—had been to her. Her heart twisted, half joy, half sorrow, as she realized that, yes, the forest had nourished his body, but her mother's words had nourished his soul.

CHAPTER TWENTY-FOUR

"Get over here, you," Rylee called, shaking out the hair salon cape quickly and tossing it over the back of the chair. "You didn't have to come in for a cut to see me. I would have come over to your place later."

Harper grinned, wrapping her arms around her friend and squeezing her tightly. "I couldn't wait. And I could use a trim." Rylee raised a brow. They both knew that wasn't true, as she'd had one right before Rylee's wedding two weeks before. "How was Mexico? I want all the dirty details." She sat in the salon chair at her friend's station and met her eyes in the mirror, raising one finger. "Wait, maybe not *all* the dirty details."

Rylee smiled, picking the cape up and securing it around Harper's neck. She moved Harper's hair aside and put her hands on her shoulders, looking at her in the mirror in front of where Harper sat. "It *was* dirty. In all the best ways." She winked. "And amazing. I hardly wanted to come back."

"When I was here waiting for you?"

"You and about ten feet of snow."

"Good point." Harper smiled. "So married life is good so far?"

"Yeah, yeah." She waved her hand around. "But we've been living together forever. It hardly feels like anything's changed now that all the hoopla's over with. Anyway, enough about that. I can't believe I'm just now getting the details about finding your parents' car." Her eyes widened, and she leaned forward. "How are you, Harper? Really? I mean, I almost fell over dead when I got your text." Rylee glanced back at Moira, the owner of the hair salon where she worked, and then grabbed a comb off the counter, running it through Harper's hair.

Harper sighed. "I'm okay. I'm good." *Better* than she'd been before.

Rylee began sectioning Harper's hair and clipping it up. "I just can't believe it. After all these years. And how was it found? You don't usually go out searching in the winter, do you?"

Harper paused, going quickly back over everything that had happened since Rylee left on her honeymoon. It was like life had turned upside down since then. "No, it wasn't me who found it. I was led there." She thought about where to start as she realized all the ways life had changed in the short time her friend had been out of town. "Did you hear about the murder in town? At the Larkspur?"

Rylee frowned as she clipped the ends of Harper's hair. "Yeah. As soon as I got back. Some woman passing through town, right? I heard someone say it was a boyfriend she might be traveling with or something? Seriously awful. But what does that have to do with your parents?"

"Nothing. Well, sort of nothing." It was all seemingly

connected to Lucas—some in bigger ways, some in smaller. Some in ways she possibly didn't understand because he wasn't the most forthcoming man. But Lucas stood right in the middle of everything that had happened or come to light in the last couple of weeks. *What does that mean? Does it have bigger implications than—*

"Earth to Harper."

"Sorry." She began telling Rylee about Agent Mark Gallagher, about Isaac Driscoll, about Lucas, and then about the necklace and how Lucas had led her to her parents' wreckage, including her mother's backpack. When she mentioned her mother's notes on *The Count of Monte Cristo*, she left out the way he'd treated them as though they were the Holy Grail. She wasn't sure why; it simply felt like something that should remain between them. *Now who's the secretive one, Harper?*

But Harper had always had secrets. She was used to keeping them.

Rylee continued trimming her hair, her eyes wide, a look of disbelief on her face when Harper was done. "Wow."

"I know. It's…crazy."

"So, if your Tarzan has been ruled out for the moment, there are no suspects in either of the murders?"

Tarzan. Harper rolled her eyes. "He's not *my* anything. And no, not as far as I know, although I'm not really privy to every single lead the police are working on. Agent Gallagher's been nice enough to keep me in the loop about my parents' case and has answered a few questions I had about Lucas, but it's not like I'm actually working every angle of the investigation."

"Even so"—she smiled—"your dad would be proud." She used her hand not holding the scissors to squeeze Harper's shoulder, her smile dimming. "I know I've mentioned it before, but…my dad's still sorry he didn't take you in," she said softly. "He regrets it. I can tell by the way his mood shifts whenever he asks about you."

Harper made a small sound of denial. "You were barely making ends meet. The loss of your mother was still fresh, Rylee…I get it. I get why it wasn't an option. I don't blame him." Was that true? She hadn't really worked that out in her mind. She didn't want to blame anyone, but the real truth? *It had hurt.* From what she knew from school reports and things her parents had always said about her, she hadn't been unruly. She'd been well behaved. Subjectively, she couldn't understand how no one in her community, people who had known and cared about her parents, had been willing to keep her.

The years she'd spent in the foster care system were at times terrifying and lonely, and she'd wished with all her heart that her parents hadn't been torn from her and that she didn't have to suffer the additional trauma of being placed in the home of a stranger—a stranger who had been anything but safe. Her uncle had been in college and then beginning his life, so he hadn't been able to offer her a home, and her best friend had lost her own mother to cancer six months before, leaving her father to raise two daughters by himself while grieving the loss of his wife.

Some people felt guilty, she knew that too. It was why Dwayne always offered her jobs that came up at his office, for instance. Why Rylee's dad had insisted she stay at their home during the summers in high school and then bent over backward to help her start her guide business, even securing her first several clients, ones who'd booked with her again and again.

But she understood why they hadn't offered to adopt her after the accident, she did. Or, at least, the adult Harper did. She just didn't know how to explain it to the little girl inside her who still ached when she revisited that time in her life. In her heart of hearts, she still felt like the little girl no one wanted.

She didn't like to think too much about the first several years after her parents died. But later…well, later she'd been placed with an older woman who had been kind to her. She'd settled into a new school, and…she'd been okay.

Rylee pressed her lips together, the look that always came over her face when she talked about Harper going into the social services system.

"Anyway," Harper said, wanting to change the subject, "I'm still waiting for the coroner to release their remains, and then I'm going to have a burial."

"The whole town will be there."

"I hope." Harper mustered a smile. "My dad would have liked that." Her smile widened. "My mom would have wanted to stay home reading." Harper was such a combination of them, she realized with gladness. Outdoorsy like her dad and a lover of books like her mom.

Rylee moved in front of her, bending forward and holding the ends of Harper's hair up on both sides of her face to measure the evenness of the trim she'd just finished. She met Harper's eyes and smiled. "She did love her books, didn't she? I remember her asking me if I missed the characters when I told her we'd read *Charlotte's Web* in class. I had no idea what she was talking about. She literally *missed* people who didn't exist." She straightened, stepping back to assess her work.

Harper smiled. Yes, that sounded exactly like her mother.

She had loved literature. And she had inspired others to love it too. That thought brought Lucas to mind, the way he'd looked so sorrowful as he'd handed the backpack to Harper containing her mother's notes, giving them to her to keep.

I should have left them with him.

Yes, of course she should have. What had she been thinking? Well, she'd been thinking that it was another precious piece of the past she was desperate to hold. Something tangible. But it seemed that those notes had sustained Lucas, when to her they were a special keepsake. Had she just done the same thing to him that had been done to her? Taken away something cherished that brought light? Her heart sank.

"So what's going to happen to Lucas now?" Rylee asked as she peeled the Velcro apart and removed the cape from around Harper. "Is he going to stay in the woods?"

Harper's brows came together as she again met Rylee's eyes in the mirror. "I don't know that he has a lot of options. I mean, the guy has no family that he knows of, no formal education or job experience... I don't know. But...there's something about him. God, it's hard to explain. He's this combination of wild and, I don't know, innocent? No, that's not right. Thoughtful?" She shook her head, frustrated that she couldn't describe him accurately or do him justice. "Sensitive."

"Your eyes are all funny right now," Rylee noted, and when Harper looked at her, she saw that her friend was watching her with an expression that was half-puzzled and half-amused.

Harper rolled her eyes. "All right. He's an enigma."

"Well, yeah, of course he's an enigma. He grew up on dirt and snow and class notes on *The Count of Monte Cristo.* He's probably confused as hell."

Despite that it felt a little mean, Harper laughed. "Who wouldn't be?" she asked, attempting to defend him, though she knew Rylee was mostly kidding. "Can you even imagine, Rylee? The loneliness he must have lived with all these years? I don't know if I could have survived."

"Of course you could have. You're the strongest person I know."

Harper appreciated the vote of confidence, but she wondered if anyone was strong enough to survive that without some major lasting effects. "Anyway"—Harper stood, taking the few steps around the chair and giving her friend another hug—"I've gotta run, but thank you for this," she said, pointing to the trim she hadn't really needed but that had allowed her to visit with her friend under the watchful eye of the salon owner.

"Stay warm," she said as Harper handed her the money for the cut and a tip, folding it into her hand so she didn't try to give the tip back like she always did. "And let me know what I can do to help with arrangements for your parents."

"I will." Harper waved goodbye to the other stylists she knew, the bell over the door tinkling as she left.

She'd only made it a block down the street when her phone rang. She pulled it from her pocket, and when she saw who it was, her heart picked up speed. She stopped, stepping close to the side of a building so she wasn't in the middle of the sidewalk. "Hello?"

"Hi, Harper. I was calling… Well, are you sitting down?"

Harper's breath caught, and she leaned against the wood siding of the hardware store. Agent Gallagher sounded…off somehow. "Yes."

"The coroner called me. Harper, there's evidence that your parents were shot."

"Shot?" For a moment, the word didn't make sense, as though he'd spoken in a foreign language she couldn't comprehend. "I don't understand."

"I don't either, but their case is now being treated as a homicide."

CHAPTER TWENTY-FIVE

Drip. Plunk. Ping.

Winter was melting all around him, falling from the forest. The ground drank it up, taking it deep down where the life of the trees and the plants and the flowers waited to live again. Jak stepped on the soft ground, his eyes looking for some mushrooms or something else to fill his empty belly. Soon there would be enough food again, and that thought brought a faraway gladness, though the heavy feeling that had weighed him down since Pup died felt like it was crushing all happiness, making it smaller, not important. The heavy feeling was bigger, shadowing everything.

Pup.

A lump moved up Jak's throat, and he swallowed it down, his steps slowing.

The wind moved, a terrible smell making his nose wrinkle, his attention turning right before he heard a low grunt. Something moved in the brush to his left. *A boar.* He went into a slow crouch, waited for the fear to come, but it did not. That heaviness inside him made that small too.

Pig meat is going for lots of money in town. If you can kill one, I'll bring you your own bow and arrows. It had been a long, hard winter without Pup. Jak had gone hungry often. Scared. Alone. His ribs could be seen easily under his skin. He needed the bigger weapon now if he was going to live. Not only to have meat, but to kill animals big enough for the furs he needed to survive the freezing cold. And if he wasn't going to live, then why wait for starvation to take him, slowly and hurting? Why not let the pig do it with one angry, squealing stab to his gut? Wouldn't that be better anyway? Quicker?

He knelt down next to a mossy tree trunk, going still and waiting for the pig to come out of the brush. He let his breath out slowly. Pinging water. Pig stink. The low growl coming from his own throat.

But the snuffling of that wild pig was not soft. It let out squeals—the ones that had always scared Jak before now. It sounded like a monster or something he had thought might be under his bed when he was a little boy. The thing he'd asked his baka to check for but that she'd told him he must face himself if he was a strong boy like she thought.

He'd done it then. He'd do it now. Face the monster. Even if it felt like he'd already faced too many monsters.

And he couldn't figure out if he hoped to win against this one. Or lose.

The pig came out from the brush. A huge male that had to weigh more than ten Jaks. Prickly white hair covered his black and white body. Short, sharp tusks sticking from his mouth. He had the biggest set of balls Jak had ever seen on any living thing. He grunted when he saw Jak, letting out one of those high squeals and shaking his head back and forth.

Pig stink. *Crazy* stink. The scent of decay coming from his nostrils like his brain was rotting. As crazy and mean as Jak had ever seen before.

Jak moved toward him, taking out the pocketknife, the blade worn small after many winters and summers of using and then sharpening it again and again against rocks. But he hadn't known he'd be facing down this beast today and hadn't brought the hunting knife.

The sharp gift of *life* the dark-haired boy had given him so long ago was all he had. It would help him live or help him die. Either was okay.

The pig raised its head, squealing again—the scream of a devil—and Jak felt the first sprout of rage begin to grow, wrapping around his insides. Jak raised his own head, letting out a scream that rang through the forest. He laughed, a crazy sound that came from deep inside his soul, a mix of the loss and fear and hurt and suffering he'd lived through. "Come and get me, you *damn* pig!" he screamed, rage exploding in him. "Do whatever you want!"

For a minute, the pig stood there grunting, its head lowered, and Jak thought it was going to turn in the other direction. He leaned forward, ready to chase it, when it suddenly charged forward, taking him by surprise. He stood his ground, planting his feet in the soft earth and bending his knees, the knife stuck out in front of him.

Fear swirled through him but so did a wild excitement. "Come and get me, you ugly thing," he said, only this time instead of yelling the words, he grunted them out under his breath, his jaw grinding. The boar lowered its head more and sped up, charging straight at Jak.

Jak had a second of confusion, his instincts screaming at him to *run*, his mind and his heart saying *no*. The forest was quiet for a heartbeat, two, like every animal, leaf, and branch had stopped to watch the beast and the skinny man/boy slam into each other, eyes stuck as the animal rushed forward as fast as its fat body would let it. And somehow, that huge animal moved with the quickness of a lightning flash.

Everything exploded through Jak as the animal ran straight into him, Jak's body flying backward and slamming into the trunk of a tree as the animal let out another war scream and kept coming.

Jak hurried to his feet, fighting to fill his lungs with the air that had been knocked out of him. He jumped to the side just as the animal came at him again, the sick smell of it following him, even though its body went to the side. Jak rolled and hopped to his feet, just as it came up too short and turned back, charging at him again, its eyes crazed, spit flying from its mouth.

Jak held up the knife and rolled again, a deep yell coming from his chest as he rolled away from the pig and stabbed his arm forward, the blade ripping across the animal's shoulder. It let out another demon scream, this time of pain.

"Come on, you dirty beast!" Jak yelled. "That's all? That's the best you can do?" He felt as crazed as that pig looked. *Nothing mattered*. He would die, but first, he'd get in as many good jabs as he could. The boar wanted to kill him, but Jak would make it a fight that nasty thing would never forget. That ugly monster would be telling his ugly grandkids about Jak someday. Jak figured he had balls big enough to make at least a hundred ugly kids as sick smelling as himself. He laughed crazy-like, spinning as the huge pig rushed him again.

Jak went the other way quickly, but he didn't move fast enough this time. As he threw his body forward, his foot caught on a tree root and he went down hard, the wind knocked from his lungs again as pain rattled his bones. He cried out, the hurt making him curl into himself as the pig head-butted him where he lay, the edge of its tusk slicing down his arm. Jak grabbed the beast, squeezing big handfuls of hairy meat as the animal shrieked, its heaviness coming down on top of Jak, crushing him, his air whooshing from his lungs.

He wrestled with the animal, fighting with all his leaving strength. *I can't breathe. I can't breathe* was the only thought rushing through his dying mind. The forest around him blinked out for a second, dark spots coming in front of his eyes as the stink of the animal filled his nose.

I'm going to die.

His head fell to the side as the pig kept up his shriek, its hoofs digging into Jak's body, its tusks scraping across his flesh, the wounds he'd opened gushing blood. Jak opened his eyes to see the glint of shininess. He was still holding the pocketknife loosely in his fist.

The dark-eyed boy from that very first night showed up in his mind like he was right there beside him.

Why are you here? Jak asked, and the boy didn't answer, but he looked down at the pocketknife still held barely in Jak's hand as the boar continued to tear at his body. *What happened to you?* Jak wondered. The boy looked down at the knife again as if to say, *I gave you that knife. My dying gift. Use it.*

Jak's final boom of strength came from nowhere, from everywhere, from the memory of that other boy and the way he'd held his hand and Jak had told him to live. Jak raised his hand, and with the last of his might, he let out a battle cry and swiped the knife across the pig's throat.

Later, he would remember only feeling nothingness as he dragged that dead pig body through the wilderness, his wounds tied with torn pieces of his clothing but still leaving drops of red in the melting snow. The gaping one at his side burning like fire.

Driscoll was outside when Jak turned the bend, and he stared at him with wide eyes, his jaw loose. When Jak made it to where he stood, dropping the dead boar at Driscoll's feet, Driscoll threw his head back and laughed. *He's as crazy as that pig.*

Jak tilted to the side, catching himself and pressing his fingers to the gaping tear at his side. "Iwantmybowandarrows," he said, the words running all together.

"Oh, you shall have them," Driscoll said. And with that, Jak turned and walked away.

The next while was spent somewhere between life and death. The dark-eyed boy did not come to him again, but his baka did, telling him he was a strong boy and not to give up. Jak wanted to give up. He was tired of living. Tired of fighting. Tired of surviving. And most of all, he was tired of the never-stopping empty aloneness.

But Jak's body didn't agree that he should give up. It kept on fighting, even though his spirit did not. There were no whispers inside, no deep-down life. Only silence. His soul had died. *Along with Pup.* He cleaned his wounds and laid clean cloth on them, changing through the pieces he had, washing them in water from the pump behind his house and drying them in the warming wind, to go back inside to sleep again. He woke only to gulp down water from the pump, clean his wounds, and eat the small bit of food he had.

Many, many days passed. He didn't know the number, but one morning, he woke, noticing he felt better, less sore, less achy. For many minutes, he lay there, staring at the wood ceiling, a beam of sunlight from the window, dancing and sparkling before his eyes. *Maybe I am dead,* he thought. *Maybe those dancing lights are tiny angels and I'm in heaven.*

A twist of hurt in his side spoke up, telling him he was wrong. No angels, just dust pieces, and two things could not be more different than those.

His belly spoke up next, telling him that it wanted breakfast. He pulled himself from bed, cleaned himself up, dressed, and picked up his hunting knife.

Another day. Many more to follow. He walked in a different way than he usually took when hunting. Maybe it was toward town, maybe not. Maybe he would walk right into the middle of enemy territory. Maybe they would kill him on sight.

Maybe...he didn't care.

He'd thrown himself in front of a huge, wild, crazy pig with sharp tusks and lived. He'd laugh, only it would open his wound back up again and he didn't have any clean cloths.

He didn't know if he could do it anymore, the constant suffering. The winters always coming, the hunger, the loneliness that felt like darkness carved deep into his bones. Why *should* he fight? For what? Why should he survive? He understood the look in the blond boy's eyes now. The *happiness* that it was finally over. Jak should have died on that cliff that night, with the other two boys, maybe three. But he had fought to live. *Why?* He didn't want to fight anymore, and there weren't any pigs nearby.

You could find a bear with cubs. A mother bear would rip you to shreds if you went too close to her babies.

But that would take too long. He didn't think he wanted to live, but he didn't want to be torn apart by a bear over a whole day either. Plus, he liked bears. He didn't want to make one mad.

He came to a canyon and stood at the edge, looking down. He could jump off a cliff. But not this one. This one wasn't high enough to make sure he died, but there were lots of others that would.

As he stood there thinking about the ways he could make sure of his death, sunlight blinked off something shiny through the leaves at the bottom of the canyon, blinding him for a second.

Curiosity made him pause, the fog that had been hanging over him clearing for a quick minute, the need to know what large shiny item was hiding underneath the leaves, a spark of…life. Jak climbed down the canyon slowly, not out of being careful but because it was all he could do. His body was still healing; he could feel a trickle of blood from the barely closed-up tear on his side sliding down his skin.

His feet hit the bottom with a crunch, and he moved toward the glint of what looked like blue metal from this closer place. He blinked in surprise when moving the thick leaves aside showed a…car. It took him a minute to put together this large thing from that other world with the one he lived in now. *What is it doing* here?

Had it been someone trying to escape the enemy, who'd driven far into the wilderness and over the edge of this canyon? *How long has it been here?*

Glass crunched under his feet, and he bent, looking inside the broken window and pulling back when he saw the skeletons inside. Clothes hung on the bones, and by their look, he could tell that the one at the wheel had been a man and the other one a woman.

Another beam of sunlight caught something shiny lying on the seat, and Jak reached for it, bringing it out of the car and opening his hand. A silver necklace with a tiny opening thing on the side. Jak used his thumbnail to pry it open, showing a tiny picture of a man, a woman, and a baby inside. *A family.* Jak's stomach knotted up with wanting as he stared at the three smiling faces.

His eyes moved over the people one by one, the man wearing a small smile, one hand sitting on the woman's shoulder. The woman's smile was big and shiny, her blond hair pretty and bright. But it was the baby who drew him in. It was the baby who made him stop and stare. There was something about her eyes...something that made his heartbeat go faster and his skin feel sweaty. He gripped the necklace in his hand and moved to the back of the car where the trunk was opened a crack.

He pushed on it, the metal creaking as it went up. There were piles of wet leaves inside, something that looked like it had once been a blanket but had rotted with wetness. He pushed that to the side and found that under it, there was a blue bag, mostly not touched by weather.

He unzipped it and looked inside. A few paper pads with writing in them. He wanted to know what they said, but he made himself wait, putting the things back into the bag, zipping it closed, and swinging it over his shoulder.

Something that felt like excitement sang inside him. It'd been so much time since his mother had dropped off those kids' books, the ones he could now say by heart. The ones he still took out many times a day to read so he would remember what words looked like. What they felt like in his mouth and in his mind. Maybe what he had in the bag wasn't a story, but to have something new to read…new words… They were…light in the dark.

He turned toward the canyon wall and started to go up. He could figure out a better way to die tomorrow. Today, he had new words. And he didn't feel as alone.

CHAPTER TWENTY-SIX

Harper knocked at the door that was now becoming a familiar sight. She stepped back, her heart skipping several beats as it seemed to do whenever she would soon be in his presence. The door opened, and he stood there, staring at her with a look on his face that was at least a little less wary than it'd been the first two times she'd shown up unannounced. Not that she really had any way to announce herself other than the sound of her truck a few minutes before she arrived, but...

"Hi."

"Hi."

She reached inside the large purse she had slung over her shoulder and retrieved the notebooks that had once belonged to her mother. "These are yours."

Surprise flickered over his face. "They're not mine. I only found them. They belong to you."

Harper shook her head and took the book she'd brought out of her purse. She handed *The Count of Monte Cristo* to Lucas and watched him as his eyes flared with surprised pleasure. "I also thought you might want this, so you can make more sense of those notes."

He didn't attempt to reject the book as he'd attempted to reject the notes. He took it and held it to his chest as though it were precious.

Harper looked over his shoulder at the dancing firelight on the walls. "Can I come in? I won't stay long."

He didn't answer, but he stepped back, and she went inside, shutting the door behind her. She put the notebooks on the empty bed closest to the door, and his gaze remained on them for a moment before he met her eyes again. "I *want* you to keep my mother's notes."

"Why?"

"Because...I think they were meant for you."

He frowned. "What do you mean?"

Harper sighed, moving closer to him. "I'm not sure what I mean. I just...have this feeling. And I'm not always one to follow my gut or my intuition or whatever you want to call it, but I think those notebooks belong with you, and that's all. I didn't think it through. I drove them out here, and I hope that's okay. Also, I found something out this afternoon, and I wanted...well, I wanted to ask you about it, to see what you think because—"

"Harper." He said her name, nothing more, but there was a gentle beseeching in his tone—*slow down, breathe, I'm trying to understand you*, it seemed to say—and that one word was enough for her to stop her aimless rambling and gather herself. She felt *seen* by him in a way she hadn't been seen by anyone in a long time, even if he didn't always understand her words.

"Agent Gallagher called me this afternoon and told me they'd found evidence that my parents were shot."

"Shot? With an...arrow?"

"No, no. With a gun."

"I thought they died in the car accident."

Harper sat on the bed next to his, the metal springs making a soft creaking sound. "I've always believed that. I've always assumed the three of us were involved in an accident and the car had never been found. I believed that all my life. Despite the location being odd"—she wrinkled her brow—"finding the car at the bottom of that canyon was confirmation of that. I'm so, so confused, and...I don't know how to feel." She paused for a moment. "Did you see anyone near that wreck? Or know anything that could explain what happened to them?"

Lucas took the few steps to his bed and sat on it, the springs making a deeper creaking sound than the springs on which Harper had sat. She became even more aware of him, his knee only inches away from her own, his size seeming to increase along with the close proximity. "I don't have any answers for you. I climbed down the canyon one day when I saw sun shine off something at the bottom. It was almost all covered with branches and leaves. When I looked in the window, I...saw them in there. The necklace was on the seat. The trunk was open, and the only thing inside was the blue backpack. I took it with me and climbed back up. I went back sometimes, I don't know why. Maybe because your mother felt...real to me. I wanted to...I don't know, Harper. I wanted to thank her. She...the words... They made me want to stay alive."

Harper blinked, tears burning the backs of her eyes. He'd told her it was so *they* weren't alone, but it was also so he wasn't either. *You're breaking my heart,* she thought with a catch of breath. "I knew I was right."

"About what?"

"That those notes are meant to be yours."

He smiled in that unpracticed way of his, and Harper smiled back, her finger tracing one of the uncovered springs. "What did you learn from her?"

"From your mother?" He squinted out the window for a moment, obviously considering her question seriously. When he looked back at her, he asked, "Have you read it? The book your mother was teaching her class about?"

"*The Count of Monte Cristo*?" Harper smiled. "Yes, twice, and I've seen the movie too."

"There's a movie."

She smiled. She liked the way he posed his questions as more of a statement, as though reiterating something to himself that he'd just learned rather than asking for confirmation. "Yes. It's very good actually, and that's not always true of books turned into movies. Have you…ever seen a movie?" She felt awkward asking it, but she wanted so badly to know about him, and she never would if she didn't ask the questions that came to her mind. She'd spent enough time with him to know he didn't offer information freely.

"I've never seen a movie, but I heard of them when I was a kid. And I've seen TV."

"A movie is just TV but on a bigger screen." How *strange* to utter a sentence like that to a man who was approximately her age, if she was assuming correctly. "Anyway, *The Count of Monte Cristo* is one of my favorite stories. It's about vengeance, but more so, it's about forgiveness."

"I had to try to understand the story from what your mother wrote about it. And from the questions she asked. I didn't know that word before—*vengeance*. It means feeling mad and then getting even. But your mother was like you.

She thought the story was more about forgiveness. Your mother thought that most humans are good. She hoped her students would think that too."

"Do you?"

His lips tipped. "Am I one of her students?"

"Of course you are. You've probably studied her thoughts and ideas—her values—more closely than any one of the boys or girls in her classrooms."

That seemed to please him. "Maybe. But…I don't know if I believe more people are good than bad. I don't think I know enough about the world outside of that one book. And I haven't even read it yet. Your mother, though, she made me feel…"

He looked to be searching for a word, and so Harper attempted to supply it. "Hopeful?" she asked softly.

His eyes met hers. "Hopeful," he repeated. "Yes. Your mother gave me…hope. She taught me that there is both good and bad in the world. Before that, I didn't know."

"Meaning you only thought there was bad in the world?"

"I…wasn't sure. Driscoll thought so."

"Driscoll?" She frowned. "What else did Driscoll think?"

"I don't know. I didn't care."

He turned his head away. He obviously wasn't interested in talking about Driscoll any further. After a moment, though, he looked back at her, and Harper tilted her head, her gaze moving over his features. He had such beautiful eyes—that blue and gold, *sunset* blue, and almond-shaped with long, full lashes. His eyes were a contrast to the stark masculinity of the rest of his face—his sun-darkened skin, sharp cheekbones, his square, scruff-covered jaw. And the obvious masculinity of his strong, muscular body. But she wasn't looking at his body. She refused to do that. She was already distracted enough as it was. Shaken up. Confused. He didn't want to talk about Driscoll, so she wouldn't continue questioning Lucas about him. "In some ways…you might know my mother better than I do. Or at least…a different side of her," Harper said, returning to the subject he'd seemed comfortable talking about. "But to me, she was comfort and home and the things I haven't had since." She looked behind him, considering her words. "I don't know, maybe I'm afraid that reading those"— she nodded her head toward the notes—"will dim those other memories of her somehow, and so I'm afraid to."

He regarded her, and she couldn't read the expression that had settled on his face. "What? Why are you looking at me like that?"

"Because you're an honest person. I can tell. I've wondered…if I'd be able to."

Harper didn't know exactly what that meant, but she felt it was a compliment. Even so, he wasn't completely right. "I'm not always honest," she blurted. "I keep things inside sometimes." She paused. "A lot of times."

"You do?" He looked confused about that, and she laughed quietly. "Sometimes I talk the most when I'm avoiding a topic or keeping something to myself."

He appeared to think about that and then smiled as though she'd cleared something up that had confused him. He was so very sweet; he really was. "Keeping your feelings to yourself is different than lies. Isn't it?"

"I suppose. What do you keep to yourself, Lucas?"

He released a breath that may or may not have contained a chuckle. "What *don't* I keep to myself? I don't have another choice."

She blushed, grimacing at her insensitivity. "That was a stupid question. I'm—"

"It wasn't stupid. The trees and the birds and all the forest animals know my secrets. I go outside and shout them to the mountaintops sometimes. They all stop to listen."

She laughed softly. "Does it feel better to get them out? Even to the forest?"

"Yes." He grinned, and her heart tripped all over itself. "Try it sometime."

"Maybe I will."

They sat there smiling at each other, the moment heavy with whatever the thing was that flowed between them. Chemistry. Awareness. Deep curiosity. All elements of the undeniable lure that had been flowing between men and women who were attracted to each other since the beginning of time. At dances and in restaurants. At bars and in offices. In caves and in cabins in the middle of the deep, dark forest.

"Anyway," Harper said, standing and grabbing the purse she'd dropped on the floor next to the bed she was sitting on. "I brought something, and I hope you'll help me. And a bribe so you won't say no."

His eyebrows lowered. "A...bribe?"

She smiled. "A payment of sorts. But I was just kidding. It's more of a gift, and there are no strings attached." She pulled the bottle of orange Crush from her bag, grinning at Lucas when she held it up.

His eyes widened, lighting up. "Orange drink with bubbles. Crush."

"Yes." She twisted off the cap, slowly so it wouldn't explode, and handed it to him. He looked at it for a second and then tipped it back, taking a big sip. He lowered it, the expression on his face...less than impressed. He held the bottle before him, studying it again as he swallowed with obvious effort, cringing. Clearly revolted.

"Not as good as you remember?" she asked, holding back a giggle.

"Not…quite."

She laughed then. She couldn't help it. She wanted to kiss him and taste the orange Crush on his lips. She moved that thought aside rapidly. "Anyway, about this thing I need your help with."

"What is it?"

"It's a map." She stepped to the table they'd eaten at the last time she'd been there and sat down on one of the stools, spreading the map over the tabletop and setting a red pen next to it.

Dusk had fallen, and Lucas took a moment to light the two candles by the window, bringing them to the table so they could see better. He sat down on the stool next to her and looked at the map. "What do you need my help with?"

"I thought it might be helpful to mark this up for Agent Gallagher. I need to do something to help solve my parents' murders." A chill went down her spine. She still couldn't believe she was saying the words or that the words were true. *My parents were murdered.* It didn't exactly make the loss sharper, didn't make her suddenly grieve them more than she had. But it lit a fire under her. She'd answered the question of *where* that she'd been asking all her life, and now she had another two she hadn't expected: *who?* and *why?* She gave her head a small shake, attempting to bring herself back to the moment. "But, um, I'd like your input before I do."

"Okay."

She picked up the pen and brought it to the map that was folded to show Missoula and the surrounding areas. "Okay, so this is the highway from Missoula to Helena Springs." She used the pen to trace the highway. There were also unnamed

211

caverns a few miles off that highway that she'd always assumed had been the ones the hikers had been looking for, but she supposed that wasn't necessarily accurate, considering where her parents' car had been found.

She moved her eyes to another area on the map. "This is the approximate location of Driscoll's cabin." She drew a square over the green area of wilderness. "And this is yours," she said, drawing another square near Driscoll's. Harper glanced up at Lucas, and he had a small crease between his brows as he concentrated on what she did.

"All right," she went on, "this is the Owlwood River." She traced the long, winding line that represented the river, going from the highway that connected Missoula to Helena Springs, down past Lucas's house and beyond. "And this is where my parents' car was found," she said, drawing an X far downriver, near the base of a group of mountain ranges.

"Okay," Lucas said, bringing his head slightly closer to hers. The candlelight flickered, and it suddenly felt intimate, the way their heads were bowed together, the way they were speaking in hushed voices, the way it was only them and no one else for miles and miles. She wondered what his lips would feel like if he kissed her, wondered if he'd know what to do.

"Okay," Harper repeated, her voice emerging on a whisper that was far more breathy than she'd meant it to be. She cleared her throat, heat moving slowly up her neck and then sweeping through her limbs with a suddenness that made her break out in chills.

"Are you cold?" he asked when she rubbed at her arms.

"No. No. Ah…" She focused on the map again, trying to get her mind on what they had been doing. "All right, so up here"—she tapped at the wilderness area between the highway connecting Helena Springs and Missoula and the Owlwood River—"is where I generally do my guide work. And where I've focused my own search efforts for my parents' car." She put the end of the pen to her lips, biting softly at the tip.

"Why?" he asked, and when she glanced at him, she saw his gaze was focused on her mouth. She pulled the pen from her lips, their eyes meeting, his widening before he glanced away.

"Why? Ah, well, because it's good for camping and hunting but also because the road that I assumed they'd been traveling is close by.

"The hikers who found me couldn't say exactly where, but the authorities picked us up here," she said, tapping the map. "It all pointed to my parents' car being in this area. I've never typically searched any farther than this because the river veers off here"—she tapped the map again—"into Amity Falls. I obviously didn't tumble into a three-hundred-foot waterfall or I'd be dead. The helicopters focused their initial search here too." Harper tapped the pen against her teeth again, thinking. After a moment, she released a frustrated breath. "In any case, I still don't know what any of this has to do with my parents being murdered. I just thought maybe drawing it all out might help in some way."

Lucas was quiet, his eyes remaining on the map in front of them, the candle flickering over it, casting the peaks and valleys that might hold answers to the many questions swirling around them both in light and shadow. When he met her eyes again, his expression was grave, a hint of apprehension in the set of his mouth.

"I think I saw the helicopters that were looking for your parents. And if I did, then I was left here on the same night your parents were murdered."

A spear of shock arrowed through Harper. "How is that... Are you sure? That seems highly...I don't know, coincidental?"

"I've never seen helicopters again. And they were flying right over this spot." He pointed to the place on the map where she'd said she always thought her parents' car had crashed.

Harper's gaze stayed on the spot where his index finger had tapped for a moment before looking up at him. She was completely bewildered. How was it possible that they'd both ended up out here on the same night? Her rescued. Him... *not*.

"I, uh..." He pressed his lips together, his eyes deep and dark in the flickering candlelight. "I've been lying to you. Lying to the agent."

She blinked. "Lying?" she whispered, fear spiking. "About what?"

"About my name. My name isn't Lucas. It's Jak."

CHAPTER TWENTY-SEVEN

Harper blinked at Jak, her pink lips taking the shape of an O as she took the pen from between her teeth. He was nervous, but even still, his blood caught fire at the look of her mouth parted that way.

"Jak? I don't understand. Why did you call yourself Lucas?" She looked worried, and it made him feel… He didn't know the word, but he knew the last thing he wanted to do was scare her when she was alone with him. *Especially* when he kept thinking about her lips and how much he liked sitting right next to her, inhaling her sweet woman scent and—

He stood quickly, moving away from her, leaning against the wall by the window. "I told the truth when I said I don't know my last name. I think a woman named Alma or Almara or Almina named me, but I don't know for sure. She did raise me, though, until I was almost eight, and I called her Baka. She talked in a different language sometimes. I don't know which one, and I don't know where we lived or why I was taken from her."

Harper's mouth stayed in the same surprised O, her eyes wide as she listened. "What do you mean you were taken from her?"

"I mean, I ended up out here, and I don't know how or why." That much was true too. He wasn't ready to tell her the rest, not yet.

"Do you think *she,* your baka, dropped you off here?"

"I...don't know."

She looked so confused. "It doesn't make any sense. Who was your mother? Your father?"

He felt torn. "My mother gave me up to my baka, I think. I don't know. And...I don't know anything about my father."

"Why did you lie? Don't you want help figuring this all out?"

He ran his fingers through his hair. He wanted to tell her about the cliff and the war that wasn't and how he'd been lied to, but he didn't know yet what was okay to hold back and what was okay to tell.

Don't tell anyone I've been here, okay?

"I lied because I don't know who to trust," he admitted. He *wanted* to trust her, he realized, and part of him already did. It was the wanting that surprised him when he'd only trusted himself for so long. But he did, he *wanted* to watch her large, dark eyes fill with...understanding. He wanted to share his worries and troubles with another person. He just wasn't sure it should be this woman, who made him feel unsure of himself, made his blood run hot in his veins.

The woman he wanted to call his own.

Her eyes ran over his face like she could read the answers to the questions she had by just looking at him. *Not yet,* an inner knowing told him. *But soon if you let her.* He turned away, grabbing a can of food she'd brought with her the last time and turning around. "Are you hungry?"

He didn't know if he could—or should—fully trust her, but he could feed her, even if she had been the one to bring the food.

Harper glanced at the can and then back to him. "Yes," she murmured. "Lucas…Jak…which do you prefer?"

"I've lived my life as Jak. Until…I went to the…sheriff building."

"Then…Jak, I want you to know that you can trust me. I'd like to help you if you'll let me." She looked back at the can he was still holding. "And, yes, I'd love some dinner."

It was dark outside now, and the candles were making shadows on the walls. How many times had Jak sat at this table, eating a meal, and it'd felt cold and lonely? Especially after Pup died. Especially then. But now, he felt a closeness with another person that he'd never felt before. It made him feel peaceful. It made him feel terrified. It made him think of the family who had been taken from him or that he'd watched walk away, and the memories made an icy-cold knife slice slowly through him, cutting, tearing, just like all the cuts and wounds that had made scars on his skin. He shouldn't get attached to this woman because he didn't want to feel pain when she left.

She smiled around a bite of food.

"What?" he asked.

"This is a first."

He tilted his head as she let out a happy laugh. "A date of franks and beans by candlelight."

"A date?"

Her smile faded. "Oh, yes. No. I mean, not that it's a date. But…I mean, it could be. I don't want you to think…

not that… Anyway, it's nice is what I mean." She lowered her eyes but then peeked up at him.

He remembered what she'd said. "You're talking a lot, which means you're not saying something."

She laughed. "Maybe I shouldn't have given myself away." But her eyes were warm, and she smiled. "I like spending time with you is what I was trying to say."

"Why?"

She blinked. "Why do I like spending time with you, Jak?"

He sat back slowly. He loved hearing his name—his real name—on her lips. "Yes."

She stared at him for a few seconds, tilting her chin a little. "Because I find you interesting and kind. You surprise me but in good ways. I like the things you say, and I like watching you discover new things. I admire how you've survived out here alone for all of these years." She looked off to the side. "No, *admire* isn't strong enough a word. I'm in *awe* of how you've survived out here all of these years, and I'm sure I don't know the half of it. I hope someday you might trust me enough to tell me. You value truth, Jak, so that's it. One hundred percent."

His lips tipped. *I like you,* he thought, amazement rushing through him. He remembered it—the feeling of…affection, was that the word? Yes, he thought it was. The warmth for another human, the…liking of them being with you. Not a wanting to mate—though that was there too. The feeling of…affection was a good one, a liking that couldn't be taken away by leaving. It would stay whether she did or not. It made him feel good knowing there was another thing no one could steal from him.

He liked her. It was his. That was all.

At the same time, he felt guilt. How could he value truth like she'd said and also be a liar? He had so many questions about the world, about life and humans, so many things that confused him. Did he believe what he'd said when he'd told her keeping information from someone was different than lying? *Was* there any difference? *No,* he thought. He knew there wasn't because both had been done to him, and in the end, the pain was the same.

So many doubts and questions swirled inside him. His mind was a tide pool, thoughts rushing here, there, in, out, going in circles. So fast he couldn't get his balance. These new feelings that had only come because he cared what this woman thought. *Human* feelings. Human questions. He wanted her trust. He wanted her to like him. "What do you value?"

"Me?"

"Yes. Above all else," he said, repeating her words.

She was quiet, looking like she was thinking hard about his question. "Stability, I think…love." Her cheeks got pinker, and she looked away.

Was she embarrassed to want love? He wondered why. She had lost people she loved too. If she still wanted it, it was brave. "Do you have it in your life…love?"

She breathed out a laugh. "You're very straightforward when you want to be."

"Am I asking the wrong questions?" He felt ashamed. He didn't know how to do this, talk about the things inside him with other people. Sometimes he didn't even know how to talk to himself.

"No." She shook her head. "No. Your questions aren't wrong. Yes, I have love in my life. I love my friends, and I love the kids at the group home I work at." She smiled again, but something sad came into her eyes too.

"Do you love a man?" *Please say no.*

"No," she whispered, her eyes meeting his. "No."

She stood suddenly and leaned close to the window. "Oh my gosh," she said, bringing his attention to the weather outside. Snow was falling quickly—the big, fluffy flakes that meant it would snow for a long time—and ice crystals stuck to the glass. Jak had seen this before, many times. He knew what it was. "That looks bad."

He stood, heading to the front door and opening it. A blow of icy wind hit his face, and he stepped back. "It's an ice storm." He'd known it as soon as he saw those fluffy flakes mixed with icy shine.

Harper came up next to him, holding her arm against the whipping wind and closing the door. "God, that came up quickly. I should go before it gets really bad."

Jak turned to her. "It's already really bad."

She met his eyes. "I lost track of time." She looked toward the window, shaking her head, her expression nervous. She took her phone from her pocket, glancing at it. "No service here, but I've gotten service in this wilderness before. Sometimes it's a matter of being in the right spot."

He didn't know what she was talking about—he knew what a phone was but not how one worked. The thing in her hand was a mystery to him, but he didn't question it. The very last thing he wanted was for her to see him as a child.

"I need to go out to my truck," she said, grabbing her jacket.

"I'll come with you."

"No, it's okay. I'll be right back."

"I'll come with you," he said again, not willing to let her walk out into the howling wind alone. He put on his coat and boots quickly and pulled the door open, squinting against the ice that burned his face. It was too easy to get lost in ice storms. One missed step or wrong turn, and suddenly you didn't know where you were and could barely see a tree right in front of you before you walked into it. He used his body to shield her as they walked in the direction where her truck was parked, not able to see it until it was right in front of them.

He'd been lost in an ice storm like this once. He'd hunkered down with Pup and barely—but he pushed his thoughts away. He didn't want to think about that right now.

Harper stepped around him, her head bent, the wind picking up in speed and sound, whipping her hood off her head, her hair going in every direction. She laughed, but it was high like a scared bird.

She climbed into her truck, and he went in after her, slamming the door and escaping from the wind. It pounded at the truck, sneaking between the cracks, trying its best to reach them. Their mixed breath came out in sharp pants. The sound of the wind got less, though the truck shook, the house invisible through the front glass.

"Good lord," she said, pushing her hair back, crystals of ice shining like jewels in the low light coming from the phone she'd brought from her pocket again.

She made a sound of unhappiness and then held her phone up in the air, moving it from side to side. "There. Damn…ah. Crap." She did that for another minute, finally dropping it to her lap. "It won't hold a signal." She turned to him. "I don't think I should drive in this. I'd probably run into a tree trying to get to the road, and even if I didn't, that road has a drop-off on both sides. I could, uh, just wait out here. I'm sure this will die down in a little bit." She

looked at him, her eyes wide as she waited for him to say…
something.

He frowned. Was she trying to get away from him? Did
she *want* to sit in her cold truck instead of with him? "Why
would you want to freeze out here when you can be warm
inside?"

"I just hate to keep showing up and forcing you to spend
time with me."

Forcing *him*? He was bigger than she was. Stronger. She
couldn't force him to do anything. He could crush her if he
wanted to. He didn't, but he could. His brow scrunched up.
He didn't understand when she said things that didn't really
say anything at all. He wasn't sure what to say back. "If I
wanted you to leave, I'd tell you to go."

She let out a breath that was taken by the sound of the
wind outside. "I was trying to be polite." She shook her head
and made a helpless sound. "I guess that in itself is a whole
language, isn't it?" She took a breath. "A dumb one most of
the time."

Jak thought about that. "So being polite is saying
something you don't mean so the other person has to say the
thing you do mean."

She laughed, the soft one he liked. "Pretty much." She
turned toward him. "So, then. Jak, I'd like to come inside
and get warm instead of sitting alone in my cold truck. Is
that okay with you?"

"I told you it was."

Harper laughed. "Right. You did. Thank you. Then let's
get back inside."

CHAPTER TWENTY-EIGHT

"Mrs. Cranley?"

"Yes. Who's speaking?" The woman on the other end of the line had an unusually deep voice that rattled. A smoker, Mark guessed.

"Hi, ma'am. This is Agent Mark Gallagher. I'm with the Montana Department of Justice."

There was a brief pause and some rustling, and then Mrs. Cranley said, "What is this about?"

"Ma'am, I'm very sorry to inform you that your brother was found deceased."

Another pause, longer this time. "Isaac?"

"Yes, ma'am."

"Did he leave something for me in his will?"

Well, that was abrupt. Mark was taken off guard for a moment. "Actually, ma'am, it appears Isaac didn't have a will. But you're listed on several documents as his next of kin."

"Well, I'll be." Mark heard some more rustling and then

Mrs. Cranley's muffled voice yelling to someone in the background, "Lester, Isaac died and didn't leave a will. I'm his next of kin."

"When was the last time you spoke to Isaac, Mrs. Cranley?"

"You can call me Georgette. And, eh…maybe twelve years ago at our daddy's funeral. Me and Isaac didn't get on real well. Guess that doesn't matter now. He was a creep, truth be told."

Mark cleared his throat. Apparently, this woman had no problem speaking ill of the dead. Made his job easier anyway. "How do you mean, ma'am? Georgette?"

Mark heard a deep inhale as if the woman had just lit a cigarette. "He just *was*. He was always watching everyone with this weird look on his face. Gave me the chills, and he was my own brother. It got worse as he got older. I was happy when me and Lester moved to Portland and I had no reason to see him anymore."

"I see."

"'Course I figured it out when I went over to his place in Missoula, oh…I guess it'd have been going on eighteen or nineteen years now and there was an old lady neighbor at his place with her grandson, I guess. Kid was just a toddler, so it'd have to be. Isaac kept staring at him with this look on his face." She made a sound that gave Mark the idea she'd just done an exaggerated shiver. "Well, that's when I said, ah, bingo. Isaac's a pervert. It all made sense."

Mark felt suddenly sick. He cleared his throat. "But you never saw any evidence of him abusing children?"

"Nah. Just that look. But women *know* things, ya know? Intuition." He heard her suck in another inhale of her cigarette.

"And this was in Missoula, you said?" Mark pulled Isaac Driscoll's file closer and noted that his last known address had been in Missoula—probably an apartment building. He'd been in Unit A.

"Yup. I don't have the address anymore, but that's the last place I seen him."

"From what I understand, your brother did volunteer work for several social services agencies in the area."

"Well, there ya go. Gave him access."

Mark cleared his throat again. He'd spoken to several people at the volunteer agencies Driscoll had done work for, but no one had said anything disparaging about him. He made a note to widen the net of people to interview who might have known Driscoll in a volunteer capacity.

"This woman at your brother's house all those years ago, can you tell me anything about her?"

"Yeah, she was real hard to understand. Had a thick accent. She left pretty quick with the kid but not soon enough for me to see how Isaac looked at him. I thought about going over to her apartment and warning her away from Isaac, but I figured people gotta learn their own lessons, ya know?"

Again, Mark was taken off guard. Maybe the whole Driscoll family was just *off*. "Um, right. Well, I'm calling for another reason. Your brother owned quite an extensive acreage of land outside Helena Springs. As his next of kin, the acreage will go to you, but Isaac was allowing a young man to stay in a cabin on the property."

She made a small huffing sound. "Yeah, I bet he was."

"There is no evidence of any sort of abuse. The man is in his early twenties. It appears Isaac let him stay there after his parents abandoned him and the man grew up without any exposure to society."

Georgette laughed, a low sound filled with phlegm. "So Isaac was raising himself a mountain man? Weird."

"I can't say Isaac did much of his raising. But like I said, he let him stay on the property. When the estate is released to you, would you allow him to remain in his cabin until he figures out what to do? His options are very limited."

Georgette sucked in another loud inhale, and Mark grimaced on behalf of her lungs. "Nope, nope. I don't want a thing to do with Isaac's weirdness, not when he was living and especially now he's dead. Nope, that mountain man's gotta go. The sooner the better."

Mark sighed. "If you reconsider, ma'am—"

"I won't. He'll need to vacate immediately. As far as I'm concerned, he's poaching on *my* land."

The internet was filled with information about the Spartans, and for fifteen minutes or so, Mark got caught up in the research. He'd needed a palate cleanse after talking to Isaac Driscoll's sister and her blackened lungs, and sad to say, stories of war and carnage were more appealing at the moment.

Sparta, Greece, was a warrior society centered around military service. Apparently, it began in infancy when children were inspected for strength, and then, at age seven, soldiers came and took the children from the caretakers, whose gentle and affectionate influence was considered a negative, and housed them in a dormitory with other boy soldiers. The Spartan child then endured harsh physical discipline and deprivation to learn how to be strong and rely on his wits. In his early twenties, he had to pass a rigorous test and only then became a Spartan soldier.

Sounds brutal. Mark could be grateful for one thing—he hadn't grown up in ancient Greece.

He looked up the Battle of Thermopylae, a military encounter with the Persians, who greatly outnumbered the Spartans. He studied the picture online, and just as it had the first time, it sent a strange shudder down his spine. It was definitely the presence of bows and arrows in the warriors' hands—that obviously could not be ignored based on the weapon used in the two murders—but it was something else too. Something that skated just out of reach. Maybe not something in the painting so much as a puzzle piece that would link all of this together. Make *sense* of it.

A mystery woman, murders, bows and arrows, an abandoned boy, a sister who thought her brother was a "pervert," government-run social studies... Had Driscoll been attempting to raise...a modern-day Spartan? But *why*? Had he been plain batshit crazy? Or did he really believe he was helping Lucas?

He rifled through the case files sitting on his desk in front of him. Crime scene photos, information obtained about the arrows used in the murders—a popular brand sold in hundreds of sporting goods stores, both locally and on the internet. All dead ends at the moment.

The ding on his phone alerted him to an email, but since he was sitting in front of his computer, he opened it there. "Well, that's interesting timing," he murmured to himself when he saw it was from Dr. Swift. When he opened it, there was a very short note, and attached was the final study that Isaac Driscoll had worked on at Rayform. Mark scrolled through it. It was a study on the incidence of incarceration in inmates raised by single mothers. There were lots of stats and graphs, none of which seemed to make a good case for single motherhood—though Mark knew that in any good psychological study, other variables needed to be accounted for or at least mentioned as contributing factors. The study did that, naming low income, gun and gang violence in the area where the inmate grew up, and things of that nature. It painted a bleak picture, and Mark realized that it was mostly because the piece of work simply offered numbers and stats—not solutions. Which, of course, was what studies were meant to do. They weren't designed to solve problems, simply identify them. He could see why Isaac Driscoll, or anyone working in that field for that matter, might become cynical about society after performing such studies year after year.

His door creaked open, and his wife peeked around it, her smile hesitant. He sat back in his chair, offering her one in return. "I made lunch if you're hungry."

Mark ran a hand through his hair. "Thanks. I'm kind of involved in this though. Will you set some aside for me?"

He didn't miss the minute drop in her smile, but he also didn't acknowledge it. The truth was, he'd gotten lost in his work, lost in the puzzle of the case in front of him, and he craved it. God, he craved it. An escape that wasn't only for him, but for two dead people counting on him for answers. *Is that how you're justifying it, Gallagher?* He heard his inner voice whisper the question but pushed it aside. Maybe it *was* a justification, but it was also true.

"Need any help?" Her smile grew, but he could see the nervousness in her eyes. He knew her. He still did, he realized. Knew her expressions and her body language. What had changed was his desire to respond to what he knew she was asking for. *Inclusion.* But he had gone to her for the same thing, during moments when she had been the one

228

unwilling to let him in. It felt like they just kept *missing* each other emotionally. He had to *focus* though. In the past, she'd been his sounding board, the person he bounced ideas off if he was stuck, the person who'd helped him so many times when he couldn't connect A to B. Now, having her around would distract rather than assist him.

It will take time. He kept *telling* himself that, and somehow it kept ringing hollow, but he didn't know what else to hope for. "No, thanks. Not on this one. I'll be out soon."

Her smile did slip then, but she nodded and turned, closing the door softly behind her. He released a breath, massaging his temples, trying to move his mind back to the case.

But his focus was gone, at least for the moment. As he was closing the study Dr. Swift had sent him, he made note of not only Isaac Driscoll's name, but also the name of his assistant who had worked on the study: Kyle Holbrook.

He put in a call to Rayform and found that the man was still listed on the directory, but his voicemail picked up when Mark dialed it. He left a message and then tapped his pen on the desk, the smell of grilled cheese and tomato soup drifting under his door as he sat staring at the wall.

CHAPTER TWENTY-NINE

The snow sparkled under the silver-gray sky, fat flakes float-ing down and melting on Jak's skin as he slid across the open field. The long, flat shoes he'd put together made it easier to walk over the ice-crusty ground without sinking into the soft, fluffy snow beneath. He wished he'd thought of making something like these a long time ago. But how could he? He learned the best he could as he went along, figuring new and better ways to survive. These shoes weren't a...what was the word? He didn't *need* to have them, but they were nice to have.

His mind drifted, the words of the woman in the picture going around in his head. He talked to her sometimes, asked her questions, tried to guess what her answers would be.

Sometimes, like today, when his mind wanted to drift from the cold of winter, he'd say the words that brought him peace. He'd say them over and over again until his heart settled and he could find something good about the day. About life. About his presence in a world that only made sense in a physical way. To Jak, the writings of the woman were his friend; *she* was his priest from the story that he'd never actually read and his teacher. He loved her, even though he'd never met her. He visited her sometimes too, in the bottom of that canyon. He sat outside the car where she'd died, said words to her and the man. He wondered if they'd died right away or if they'd suffered. He wondered where their child was—the girl. He felt so much sadness. He wished he could have saved them. He wished they were alive and he could meet them. He would ask the woman all the questions in his mind and heart. She had so many more words than he knew.

In his pretending, she answered. He closed his eyes and heard her speak, clearer now than the faded voice of his baka.

It had been five winters since he'd found the car and the blue bag, and while he would never say his living was easy, the writings he'd found had made things…better. He wasn't sure exactly why. He only knew that the writings had changed his mind about wanting to die. *Had* he really wanted to die though? No. He had wanted the pain to end, the loneliness. The writings had made him care about living.

His muscled legs pushed one board forward, then the next, sliding across the snow, his breath puffing white in front of him for only a brief second before it was snatched up by the wind.

Movement caught his eye, and he slowed, his muscles tensing as he spotted a person far off to his right. Hide? Slink? *No.* He crouched low as he loaded an arrow into his bow, looking through the scope.

It was…a woman?

Jak lowered the bow and arrow, standing back up,

his fast heartbeat slowing down, questions circling in his mind. *Fear.*

The woman was fast-walking toward him, taking big steps in the snow, sinking down and then, with a lot of trying, lifting her foot again and again. Jak was still with shock and confusion. As she got closer, Jak saw that she wasn't wearing any winter clothes and much of her skin was showing. And she looked like she was crying, big chest-moving wails that came to where Jak was standing.

Jak took two steps toward the woman at the same second that she spotted him. She stopped and then moved toward him again, picking up her footsteps, tripping and getting back up. "Help!" she called. "Help!"

Jak moved toward her quickly, and she tripped again, pulling herself up, her wails getting clearer the closer she got. "Please, please!" she cried. "I need help!"

"What happened?" Jak asked as the woman collapsed in his arms, shivering and crying, her skin purple-red and covered in goose bumps. Her wide gaze moved over his face, her lips shivering so hard her whole jaw was shaking.

"Lost... The enemy chasing me..." Another big shiver went through her, stopping her words, and Jak's skin prickled with unease. The enemy? He looked behind her, from where she'd come. He'd always felt mostly safe from other people in this wilderness, safe from the war and whatever might be going on out in the world. *Nature* had been his enemy...any other danger seeming very far away. But now... here was a woman running from this enemy that he'd only thought of as the booming voice behind him telling him the only goal was survival.

"Please *help,*" she cried softly, looking at him in a strange way. Jak took off his animal-skin jacket, the one he'd made himself, held together with long strips of the tough, stringy parts between deer muscle and bone that he'd bleached and dried in the sun. He wrapped the jacket around the woman as her knees gave out, but he caught her, lifting her easily into his arms and heading toward his cabin.

When he got there, he set her down in front of the open wood stove, wrapping his blanket around her bare legs and throwing another log on the fire so it leaped and grew, the warmth traveling farther into the room.

The woman began to move, pushing her long red hair out of her face and sitting up slowly. "Where am I?"

"My cabin. Who's chasing you?"

Her eyes flew to the window. "I don't know who they are. I think I lost them, but"—her gaze moved quickly to the side—"uh, I got all turned around, and then I just kept walking."

Jak had an odd feeling about the woman. It was like…he sensed danger, but…that was stupid. This woman was half his size. No threat to him. But he felt…not right, and he wasn't sure why. "What happened to your clothes?"

"The enemy took them before I got away."

Jak frowned. "Tell me about the enemy."

She blinked. "What?"

"I—" He ran a hand over his jaw, trying to figure out how to explain things to her. "I don't know anything about the war. I've been living here since I was young." He sat on the edge of the bed next to where she sat against the wall. "Can you tell me what's going on? Does anyone talk about when it might end?"

She stared at him for a minute, a line coming between her eyes. "I don't know a lot either. I'm, uh"—she did that weird moving thing with her eyes again—"from somewhere else."

"Somewhere where the war is not being fought?"

"Right."

"Do you know *why* we're fighting? And who we're fighting against? There was a time when they were killing children. Is that still happening?"

"Listen, I don't know anything else, okay?" She sounded kind of...mad.

The coat Jak had put around her shoulders slipped, showing the white skin of her breast, and Jak's breath stopped. He'd never seen a woman's body before, and he wanted to take the coat from around her shoulders and the blanket from her legs and look at her naked, study how she was different than him. Suddenly he wasn't thinking about war or the enemy or anything else outside his cabin. His body felt hot, tight.

But *this* woman, she'd just been running from an enemy who had been bad to her in some way. And she was trusting him to help her. He stood, turning his back on her and walking to the window where he looked outside. The snow glittered, white gray and not touched except for the lonely footprints that led to his door. His own. At least if anyone came here, they would think it was just him. He could protect her. He looked to the place where he stored the bow and arrows Driscoll had given him a long time ago. He had spent hours and hours getting good with the weapon, becoming *so* good with it that when he used it, it felt like another part of his own body. He'd shoot to kill if he had to. His shots were strong. He never missed.

He smelled her approaching. She tried to be quiet but was not. She was no wolf. He waited...tensed and felt hands come around his waist. He turned fast, the woman very close to where he was. She'd left the coat and blanket on the

234

floor and now stood before him naked. Surprise shivered through him, along with a jolt of heat. His eyes moved over her body, confusion rising like pinpricks on the inside of his skin. *What is she doing?*

"What's your name?"

She seemed surprised that he'd asked the question, but after a second pause, she said, "Brielle. What's yours?"

"Jak."

She stepped closer and then ran her hands up the front of his shirt, over the muscles of his chest. "You're different than I thought," she said so quietly he almost didn't hear.

"Different? What...do you mean? How would you know about me?"

Her gaze shot to him, and she laughed in a nervous way. "I mean, from when I first saw you out there in the snow. I thought you were uncivilized, but you're not."

Uncivilized.

He didn't understand. And she was still standing in front of him naked, and though it was making his body feel too heated, his mind was able to stay away like he'd learned to do when he stalked and hunted. It was easy for him now.

A naked woman was touching him, but that whisper of confusion wouldn't let his thoughts quiet.

"What are you doing?" he asked her, his gaze moving over her nakedness again, seeing the pinky-brown tips of her breasts, the way her waist turned inward, the tiny black dots between her legs that showed she'd removed the hair there. He wondered why she would do that. That's where the scent was that told a male whether he wanted to mate with the female. Those smells told the male if the whispers spoke between them, if their offspring would be healthy and strong, and other things Jak didn't know because he hadn't smelled his mate yet.

"I'm thanking you for rescuing me," she said, taking the bottom of his shirt in her hands and pulling it up and over his head. Her eyes ran over his chest, her gaze stopping on each scar one by one. Something came over her face, and he didn't know what it was. She swallowed and took a step back, reaching out to run a finger along the worst of them, the ugly raised skin on his side that had come from the wild boar's tusk, the one that had almost killed him. He watched her like she was a snake and he wasn't sure whether she was going to slither by or strike at him.

Her finger moved slowly, and he hissed out a breath, the feeling of being touched by another human for the first time since he was a child making him want to fall to his knees. He wanted to push this woman—this stranger he didn't trust—away, and he wanted to beg her not to stop. "You've been to battle," she said.

He looked at her, taking his own finger and running it along the pink scar right over the removed hair between her legs and then lifting her arms where scars crossed the skin on the insides of her arms. "So have you."

Their eyes met, and her face went lighter. She looked sad. She dropped her hands. "I...yes." Her voice came out choked, and the smile she wore looked like a lie. She took a deep breath and moved forward again, returning her hand to his naked skin. "Do you want me, Jak?" Before waiting for an answer, she stepped forward and put her lips on his, running her tongue along his lower lip. She gripped his head in her hands, dragging her fingernails through his hair. He wanted to pull away, but he didn't know why. He should want this. To mate. *Shouldn't he?*

The feeling of her soft, wet tongue on his mouth sent lightning shooting between his legs, making him swell

236

and harden. But even though his body *wanted*, there was something not right in the way she smelled to him. She smelled like berries, but ones that were too ripe and had already dropped to the ground. *Too sweet. Too much.* He didn't like it. He didn't want to mate with her. And she was shaking again, but there were no goose bumps on her skin, and his cabin was warm from the fire.

Something was wrong. Very wrong.

He wrapped his fingers around her small wrist, taking her hand off him, and her lips came away from his. "I'm not like them," he said, rough sand in his voice, taking her by the upper arms and setting her away. He brought the blanket to her, wrapping it around her shoulders again and covering her nakedness. He didn't know exactly who "they" were, but whatever enemy she'd run from had taken her clothes and made her scared enough to run mostly naked out into the snow, made her offer her body to him though he had not asked for it or done anything to make her want to give it to him. He hadn't fed her or hunted for her or brought her gifts that made her dance.

She stared up at him, and he saw tears shining in her eyes. She nodded and walked to where she'd dropped her clothing. He grabbed a pair of jeans and a shirt he'd outgrown long ago and handed them to her. "The seams are gone in places because I used the thread, but they'll keep you warm. You can stay here for a little while if you need to. I have weapons."

She smiled, and to him, it seemed sad. "You'd fight for me, wouldn't you? A stranger."

"Yes."

She smiled again and used her hand to touch his cheek. "You're very attractive, you know that? Not just here"—she

237

turned her hand over and ran it down his face and over the bone of his jaw—"but here." She patted the place where his heart beat under his skin.

Jak didn't know what to say to her, was unsure why she seemed so sad suddenly. He was confused about all of this. Part of him wanted her to leave right away so things would go back to normal, and the other part of him hated his normal. "Do you think they might need me to fight in the war? Are they looking for soldiers?"

"No, I don't think so. I really have to go. My family will be looking for me."

He frowned, not understanding how she suddenly knew her way back when they hadn't even stepped outside his house, but before he could ask, she said, "You're not uncivilized at all, Jak. Don't ever let anyone tell you that you are, okay?"

He didn't answer. Who was he going to tell? As far as he knew, he might go his whole life never talking to anyone except Isaac Driscoll again.

"Let me walk you to—"

"No." She took a quick glance around the room they were in, her eyes moving over the ceiling like she was looking for something. "I'm fine now." She walked to his front door and opened it, turning around after she'd stepped onto his porch. He stood in the doorway, watching her. She gave him a shaky smile, reaching her hand out. He looked at it, not knowing what she wanted. "Shake my hand, Jak. This is what people do."

He reached his hand out and took hers, and she grasped his hand, holding on and moving her eyes up and to the side like she was telling him to look somewhere with her eyes. But before he could figure what she was telling him to look at, she pulled him to her, and as she hugged him, she whispered, "There's a camera in that tree behind me. Don't make it obvious you know it's there. I saw one down by the river too as I was on my way to you."

On your way to me? "Camera?" he whispered. A camera took…pictures. He remembered. He remembered that word.

"You're being watched. Please don't tell anyone about me."

Before he could ask her anything, she turned and ran away, going through the trees toward the road in the not too faraway.

He watched her until she disappeared, his heart pounding. *They're watching you.* What did *that* mean? Watched by who? *I saw one down by the river too.* A camera. A camera watched.

Jak closed the door and then sat in his cabin, doing the numbers his baka had taught him in the long ago as he tried to clear his mind and slow his speeding heart. *What is going on?* He counted to one thousand, twice, and then took his bow and arrows and his coat and went back outside. He took a few steps in the snow and then bent down like he was fixing something on his boot, but while his hands moved on a tie, he looked upward through his hair that hid his face.

He didn't know what he was looking for, and it was a few minutes before he saw a small flash of something dark that was not a material found in the forest high up in the branches of the tree. He stood, putting his bow and arrows on his back again and walking toward the river.

His thoughts rolled and jumped like a downhill stream as he tried to make sense of what was happening with what was too little knowing.

Should he ask Driscoll? Maybe he was being watched

too. But Jak threw away the thought. He hated the man, and he'd been trading with him for less and less as the winters had passed. Jak had either figured out how to do without things he'd gotten before from Driscoll, or he'd learned to make them himself using things he could find in the forest.

For all he knew, Driscoll was the one watching him. His skin prickled. *Driscoll is bad.* He'd known that, though, figured it out a long time ago. But…what did Jak have to fear from Driscoll's *badness,* whatever it was? Jak was way stronger than him now, though he'd never tried to hurt Jak even when he wasn't.

The river came up, the low roar of the icy water splashing over rocks and around small raised pieces of land in the middle. He'd bet there was a name for those, but he didn't know what it was. He'd bet there was a name for *everything,* if he only knew where he could find the answers. The notes had given him lots of new words, ones he had to figure out the meaning for by how they were used. But he was good at figuring things out—he always had been.

Jak took off the bow and arrows from his back and sat on a fallen tree. He took out one of the arrows and picked up a flat rock from the ground and started pretending to sharpen the arrow as his eyes moved around, looking here and there, in a way someone watching him couldn't tell.

It took him a long time before he saw the tiny flash of dark something that didn't belong. It was in another tree to the side of the river bank. He'd have never seen it if he wasn't looking for it. It was high up in one of the evergreens—just like the one in the front of his house—that stayed green all year round, so it'd never be uncovered by falling leaves.

His head spun. *What does this mean?*

CHAPTER THIRTY

Harper opened both eyes, blinking around. Reality filtered in in small pieces. An ice storm. No signal. Missed shift. Lucas. *No, Jak.* "Damn," she whispered, concern bringing her fully out of sleep and prompting her to sit up and look around. Her head turned immediately to the bed where Jak had slept the night before, but it was empty.

Why did she always sleep so hard when she couldn't manage more than a few hours at a time at home? *Because you're alone. Listening for...danger.* All right, so she knew the problem, just not how to fix it. Apparently her subconscious felt no danger here, though, and she slept soundly. There was a piece of fur on the floor under her, and she'd been kept warm by his blanket once again, while he'd slept without it. She'd tried to resist taking his blanket, but Jak had simply shaken his head and shoved it at her. She'd eased her guilt by telling herself he was right by the fire. And he *was* bigger than her. Quite a lot bigger.

Where *was* he? Harper got up, pulling on her boots and

her jacket and opening the door to his cabin. She sucked in a small gasp as she took in the surroundings: a world shimmering and sparkling and seemingly made entirely of ice.

She took a tentative step outside, awestruck by the gleaming forest floor and the icicle-laden tree branches. It felt like a wonderland, and a spark of childlike delight flared inside her. She took the steps slowly, holding the railing, being careful not to slip. Her feet crunched into the thin layer of ice covering the snow as she walked around the side of his house, headed toward the outdoor "facilities."

When she stepped around the corner, she came to an immediate halt, her eyes widening as her mouth opened on a sudden intake of air. Jak was standing in the snow, shirtless, his jeans still unbuttoned and resting low on his hips, rubbing a piece of cloth over his wet hair. He raised his head at the small sound of surprise, the cloth he held lowering as his blue eyes speared her.

"Sorry," she said breathlessly. "I didn't know"—she raised her hand, indicating his half state of undress—"that you were, um…" She tried to look away, she really did, but his shoulders were so broad, his chest so beautifully sculpted, each muscle defined, his skin reddened from the cold, his small, flat nipples—

"Showering?"

"What?"

He looked at her in confusion, his brows knitting together. "I was showering."

"In the *snow*?"

He moved closer, and it surprised her that she experienced no impulse to move away. "I have to if I want to stay clean in the winter."

"Yes. Oh, of course. It's just… It looks very…uh…uh…"

"Cold?" He lowered his head, his lip tilting up a bit, teasing.

"Huh?"

He frowned again, his eyes running over her. She was obviously confusing him. She was just sort of…slack-jawed and useless with him standing there like that. A half-naked snow warrior, scarred and exuding so much testosterone it must be addling her brain. Unbidden, her gaze dropped to the sparse line of dark hair on his flat stomach, following it slowly downward. "You can use it…"

Her gaze shot to his, eyes widening. "What?"

"I keep it dripping so it doesn't freeze." He nodded back over his shoulder to where the pipe ran up the side of the house.

Right. She glanced at the still-dripping pipe and wondered if he'd stood under it naked only moments before. She swallowed. *Of course he did, Harper. Who showers in their pants?* "No. I mean…I…don't think I could stand it. I'd die of cold. I'd freeze like an icicle."

He smiled slowly, that unpracticed one that was boyish and sweet and totally at odds with his appearance. She did step back then. Away from that smile that made her stomach muscles dance.

"I'll just wash up."

"Okay." He stepped around her, and she turned to watch him leave, letting out a gasp when she saw his back. He halted, turning his head.

"What happened to you?" she asked, moving closer and running her finger across a long, jagged scar that ran from his lower ribcage to the middle of his back. He had other scars on his back as well, but that one was by far the worst.

He turned toward her. "A pig. It tried to gut me."

243

"A pig? One of those wild boars?" She shivered internally. She hated those things. They were crazy and unpredictable, and she'd heard awful stories about people being horribly maimed or even killed by them when they'd unexpectedly encountered one.

"He was wild. But so am I." Something came into his eyes then, something challenging, though she wasn't sure whether the look had to do with the memory of being attacked by the wild boar or a warning he was issuing to her.

She raised her chin, meeting his eyes. "Clearly he didn't get the best of you."

He watched her for a few moments, and then he let out a breath, turning. Over his shoulder, he said, "I'll be inside."

She stood there for a moment, watching him walk effortlessly through the snow, knowing he'd done it a thousand times, under a thousand different winter skies. *Why had he made a point to comment about being wild?* she wondered as she turned and made her way inexpertly to the water pump a few feet away. Was it a warning? Why? Did he want her to go because she bothered him by interrupting the way of life he'd become familiar with and had no desire to change? She thought about what he'd told her the night before. How someone had taken him from his baka and left him out there. She supposed it wasn't much worse than what she'd already thought she understood: his parents had abandoned him to the elements. But didn't he want answers to the questions of *who?* and *why?* Who had been cruel enough to do that to a little boy? And *could* it be a coincidence that he'd seen the helicopters looking for her parents on the same night he'd been left out there?

She pondered on what little she knew of the mystery as she splashed frigid water on her face, letting out a sharp squeal as it hit her skin. She smoothed the water back through her hair, rinsed her mouth, and used her finger to clean her teeth as best as possible. He had a toothbrush in a cup next to the water pump but no toothpaste. No products at all. Apparently, he hadn't been willing to trade with Driscoll for shampoo. She used the other rustic amenities before heading back inside.

When she got to his door, she knocked, feeling uncomfortable with just opening it and letting herself inside. Jak pulled it open, now having put on the same long-sleeved shirt. She gestured over her shoulder. "It looks like a winter wonderland out there."

He looked past her for a moment, his gaze softening. "Things aren't always…the same as they look."

She stepped inside, and he closed the door. "Yes. I know. I mean, it's beautiful, but no less harsh. Is that what you mean?"

"Yes." He turned away.

As she was removing her coat and boots, she noticed two long, flat boards sitting against the wall in the corner. As she eyed them, she realized they had handmade "straps." Had he fashioned his own version of snow shoes from long pieces of wood? She was amazed. He really was…incredibly industrious. It was humbling to get a personal glimpse at the lengths he'd gone to to survive.

He set something in his bowl and mug on the table, and Harper walked to where he stood, sitting on one of the stools. He'd opened one of the cans of pears she'd brought and had put some of the smoked fish next to it. She smiled her thanks, and he looked pleased as he sat next to her. "Thank you, Jak. I appreciate your hospitality."

His eyebrows did that funny thing where one went up

245

and one went down. She was beginning to recognize it as the expression he made when he was trying to put a word he didn't know into context. She resisted defining *hospitality* for him. He was clearly intelligent and possibly more well read than some people walking around Helena Springs, conducting perfectly successful lives, so she would allow him the time to deduce the meanings of words he didn't know. Or he could ask her. "Speaking of hospitality, I hope you're okay extending a little bit more." She shot him a slightly embarrassed glance. "My truck is under a sheet of ice, and I can't imagine those back roads ever get plowed. They're too far out of town."

His gaze was now focused on a pear as he sniffed it suspiciously and then, apparently happy with the scent, put it in his mouth. His lips curved as he chewed, his gaze meeting hers. Harper's stomach flipped at the pure joy contained in his expression. His smile grew, and he said around the mouthful, "You can stay here as long as you need to."

"Thanks."

After she'd taken a few bites, she turned to him, wiping pear juice from the corner of her mouth. "Jak, what you said out there about being wild. You know, it's nothing to feel ashamed of. The way you grew up was not your fault. You did what you had to do to survive. Most people wouldn't have been able to."

"Survival is the greatest training of all," he murmured.

His statement confused her. "Training? For what?"

He shook his head as though bringing himself back to the moment. "What happened after your parents died?"

"Me? Oh, I…grew up in foster care in Missoula."

"Foster care?"

246

She bobbed her head. "Yes. It's a state-run program for kids who don't have anyone to take care of them. Group homes or private residences."

"Which one were you in?"

"Uh, both. I moved around a few times."

He watched her closely, and she fidgeted for a moment, feeling exposed. Something stuck in her throat.

"And now you work at one?"

"Yes. I mean, part-time, mostly for something to do to fill my time during the colder months when my business slows down. I help out with the kids there."

"But you work at night when they're sleeping."

She blinked at him. He didn't miss a beat, did he? "Well, yes." She felt like she was on shaky ground very suddenly. "They need night shift workers too."

"You watch them while they sleep?" He tilted his head, his eyes running over her expression, *reading* her. Figuring her out, the same way he figured out words and customs and things he knew nothing about until he came upon them in the new world he'd been thrust into. Or, more specifically, had been thrust *on* him in the form of *her,* showing up at his home over and over again.

"Did you survive too, Harper?" he asked, his blue eyes piercing her.

She swallowed. She'd always sugarcoated her time in foster care to her friends and others she knew. But with him, she felt no need to. He'd called her honest, and she wanted to be. Not only with him, but with herself. Maybe brushing off her experience all these years as *no big deal* had done a great disservice to her own spirit. "Yes. I had to survive too. In different ways, but...yes."

Their eyes met, and an understanding moved between

them. "Are those the things you keep inside? The things you don't tell people about?"

Harper nodded before spearing her last pear. She felt close to tears. Edgy. The way he was *looking* at her…like he knew every fearful, lonely moment she'd experienced, like he'd *been* there. She swallowed the pear with effort. If she kept sitting there, the emotions filling her chest were going to bubble over. They *needed* to bubble over. They were demanding to be set free. Just not there…not with his eyes probing her that way.

She stood so suddenly the heavy stool rocked backward before settling on the floor. His face filled with surprise as she took him by the hands. "Come on. I want to try out that thing you told me about."

"What thing?"

"Yelling my secrets to the mountaintops."

He gave her a quizzical look but didn't resist when she led him to where his coat and boots lay discarded on the floor by the door.

They put their winter gear on and then descended the steps, walking to the back of the house again. The sun was higher in the sky now, and the ice sparkled golden instead of silvery white. Winter birds twittered in the trees, and the sounds of dripping water could be heard all around. She suddenly felt silly. The crisp air had made her feel better, helped her zinging emotions settle, and now she hesitated. *What am I doing?*

But as soon as the thought went through her mind, she spotted a rock sticking up out of the snow. *Well…why the heck not?* She took a deep breath and stepped up onto it, facing toward the blue-gray mountains in the distance. As if each and every sorrow demanded release, swirls of emotions rioted for first place in her mind. She cupped her hands around her mouth and yelled, "I'm so hurt and...and angry that no one in town wanted to take me in when my parents died! Sometimes I want to move far away from this damn town and never look back!"

She let out a huge heaving breath, watching the tips of those mountains, imagining she could see the vapor of her words—the long-held truth—floating away from her body to take residence in those dark peaks. She turned, stepping carefully off the rock where Jak stood looking at her thoughtfully.

"Better?" he asked.

She sucked in a big breath, her chest rising and falling. "Yes. I think so." She paused. "Yes. You were right. It helps. I feel better al—"

"Keep going."

She nodded once, climbed back up onto the rock, and turned toward the mountains. "Sometimes I hate God for taking my parents from me! I..." A sob came up her throat, but she tried to stop it from escaping. "Sometimes I wish I'd died that night too." Her throat felt tight, as she instinctively tried to resist more painful words spilling from her tired, love-famished soul and simultaneously made the effort to force them out. "I've been so scared and alone." And that was all she could do. The sob that escaped then was followed by a small hiccup as she tried desperately to get her emotions under control. She turned back toward Jak, but too quickly, slipping on the ice-covered rock, losing her footing, and plunging forward.

Jak caught her, his arms wrapping around her waist as she wept. "You're not alone," he whispered. The whimper died on her lips as she opened her eyes to his face directly in front of hers, his mouth mere inches from her own. Her heart stuttered, swelled. For a suspended moment, their quickened breaths mingled in the air between them. She blinked in surprise, her body stilling. He glanced at her lips, his gaze heating and his arms squeezing her just a little tighter. *Kiss me,* she thought. *Oh please, kiss me.*

She could see the indecision on his face but knew *he* had to be the one to advance whatever it was between them. For a frozen moment, the entire forest stilled. The whole world waited. And then as quickly as that, their mouths were meeting, and Harper exhaled a breath of relief and joy over the sudden, overwhelming pleasure of his mouth against hers. The knowledge that he had *chosen* her. And she had chosen him.

For a second, they were both still; then he let out a small sound, a combination of a grunt and a groan as he opened his mouth very slightly and rubbed it over hers. Despite the completely unpracticed nature of the kiss, sparks shot through her veins, her blood heating. She didn't want to take control of the kiss. The waiting, the discovery of what he would do instinctively, was more arousing than anything she'd ever experienced.

He was holding her off the ground easily with his arms wrapped around her waist, and she sought even more closeness with him. She wrapped her legs around his body, bringing their cores together. He breathed out a harsh breath but didn't disconnect his lips from hers. The meeting of their bodies seemed to give him more confidence in their kiss, and he tilted his head, his lips parted from the escaped breath. His tongue flicked hers, and she couldn't help it then, taking his face in her hands and meeting his tongue with her own, showing him what to do. What she was practically dying for him to do.

His breath stuttered again, and then their tongues were twisting and dancing, and the moans that they were making echoed in the quiet of the ice-shrouded morning.

"Take me inside, Jak," she managed to say.

CHAPTER THIRTY-ONE

He kicked the door of his cabin open, his kick so strong the door banged against the wall, bouncing back and hitting him in the shoulder before he could carry Harper inside.

A grunt sounded somewhere. It must have been him because she answered with one of her own, wrapping her legs tighter around his waist.

She was everywhere. All around him, inside him. Her scent. Her heat. *Her.* He felt the wildness—the thing he'd tried so hard not to be—tearing at him from the inside, shouting for him to give in to it. "Jak," she whispered between kisses. The sound of his name on her lips made his chest squeeze so hard he had to suck in a breath. He couldn't believe this. She was here. With him. Letting him touch her and kiss her. Hot. Beautiful. *His.* The wildness moved forward, taking over.

He threw her on the bed, and she let out a surprised laugh as she bounced once, then twice. She stilled and her eyes went wide as she stared up at him, but not with the fear he thought he'd see. He wasn't sure he was glad of that or not. He needed her to tell him if what he was doing was right or wrong because he didn't know how to do this. All he knew were his instincts—that wild wolf inside him—and his *instincts* wanted to *take*, wanted him to lose control, to feed the hunger pounding through his veins.

"You're trembling," she said, so soft he almost didn't hear her for the blood whooshing in his head. She took his hand and pulled him down to her, bringing one hand to his cheek and tracing his cheekbone. He closed his eyes at the shocking happiness of this woman touching him with...sweetness. "Have you ever seen yourself in a mirror?" she asked, smoothing a long piece of hair back from his forehead.

He shook his head, unable to speak, his world turning back to only pictures, only feelings and smells, the way it'd started to become before he'd found the car, the words. The notebooks that had made him human again. Before her mother brought him from the darkness.

She smiled, a slow curving of her lips, the ones that were plump and pink from kissing him. He felt pride in his chest that he had made her look that way. Him. He had claimed her. He wished other males could see. *Know* that she was his. "You're beautiful."

"Beautiful?" He frowned. He thought that was a word used for females, and he didn't know if it meant she thought of him as a woman. That was definitely not what he wanted.

Harper laughed, running a finger down his scar again. "Handsome. Sexy. Beautiful in a masculine way." It was like she knew what he had thought, and it made him feel happy. The light from the window made her skin look golden, and her eyes sparkled. She was the beautiful one. He leaned forward and kissed her because he could. That fire in his

253

veins grew hotter again, and when she let out a moan, it caused some of his control to slip. *Hold on. Hold on.*

He needed to smell her. Everywhere.

He moved his nose to her neck and inhaled, and in that spot he could smell her, not the things she wore on top of her smell, but the scent of her skin. Her and only her. The scent that brought the whispers moving fast through his blood. "I like the way you smell," he said against her throat. She let out a small sound that might be a laugh, but the good kind. And she put her fingers into his hair, her nails scraping over his scalp. He growled, low in his throat, and then went lower, stopped by the top of her sweater.

"You can take it off," she whispered.

He didn't pause, sliding the material up her ribs and over her head as she lifted for him. His blood spiked as he threw the piece of clothing aside, but then he frowned when he saw she was wearing something else underneath it—something white that covered her breasts. She laughed again, but as he looked up, her eyes were happy. She put her hands behind his head and brought him down to her.

They kissed for a while longer, him following her lead and quickly learning what she liked by the way she moaned and pressed her body into his. He loved the taste of her tongue. The way it was soft and wet and twisted with his. He loved the feel of her, so much smaller and more delicate than he was. It made him want to protect her and fight for her.

He wanted to do whatever she told him to do. From that moment until forever.

He brought his head down to between her breasts and inhaled there, her true smell even stronger. It made his head dizzy. It made him want to thrust and take.

He let his instincts lead him then; he couldn't help it. He removed her clothes, needy to know her, to smell her every secret place, to have her. He didn't want her to keep secrets from him. He wanted to know them all. To take, and then take more and more and more. To feed himself until he was finally full and then sleep and feed himself some more. On her. *Animal instincts,* he reminded himself. *I might scare her. Woman is sacred,* he whispered in his mind, the quote from the notes her mother had written about the book he hadn't yet read.

Sacred. Something that was a treasure. To him, she was. And he was still hungry for her. He didn't know how to balance the two sides of himself. Not when she was lying beneath him, making sweet sounds and running her fingers over his arms, through his hair.

"Jak, yes," she moaned when he removed her boots and then her jeans, sliding them down her legs and tossing them on the floor. He came over her again, and her eyes showed a flash of fear then. He hesitated, trembling. *Please don't make me stop.* But she reached for him, bringing him back to her.

He moved down her body, sniffing all the places he wanted to know, going back over her belly when she gasped. He licked her skin, tasting the sweet and the salt, nipping at it lightly so her backside came up off his bed.

He could smell the place between her legs, and the scent of it so close to his nose made him growl from the pleasure—*pain*—of the way his body swelled and hardened like he'd never experienced before. He ran his nose over the womanly mound beneath the cloth of her underpants, and she gripped his hair in her hands, tugging. The need to smell her there was a hunger he could not ignore, and with one quick movement, he brought the material down her legs and tossed it on the floor.

He nuzzled her with his nose and his mouth, inhaling, learning her scent so it became a part of him, and she jerked when his nose rubbed the spot below her mound.

She smelled like *life*, like sweet water, like fertile earth and perfectly ripened berries that would take away the pain of hunger. Her woman scent was the beginning of everything and the place where he wanted to draw his final breath. She was meant for him; he knew that now. No other woman. Only her.

He waited for the fog to clear enough that he could focus on her sounds, the way she gripped his hair and raised herself to meet his face. He moved more slowly, going lower, breathing her, his tongue darting out to taste her, to lick her sweetness. *Mine, mine, mine,* the whispers sang low and old like time and earth. She made a sound deep in her throat and gripped his hair more tightly, and so he lapped her again. *Again. Again.* He loved the way she tasted. It spoke to both sides of him—both the animal and the man. For that minute, it made him believe he could be both, that he didn't have to choose which part of himself to turn away.

Her whimpers grew louder and closer together until finally she screamed his name, her thighs clenching around his head and then loosening slowly, her hands letting go of his hair.

He knew what had happened because it'd happened to him, that explosion of pleasure that made his skin prickle and stars burst inside his mind. And he'd made that happen to her. He felt proud. He grinned against her thigh, rubbing his lips across her silky skin.

She pulled on him, and he moved up her body, lying next to her on the bed. She turned, her eyes half lowered and a small, happy smile on her lips. She pushed his shirt up, and he removed it, tossing it on the floor, holding his breath. She ran a hand over his hair and down his face. She brought her mouth to his and kissed him slowly, and for several minutes there was nothing but her lips, her tongue, the blood pumping hotly through his body, the snap of the dying fire, and the lowering light of the cabin as the sun moved somewhere else in the sky. Her warm skin was pressed to his, and Jak had never felt anything better. Never.

Without taking her mouth from his, she unbuttoned his jeans and slid her hand inside, gripping him, rubbing him. He groaned, his lips breaking from hers as he opened his eyes. She was watching him, and for a minute, their gazes stared as her hand kept moving. It was almost too much, too much...closeness when he'd had none, too much pleasure when he'd only ever given it to himself. *Too much, too much.* He couldn't believe this was real. He thought it must be a dream. *Please don't end. Please don't end.* He broke their gaze, squeezing his eyes shut as she kept stroking him, up, down until he jerked and shuddered, pleasure bursting over him like he was one of a thousand falling stars, streaking toward the earth below. But he wanted to fall because when he opened his eyes, she was waiting.

His breath slowed, the world coming back together in small pieces, the crackle of fire, the light, the cold wetness of his pleasure, the feel of Harper's hand moving up his stomach. He opened his eyes, and she smiled at him, kissing him once, softly, quickly.

They'd mated...but they hadn't. He knew they had not done the thing the animals did when they mounted and thrust. The way he'd thrust into his own hand when he thought about mating with a woman he wanted to call his own.

"What?" she asked. "What are you thinking?"

For a minute, he wasn't sure he could speak, so taken over by what they'd done, by the way they were still lying together, her mostly naked, her hand moving over the scars on his chest. "Do humans…mate in all kinds of different ways?"

She smiled, a sweet one, her hand moving to another scar, her finger going along it. "Yes, I suppose so. It's not called mating for humans though. It's called sex. Or making love. There are different terms too, but those are the best ones to start with, I think." Then her smile turned to a frown, when her finger moved to the part of the scar on his ribs that the wild pig had made. He didn't want her thinking about him fighting with wild pigs right then—or ever actually—and so he turned a little so her finger fell away from that scar. Her gaze met his, and she said, "We didn't make love though. That's"—her eyes moved to the side and then back to his—"different. It's when—"

"It's when a male mounts a female and thrusts inside her." He paused for a moment. He wondered if she wanted to do that but wasn't sure he should ask. *He* wanted to. He could feel his body hardening just thinking about it. That had never happened to him before—getting hard right after he felt the rush of pleasure that made his seed burst from his body.

"Yes, that's right." A blush moved up her neck, and it confused him after what they'd just done. *I said things the wrong way, that's why,* he thought and felt a little bad, but that feeling wasn't as strong as the happiness he felt at having her in his arms, of whispering to each other as her hands ran over his skin. "We didn't make love, but we touched each other intimately, and that's a very special thing. To me, it is anyway." She looked down, so he couldn't see her eyes and that blush that had moved up her neck, stayed in her cheeks now. He couldn't understand why she was acting shy *talking* about it when they'd just done it. That seemed…backward. Another rule he'd have to figure out.

"It's special to me too," he said. "I want to do it again with you. And…again."

She laughed, a happy sound, her eyes shining as she met his gaze. "Me too. But first, feed me, Jak. I've worked up an appetite."

He grinned. He could do that. He could feed her. Nothing would bring him more happiness.

They spent the day taking turns reading aloud from *The Count of Monte Cristo*. Jak read slowly, carefully, and would halt when he came to a word he didn't know, his eyes moving over it several times before he'd attempt to say it out loud. Nine times out of ten, he'd say it correctly the first time. *He's smart,* Harper thought over and over. *More than smart.* If he ventured into the world, he would adeptly figure out modern-day society in a matter of weeks. As they read, he brought up questions that were both sophisticated—considering how he'd lived—and extremely insightful. He was a complete dichotomy—wild and sensitive, uneducated and astute—and he fascinated her to no end.

Her skin flushed when she thought about what they'd done, the way the lust she'd experienced with Jak was all-consuming. Since she'd graduated from high school, she'd had this idea that enjoying sex with partners of her choosing and then controlling those relationships was the key to her healing. She'd take back her power, she thought.

And yet...she'd always felt...removed from her partners. Emotionally disappointed in the aftermath. As alone as ever. So, for the last couple of years, she'd abandoned sex entirely. She knew *why* she had sexual hang-ups, of course, but the knowing had never altered her reaction to a man touching her. *Until now.*

Something about it had felt so...decadent. It was funny that that particular word would come to mind in a sparse wood cabin in the middle of the forest, not a scrap of luxury to be found. But, yes, that description felt right. Lying there with him, touching each other's skin in the golden light of afternoon had felt like the most decadent thing she'd ever experienced. Their *bodies* were decadent, she realized. They were made to feel that way. It was a revelation.

She liked his uninhibited joy at touching her. She liked his frank questions. They aroused her. Excited her.

Jak was obviously inexperienced, but there was something amazingly erotic about watching him follow his instincts when it came to sex, to touching her body, to taking pleasure for himself. *I could fall in love with this man,* she thought, but pushed the notion aside. There were too many questions, too many uncertainties when it came to how a relationship with him might work. And somehow it felt...unfair to think too much about her own desires when it came to him. He had lived a life of strife and struggle, and he had so many more—albeit of a different kind—in front of him. It was going to be challenging, to say the least, to learn the many things his life thus far had not taught him.

But for the moment, those were topics too vast and removed to think about. For right then, there was Jak, his head bent toward hers, his forehead wrinkled in concentration, his beautiful lips mouthing a word he'd never said before. There were the warmth of the fire and the bright, shiny, icy world outside the window. Frozen. Just like time seemed to be that day. There was the achingly sweet way he smiled so shyly at her when she caught him staring. The way canned pears made him lick his lips with delight and the way his kisses became more bold, more practiced, more toe-curlingly delicious as the day wore on.

They trekked the few miles to the old logging road, unobscured by the thickness of forest, and Harper was able to get a signal. She called the group home and explained why she hadn't made her shift, and then she called Rylee and left her a message when she didn't answer. She thought about calling Agent Gallagher, but he hadn't left a message for her, and she knew he would have if he had any new information about her parents.

A bird called out, a beautiful warbling sound that echoed through the trees, and Harper smiled. Jak caught her eye and raised his face, putting his hands around his mouth and mimicking the song. It was so exact that Harper's mouth fell open. "How'd you do that?"

He smiled, shrugged. "Practice. I wish I knew the names for things," he murmured, almost to himself. "I know what they sound like and what they do but not what they're called."

"I can help with some," Harper said, "but I don't know the name for that particular bird."

They walked slowly back through the forest to his cabin, a red fox spotting them, staring with wide eyes and darting away. Harper smiled, wondering if it was the mother fox out hunting for her babies.

"Foxes mate for life," Harper said. She'd always liked that about them.

"Not all of them," Jak answered.

Harper turned her head. "What? Yes, they do."

"Where'd you learn that?"

"In a book."

"The book lied. *Some* foxes mate for life. But not all of them. I saw this gray one with four females last summer. They were in three different directions. That guy was always running somewhere."

"What was he doing?"

"*Mating.*"

"That *devil.*"

Jak laughed, the most open and honest laugh she'd ever heard, and Harper's stomach flipped. "So what's a female fox to do? How does she separate the monogamous male foxes from the chronic bachelors?"

Jak shot her a smile, obviously having garnered what *monogamous* meant and what a chronic bachelor was. "All males have to make a...case for themselves. Why should a female choose *him*? They do it in different ways. Birds sing or fluff their feathers. Some animals walk fancy or dance around." He shot her another playful smile. "Males have a hundred ways to beg. But it's always up to the female to give her signal that she chooses him. Until that moment, he... circles."

Harper stepped over a rock jutting from the snow. "Not in the human world. There, men take what they want," she murmured. She hadn't planned to say that, but she'd been lost in the moment, and it had rolled off her tongue.

Jak gave her a curious look and then stopped, turning toward her. She came up short too. "Do you mean me?"

"Oh, no. Please don't think that. No. I..." She pulled in a deep breath and then let it out. The forest was silent around her, the trees overhead shutting out the blue of the sky. It felt like a different world, somewhere she could be different too. It felt like a place that would keep her secrets safe. And she found she didn't *want* to keep secrets from him. She wanted him to understand her, to *know* her. "After my parents died, the first house I was placed into was owned by a woman with a teenage son. He would come into my room at night and…touch me."

Jak stared at her for a moment, his expression growing dark. "Touch you? Like…I touched you?"

Harper nodded, biting at her lips, struggling to keep eye contact. It was not her fault, she *knew* that, and yet, God, why was there still so much shame?

"But…you were a child."

Harper bobbed her head again. "Yes. Some people have sicknesses that they carry inside. Sicknesses of their soul. That boy did."

He studied her intently for another moment, and she could see the wheels of understanding turning in his mind. "Your parents weren't there. You were alone."

"Yes," she breathed. "I mean, it would have been hard under any circumstances, but yes, with no one to turn to"—she lowered her head, shook it—"it was…awful." The last word died on her lips, and Jak stepped forward, though haltingly. He raised his arms, his expression uncertain before he enfolded her in an embrace, pulling her against his large, solid chest, the chest that held the proof that he himself had *bled* and *hurt* so many times. Alone in a way she really had no concept of despite her own feelings of loss and abandonment.

He held her tightly, and she felt the tension seeping from her body, from her soul maybe if that were possible. Being held… When was the last time she'd been simply held close like this? Not in a romantic way, but for the sole purpose of providing solace? By her mother or father, she supposed. And, oh, how long ago that had been. Part of her wanted to weep with the sweetness of it, of the way it felt so *necessary,* when she hadn't known how desperately she'd needed it. And the other part of her marveled that this man knew to provide her with it. When had *he* last been comforted, if he even remembered it? And if he didn't, was this an instinctive act? The same way he'd figured out—*quite adeptly*—how to pleasure her body?

She hugged him back, giving him—she hoped—the same thing he was giving her.

After another minute, she pulled back, tilting her head and looking up at him. "Thank you."

He nodded, releasing her, and she felt the loss of his body heat—the way he'd felt so strong and solid against her—immediately.

"Do you think I can ever be normal?" She turned her head and saw that he was squinting off into the distance, in the direction of Helena Springs. Civilization.

"Of course you can be normal, Jak. You already *are* normal. It would be an adjustment to live among people, to…adapt to society, but I don't think it would take you long."

He looked at her, his expression full of vulnerability. He could school his expression if he wanted to, but lord, when he didn't attempt to, he was such an open book, each thought skating so transparently across his handsome features. "You believe in me."

"Yes. I believe in you."

"I believe in you too."

She laughed, and he smiled, as though the sound brought him joy. Truly, though, his words made her feel powerful.

He had both internal and external scars to contend with, and she did too. But they would both adjust, both overcome, both thrive. In that moment, she believed it with every fiber of her being.

Jak's smile faded, and she saw worry in his eyes. "I don't know where to start."

"I'll help you." Her mind spun. He'd need an ID first. She'd bet Agent Gallagher would be able to help with that. He'd need… She cut off her cluttered thoughts. He'd need help, guidance, yes, and she'd have to consider how big a role she should play in that, but in any case, she could point him in the right direction. She had faith that he could take it from there. She'd *meant* it when she'd said she believed in him. "I'll help you help yourself. You can do anything once you know where to start."

That same worry and vulnerability appeared in his expression.

Harper stopped, bending and retrieving a long twig on top of the crust of snow. She formed it into a circle and then gestured for Jak to bend. He did, a look of curiosity on his face, his gaze intent. Their breath mingled, chemistry sizzled the way it simply *did* whenever they were close that way, and she placed the makeshift crown upon his head. "There," she said, a slight hitch in her voice. "I, Harper Ward, appoint you King of your Own Destiny from this day forward. May you rule your subject with dignity, kindness, and…patience."

He stood to his full height and then removed the crown from his head. "And I, Jak, appoint you Queen of your Own Destiny from this day forward. Be good to your subject." He smiled a bit bashfully, and Harper laughed as he placed the "crown" upon her head.

She took his hand in hers again, and they walked through

the snowy forest hand in hand. She had no idea what would be in their future. In his. In hers. But she'd never felt so... embraced. And in that moment, with the white of winter surrounding them, she didn't feel the cold. Because neither Harper nor Jak was alone to face whatever came next.

CHAPTER THIRTY-TWO

Mark lifted the ornate gold knocker and rapped at the massive carved door, glancing back at the security gate he'd driven through, the name of the estate spelled out in scrolled letters above: *Thornland*. The door opened, and a man in a butler's uniform stood before him. He inclined his head. "Sir, please enter. Mr. Fairbanks is waiting for you in the parlor."

Mark stepped inside, feeling as though he'd just entered a game of Clue and Miss Scarlet was going to glide down the grand, curved staircase at any moment with a candlestick.

The butler led the way, extending his arm toward another grand door that Mark guessed led to the parlor where the owner of this estate and the many acres of surrounding ranch land lived. He'd called the contact number from the website the woman at the library had visited and spoken to Halston Fairbanks's secretary. He'd been out of the office at the time, but Mark had received a call back a few hours later, saying Mr. Fairbanks could meet with him at his home outside Missoula.

"Thank you," Mark said to the butler as he entered the room. An older man was standing at a bar cart near the window, and he turned as the door clicked shut behind Mark.

"Mr. Fairbanks," Mark said, walking to the tall, broad-shouldered older gentleman and extending his hand. "Agent Mark Gallagher. Thank you for seeing me."

They shook, Mr. Fairbanks's grip strong, his eyes assessing. "Agent Gallagher."

"Please call me Mark."

Mr. Fairbanks nodded as he turned, moving back to the bar cart. "Call me Halston and you've got a deal. I was just pouring myself a drink. It's about happy hour, wouldn't you say?" He smiled, large, straight white teeth flashing. "Join me?"

"No, sir, thank you." It was only four o'clock, and Mark didn't drink on the job, but he figured this man was rich enough to designate happy hour to whatever time he chose.

"How long has your family lived here at Thornland?" Mark asked, as he heard ice dropping into a glass.

"It's been in the Fairbanks family for four generations now. Almost one million acres of prime Montana land that stretches over six counties." Mark knew that part because he'd looked it up before coming out there. He also knew that the Fairbanks family had earned its substantial wealth as owners of one of the top ten lumber companies in the United States. The current CEO of Fairbanks Lumber turned, smiling and swirling a crystal glass of amber liquid. "But I'm sure you're not here to discuss Thornland. What is it I can do for you, Agent?" He inclined his head to a seating group, and Mark took a seat in one of the blue-velvet chairs, Halston sitting across from him as he took a sip from his glass.

"Mr.—Halston, I'm here because a woman was found

dead in Helena Springs a little over two weeks ago, and I have reason to believe she contacted your office the day before she died."

"Died?"

"Yes, sir."

Halston Fairbanks regarded Mark over the rim of his glass, taking another small sip and then setting his glass aside. He let out a sigh. "Emily Barton."

Mark was caught by surprise. "We don't know the victim's name yet. We recovered some prints, but so far—"

"It was Emily Barton." Halston sighed, rubbing at his eye. "How'd she die? Overdose?"

"No. It was a homicide."

That seemed to surprise Halston, and for a moment, he simply stared at Mark. "Murdered? Why?"

"We don't know that yet."

The color had drained from Halston's face, and for a second, he simply gaped before reaching for the glass again and downing the remaining liquid.

"We're still gathering information about the victim and the crime. The name you supplied—if correct—will go a long way in helping us do that. Can you tell me how you knew her?"

Halston sat back in his chair, seeming to need a moment to gather himself. Mark gave it to him, glancing around the room, taking in the paneled walls, the rich drapes, the two groupings of luxurious furniture, the grand piano in the corner. He couldn't imagine waking up every day in a place like this. It would feel like living in a museum.

"Emily Barton," Halston mumbled. "She's the woman who ruined my son's life. And mine, though I own most of the blame for that."

Mark leaned forward. "I think you need to tell me about Emily."

Halston sighed, meeting Mark's gaze. He looked weary suddenly, older than he'd first appeared. "My son, Hal Junior, took up with Emily Barton when he was barely eighteen years old, his whole life in front of him. I told him to cut her loose. She was pretty to look at, but trash is trash. I don't know how many times I told him not to let some two-bit whore with dollar signs in her eyes trap him. The boy didn't listen." Halston's gaze grew distant, his expression set, deep sadness in his eyes. "Wasn't even six months before he knocked her up, the dumb fool. I offered her money to get the hell out of town. Told her she'd never get a dime otherwise. As expected, she took it."

When Halston lapsed into silence again, Mark asked, "What'd you hope she would do with the baby?" *Your grandchild. Your blood.*

"At the time? I didn't care as long as she didn't give him or her our name. I wasn't even convinced the baby was my son's. Girls like that…well, anyway. Now? Time and circumstance change things, don't they?" He paused, and when he began speaking again, there was a hitch in his voice. "Hal never was quite the same after she skipped town. Fancied himself in love with her, I suppose. He'd dabbled in illegal substances, thanks to her, but when she disappeared without a word, he started the heavier stuff." His shoulders sagged. "He was killed in a high-speed drag race, heroin in his system."

Mark took a deep breath, his heart going out to the man. "I'm sorry for your loss. I lost a daughter myself. I know the agony."

Halston met his eyes, an understanding flashing between

the two men who'd survived the unsurvivable. Despite the difference in the way Mark would have handled the situation Halston spoke of, the loss of a child was something Mark wouldn't wish upon anyone. He'd made the offer that drove Emily from town and perhaps led to his son's spiral downward, but Emily Barton had accepted it.

But now? Halston looked like an old man filled with regret. "What'd she do with the baby?"

"I didn't know until two weeks ago. Turns out the boy was less than an hour away from me his whole life. Emily gave him to a man who raised him off the grid, away from society. He grew up in the woods outside Helena Springs."

The boy. Raised off the grid. Mark sat in shock for a moment, digesting the information.

Lucas.

Holy Christ. Lucas had family. Lucas was a *Fairbanks*. The woman at the bed-and-breakfast with an arrow through her throat had been his *mother.* But if she gave him up for adoption—legally or not—why in the world had she opted to give him to Driscoll instead of a nice family in the suburbs? Had it simply been a matter of money? Mark flinched internally, picturing some of the unthinkable things he'd seen mothers do to their children for drugs over the span of his career.

Halston had just provided several answers and ushered in a whole slew of new questions.

"Isaac Driscoll."

"Excuse me?"

"That's the name of the man whose property he's living on. Although to say he 'raised him' is a stretch. Lucas, that's the name of your grandson, said he barely had a relationship with the man. And Isaac Driscoll was found dead a week after Emily Barton, murdered in the same manner."

Again, Halston gaped, but then he shook his head, released a loud whoosh of breath. "Can't say I'm sorry."

Mark understood that. Now that it was becoming clear that Driscoll had had far more to do with Lucas living alone in the woods the way he was and that his motives were more than likely nefarious in some way Mark was still trying to figure out, he couldn't muster much sympathy for the dead man either. Lucas was a different matter. Lucas had never been given a chance to live a normal life. But *why*?

"Today is the first time you're hearing his name? You didn't know anything about him prior to two weeks ago?"

"Not a thing."

"Do you know what Emily's connection to Driscoll might have been? Did she give you any indication why she'd given him her baby?"

"Because she was an addict. He probably paid her. Who knows?"

They were both silent for a moment, Mark attempting to piece together this new information. He was surprised that the victim's fingerprints hadn't gotten any hits. It was rare that a person with a lifetime of addiction—if Halston was correct—avoided at least a run-in or two with the law. She'd gotten lucky. On one front at least. "What did Emily want the night she called from Helena Springs?"

"Money. She always wanted money."

Mark frowned. "Why did she think you'd give it to her?" His son was dead. It'd been two decades. What could she threaten him with?

"To make a life for her and the boy," he said. "She'd burned through the money I'd given her originally and whatever money she might have made from the adoption and had caved to her addiction again. She'd come back to town before, asked for money, but wouldn't give me any information about the child then except that he'd been adopted. Two weeks ago, she told me how he'd been raised—if you can call it that—in the woods like some goddamned animal. But not by whom." The words had emerged through gritted teeth, the final one sounding choked. Halston dropped his head, taking several deep breaths, his shoulders quaking with the movement. "She said she'd caught a ride from a friend and only had enough money to pay for a week's stay in town, but not a dime more. It was *my* fault, she said, that things had turned out the way they had. It was because of me she'd been forced to make the choices she'd made. I'd backed her into a corner, and now lives were ruined. She said she was back to right the wrongs, and I could do the same if I gave her and the boy enough to start a new life." Halston's last word emerged on a broken whisper, and Mark gave him a moment to compose himself.

After a minute, Mark asked, "Lucas is in his early twenties, if I'm doing the math correctly. Do you know why Emily wanted to set up a life for them *now*? Why she'd waited so long? He's an adult."

Halston shrugged. "Because in the past the girl couldn't get clean. This time, she told me that she'd been clean for a year, though I didn't believe her. Or if she was, it wouldn't stick. As far as Lucas, he's an adult, yes, but what prospects does he have to make a life for himself? The boy must be completely uncivilized." He looked defeated, not like a man who'd built an empire.

"He's not. I've met him. He's…lived an unusual life, yes, but he's no animal."

Halston regarded Mark, something that looked like the bare glint of hope coming into his eyes.

"What's the likelihood he'll ever live a normal life?"

"Normal? I'd say it depends on your definition. I'm not a psychologist, Halston, and I can't begin to guess what type of psychological harm came to him after the severe isolation he's experienced. But he's intelligent. He's obviously a survivor. I'd hazard a guess that he could adapt to society if he chose to do so."

Halston sighed, looking off to the side again, seeming to be deep in thought.

Mark leaned forward. "You regret rejecting your grandson? Letting Emily give him up for adoption?"

Halston pressed his lips together. "I acted hastily, with selfish motives in mind. I…don't suppose he'll ever really be one of us, but the least I can give him is his name. Whether he chooses to accept it is up to him. What does he go by now? Barton or Driscoll?"

"Neither. Only Lucas. He's never had a last name. He's been alone for a long time."

Halston steepled his fingers and mumbled a curse under his breath.

"Along with a name, you think you might find it in you to give him a home too?"

Halston looked up, appearing surprised. "A home? Why? I was of the understanding that he has a home."

"The cabin where he's lived most of his life belonged to Isaac Driscoll and now belongs to a sister who is uncompromising about allowing Lucas to stay there."

"I see." He pressed his lips together, looking Mark in the eye. For several beats, he said nothing and then, "If the boy will accept it, he has a home here at Thornland."

CHAPTER THIRTY-THREE

The white car he'd seen parked next to Driscoll's house was gone, which meant Driscoll was too. Jak watched the house from the low light of the forest for a few minutes, making sure he didn't see movement through one of the dusty windows. His gaze moved to the trees, squinting into the light as he looked close at those too, looking for that tiny flash of something that didn't belong. He didn't see it, but the day was overcast and cloudy, and he wasn't sure if he'd see a camera, even if one was there.

He'd have to take his chances.

He'd spent the last few days going over the things the redheaded woman had told him, the way she had made him feel, the questions she'd brought to his mind. He'd felt like she was lying to him, and he didn't have enough under-standing of the world to make sense of it. But he felt in his gut that it led to Isaac Driscoll.

Isaac Driscoll was the only one who gave information to Jak. Isaac Driscoll was the only one who explained what happened in the world outside the forest—what was safe, what was not, and who and what to stay away from. He'd given Jak shelter, fire, so he had no need to leave.

But what if Isaac Driscoll was crazy?

What if *he* was lying?

But why would he? Jak couldn't figure out a reason, so he wondered if asking the question made *him* the crazy one. He didn't think so.

He'd thought about trying to walk into town, into the faraway, however many days or weeks that might take. His old fear about the enemy killing children could be behind him now. He wasn't a child anymore. He was a man. His body was hard and muscled. He knew how to use a weapon. He could fight. He could kill if he had to.

Whenever he'd had the thought before, he'd always talked himself away from it. Even though he was lonely, he'd found some peace in his life, and there didn't seem like there was a good reason to walk away from everything he knew into a war. He still fought and struggled because there was nothing you could always count on about nature, but he'd learned to get ready for the winters as best as he could, and he was the master of his small world. Why risk it?

But now…

Now things had changed, and Jak had to know.

He moved quickly from one tree to the next, a wolf in the shadows, as he kept looking for cameras or anything else that might not belong, something he'd never looked for when he'd gone to see Driscoll before. After he'd watched the house for a time, he put on his flat shoes and walked out into the snow like he'd come to trade something or another. He didn't think Driscoll was home, but he'd rather be sure before breaking in.

In the bag hung on his back, he had a hat made from soft rabbit fur that he'd tell Driscoll he wanted to trade for matches if the man *was* home.

He stepped sideways as he walked up the steps, not removing his flat shoes so he wouldn't make any footprints. He knocked on the door, his gloved hands making the sound soft, but not enough so Driscoll wouldn't hear if he was inside. Jak waited a minute before knocking again to be sure. When there was still no answer, he tried the handle, but it was locked. He stood there for a minute, trying to figure out a way to open the door other than breaking it down. Unsure, he stepped carefully down the steps and walked around the side of the house, trying each window along the way. The second window on the side slid up when he pushed hard. "Yes," he murmured. He untied the flat shoes and left them on the ground. In a minute, Jak was standing in Driscoll's living room.

He walked through the room, not making a sound. Jak knew how to be silent, quick. His life depended on it. There was no one in the main room, and the kitchen area was empty. Jak blew out a breath and started looking around. Things looked the way they always had when he'd been there to trade. Except...he spotted a pile of notebooks on a small table next to the one chair. He opened the one on top, and a pile of pictures fell out, dropping to the floor. Jak began taking his deerskin gloves off when he stopped, the face looking up at him from right next to his foot...familiar. He'd seen it before, staring back at him from a clear patch of water. And he knew the clothes. He was wearing them now. Shocked, he reached for the picture, turning a few of the others over and freezing when he saw that they were all of *him*.

He stood slowly, looking through the pictures, insects starting to buzz in his head as his skin got cold. In one, he was dragging a deer through the forest, a long trail of blood left behind it; in another, he was sitting on a rock on the riverbank taking scales off a fish. He went through them faster, blinking. They went back to when he was just a young boy, still in the same jeans he'd been wearing the night he was taken and woke up on the edge of the cliff. Pup was in most. Driscoll *had known* he wasn't wild. He'd *known* he belonged to Jak. He'd killed him on purpose.

Jak gripped the pictures, deep confusion and anger rocking through him. He set them aside and started reading the journal on the top of the pile...about a possum and a deer and a wolf. All the journals were the same. He read a few of the entries, a lump filling his throat. He stuck the pictures in his pocket—they were *his,* proof of everything he'd done to survive. Looking at them brought him back to those times and made him feel dizzy. Sick.

He put the journals back where they'd been and then stood, holding his hair in his hands. Driscoll had watched. He'd watched, and he hadn't helped. Jak felt a howl rising in his throat, but he swallowed it down, made himself stand still instead of tearing the house to shreds, breaking furniture—

He heard a noise from the bedroom and went into a crouch, a low growl coming from his throat, too soft for anyone to hear. He turned his head so his ears faced up, sniffed the air.

He let out a slow breath. Just a tapping bird in the near faraway.

He stood slowly, walked to the bedroom on legs that felt stiff like tree trunks. The room was empty. Jak moved to the dresser, pulling drawers open, looking for what, he

body, wanting to pull at her pants, to kneel behind her and put his tongue between her legs from that position. Would she let him? Would her knees shake? Would she touch him again the way she had before? He wanted to make her shake and cry out his name again. Male animals made it known what they wanted and waited for the female to give a sign she wanted it too. But how did a *man* ask for something like that? Words had made her blush before, and he still wasn't exactly sure why, but he didn't think asking for it with words was the right thing to do.

Should he just...touch her? Would she like that?

Animals made it easier than people.

She turned, giving him a smile over her shoulder, her eyes widening as she caught his gaze like she'd read the thoughts on his face. The quiet sound of footsteps in the snow caught his attention, soft but coming closer. He turned from Harper, moving toward the door. Listening. Waiting for a scent. The sound got closer, and then someone was climbing his steps. A man. That was followed by a knock.

Jak tensed, a growl rising in his throat. When he saw that Harper was looking at him, he snapped his mouth closed, making his body loosen.

He moved closer to the door just as a male voice called, "Lucas, it's Agent Gallagher."

Lucas.

He'd already forgotten that name.

He frowned as he went to his window and peeked out. The man was standing to the side of the door, in a huge puffy jacket and boots with fur at the top that came from a type of animal Jak had never seen in nature. No weapon and...no car, which meant wherever he'd come from, he'd walked.

"You can trust him, Jak," Harper said, coming up behind him and putting her hand on his arm. "I do."

He realized how tightly he'd been holding his body and met her eyes, nodding. When he opened his door, the agent's gaze went quickly behind him to where Harper was standing. He let out a breath. "Good, you're here." He looked at Jak. "May I come in?"

Jak opened the door wider, and the agent came in, looking around the cabin as he took off his big coat. "I was concerned," he said, again to Harper, giving Jak a look that he knew meant he didn't trust him all the way. Jak could understand that, but he didn't like this man worrying about the woman he was already thinking of as his own. He wanted that to be his job.

"I'm fine," Harper said, taking his jacket and hanging it on the hook on the wall next to where she'd hung hers. Jak liked that she already knew his house, liked that she was acting like she lived there. "Were you looking for me?"

"Yeah. I've called you several times. When you didn't answer, I got worried. I remembered you said you were thinking of coming here."

Harper frowned. "Oh, I didn't see that I had any missed calls. The reception is so spotty out here. Maybe your messages hadn't come through before I moved into a spot where there wasn't any service."

The agent gave Jak another look that had something in it Jak didn't know the name for. It wasn't a good look though. It told Jak the agent had wondered if Jak had hurt Harper and had come to rescue her if she needed rescuing. Jak had thought he'd had nice eyes in the sheriff building, but now he didn't like him.

"I've sort of fallen down on the job you asked me to do

if you're driving yourself out here." Harper looked back and forth between the agent and Jak with a nervous smile on her face like she wanted them to be friends.

The agent laughed shortly. "No, it's okay. I see why you stayed here. I had the deputy drop me at the nearby road, and then I walked. It's like an ice forest out there."

"Oh." Harper frowned again. "I hate that you had to do that because of me. Thank you for your concern." She looked at Jak. "But really, I'm just fine." She smiled at him, and then she blushed. Jak looked at the agent, hoping he'd seen it and knew what it meant.

"I'm actually glad I drove out." He gave Jak a smile. "Or walked, as the case may be. I wanted to talk to you anyway. I've found out a few things that I think you should know about. And I'm hoping you'll answer a few more questions."

"Do you want to sit down?" Harper cut in, leading the agent to Jak's table. He watched them for a minute as Harper pointed to one of the stools, making sure he was comfortable. That's where Jak had sat with Harper, and he felt something odd bubbling in his chest. No, not bubbling...but...he hated that he couldn't even explain to himself how he felt from minute to minute. Maybe if he could explain how he felt, he could talk himself out of it. As it was, all he had were the feelings. Nothing else.

After they'd both sat, Jak walked slowly to the table, joining them. The agent was watching him, the look on his face not mean, and Jak stared back. He knew that if another male stared at him, he could not be the first to look away, or it would show fear. The agent knew that too; he could tell.

"Lucas—"

Harper cleared her throat, giving Jak a look.

"Am I missing something here?"

Jak sighed. He had told Harper his name and didn't want her to have to lie for him. "I lied about my name. My name is Jak. I told the truth when I said I didn't know my last name."

The agent tilted his head. "Why did you give me a false name?"

"I didn't know if I could trust you." *I still don't.*

The man looked at him for a beat, two, but then nodded. "I understand." Jak watched him, nodded back. "Jak then... can you tell me again what you remember about being left out here by your parents?"

"I...don't remember anything, except being alone and having to...survive."

"That's all? Nothing more? Nothing about...being dropped off out here? Nothing before that?"

Jak shook his head, not looking at Harper. He hated lying in front of her. It made him feel bad inside after they'd shared truth, after she'd told him her secrets. He battled inside his own mind, not knowing what to do, trying hard to go through the reasons he should tell the truth and the reasons he should not.

Agent Gallagher sighed, and they were all quiet for a minute, something in the air that made Jak...unsure. The older man laced his fingers together, his hands on the table. "Jak, can I tell you why I moved here to Montana? Why I took a new job at fifty-four instead of staying in California at a job I loved? In the house my wife and I had put so much work into? The place where we'd raised our daughter?"

Jak tried to hide his surprise. He nodded slowly. Harper seemed surprised too as she watched the agent.

Agent Gallagher let out a long, slow breath. "Our only child, Abbi, died of leukemia three years ago. She was twenty years old. She'd been battling the disease since she was seventeen and a senior in high school. We—" His voice broke off then, and Jak could hear the breakable sadness in it, like the distant snap of something in the faraway that you couldn't name but knew had lost a piece of itself. "We buried her, and we tried to find a reason to go on living." He was quiet for a long time as he looked down at his hands.

Jak noticed Harper had the same look of sadness on her face as Agent Gallagher's. *I understand you,* her look said. She was kind. Good. It made Jak feel...soft toward her.

"One day my wife Laurie and I were in the grocery store, and we ran into one of Abbi's best friends, Ella. We hadn't seen her since the funeral, and...well, she was six months pregnant, excited to be expecting her first. We said all the right things, I suppose. Smiled. But...it broke us. My wife and I went home and sat there, and it was"—he shook his head—"it was like losing her all over again. Losing what would have been. We lived in a tight community. We knew we'd watch—even if from a distance—all of Abbi's friends get married, have children, and it...it felt unbearable."

He looked up at Jak and Harper, giving them a sad smile. "Laurie's sister lives in Montana and is raising two boys on her own. She'd been a great support to Laurie, and Laurie had been a great support to her when she went through her divorce, but she was far away. I thought I was doing the right thing when I applied to the Montana Department of Justice. I thought...a new start is what we needed. Somewhere the memories aren't crushing at every turn. Somewhere we have family. And"—he took a deep breath—"all that's been good. But the problem is, we still look at each other and all we see is Abbi. All we see are those hospital rooms, our daughter slipping away, and then that...casket."

He was quiet again, and then he looked at Jak. "That's

287

what brought me to Montana, Jak. I'm here because I was running away, but I didn't get far enough. I'm here because the thing I loved most in this world, my *complete* family, is no longer in it, and I can't make sense of how we'll ever be happy again. I'm lost, and I think you are too. And I'm not sure what can be done about my own situation, but I hope you'll let me help you with yours."

A tear slipped down Harper's cheek, and she wiped at it quickly.

"I'm sorry," she whispered, and Agent Gallagher nodded, giving her a sad smile.

Jak ran a hand over his jaw, still confused but feeling... like he had two people who might...who might be on his side. A breeze blew through him, carrying happiness. Fear.

"I woke up at the edge of a cliff. There was a man. He told me it might be the day I would die," he said, the words tumbling over each other like they'd been a pile of sticks dammed up for a long time and finally been pushed free.

Harper's eyes went wide, and she tilted her head, surprise so clear on her face. He pressed his lips together, not moving his eyes from hers. "But a huge piece of ice moved, making snow slide. I...went over." He looked away. He wouldn't tell about the other kids. If they knew about them, they'd find out he killed one of them. They'd find out all the other bad things he'd done. And if they found all that out, he'd stay in that tiny cage with the bad smells. He'd die there. Alone.

Harper's face had lost color, and her body was held stiff. "I don't understand."

Agent Gallagher gave her a look that Jak didn't understand. But the words inside him were moving—the dam had broken. He'd never said these words to another living person.

"I didn't then. I still don't. I know that Driscoll was...in on it somehow, but he wasn't the man on the cliff. Driscoll told me there was a war."

"A war?" Agent Gallagher asked, and Harper seemed to lose more color.

Jak looked away from her. He hated the look on her face—unbelieving. He didn't know if she couldn't believe what was done to him or if she couldn't believe he'd fallen for it. Maybe he didn't want to know. For the first time since he'd started talking, he wasn't sure he should go on. But there didn't seem to be a way to go back now.

"Jak," Agent Gallagher said, and Jak looked at the man instead of Harper. That made it easier. He wanted so much for her to think good things of him. But he didn't want her to leave either. He wanted her to know him, to understand him.

Maybe not all. Not that wild part he kept hidden inside. The part that had come out when he was starving and suffering, the part that he never wanted to come out ever again. But most. As much as he could let her and still have her want him.

Jak told the agent about Isaac Driscoll, about the war, about the enemy and what had kept Jak alone all this time.

"Do you know why he would do that? Lie to you that way?"

Jak shook his head, the anger rising like a wave. "No. He was watching me though. There were cameras in the trees."

"Cameras?" Agent Gallagher leaned forward, putting his hands on the table. "Where?"

"I can't see them anymore. They're gone. I think Driscoll took them down." He must have noticed Jak had stolen the pictures. Known he'd been in his cabin. Known he'd found out the truth.

Agent Gallagher frowned. "Okay. Do you have any idea where the recordings were going?"

Recordings? Jak didn't know what that word meant. "I thought they took pictures. I don't know where the pictures are," he lied. He'd torn them into little pieces and thrown them in the river, watched them float away.

"Okay. Okay. And the man on the cliff, you've never seen him again?"

Jak shook his head.

"Jak, can you tell me what you remember before that?"

Jak glanced at Harper, the sight of her there beside him helping him feel brave. "A woman raised me until I was almost eight," Jak said. "I don't know her name. I think it was something that started with A. She said words different than the people on the TV, and she told me to talk like them, not like her. I called her Baka." He told Agent Gallagher about how she'd taught him to read and how to count and to believe that he was strong. "That's all I remember. I haven't seen her since the night I fell asleep in my bed and then woke up…out here."

Harper looked sad, and so did Agent Gallagher as he nodded. They were quiet for a minute before he said. "Thank you, Jak, for telling me the truth. You've given me lots of good information to work with." He paused for a second. "One of the things I need to tell you is that the woman murdered in town, the one we questioned you about? Jak, she was your mother."

Harper let out a small gasp. His mother. *His mother.* The hairs on Jak's neck stood up. "My mother?" he asked, rubbing his hands on his thighs. They felt cold and sweaty. His mother was *dead*? The woman who had brought him books and told him she would come back for him? Ice ran down his spine.

"Yes. Jak, do you know anything about your mother?"

"I..." He looked at Harper, and her mouth was open. His mother was dead. No one could hurt her now. "She came here. I never met her before that."

Agent Gallagher pressed his lips together, his eyebrows moving closer to each other. "When did she contact you, and how?"

"She came to see me five...years ago. She told me she was trying to find a place for us to live. She brought me kids' books. She promised to come back and bring me more books. She told me not to tell anyone about her."

Agent Gallagher frowned again. "I see. And did she indicate why?"

"No. I thought..." He looked at Harper. "I thought it was something about the war. The war Driscoll told me was being fought." He looked back at the agent. "I said something about it, the war, and she agreed, or..." He frowned, looking away, trying to remember what he'd said and what she'd said back. "She said, yes, the world is on fire."

They were all quiet for a minute before Agent Gallagher asked, "Do you think your mother was working with Isaac Driscoll somehow?"

Working? Did she have a job with Driscoll? Is that what the agent meant? Jak thought about it. "I don't know. She didn't seem to like him. She said she'd followed him from town. But...there was another woman too..." He kept his gaze on the agent instead of looking at Harper, feeling heat rising in his face. He didn't want to tell them about the redheaded woman, but he knew he had to. He told the agent and Harper about thinking the woman was hurt, about bringing her back to his cabin, and then about her offering her body to him. He didn't look at Harper while he told the story, not wanting to know if she was angry or, worse, if she didn't care that he'd touched someone else. He was not like the gray fox, he wanted to tell her. He only wanted to touch her.

And he knew now why the other woman had felt wrong. *Smelled wrong.* She hadn't been meant for him. She wasn't Harper.

"Did you get the feeling the redheaded woman was involved with Driscoll somehow? And if so, why would she tell you about the cameras?"

Jak shook his head. He had no idea. Most of him hoped the agent could put it together, find answers. But another part just wanted it all to go away. Driscoll was dead—his life was better without him—and he wanted to figure out where to go now.

"Okay, Jak, thank you. I appreciate all your honesty. I'm going to try to figure out what was going on. I'm going to do my damnedest, okay?"

Jak nodded, running a hand over his prickly jaw, the question he wasn't sure he wanted an answer to falling from his lips. "Who was she? My mother?" It still caused hurt to echo through him when he thought of those words—*my mother.* She'd never been a mother to him though. She'd never come back.

"She was a troubled young woman, Jak. She made a lot of very bad choices, but I think she was trying to make them right. I think she cared about you and carried a lot of regret."

Jak didn't know how to feel about that. He wasn't sure he could miss someone he'd never known. He wasn't even sure he could be angry at someone he'd never known.

When Jak looked up, Agent Gallagher was watching him, a worried frown on his face. But when he met Jak's eyes, he gave him a small smile. "There are some other things I've found out about your past and where you might go from here."

Jak felt a jolt of fear. "Do I have to leave the cabin I live in now?"

Agent Gallagher sighed. "I'm afraid so. I spoke to Isaac Driscoll's sister, who's his next of kin, and she was unwilling to let you remain on the land." Why did he look mad? What did he care if Jak couldn't live in his cabin anymore? It wasn't really his anyway. Maybe he should have left it the second he found out Isaac Driscoll was watching him, had *lied* to him. But he hadn't wanted to let the man know he'd found out what he was doing, had thought he could hide it, so he'd acted normal…tried to understand what to do. And then… Driscoll was dead.

And now, he couldn't be sorry he'd had somewhere to be with Harper. If he hadn't had this cabin, he wouldn't have been able to protect her from the cold.

Take me inside.

At the memory of the words, Jak's skin flushed.

But now…now the cabin wouldn't be his anymore.

He'd go back to the forest. He'd survived it before. Survived it with less knowing than he had now. The only thing that made his heart speed up and his throat go dry was the woman sitting next to him, the woman who he wanted to call his own. The woman who he would *never* let visit him in a cave in the woods. When he thought of it, he felt ashamed. He could feel her eyes on the side of his face, but he wouldn't look at her.

"How long has she given Jak to vacate the land?" Harper asked, and he heard anger in her voice too. They both thought that woman should let him stay. But…now that he was really thinking about it, maybe he didn't want to stay. Not in a place where he had been lied to, watched. He didn't want to live in a cave in the woods because it would mean leaving Harper, but...he didn't want to live on Driscoll's land either.

"A week," Mark said.

Harper gasped as she brought her hands to her mouth. "A week? What kind of horrible *witch* is she?"

Mark Gallagher laughed, but it didn't sound like a regular laugh. There was no happiness in it. "Class-A."

"I guess so. Does she know what her brother *did*?"

"I didn't get the notion that she cared. They weren't close. She's interested in her payout, and that's about it."

Harper was quiet, but he could see her teeth grinding. She was mad *for* him. It made a warm feeling in his chest. "Okay," he finally said. What else could he say?

"I have some other news for you," Agent Gallagher said. "And it's good. Or, at least, I hope you'll see it that way. You have a grandfather, and he wants you to come live with him."

"A grandfather?"

"Yes. Your father's father. Unfortunately, your father passed away many years ago."

Jak felt a tightening in his chest. But he hadn't known that man. "My father's father," he repeated, trying to picture unknown people who were somehow part of him.

"Yes. He knows how you've been living, knows about Isaac Driscoll. He'd like to offer you a home with him for as long as you want to stay."

Jak didn't know if he should trust this. He kept trying to tell himself that there was no war, no enemy, and then he had to tell himself that not *everyone* was lying to him. If he couldn't, how would he ever make it through the world?

"Who is he?" Jak asked. "My…grandfather?"

"Turns out your family is very successful. They live outside Missoula and own the Fairbanks Lumber Company."

"The Fairbanks Lumber Company?" Harper repeated, surprise in her voice. "That's…that's huge. Wait, Jak's *father* was a…Fairbanks?" She looked at Jak. "So that means you are too?"

"A Fairbanks?" Jak asked. "Lumber company?" He frowned, his head spinning. "I don't want to live with strangers. I don't know them."

"You'll get to know them. And…if you don't enjoy their company, you can move out." The agent paused. "Jak, I think this is a really good opportunity. I think…well, having family on your side—especially a family like the Fairbanks—is going to open a lot of doors for you."

Enjoy their company.

And open doors? What doors?

Harper was chewing at her lip, a small wrinkle between her eyes. "You don't think I should move in with them, Harper?"

Her eyes met his. "What? No. I mean…I think Agent Gallagher is right. I…I know what it's like to move into a house with strangers, that's all. But Jak, you're an adult, and Agent Gallagher is right. If you don't like it there, you can leave."

He felt sad for her. When she was a little girl, Harper had to move into a house of people she didn't know. She had been scared. *But she was a little girl. Like I was a little boy when I lost my baka.* That reminded him of how scared he'd been. He wanted to go back in time and protect her. He wanted to rip the throat out of the man who had done bad things to her. *If you don't like it there, you can leave.* Harper hadn't been able to leave.

295

There were so many words he hadn't understood from Agent Gallagher, and his heart felt like it was beating too fast. He needed air. To see the sky. He wanted to watch as the sun went behind the mountains and the stars came out, one by two, by ten, by a hundred, then a thousand, and an endless number he could never count to even if he learned them all. He wanted to empty his mind and figure out what might be waiting for him out in the world. *A family,* his heart whispered. *Your own pack. No,* people *to call my own.* Could he learn how to trust them? Could he learn how to be one of them? Would they want him to?

"Jak, listen, take tonight to think about it. I've laid a lot at your feet, and you've given me some more leads I need to follow up on. However, I recommend that you take your grandfather up on his offer." He glanced at Harper. "Were you planning on staying or—"

"No. I need to get back. I can give you a ride. I think the ice has melted enough that it's safe to drive." She looked at Jak, her cheeks going pink. "How about I come back first thing in the morning and we can drive to Helena Springs? I can show you around. Maybe you'll have made a decision and we can call Agent Gallagher."

Jak nodded. He didn't want her to go, but he needed time alone. He needed to think. He needed to decide. About his life. A life he had never known was possible for him.

"There's one more thing," Harper said, and then she told the agent about the helicopters, about Jak seeing them the morning after he'd been dropped off on the cliff.

Agent Gallagher frowned, looking confused. "That can't be a coincidence," he murmured. "Two mysteries beginning on the same night? In the same wilderness?"

"Well," Harper said, standing up and getting the map

she'd marked up with Jak, "they occurred quite a ways from each other, but yes." She set the map in front of him, and he looked at it for a few minutes. "Can I take this with me?"

Harper nodded. "Of course. I drew it up hoping it'd be helpful."

"It is," he said, "if for no other reason than it helps me picture where everything occurred. Thank you."

Agent Gallagher looked between them for a minute and then put his hands on the table in front of him, his eyes on Jak. "Is there anything else you need to tell me? Anything that might help with the investigation?"

Jak's heart quickened. He looked away, shaking his head. There were things he couldn't...wouldn't tell. If he did, who would ever want him as part of their family? Part of society? They'd lock him up. They'd call him an animal. A beast. And maybe he was. Or at least, he could be. And that had to be his secret. That was all.

The agent nodded. "All right. All of this, it's a lot," he said. "Are you okay?"

Okay? Right then he was. "Yes. I'm okay."

Agent Gallagher smiled. "Good. Think about all of this, and then we'll talk." He looked between Jak and Harper again. "By the way, what are you two doing for Christmas?"

Harper glanced at Jak. "Christmas?" he whispered.

"Do you remember Christmas, Jak?" Harper asked softly. He shook his head. "I don't know Christmas."

Something sad came into Harper's gaze. Christmas must be very good. Lots of things must be very good that he'd never known about before. "It's the holiday of Jesus's birth."

"Jesus?"

Both Harper and Agent Gallagher laughed, but their laughter was the nice kind, Harper's eyes dancing. Jak smiled too. "Never mind that for now." She looked at Agent Gallagher again. "I usually go to my friend Rylee's house. But it's her first Christmas with her new husband's family… so I don't have any plans."

"Well then, it's settled," Agent Gallagher said, standing. "You'll spend it with me and my wife. I insist."

CHAPTER THIRTY-FIVE

The old woman peeked through the crack in the door, peering at Mark, eyes narrowed with suspicion.

"Hello, ma'am. Almina Kavazović?"

"Yes."

"Agent Mark Gallagher. I'd like to ask you some questions if I may."

"About what?" she demanded in a heavily accented voice, not widening the door an inch.

"A man who used to live in the apartment next door to you."

Her eyes widened almost imperceptibly. *Almost.* Mark caught it and knew his hunch had been right when he'd gotten the list of tenants at the apartment building Driscoll's sister had mentioned and found the name Kavazović on it.

"Dr. Driscoll? What about him?"

"Ma'am, this conversation would be a lot easier if you'd let me come in for a few minutes. I have—"

The chain lock disengaged with a soft clatter, and the

door opened before Mark could finish his sentence. The woman stood back to allow him entrance, an old lady in a flowered house dress, her hair tucked into a dark handkerchief wrapped around her head. "I knew this day would come," she said, her voice suddenly holding none of the suspicion, only resignation. She turned, and he shut her door, following her to the living room, where she'd already sunk down into an easy chair that faced a flowered love seat. The furniture was well worn, but the room was neat and tidy, lace doilies atop almost every flat surface. Mark sat and waited for her to speak.

"What did he do?" she asked.

"He's dead, ma'am."

She met his eyes then, though she didn't appear shocked. "Yes," she said matter-of-factly, "it is for the better then."

"Will you tell me about Dr. Driscoll? How you came to know him?"

She sighed, a weary sound that rattled in her throat. "He was my neighbor, like you say. I didn't know him much, just that he work for government. I come from Bosnia in nineties during the war. My family try to come, but they..." She trailed off for a moment, and Mark waited until she continued. "They cannot."

Mark didn't ask her to elaborate on that, and he could imagine the reasons her family had run into trouble attempting to immigrate. Red tape...holdups...inadequate finances... He wondered how she'd made it out, but that was somewhat immaterial.

"I go to Dr. Driscoll, ask him if he can help since he have government job. At first he say no. He cannot help. Then he come back later and say yes. He can help me if I take a job for him, follow his rules, and tell no one."

"What job was that, ma'am?" he asked, his heart sinking, figuring he already knew what she was going to say.

"To take care of baby. To raise him until Dr. Driscoll is ready to train him."

Train him? Mark had expected her to tell him about raising the baby, but not about…training. He remembered back to his own roaming questions about Driscoll's interest in the Spartans. "What kind of training?"

"He do not say. He just tell me I must not coddle the boy or I would be doing him disservice. He tell me to feed boy and care for him, but no more. Do not coddle," she repeated. "That is very important, he say. It is the good way."

"And in exchange for that, he would help get your family here?"

She bobbed her head. "Yes, and get me visa so I can work. I sew the lace and sell to small shops. Now internet too but not so much since hands don't work so well."

Mark glanced at her gnarled hands, clutched together in her lap, knuckles white.

"I…see. And did he pay you to care for the boy?"

"Expenses only."

"And did he arrange for your family to come here?"

She shook her head, looking away from him. "He was not able to after all. I find out later they were killed in war."

"I'm sorry."

She didn't acknowledge him, her shoulders held rigid. "But I get my paperwork. I am U.S. citizen now."

Mark waited a moment and then asked, "So you raised this boy until he was how old?"

"Seven, almost eight."

"And then Driscoll took him to begin this training?"

"Yes," she said, a catch in her voice, and where she had

301

not shed tears when speaking of her family killed in her home country, her eyes glittered when she spoke of the boy.

"Do you know if Driscoll was working with someone else?"

"No. No one else. Just him."

"Did you have any idea what this so-called training entailed?"

"No. I do not know. Dr. Driscoll come here at night when boy sleeping. I try to stop him. I…do not want to let him go. I will raise him, I say. But Driscoll push me. He say he will revoke my work visa. I will starve with no work. No family." She hung her head. "He give the boy medicine so he will not make fuss and then he take him." The look on her face was so bereft that despite what she'd done, Mark couldn't help but feel a twinge of sympathy for the old woman in front of him. No country. No family. Left to live with the terrible choices she'd made out of desperation. Left with not knowing what had become of the boy she'd obviously loved, though she'd been instructed not to.

"Do you know what happened to boy?" she asked, not meeting Mark's eyes, her body tense and unmoving as though she was holding her breath as she waited for his answer.

"He's alive. He had a very harsh upbringing, as you have probably imagined. But he's a survivor. He's very strong."

A tear escaped her eye and ran down her wrinkled cheek. "Yes. Strong. That's why I call him Jak. Means strong in my language." She took a moment as she obviously gathered herself. "He very smart boy. Good boy." The expression on her face was one of pride as she said it. "Driscoll move from here, he say he building nice house to raise Jak soon. He say no school, it interfere with training. But I teach the boy to read, and I teach him numbers in the English. I tell him not to talk like me but like the TV. He very smart and learn fast. I say the words are very important. I try to teach him what I can with books about tying knots and building things. What I think will help him. And I make him stay outside many hours every day so he climb trees and build forts and grow even stronger. I try...I try to give him what I can."

What she should have done was call the police and report Driscoll. But...Jesus, there were always so many shades of gray involved in the cases he worked, so many stories, so many situations that most people couldn't even imagine surviving. "From what I know, what you did helped him."

"Good." She paused for only a moment before asking, "He killed Driscoll then? My Jak?"

"He says he's innocent of the crime, and there's no evidence to say otherwise. Driscoll's murder is unsolved right now."

She looked vaguely surprised at his answer, as though she'd assumed Jak had killed him. Hell, after finding out what he had, he was surprised Jak *hadn't* killed him. If that turned out to be true. And though there was no evidence against him, he had one hell of a motive. The man had not only watched on as Jak had suffered, but he'd deceived him about there being a war. *Enemies.* He'd planted the fear in him when he was just a child so it was all he'd ever known. It was really a wonder Jak wasn't stark raving mad.

"He...remembers me?"

"He does, yes."

The old woman nodded, tears shimmering in her eyes again. "Will you tell him Baka is sorry. So very, very sorry."

"Yes, ma'am. Of course I will."

Once he'd said goodbye and left the small apartment of the woman Jak had once called Baka, Mark descended the steps, walking slowly to his car, one of the pieces of the puzzle of Jak's life sliding into place.

He turned the ignition and sat for a moment staring up at the apartment building where Jak had been raised, unknowingly being prepared for a "training" program devised by a sick and/or evil mind. What the hell did that mean? What had Driscoll's point been? Why had he done what he'd done to an innocent boy? He glanced at what he could see behind the building. A vast expanse of woods…the place Jak had first played at what would become his only existence.

Jak was the common denominator in all of this. *How? Why?* Who else knew what Driscoll had set up other than the woman found murdered in town? Jak's mother. Had there really been cameras in the trees? If so, who removed them? Driscoll? Who was the man on the cliff? Or had that actually been Driscoll and Jak's young mind had misremembered?

Mark pondered on all he knew and what he'd just learned, his mind then turning to Harper Ward and how her parents had been murdered too. Driscoll had been particularly bothered by the foster care system, Dr. Swift had told him. Harper Ward had grown up in social services. Did that mean anything? Were the two cases random and unconnected? They very well could be, but Mark had a feeling they were twisted together in some sinister way he could not yet fathom.

A shiver rolled through him as he backed out of the parking space at the apartment complex, the old woman in the apartment he'd just visited staring at him from her window. When he'd first started investigating the homicides, he'd believed them to be crimes of hate. He'd find the perpetrator and then move on to the next case. But with each week, with more and more puzzle pieces emerging, he became increasingly disturbed. Jak had been taken and mistreated and had probably nearly died while trying to survive. A woman had been manipulated to believe that in taking in a baby, she'd find joy in a reunion with her family. Families broken. Parents grieving. *But how was it all linked? What was first? Who was responsible? Would anyone pay for these crimes of cruelty?*

And was there a bigger picture he wasn't yet seeing?

CHAPTER THIRTY-SIX

Mark and Laurie Gallagher's home was a charming ranch at the end of a curved driveway, woods stretched out around it. Harper pulled up in front and shut off the engine, looking over at Jak, who sat next to her, his palms flat on his thighs. The first time she'd seen him in the sheriff's office—what now seemed like a decade ago—he'd been sitting the same way. She now recognized it for what it was—nervous body language. He was grounding himself.

She reached over and put her hand over his, linking their fingers. "This is going to be fine."

He gave her a nervous smile. "What if I do something wrong? I don't know about going to someone's house for dinner."

"Jak, these people know that. They want you here. They're not going to judge your table manners. Just do what everyone else does."

He nodded but still looked doubtful. She squeezed his hand and then grabbed the bags she'd placed in the back seat. "Come on. I'm with you."

He glanced at the bags the same way he had when he'd first seen them, a mixture of curiosity and uneasiness, but followed her lead when she opened the truck door and got out.

Harper smiled when they stepped onto the porch, decorated with two potted evergreen shrubs flanked in twinkle lights on either side of the porch and a large wreath on the front door. She knocked and then took Jak's hand in hers again, giving him another encouraging smile. If he was going to begin stepping out into the world, he had to start somewhere, and the best place—she thought—was the home of people who understood his situation and would strive to make things comfortable for him.

So far, the only thing he'd done was to ride through town with her as she pointed out the different shops and businesses. She knew he had a million questions; she could see it in his expression that morphed from shock to bafflement, to delight, back to shock. He didn't ask her anything though, and she figured he was taking it all in, attempting to figure things out for himself—or perhaps bring back memories of what he already knew and put them back into context. Not only that, but he also had to be struggling with the fact that he'd been given up, used, lied to in ways she still didn't understand. There were so many unanswered questions remaining about what happened to him. Not to mention what happened to his mother and Driscoll. It was all *so much*. She didn't want to rush him. He had to be completely overwhelmed.

The door swung open, and Agent Gallagher stood there, smiling out at them. "Come in. Jak, Harper. Merry Christmas."

"Merry Christmas, Agent Gallagher," Harper said, stepping over the threshold, Jak behind her.

"Merry Christmas," Jak mimicked, and Agent Gallagher smiled more broadly, giving him one of those manly shoulder pats as he entered his home.

"Please, you're in my home. No Agent Gallagher." He smiled. "Call me Mark. And come meet Laurie. She's in the kitchen."

They followed Mark through the foyer and down a short hall. "I'll put these under the tree real quick. Hold on." He took the packages from Harper's hand and stepped into the living room, a beautifully decorated, brightly lit tree in the corner, and then met them again in the hall. "Right this way." He smiled and led them into a large, open kitchen at the end of the hall. A pretty woman with straight, shoulder-length blond hair wearing a red apron was taking something out of the oven, and she turned, placing the tray on the counter and smiling when she saw them.

"Laurie, this is Harper and Jak," Mark said, as Laurie took off the oven mitt and came around the island.

"Mrs. Gallagher," Harper said, taking her hand. "Thank you for having us to your home."

"Thank you for coming, dear. We're so happy to have you." She shook Harper's hand and then held her hand out to Jak, who took it tentatively. "Merry Christmas. Please, call me Laurie." She smiled again, and though her smile was bright, there was a sadness in her eyes that was unmistakable—a very slight rim of red that made Harper think she'd cried recently.

"Can I get you something to drink?" Mark asked. "I've mixed up a special batch of my eggnog."

"Sure," Harper said. "I'd love some."

"I'd love some too," Jak said, looking unsure. Harper grabbed his hand discreetly between them and squeezed.

"You three go on in to the living room while I finish up the appetizers," Laurie said.

"Can I help you with anything?" Harper asked.

Laurie hesitated, glancing back at the counter. "Oh sure, if you don't mind. I just need to lay a few things out on trays."

"Great. I can definitely handle that."

"Come with me, Jak," Mark said. "The drink cart is in the living room. Harper, yours will be waiting."

Jak glanced behind him as he followed Mark out of the room, and a warm flush of tenderness washed over her at the uncertain look on his face. He felt comfortable with her over anyone else. Anyone else in the *world,* she realized, and the thought caused a feeling of deep honor to fill her.

Laurie told her what she needed done, and they chatted easily, getting to know each other, Laurie telling Harper how the adjustment between sunny California and snowy Montana was going. Laurie Gallagher was warm and kind, and Harper liked her immensely after only ten minutes. Her heart broke to know that such a motherly woman had lost her only child.

They each carried two trays of appetizers into the living room, where Mark and Jak were standing by the Christmas tree, both holding a glass of eggnog. Mark helped them set down the food and then handed them each a glass. "Merry Christmas. Thank you both for joining us and brightening our home." He looked at his wife, and a flash of sadness moved between them before they both smiled, raising their glasses. Harper and Jak raised their glasses as well, and then Harper took a sip of the rich, creamy drink with the barest hint of alcohol. She was glad it was subtle. She wasn't much of a drinker, and anything more would have been too strong for her.

As she was lowering her glass from her lips, she glanced at Jak, who had just taken a drink. A look of pure horror crossed over his face before he sputtered, a spray of eggnog raining from his mouth as he coughed and retched and tried to catch his breath.

Harper took the cup from him, as Mark began patting his back and Laurie rushed forward with a napkin. He took it, wiping at his mouth as tears from coughing filled his eyes. "Oh dear," Laurie said. "Are you okay? Let me get you some water. You must have swallowed it down the wrong tube."

She rushed off, and Mark ceased pounding on Jak's back as he coughed once more, taking a deep breath. "What *is* that?" Jak asked, eyeing the glasses in Harper's hands as though she was holding two big goblets of poison that he'd just drunk from.

"Just cream and eggs and well..." Harper looked helplessly at Mark who glanced back at her, sheepish.

"I should have realized that this might be a taste you're not quite used to," Mark said. Laurie came back into the room and handed Jak a glass of water, which he took, a grateful look on his face before he tipped it, drinking it all in three quick gulps. Jak let out one final shudder as Harper placed the two glasses on the table, looking at the trays of food with new eyes. There was an array of cheeses, but there were also vegetables and crackers and a few nuts and dried berries. She let out a sigh of relief. He had plenty of options there of foods that wouldn't cause his stomach to protest. Hopefully. She wasn't a medical professional, but she knew his diet had been limited and his body would probably react poorly to things it wasn't used to.

Damn, I should have thought of that sooner, she admonished herself. By the look on Mark's face, she could tell the same thought was crossing his mind.

"Why don't we open a few gifts before Laurie's sister, Pam, and her boys get here," Mark said, leading them to the tree and, Harper knew, trying to ensure Jak didn't feel awkward about spitting out the eggnog. He didn't look awkward exactly—yet—more aggrieved that they'd all tried to poison him on Christmas. But Jak was self-conscious, and as soon as he had a moment to wonder if he'd reacted wrongly, he would. Not that he *had* done anything inappropriate, considering *they* should have thought a few things through—but, regardless, Jak would wonder, and she was glad Mark was moving on quickly to something else.

"Great idea, Mark," Laurie said, heading toward a grouping of bags under the tree near the back.

Harper grabbed the pile of gifts she'd brought, and when she went to hand Jak the gift she'd gotten for him, he was standing at the tree, a look of utter bafflement on his face as he rubbed the "needles" of the fake tree between his fingers. He leaned forward and tentatively sniffed at it.

"It's not real," she whispered, leaning toward him.

He glanced at her. "Not real?"

"Right, it's, um, made of..." *Plastic? Nylon?* Harper actually had no idea.

Jak's brow wrinkled, but then his fingers found one of the twinkle lights, and he touched it lightly as though he thought it might burn him. "They're like tiny stars, cold enough to hold in your hand," he murmured. He seemed pleased by them, and Harper's lips tipped as she watched him. She gazed at him, studying the look of childlike wonder on his strong, handsome face. *I'm in love with him,* she thought. It was too quick, too much too soon, too risky in so many

311

ways, too…oh, so *many* "toos," but it was true and real. *I love you,* she thought as he gazed at the fake tree, a look of awe and perplexity mingling in his open expression. The strength of the feeling almost brought tears to her eyes.

When did it happen? she wondered, trying to pinpoint the exact moment she had fallen. It should have been…*momentous,* wasn't that true? But no, she realized dreamily, it hadn't been one singular stopping of time. It was a beautiful string of moments, each one opening her heart to him little by little. And this was one. Watching Jak under the twinkling lights of his first Christmas tree, it was suddenly clear. Sometimes miracles—like love—arrived gently. Softly. Without fanfare. Without a lightning strike. For true miracles needed no such thing. Their eyes met, and her heart sang. *I love you,* she thought again. And it was as simple and as wondrous as that.

"Here," she whispered, and his gaze moved downward as she placed a wrapped gift in his hands.

He blinked at her and then considered the package wrapped in bright-red shiny paper, tied with a white-and-red bow, a look of pure delight coming over his face. "Thank you," he said. "I love it."

She laughed softly. "There's something inside."

"Inside?" He turned it over.

"Have you never received a gift before, Jak? Even when you were a child?"

"No."

Her heart squeezed—even she, a foster child, had received a few Christmas gifts—but she didn't want to make him feel strange, and so she smiled. "I'm honored that I'm giving you your first one then. Let's sit and you can open it."

Laurie had collected her bags and was seated on the couch, and the rest of them joined her, passing gifts around. Jak watched them, the first hint of uncertainty coming into his eyes. Harper knew what he was thinking: he had nothing to give to them. *I should have helped him with the whole gift thing.* She hadn't anticipated that he'd feel bad for not reciprocating. God, she really needed to start considering his situation more. Considering that he watched everything so *closely,* that he wanted so much to fit in. She was just really getting to know him, but she should have realized *that.*

"This is from me and Jak," she said quickly, handing the gift she'd brought for the Gallaghers. It was a beautifully photographed coffee table book of Montana, done by a local photographer.

Laurie ran her hand over the top of it. "Oh, Harper, Jak, it's lovely. It's the perfect addition to our new home. Thank you."

She smiled. "In the summer, if you'd like, I'd be happy to show you some of those spots. There's a beautiful waterfall a short distance from here. You can see a picture of it in there."

Laurie glanced at Mark, and Harper thought she saw something that looked like hope in the older woman's eyes. Had Harper's gift made her glad—even for a moment—that they'd moved to Montana? Oh, she hoped so. "We would absolutely love that."

Harper turned toward Jak. "Open yours," she said softly.

Jak looked down at the gift in his lap and then slowly, so slowly and painstakingly, removed the bow and then the wrapping paper, turning over the book she'd picked for him. *The Montana Wildlife Guide.* "I…thought you could look up the names of the things you've come to know," she said very softly.

Jak stared at it, touching it lovingly before looking at her.

"Thank you," he said, and the absolute and utter joy on his face made her heart skip a beat.

"You're welcome."

"I…don't have anything for you."

She took his hand, squeezing it. "Oh, Jak, you've already given me so much. You gave me my life back." She smiled at him, tears springing to her eyes, and he smiled back, so sweetly it broke her heart. This big, strong, and competent man was so very out of his depth.

The Gallaghers gave Harper and Jak gifts next—a beautiful handmade scarf each—that Jak touched delightedly and then put around his neck, smiling at them and not removing it. They all grinned and then talked and laughed and snacked on the appetizers for a while before the doorbell rang and Laurie jumped up. "Oh, goodness, time got away from me. That'll be my sister, and I need to check the turkey. Mark, will you grab the door?"

Once they were alone for a moment, Harper took Jak's hand in hers and leaned over, kissing him quickly on the mouth. "You okay?"

He nodded, his gaze lingering on her lips and making her wish they could leave right that second. She wanted him. In a way she'd never wanted anyone before. And the joyful anticipation of making love with him set off a burst of fireworks in her belly.

The twinkle lights sparkled more brightly, the candles on the mantel glowed so warmly, and joy glimmered and danced inside Harper.

This Christmas was the first in many years that she'd felt true happiness, something she hadn't thought she'd feel again. Having this time with the Gallaghers was also feeding another part of her soul. *Family. Parents.* Not hers, not Jak's, but a home she felt so welcomed into.

She was startled from her ambling thoughts when a boisterous group of three burst into the room, the woman who looked like a slightly younger version of Laurie talking exuberantly as two boys followed her, also talking excitedly. "It wasn't supposed to snow today, and I could barely see out of the windshield driving here. I swear, those weather people should—" They all quieted as they caught sight of Harper and Jak sitting in the living room, but after a moment's pause, they rushed over, introducing themselves. Jak and Harper stood, and Pam gave them each a big hug, smothering them against her chest for a moment before letting go and making Harper laugh in surprise at the enthusiastic show of affection.

The two boys—or, rather, young men—Oliver and Benji, introduced themselves, grinning and then giving Jak curious glances as they moved aside. Oliver looked to be in his late teens, and Benji looked to be about eleven or twelve. They both had their mother's blond hair and open smiles.

Mark got everyone drinks, and then they chatted for several minutes, laughing and getting to know each other. Pam was as kind as Laurie, but with more of a boisterous, outgoing personality, and her boys were polite and friendly. The Gallaghers had obviously told them a little bit about Jak's situation because they skirted around introductory questions that would have been awkward. But after they'd been chatting for a while, Benji obviously couldn't help himself and blurted out, "Have you really lived in the *woods* all your life?"

There was a moment of silence as all eyes turned to Jak. Jak nodded, seeming slightly tense, but then Benji let out a laugh and said, "That's so cool. Was it cool?"

Jak nodded very seriously before answering, "Yes, in the winters it was always very cool."

Harper wanted to simultaneously laugh and shed a tear, and by the looks on the other adults' faces, they felt the same way. Benji shook his head and looked confused, although his eyes were still shining with interest. "But did you, like, make friends with wolves and stuff?"

A look that Harper couldn't read passed over Jak's face, but as quickly as she'd seen it, it was gone, before he answered. "Yes. My best friend was a wolf. His name was Pup."

"Pup," Benji repeated, a note of awe in his tone. "Will you tell me about Pup?"

Jak seemed to struggle with the decision for a moment before finally answering, "Yes, I'll tell you about Pup." Benji grinned, and then Pam asked Harper a question, and her attention was drawn away from Jak.

When Laurie entered the room ten minutes later to tell everyone dinner was ready, Jak and Benji were still standing together, Jak speaking slow and seriously and Benji gazing up at him with such a blatant expression of hero worship that Harper almost laughed. But with happiness.

They all helped bring dishes from the kitchen and place them on the large mahogany table in the dining room and then joined hands as Mark said a prayer. Harper swore his eyes got just a little misty as he held up his glass, wishing everyone merry Christmas.

They all began conversing again as dishes were passed around, Harper helping herself to thick slices of turkey, fluffy mashed potatoes, rich gravy, and—

She halted, a serving spoonful of stuffing suspended in midair as Laurie let out a sound of distress. Harper looked at Jak, whose fork was also frozen in front of him. And when she looked at his plate, her eyes widened as she tried to make sense of what he was eating, understanding dawning about the sound Laurie had made. On his plate were the half-eaten, raw turkey innards.

"I...I left those aside for the dogs," Laurie said helplessly. *Oh God,* Harper realized, in the hubbub of the group effort of bringing the food from the kitchen to the dining room, Jak had brought the plate of uncooked meat.

Harper swallowed. The table grew quiet as they all sat frozen, staring at Jak. And then suddenly, a giggle erupted. Benji. Jak's eyes flew to the boy, and Harper saw Pam look sharply at him too. But then her own lip shook as she tried to hold back a laugh, and suddenly more laughter joined in, and it was all so ridiculous that Harper felt a giggle rising in her own chest. Jak looked around one more time, and then his own lip quirked upward and he started laughing, softly at first but then more loudly, his deep chuckle filling the room, warming Harper's heart as they all collapsed in a fit of giggles.

"Well, what the hell?" Oliver said, breaking off a turkey leg. "If he can eat that, I'm taking the leg. No one's telling me no this year." And with that, he brought it to his mouth and took a huge bite, beaming at all of them, to which they only laughed harder.

Two hours later, after eating and more laughing and talking, Pam and the boys left with hugs all around. Harper excused herself to use the bathroom before she and Jak left, and as she was on her way back to the living room, she spotted a portrait hanging in the hall. She stopped, gazing at the beautiful blond girl who looked so much like her mother.

"Abbi," Laurie said, coming up behind her. Harper

turned, slightly embarrassed though she wasn't sure why. "She died of leukemia."

"Yes." Harper nodded. "Agent—Mark told us about your daughter. I'm so very sorry."

Laurie looked surprised but then nodded. "Nothing is quite the same without her."

Harper heard the small break in her voice, and the words resonated with her. How often she'd had the same thought about her parents. *Nothing,* all her life, would ever be the same as it would have been had her parents still been with her.

"Mark was a little worried about having Jak here. Not because of the life he's led, but because he was worried about how it might look as far as the case. We talked about it." Happiness came into her eyes, and it made Harper wonder if she'd seen the conversation as a move back toward their connection as a couple. She remembered Mark saying how far they'd drifted, and she hoped very much she was right about it being a small step. "We decided it didn't matter. Our hearts, our souls, would not and could not allow a person without any family to experience loneliness when we could prevent it."

Harper's heart warmed at the words. They'd saved her from loneliness too, when she'd felt alone so often in her life, and she was grateful. She once again gazed at Abbi's picture, taking in the smile of the beautiful girl on the wall who was still so very, very loved.

"You might know, because of your husband's work, that I lost my parents when I was seven."

"Yes," Laurie said, taking Harper's hand in hers and squeezing it. "I'm so sorry."

Harper gave her a sad smile, nodding. "I was just

wondering if maybe…" She shook her head, suddenly feeling silly when she started to put her thought into words. Feeling like she might be stepping out of bounds to say what had entered her mind. Her heart.

"What, dear?" Laurie squeezed her hand again, spurring her on, looking at her with hopeful eyes.

"Well…I guess it sounds sort of fantastical, but do you think that if people meet here on Earth, the people they've loved and lost meet too because they're watching over their loved ones? Does that make any sense?"

Tears came to Laurie's eyes, but there was happiness—*hope*—in her expression. "Yes. Yes, I'd like very much to believe that."

Harper expelled a relieved breath. "Good, because my parents, they were wonderful, and I'd really love to believe they're meeting Abbi right now and making her feel as welcome with them as you've made me feel here with you tonight." She blushed, hoping the woman didn't take what she was saying as a desperate—and perhaps unwanted—attempt to make her invite Harper back again or something like that. She laughed, feeling awkward. "I hope—"

"Oh, my darling girl." Laurie's voice broke as she pulled Harper to her in a big hug. "I can't tell you how much you've filled my heart by saying that. Thank you."

Then they returned to the room, tearful but smiling, where the men were waiting for them, both with equally perplexed looks on their faces, to which Harper and Laurie responded with another bout of giggles.

CHAPTER THIRTY-SEVEN

Because of the newly falling snow—and that the plows weren't out on Christmas—the ride to Harper's apartment was slow and quiet, though pleasantly so. Harper was basking in the glow of having spent the happiest Christmas she could remember, and Jak looked happy too, a small smile curving his lips as he watched the snow streak by his window.

They pulled in front of the house where she rented a room, and Harper took his hand, laughing as they ran from the truck, the snow a white flurry all around them. She unlocked the door, and they spilled inside, Harper taking her finger and bringing it to her lips as they tiptoed up the stairs.

The old house had been converted into a duplex, and the old woman who lived on the main floor was a distant relative of the original owners who had built the home. The studio apartment Harper rented was up a flight of back stairs and featured a main room, a very small kitchenette, and a bathroom, nothing more. But it worked for Harper's needs.

She unlocked the door at the top of the stairs, and they entered her apartment, removing coats and scarves, though Jak left his new scarf on. He hadn't taken it off since he'd received it. Harper loved how much he valued the gift. She was sure he'd keep it on indefinitely.

Harper watched as he looked around, moving from the small tree with twinkle lights in front of the window to her bed, made up with an antique, handmade quilt she'd bought at an estate sale on the last day when prices for the remaining items had been slashed to the thrifted furniture items she'd picked up for pennies and painted. He ran a hand over the high pile of books on her nightstand, and then he peeked into the tiny kitchen and then the bathroom. She watched him, his eyes moving everywhere with interest. He looked… impressed, and she couldn't help the smile that tilted her lips.

Jak walked to the window that featured a very small false balcony and opened the latch. There was a portico above the window that kept the snow from coming inside, and so although the wind whipped the curtain, the snow fell just beyond it.

"Don't step onto that balcony," she warned, coming up beside him. "It isn't safe."

He looked over at her and smiled and then back out to the snow, watching as it swirled and tumbled, the lights of the town twinkling beyond, giving everything a dreamy glow. "It's so beautiful here," he said, a note of awe in his voice.

She laughed, wrapping her arms around his bicep and pulling him close, resting her head on his shoulder and looking into the twinkling white. She'd tried to make her small home pretty despite having little money to spend on pretty things. But she had never considered it *beautiful*.

Homey, yes. *Hers,* yes. As good as she could do with what little she had. But now, standing there as the lights and the snow blurred in front of her, the wind cold but the warmth and comfort of home a few footfalls away, she realized it *was* beautiful. She had everything she needed. She'd done her best, and she was proud that she'd never stopped trying.

"It is, isn't it?" she whispered, a small hitch in her voice at the emotion the whole night had elicited. She wanted to show him other things, experience everything that, for him, would be brand-new—pie in diners at midnight, picnics in sunny parks, late-night movies, barbecues, and a thousand other things people took for granted. She wanted to watch his face as he took it in, to see the delight in his eyes, the confusion, the understanding. She wanted to watch as he worked things out in that quick mind of his. And yet another part of her wanted him just the way he was, always—innocent, beautiful, untouched, *hers.*

He shut the window against the cold and turned to her, bringing his hands to her face and looking at her as if *she* was the *most* beautiful thing he'd ever seen. "You make me see beauty where I didn't see it before, Jak," she said, turning her face and closing her eyes as she kissed his palm. "You make everything new. Even me."

He tilted his head, and in the dim light of the room, shadows played over the lines of his face, his light eyes burning into hers, the only fire she needed to keep her warm. "Is that good?" he asked. "That I make you new?"

"Yes, it's very, very good." She was transforming, she realized, and she still wasn't certain about all the ways he was helping her grow, but it felt good. It felt right. Since he'd come into her life, more questions had arisen, and yet it finally felt like she was figuring out her life when before

322

she had been flailing. Maybe part of it was the deep gratitude he'd opened up in her. Maybe it was her perspective on her own life and the struggles she'd endured. She wasn't entirely sure yet, but it had *everything* to do with him. She felt like a blooming flower, gently opening, her petals reaching for the sunlight she hadn't even realized was there because she'd been curled up so tightly, a bud protecting herself from the very thing she needed to blossom.

"Did you enjoy tonight?" she whispered, her finger moving along the wool of his new scarf.

"Yes. Very much." He looked thoughtful for a moment. "When you were in the kitchen, Agent Gallagher told me about the woman who raised me. He...found her. She was a refugee of a war. A...real one." He looked away for a moment. "Isaac Driscoll used her. She was wrong too. But for some reason, I can't hate her. She gave me what she could."

Harper regarded him, considering his innate goodness. His gentle heart. Him. "I'm glad you're getting answers, Jak. You deserve them."

His eyes met hers, vulnerability filling his expression. "Everyone gave me away. No one kept me."

Her heart stuttered, squeezed. "I'll keep you," she whispered, the words that had spilled from her lips making her feel shy suddenly. She looked down.

He nudged her chin up with his hand, so her eyes met his once more. "Promise?" he asked.

She nodded, their gazes holding. And she knew she would. No matter what the future held. No matter whether *he* decided to keep *her* or...not. He would remain part of her. Forever. She'd keep him. She'd never let him go because she wouldn't know how.

They stood at the window for a few minutes longer, living in the shared moment of vulnerability, looking out at the dark night. He traced her fingers, his hands moving up her arms, the heat of him all around her. Yes, she wanted him. Wanted every minute of the coming night.

She turned, kissing him slowly, and he groaned, pressing himself toward her, their bodies meeting, her softness molding to his hardness so they became one—two perfect parts of a whole. Their tongues tangled and danced, and she pulled away, laughing and yanking at his scarf. "I know you like this, but if I'm going to kiss you properly, you need to take it off."

Harper had never seen a scarf come off so quickly.

Her laughter was cut short by his mouth.

They kissed and kissed, their hands roaming, both wearing far too many clothes. Harper felt the proof of his desire and rubbed herself against him. He hissed out a sound of tortured arousal, his lips breaking from hers.

She ran a finger down the scar under his cheekbone, gazing at him, beautiful and fierce, and for a moment—but only a moment—she was fearful of the deep need she saw in his gaze. He wanted to take her, to claim her, to *mate* fiercely and with wild abandon. She saw it in his eyes, in the set of his jaw, but then his expression gentled, and the fierceness in his eyes diminished. Her breath came easier, her heartbeat slowed, but something deep inside had spiked in response and then dipped as it faded. She didn't know what to call it. All she knew was that she wanted him too.

"Take me to bed, Jak," she murmured. "I want to be with you."

His eyes widened, and he took one small step back, as if he needed to be able to see her better, to read the expression on her face to know that she meant what he thought she did. "Make love to me," she clarified.

"Yes," he said, and the simplicity of his answer when his eyes burned so bright and his body trembled made her smile.

He raised his hand and then dropped it. "Where…where should we start?"

"Removing our clothes is probably a good place to start."

His smile was sweet and unsure. *Boyish.* But he raised his hands and pulled off his shirt, exposing his beautiful chest to her, his scars standing out white and raised in the dim light. She leaned forward, trailing her tongue along one and then another. He pulled in a breath, bringing his hands to her scalp and dragging his fingers through her hair. She made a purring sound, raising her head and trailing her fingers down his sides.

"Harper," he moaned, a note of desperation in his tone.

"Yes," she said, "I know." This wasn't going to last long. But after this time, they had all night. The muscles between her legs clenched at the thought.

"This might…" He swallowed, seeming suddenly unsure, gathering his control. "We might have a…" His brow furrowed, and her breath paused. "Offspring," he finished.

Oh. She exhaled, her heart filling with tenderness. "No. I'm on, uh, I take something so that won't happen."

He regarded her quizzically for a moment but then nodded, his eyes heating once more as she began to undress.

She removed her clothes as he watched, his eyes devouring every part of her as it was revealed, his breath releasing in soft pants. A look of such deep approval in his eyes that she felt beautiful. Worshipped.

She took his hand, and they walked the few steps to the bed. He pulled off his boots and then his pants so fast a giggle bubbled up in her chest but died when her gaze fell to his erection, jutting toward her, large and flushed reddish-purple with the intensity of his lust. For her.

She swallowed. "Do you know how to do this?" she whispered.

He stepped toward her, his voice gravelly, thick. "I... know the basics. The rest, you'll have to show me. I have... questions."

"Like what?" she whispered. Why was she stalling now? *Am I scared?* she asked herself. *Not of him, not of this,* she realized. It was just that she'd never felt this kind of...*gravity* when it came to sex. Maybe she hadn't wanted to. Maybe she'd made a point of avoiding it for the lack of control it brought. But now, she realized she'd denied herself the very thing that might have helped heal her.

As he moved his finger under her breast, he watched in rapt fascination as her nipple stiffened and she shivered with delight. "I'll let you know as they come up."

He took her hand, and now he was leading her to the edge of the bed, where he pulled back the blankets and guided her to lie next to him. He pulled the covers over them, and for a few minutes, they simply gloried in the feel of naked skin against naked skin, in the warmth they shared, the safety of her room, the hopefulness that stretched before them. The long, delicious night that lay ahead. Harper's skin prickled, and a sigh fell from her lips as his mouth nuzzled the swell of her breast, moving around it. She watched him for a moment, realizing that he was avoiding her breasts. "You can kiss me there," she whispered, turning her body slightly, offering her breast to him. He looked briefly puzzled, but then his eyes darkened, lust flaring, and he lowered his mouth to her nipple, sucking gently. She moaned.

"You like that," he noted, his voice gravelly, a note of awe in it.

"Yes," she breathed. He lowered his head again, spending long minutes nuzzling, rolling his tongue around her nipples, driving her crazy with desire, the vibration between her legs heightening to a feverish pitch.

"Jak," she gasped, pulling at him, needing him to fill the emptiness inside her.

He rose up over her, a shadow in the darkness, his eyes glittering with intensity, and though she would have expected her heart to stall, her desire to fade, in fact the opposite happened. Her body *thrilled*. Answered to him in some primal way she couldn't define. She felt a heady rush of arousal, and her need for him made her writhe, the hot pulsing between her legs causing a sweet ache. She opened her thighs, giving him invitation, asking him to take the most tender part of her and make her his. *I trust you,* she thought. *With every part of me.*

She took her hand and lined his erection up at her entrance. "Slow," she whispered.

He did as she instructed, but she could tell it was costing him, his breath coming out in fast pants, his limbs trembling as he entered her one slow inch at a time, stretching her so it was a delicious pleasure…pain. Her body adjusted, muscles clasping as he penetrated her to the hilt, grunting, an animal-istic sound of profound pleasure, of joy, of relief and surprise and desperation all mixed together.

She didn't have to instruct him what to do then. His body took over, as he pulled out slowly and then pushed back in, his movements corresponding to long masculine groans of ecstasy and short grunts of exclamation as he buried himself inside her and then pulled out again. He moved with such singular focus, and the sounds he made set her on fire. And *oh God,* he felt so good, his body big and hot and hard, filling her, his rough skin rubbing on her most sensitive parts, back and forth, back and forth, but too slowly. Too torturously slowly. "Faster," she groaned, a pleading note to her voice. "Faster, faster, faster," she panted.

"I'll…"

"I *know,*" she said. "I want to feel it. I want to feel *you.*" She wanted to watch him as he fell apart inside her for the first time. She couldn't wait.

She felt him hesitate, something almost fearful crossing his expression, but only for a second as he finally—finally—sped up, his hips bucking as he began to thrust in earnest. *Yes, yes, yes.* She tightened her thighs around him, watching his face, waiting for the moment it would tense with unbearable pleasure. But to her surprise, it was her *own* intense pleasure that swept over her, an orgasm rising so quickly, it took her unaware as she cried out, the pulsing bliss exploding and then receding.

His eyes grew heavy, his lids half closing as his mouth fell open and he plunged into her, once, twice, an animal roar of pleasure erupting from him, as he threw his head back and pressed himself into her one final time.

With one last groan, he collapsed on top of her, rolling his weight to the side as their hearts beat together, their quickened breaths mingling, slowing, sweat cooling on their skin.

She felt his smile against her neck, and it elicited a small laugh from her as she used her inner muscles to squeeze his softened flesh, still halfway inside her. He grunted against her throat, chuckling, the movement causing him to slip out of her body.

He rolled to the side and propped himself up, gazing down at her, the look of stunned joy on his face so stark and clear that she laughed out loud. She lifted herself up and kissed him once, hard on the mouth.

"Let's do it again," he suggested, his voice slow with satisfaction.

She laughed, kissing him again, tracing his lips with her finger. "Hold me for a while first."

He did, and she knew he relished the intimacy, his joy so close to the surface that she could read every nuance on his handsome face. His joy inspired hers, and she'd never felt so contented in all her life, lying there with him in the warmth of her bed, sharing, touching, making love again and again.

The night deepened, wrapping around them so it felt as if no one else existed. Only them. "This. Here," he breathed, looking at her with deep intensity, their bodies connected, their hearts entwined.

"What?" she asked on a breath, the moment slowing, though everything physical about her was rushing, quickening.

"This fills my soul. You…you fill my soul."

Oh, Jak.

He began moving then, and her thoughts tumbled, drifted away as pleasure engulfed her, joy spiraling wildly. *You fill my soul too,* her heart whispered just as her body flew to the stars.

They whispered in the dark. He told her about his beloved Pup and kissed her tears away when she cried for his loss. She told him more about her childhood, how hard it had been every time she had to pack up and move somewhere else.

When the sun peeked through her curtains, they had

hardly slept. Her muscles ached, and she was sore in places she hadn't even known existed. And yet Harper had never opened her eyes to a morning that held more exuberant joy than that one.

CHAPTER THIRTY-EIGHT

Jak's grandfather lived in a castle. Though Agent Gallagher had called it an "estate." *Estate* was another word for *castle*, he figured. It had to be. There couldn't be a house bigger than the one he was standing in.

He squeezed Harper's hand, and she looked at him, her eyes both sleepy and bright. His blood got hot, and he wanted to mate with—no, make love to—her again, even though they'd done it four times, once just before Agent Gallagher had picked them up. Harper had asked if he wanted to go alone to meet the grandfather, but he wanted her there. Wherever he was, that's where he wanted her to be.

Clicking sounded on the floor, and a second later, a man came into the room. He was almost as tall as Jak with gray hair and clothes that looked like a uniform, only...not. His gaze turned to Jak immediately, the look in his eyes sharp like an eagle. He walked to him and held out his hand. Jak shook, gripping firmly like Agent Gallagher did. The shaking thing, it was becoming familiar. It was what people did when they met or saw each other again.

"My God," the man murmured, his eyes traveling all over Jak's face. His voice sounded surprised and sad and happy all together. "It's uncanny. Come." He turned and made a hand movement that Jak thought meant he should follow him. Jak glanced once at Harper, and she gave him a nod before he followed the older man. He walked to a desk and picked up a photograph, handing it to Jak. The picture was of a man about his age, he thought, standing in front of a car and smiling.

Jak looked at it, trying to figure out what the older man was showing him. "That's Halston Junior. Your father." Jak's eyes widened, and he brought the picture closer, looking at the face of the man who had fathered him. "You look like him," the older man said. "Just like him. There are more family albums in the drawer if you want to look through them later." Jak stared at the photograph again, bringing his hand to his bearded jaw, his eyes moving back to the man in the picture, curious. Jak wasn't sure if he looked like his father. He still pictured his own face looking back at him from the wavy water. He couldn't remember what he'd looked like in the pictures he'd found at Driscoll's house, and he didn't like to think about that anyway. He'd only glanced at himself in the mirror in Harper's bathroom. He hadn't taken the time to study himself—he'd wanted to, but he wanted to get back to bed *more*. To her. He handed the photograph back.

"I'm your grandfather, son. Call me Hal. Welcome. Welcome to the family." His voice made a weird crack, and then he stepped forward, surprising Jak by wrapping his arms around him. Jak remained stiff for a second but then let the man hug him quickly before he stepped back again. "Well, I'm sure you have hundreds of questions, and we can sit down and talk after I've shown you around your new home. How's that?" He thought of his real home—his *old* home, he kept having to remind himself. Right now, the forest would be filled with the noise of the hunters and gatherers going about their work. The sun would be at its warmest. If he closed his eyes, he could feel it, smell it, remember the times of peace when his mind was quiet and his heart was calm. There, he felt connected to all living things, when the whispers weaved through him, wrapped around him, and he became part of it all. No end. No beginning. He'd drawn the feeling on Harper's mother's notes. He wondered if he'd ever have that feeling again. This new place felt like the opposite of that.

The grandfather—Hal—smiled at Agent Gallagher and Harper, who was standing next to him with her hands together in front of her. "Thank you for everything," he said. "Nigel will show you to the door." The man named Nigel in the black-and-white uniform stepped forward from the doorway like he was a shadow who had just come to life.

"Thank you. Jak, give me a call if you need anything," Agent Gallagher said, giving him a nod and starting to turn away.

Jak's heart leaped, and he stepped toward Harper. "Do you want me to stay?" she asked softly, leaning in to him.

Yes. He did. But he remembered she had gifts for the kids at the group home. Gifts in shiny green paper with red-and-white bows. She'd put them behind the seat in her truck and said she'd been away from them too long. He wanted those kids with no parents—like him and Harper—to have those gifts. To know she hadn't forgotten about them.

But he didn't want to be alone with these strangers in this big castle that felt cold and lifeless. He felt...stuck. He stared at Harper. It'd only be for a little while... "Will you come back?"

Harper smiled, but it looked like she was making herself do it. "Yes, of course I will. I'll call you."

Call him? He felt panicked. He didn't even know how phones worked, didn't know *what* phone or where...

"Agent Gallagher gave me the number here," she said, as if she could read his mind. "I'll call you."

"Okay, then, it's all settled," the grandfather said. "Nigel."

He held out his hand to Harper, feeling unsure, wanting to kiss her. She looked unsure too, but she moved forward, hugging him quickly, squeezing, and then she was turning. Walking away. Gone. *Harper. I should have asked her to stay.*

"Follow me," the grandfather said. "I'll give you a short tour, and then we can sit down and talk before my one o'clock appointment." *Tour. Appointment.* So many words he didn't know. His head hurt. Jak followed the grandfather out of the room with all the couches and chairs and blue and gold colors into a huge, open area that was so tall, Jak had to bend his neck to see the ceiling. Everywhere there was shiny stone, white and gray with streaks and rivers inside it. Jak wanted to reach out and touch it, to feel it under his fingertips—how did rock get that smooth?—but he didn't, instead holding his hands behind his back the way the grandfather was doing.

There were carpets with whole forests under his feet—birds and trees and flowers in reds, blues, yellows, and starless black.

The grandfather showed him another room with sitting furniture, this time in green and white colors, and then he walked him into a room with shelves so high they reached the ceiling. They were filled with…books. Jak's eyes widened, and his heart jumped. So many, many books. More books than he knew were written in the world. "Agent Gallagher said you're able to read."

"Yes," Jak murmured, his eyes unable to move from the shelves to the man speaking to him.

"Well, help yourself to any of these. Lord knows no one around here reads them."

Jak felt his eyebrows shoot up. "No one reads these?" He couldn't understand. His heart was jumping and speeding at the news that so many books even existed. He was still in the middle of *The Count of Monte Cristo*, but he wanted to start looking through these. He wanted to pick his next book and the one after that. He wanted to stack them into a big pile and start reading right away.

"All too busy, I guess. The young people are always on their phones. Lord only knows what they're doing. Social media, I guess."

Jak didn't know what that was, so he made his face look understanding and nodded. The grandfather led him out of there, but Jak looked around the big hall so he'd make sure he could find his way back.

The grandfather took him to a kitchen so big that Jak stood in the doorway staring. It was bigger than two of his cabins, bigger than five of his baka's kitchens. It had more of the shiny stone, a bright silver stove, and a refrigerator that looked like a small house. Jak swallowed. There was so much food. Right there, for the taking. He turned away, something about it making sadness pinch his chest. He pretended he didn't feel the way he did. He didn't even know what he felt anyway.

"Jak, this is Marie. She's our chef, and anything you'd like to eat, you just let her know." *A chef?*

The round woman with red cheeks smiled and held her hand out. Jak shook it. "I make the food here," she said, winking her eye. "Any favorites I should know about, Jak?"

"Uh." He searched his mind. He knew he'd done the wrong thing when he'd eaten the raw meat at the Gallagher's. He'd be expected to eat cooked meat from now on; he understood that. Understood that it was *uncivilized* not to. Except sushi, Harper had told him. He didn't know what that was, but if it was raw, he figured he would like it. "Sushi."

Marie's eyebrows did a funny thing, but she smiled again. "I'll be sure to add it to the menu then."

"Very good," the grandfather said, and then he led Jak out of the kitchen, down another hall. Jak didn't know how he'd find his way out if he decided he wanted to leave. The grandfather opened a big set of doors with glass at the top, and Jak smelled the birds before he heard them. He stopped, confused. The grandfather laughed. "Hear the singing? Lovely, isn't it? It's coming from the aviary," he said. "It's where my wife, Loni, will be. Come with me."

Aviary? The bird cries got louder, and Jak's heart stumbled. They weren't like any bird language he'd ever heard before, and the birds he was listening to weren't singing…they were…crying. *What's happening?*

He followed the grandfather into another large room with big trees that didn't grow in the ground but instead in… pots all around the sides. He wondered how they whispered to each other that way when they had no deep-down place to meet. In the middle of the room were three giant cages that almost reached the ceiling. Bird castles made of bars.

Inside were hundreds of birds in colors Jak had never seen birds in before. "Flower birds," Jak murmured, his eyes wide, their cries twisting his heart.

A woman wearing all white glided from behind one of the cages and held her hand out to Jak. Her eyes moved all over him, and he got that same feeling he used to get when he thought someone was watching him. The hairs on the back of his neck stood up. "Hello," she purred like a fox when it was eating its kill. "Look at you. You're just everything I thought you'd be."

"Spitting image of Hal Junior, isn't he?"

The woman glanced at the grandfather. "Mmm," she purred again. "I'm Loni."

"She's your step-grandmother," Hal said, and she gave him a look like she was mad because what he said wasn't true. She did look a lot younger than the grandfather. She reached her hand out, and Jak took it in his, noticing her nails were long and sharp and bright pink. She used one of them to tickle his palm as he was pulling his hand away. Maybe she was trying to make him laugh, to tell him it was all a joke. He hoped so, but... "Her son, Brett, and daughter, Gabi, live here with us as well. You'll meet them later tonight."

"You must be an animal lover, Jak," Loni said. "We have that in common." She waved her hand around at the crying birds. "I can't wait to find out what else we have in common."

Jak had no idea what to say to the bird woman with the claws, so he simply stared.

"You let me know if you need anything settling in, you hear?" Loni winked at him, but it was different than the wink Marie had given him, and he wasn't sure how, but it was.

He nodded, wanting to get far away from the woman who enjoyed making beautiful things cry.

He hurried after the grandfather, finally taking a full breath once the bird cries faded. They went into a smaller room with two couches and two chairs. This room was yellow, all different shades. Jak sat in the chair the grandfather pointed to. "Can I get you something to drink?"

"Not eggnog, please."

The grandfather laughed. "Not a fan, eh? Me neither." He handed him a glass of water, and Jak took a grateful sip.

"I'm sure you have questions, Jak. What can I answer for you?"

"I'd like to hear about my father," he said. "Agent Gallagher told me what happened with him and my... mother, but...what was he like? Who was he?"

The grandfather had a sad expression on his face, and Jak wondered if it had been wrong of him to ask, but then the grandfather's lips tipped upward, and he leaned back in his chair. "Smart as a whip," he said. "Everyone said so from the minute he was born. He picked up everything quickly, was good at whatever he put his mind to. He had so much..." His voice faded away, and then he sat up straighter and his voice sounded strong again. "Potential."

Potential. His father was smart. He picked things up. He had...potential. Hope. Hope for...a good life. Jak stored the word away. He liked that one. And he wondered if he had potential too. Maybe he'd gotten that from his father, along with the look of his face. He ran his hand along his jaw.

"You'll want to shave, I imagine, once you get settled in your room."

Jak nodded slowly, unsure. He kept his beard short with his pocketknife, but he hadn't shaved his face since he'd grown face hair. It kept him warm in the winter. It told others he was a man who could mate and have his own offspring.

But the men he'd seen in civilization so far all had shaved faces. He guessed females in civilization thought other things were more important than mating and offspring. Jak ran his fingers along his jaw again, wondering what Harper would like.

"Anyway," the grandfather sighed, "your father was a good man. He would have led a good life if that woman…" He seemed to grind his teeth together for a moment, and then he brought his own hand to his jaw, rubbing it before going on. "Well, suffice it to say, I wish things had been different, but here we are."

Here we are.

The grandfather didn't look happy about that, and Jak suddenly felt even more out of place. *Be still, don't move. Don't become prey.* He knew that wasn't the right word, but it was the best one he had. Animals smelled confusion and fear, and they took advantage of them. Humans did the same, he knew, but they couldn't smell it. They used their eyes and their brains instead.

Jak didn't yet know if the grandfather was good or bad, and he hoped he was good, but until he knew for sure, he would watch him. This house made him feel funny with its big, cold walls and its beautiful caged birds and the people who made strange looks and said things that made him think they were saying other things underneath if he knew how to listen right.

"Speaking of your father, Jak, his downfall began because of a woman." He seemed angry. "I would hate to see the same thing happen to you."

Jak sat back, staring at the old man. *Harper.* He was talking about Harper. A sharp prick of anger made his chest tight. "The woman you brought here today, she's obviously not of our ilk."

Jak had some idea what the man was saying but stayed quiet. Waiting for all the words so he could put them together in his mind. Understand. "The name Fairbanks comes with much privilege, but it also comes with its share of difficulty. Namely, others will want to use you for what you can do for them. It's why your father ended up on the path he did." The grandfather gave him a stare and then sighed. "Do you know what a gold digger is, Jak?"

Gold digger. Someone who digs for gold? But he didn't think the grandfather meant that. He shook his head.

"It's a woman who wants you for your money, son."

"I don't have any money," he said slowly.

"You *didn't* have any money. But you're a Fairbanks now. All of this"—he waved his hand in the air—"is at your fingertips."

"What?"

"What is at your fingertips? Why, this house, the opportunities the Fairbanks name opens up for you, perhaps the Fairbanks estate someday, Jak." He leaned forward, looking thoughtful. "I'll teach you the basics." He raised an eyebrow. "And someday maybe…you can hire good people to deal with the business specifics." He sat straighter, looking more… hopeful. "Someday you'll have a son of your own, and then all of this will go to him. It's the way estates work, Jak. It's the way a family name goes on and on."

Jak ran everything the grandfather had told him through his mind. The grandfather believed his mother had ruined his father's life. He thought Harper would ruin Jak's life too.

That she was a *gold digger* who wanted him for his money. But Harper, she had kissed him before she knew he had anything. Before she even knew he was a Fairbanks. Before he had a last name at all.

Plus, he trusted her. She was honest and sweet, and she'd cried for Pup because Jak had loved him. And even more than that, he'd scented her. She was his mate. That was all.

The grandfather stood. "In any case, you must be tired. We can talk about this another time." He looked at the watch on his wrist. "I've got to get going. Let me show you to your room. I took the liberty of having our housekeeper, Bernadette, pick up some clothing and whatnot for you." Jak stood too. He followed him when he left the room, leading him to a staircase so big and wide, he could have lived right there.

His room was down a long hallway with carpet so soft it felt like springtime grass under his feet, even through his shoes. He hopped on it lightly as he walked, and the grand-father gave him a look that made him stop. "I hope you'll be comfortable here, Jak," the grandfather said as Jak followed him into a large room with a huge bed in the middle with not just one blanket, not just three like Harper's bed, but so many it looked like Jak would be sleeping on a cloud.

Jak stepped slowly inside. "The bathroom's behind that door. Your new clothes are in the closet. Just leave your old ones on the floor and the maid will…take care of them." Jak turned back to the grandfather, whose face looked like he'd eaten something bad, but then he changed it to a big smile that only moved his lips. "Welcome home, Jak." Then the grandfather left, closing the door behind him.

Jak took a minute to look around the room and then inside the bathroom, walking to the mirror. He stood in front of it, turning his face slowly one way and then the other. *Did* he look like the man in the photo? His father? He couldn't see it, but the grandfather said he did. Jak's face was dark from the sun—both winter and summer—darker than the grandfather's or Agent Gallagher's. His cheeks were chapped from the wind, and his beard was rough and... uneven. He had cut it using only the feel of his fingers.

Jak had a scar under his cheekbone from where the blond boy had cut him that terrible day.

He looked different than all of them. *Strange. Wild.* And that's because he *was.*

He thought of the things he'd done—some because he'd had no choice, others because he had wanted to *live.* But he could be different now. He could be like them. Harper had accepted his looks and the part of himself he'd shown her, but she never had to know about the way he'd both crawled and killed. Never had to picture him the way he'd been in his lowest times. Never had to know that part of him even existed. Here...at Thornland, he could leave all that behind. Only Driscoll knew about that part of him, and Driscoll was dead. He could be...civilized. He could be a man—*all* man, *only* man—so Harper never caught a glimpse of that beast within him.

He picked up a can of something that said shaving foam, looking at the other bottles on the shelf over the sink, swallowing thickly when he saw the things he'd lived without for so many years. Everything felt...big. *Smelled* big. All of it was *huge,* bigger than he remembered, shinier, *more. Very.* He stepped back into the bedroom, closing that door behind him.

Welcome home, the grandfather had said.

So why did he still feel lost?

CHAPTER THIRTY-NINE

"Come in," Mark called, taking his hands from the keyboard and sitting back in his desk chair. Laurie peeked inside.

"I'm running to the grocery store. Anything specific you want for dinner?" She smiled. "I think we've officially finished off all the holiday leftovers."

Mark chuckled. They'd been eating turkey for breakfast, lunch, and dinner for the last few days—and November had brought its fair share of turkey too—and he had seen about all of that particular bird he wanted to see for a while. "How about steak tonight?"

"Sounds good." She turned to leave, and Mark sat forward.

"Laurie?"

She turned, her expression surprised, questioning.

"Uh." Jesus, had he forgotten how to do this? How to talk to his own wife? They'd had a few conversations over the last few weeks—stilted ones, but those counted too—but they were still out of practice. "Other than Jak's obvious lack of knowledge about common things, what did you think of him?" It'd been several days since Jak and Harper had been to their house, and though they'd recounted the holiday warmly, he hadn't talked to her about the specifics. But now he was officially back to work, and for the last few hours, he'd caught up on emails and wracked his brain about what avenue to follow next. He refused to let these cases grow cold.

Laurie came back into the room hesitantly, as though she was afraid she'd misheard him ask her opinion about a work matter—or, sort of a work matter anyway. She pursed her lips as she thought about his question. "He has a sweetness to him, an…innocence…" She sat in the chair in front of his desk, and seeing her there, that thoughtful look on her face, made his chest constrict. "Although he's clearly all man." She shot him a raised eyebrow look and he chuckled. He figured any woman would have noticed that. "But…I don't know. He has…secrets in his eyes. There's almost something…he *wants* to hide from everyone else. It could be his lack of confidence, but"—she shook her head—"oh, there I go again, offering up my intuition when you're asking for facts."

"No, I was looking for your intuition."

She looked down, a flush coming to her cheeks as she smiled shyly. And at the look of happiness on her face, he swore at himself. *When was the last time you made her look that way?* He couldn't even remember.

She looked up. "And, oh, the way he looks at Harper, Mark. He worships her."

He laced his fingers. "Do you think that's a good thing?"

"You mean do I think he could make her his whole world when he should be focusing on, well, the whole world?"

344

"Yes, exactly."

She looked to the side, thinking again. "Maybe. But I think Harper's an intuitive girl. I think she'll help guide him and step back if that's the case."

"I hope so."

She nodded. "Me too."

For a moment they sat there staring at each other, both smiling, things needing to be said, though Mark wasn't sure where to start, not sure he *wanted* to do this. Not yet. Not now. *Then when?* The ringing of his cell phone saved him from having to answer his own internal questions.

"You get that." Laurie stood, seeming relieved by the interruption too. "I'll be back in an hour."

Mark nodded, reaching for his phone as she slipped out the door. He felt her loss but simultaneously was glad she was gone. Although that'd been a step on both their parts, and Mark was glad for it. "Mark Gallagher."

"Agent Gallagher. This is Kyle Holbrook, returning your call."

Isaac Driscoll's former assistant. Mark was momentarily taken aback by the deep tenor of the man's voice. He sounded much older, but Mark knew from his online portfolio that he was in his thirties.

"Yes, thank you for calling me back, Mr. Holbrook."

"Of course. I would have called you sooner, but I was away for the holidays. This is in reference to Dr. Driscoll?"

"Yes. Unfortunately, I'm investigating a crime. Isaac Driscoll was found murdered. I understand you were his research assistant sixteen years ago."

There was momentary silence on the other end of the line. "Murdered? Jesus. I didn't expect that. I assumed you were calling because he'd done something…weird."

Weird? "Why would you assume that, Mr. Holbrook?"

Another pause. "Well, to be honest, I hadn't thought about Isaac for years, so I had to think back when I heard your message. But he had grown increasingly...odd at the end here. I feel bad saying that now that he's...dead. But, honestly, I was happy to see him go. He was always going on about war and how we were all going to die off because people were selfish and stupid and couldn't think beyond their own needs. But most disturbing of all was he tried to convince me that we should start doing research on *people,* like, not just have them fill out questionnaires or surveys but, like, put them in real-life situations and see how they'd react. But, like everyone knows, that's not how social science works. Or even psychological study. You can't emotionally scar human beings for the sake of research."

Mark nodded, a cold feeling settling in his bones. "Do you have any reason to believe he acted on any of this talk?"

"No. In fact, I thought that was the reason he retired early. He realized the job was causing him to entertain unhealthy ideas. But when I heard you mention his name in the message, I feared he might have gone back to work somewhere else and done something unethical, if not... immoral. I'm glad to hear that's not the case, though I'm sorry to hear something so terrible happened to him."

Mark's mind was racing. "Mr. Holbrook, if I email you a couple of photographs, can you let me know if you've seen either of the people in them?"

"Of course. I have my email open now, if you'd like to send them over."

"Okay, great. It'll just take a second." Mark drafted a quick email and attached the photographs of Jak and Emily Barton saved to his desktop and pressed send.

"Got it," Kyle Holbrook said a second later. There was a pause, and then the man came back on the line. "No, I don't know either of them. I don't suppose you can tell me who they are?"

"The woman was murdered in Helena Springs in a similar manner to Dr. Driscoll."

"Christ. Two murders?" He sounded genuinely shocked, but, of course, Mark was only going by his voice. "This other photograph you sent me, is he a suspect?"

Mark hesitated to call Jak a person of interest, though in actuality he still was. *He has secrets in his eyes.* "He lived near Dr. Driscoll," he answered with a nonanswer.

"Ah. Well, I'm sorry I couldn't be of more help."

"No, you've been a great deal of help. If you think of anything else, please give me a call."

"Absolutely. Good luck, Agent Gallagher."

Mark hung up the phone and then sat staring, unseeing, at his computer for minutes.

He tried to convince me that we should start doing research on people.

Mark had a sinking feeling about what Isaac Driscoll's research had focused on. Or, rather, whom.

To raise him until Dr. Driscoll is ready to train him.

Was Driscoll *studying* Jak? Or just "training" him? Both? To what end? He'd found the notes on the strange animal observations in Driscoll's cabin, but nothing more. He'd go back and look under all the floorboards, in the *rafters,* he decided, before officially clearing it as a crime scene. There *had* to be more. If Jak wasn't mistaken, the man had had cameras set up, for God's sake.

Jak…he has secrets in his eyes.

"What secrets are you still keeping from me, Jak?" Mark

murmured to himself. Did Jak know more about what Driscoll had been doing? Or had he himself done something he was ashamed of?

The picture of the Battle of Thermopylae that he'd printed was on his desk, half obscured under a pile of papers. He picked it up, gazing at it for a few moments, remembering what he'd read about the Spartans.

They'd trained their children to become soldiers; they'd made them endure harsh survival exercises to strengthen them, to discover their worth.

Children...not *child*.

He pictured the cabin where Jak lived, the unused beds. The dormitory setup that only housed one person. If Driscoll had set the place up like that, who else had he intended Jak share it with? And why hadn't they?

Mark dug out the "map" that had been found in Isaac Driscoll's drawer, looking again at the one word printed at the bottom: *Obedient*.

Isaac Driscoll had been fascinated with the Spartans, had possibly been doing his own studies on children, somehow mixing up the ancient rituals with his current project, whatever that might have been. The possibility was almost too sick to consider, too demented to contemplate the details until Mark had more answers. He did another Google search, this time looking for phrases related to Thermopylae and the word *obedient*. After a few minutes, he found it, a monument that was erected to the soldiers who'd died at Thermopylae: *Tell the Spartans, stranger passing by, that here obedient to their laws we lie.*

A monument to the dead. Obedient soldiers. A map that marked the places they lay?

A cold feeling wound its way around Mark's bones. He

could be wrong. It was just a *word*. Just a…hunch based on unconnected pieces to the puzzle that was this case. This was going to be a shot in the dark. Still…he picked up his phone, dialing his office, willing to put his ass on the line. His blood was humming in that way it did when he knew he was onto something. He asked for his boss, and when he picked up, Mark got straight to the point. "I think we need to get some cadaver dogs out to Isaac Driscoll's land."

CHAPTER FORTY

She almost didn't recognize the man in the khakis and the white button-down shirt as he came toward her, but it *was* him. She knew that stride, the way he seemed not to walk but to *prowl*. And then he smiled—that boyish unpracticed grin full of open pleasure—and her heart leaped. She rushed forward, and he did too, taking her in his arms, both of them laughing, as though they hadn't seen each other in months when in fact it had only been three days.

He swung her around once, and she laughed, leaning forward so he could kiss her. He did, both of them sighing as their mouths met. When the kiss ended, he placed her back on the marble floor of the Fairbankses' foyer.

"You shaved," she said, bringing her hand to his smooth cheek, just the bare hint of dark stubble underneath his skin. He was ridiculously handsome, his jawline strong, his cheekbones high and sharp, but a part of her mourned. It was the first outward proof of his *changing*. She knew it was inevitable now that he was living as part of society. She knew it was good and positive. She knew he'd learn and grow and change as he should. As he deserved. She *knew* all those things, but she still felt the loss of the part of him he'd leave behind to become the man he was meant to be.

He laughed, releasing her, his gaze roaming over her as though his eyes were starved for the sight. "You didn't call me," he said, and she saw the hurt in his expression.

She stepped back, frowning. "I did call you. I left four messages."

Jak frowned too, glancing over her shoulder. She looked back. She'd forgotten the butler was still standing near the front door. What was his name again? His gaze was directed elsewhere, but she felt momentarily embarrassed for the public display of affection.

Jak took her hand, leading her out of the foyer. "He's like a weasel," he said under his breath, leaning toward her as he glanced back again. "Always *slinking* through the house." He put the emphasis on the word slinking as though it was a new one and he had looked it up specifically to describe the man. He grinned proudly, and Harper laughed, covering her mouth.

He opened a pair of wide mahogany doors that went all the way to the tall ceiling of the hallway and ushered her inside. She sucked in a delighted breath as she looked around at the impressive library, bookshelves filled with books from floor to ceiling. There was a reading light on in the corner, next to an overstuffed red-velvet chair. "Is that where you've been?" she asked, nodding toward the chair.

"For three days," he answered, letting go of her hand and walking away, his face tipped upward as he looked around at all the books. "Isn't it incredible? It would take me the rest of my life to read all these books."

"Oh, I don't know, it looks like you're making pretty great progress." She looked pointedly at the teetering stacks of books next to the red chair. "Did you really read all of those?"

"Not all. Some I didn't like as much as others. The pile in front are the ones I want to read again."

She laughed. "Well, if you're rereading, it *might* take you the rest of your life to get through this collection."

He smiled happily. "I've learned so many new words, Harper." He looked up, recalling. "*Distressed* and bewildered. Anxious. Accepting. *Indignant.*"

She studied him for a second, noting the words that seemed to matter to him the most were emotions. Her heart flipped. She wondered if he'd tried to describe his own feelings to himself all these years and had come up short. *I love you*, she thought for the hundredth time since she'd first realized it, and, yes, it was as simple as that. She took in his smile as he gazed around. "Do you like it here, Jak?"

He sat on the edge of the table behind him, crossing his arms casually over his chest, his biceps straining the material. In that moment, he looked so unlike the caveman she'd watched in that cell what seemed like a thousand years ago. In that moment, he looked like a…well, like a Fairbanks. He appeared thoughtful and then spoke haltingly. "I like some things… I like the shower." He grinned. "And…I like this room the most. Some of the food is good. But…I'm not sure about the people who live here or…the birds."

"The birds?"

"My grandfather's wife is a bird woman. She has a roomful of hundreds of birds. They're called *tropical,* and they live in cages." He shivered.

"Ah. An aviary." Yes, she could imagine that would be

very strange to him. Strange and possibly sad to see caged birds when he'd only ever known them to fly free. *She* found it sad.

"Aviary," he repeated. "Yes, that's the word." He stood suddenly, moving forward, taking her in his arms, and though he looked like a Fairbanks, she was glad he still moved like a hunter. "I missed you," he growled against her ear, walking her backward until her butt hit the edge of another table. She thrilled at his words, his touch, the hard length of his body pressed to hers. She opened her legs so he could step between them.

"I missed you too. When I didn't hear back from you, I thought maybe…" She turned her eyes from his, vulnerability making her feel shy. He moved his head to the side, lining their eyes up again so she was forced to look at him.

"What?"

"Well, just that you were getting acquainted with your new life…that…"

"That I didn't want to see you?"

She blushed. "Yes." She shook her head, grimacing. "No, I understood." She let out a small uncomfortable laugh. "I mean, you *should* take all the time you need to get acquainted with your new life."

A crease formed between his eyes. "It feels like I have *more* time now. I don't have to hunt for food, and before…I lived by the sun's rising and setting, so I've been very…tired here." His brows dropped as though he wasn't satisfied with the word he'd chosen. "The days feel…strange. But, Harper, I *want* you to be part of my days. *All* of my days. Do you want me to be part of yours?"

"Yes," she answered, a catch in her voice.

He smiled, and she guessed that was that. He leaned

forward again, rubbing his lips on her throat, inhaling her scent. She leaned her head back, offering him as much access as he needed. "I need to ask who to get my messages from," he murmured. "So I don't miss one of yours again."

"Mm," she hummed. "I'm glad I got up the nerve to stop by."

"Me too," he whispered back, licking slowly up her neck, causing her to gasp, a surge of moisture accompanying a deep throb between her legs. She clawed lightly at his back, and he emitted a low growl in his throat. Thrill and fear coursed through her as they seemed to do when he did something decidedly...animalistic. Another throb made her moan.

"Jak," she sighed.

"You make me feel exultant," he breathed against her neck.

She let out a small laugh that was part whimper as he nipped at her skin. "Exultant?"

"Mm," he hummed, bringing his head up and meeting her eyes, a smile teasing his lips. "It means happy but *more*. I feel exultant when I'm with you."

Oh, God, he was sweet. And sexy. And...yes, she felt exultant too.

He brought his mouth to hers, kissing her deeply, thoroughly, the world fading away around her. He tasted like cinnamon and smelled like something new...a soap or an aftershave, a product he hadn't had before. It was subtle, and it smelled good, but she remembered the heavenly night they'd spent in her bed, the way his masculine scent had still been on her skin the next morning—clean male, sex...*him*. She knew a person could hardly go through life not smelling like something other than themselves—soap, laundry detergent—but she'd miss the way he smelled before a million products got a hold of him.

"I missed kissing you," he said, trailing his lips down her throat again. "I missed being inside you, making love. I want to be inside you now." He took her hand and led it to his erection, hard, straining the material of his pants.

A flush of heat blossomed under her skin. *Oh, yes.* She wanted him too. "We can't, Jak," she moaned. "Not here."

"Why not? No one will come in here."

She laughed, and it ended in a moan as he moved his hips, rubbing his erection between her open legs. Her hardened nipples grazed his chest and lightning arced downward to the place that was aching for him to fill. "Because it's your grandfather's library. It's just…it's not…"

He pulled back, looking at her. "People only make love in beds?" he asked, looking truly interested, perhaps a little outraged. It made her want to giggle.

"Well…no, not only, but…usually. *Normally.* I mean, people can do it wherever they want except in public. Even then…some people do, just discreetly. They, er, enjoy the thrill of, oh, being caught."

He was staring at her with great interest now. His cheeks were flushed the way they got when he was aroused. "The thrill?"

"Well, some people find thrill in that."

"Do *you* find…thrill in that?"

She laughed and shook her head. "No, not generally. Although, you know, don't knock it 'til you've tried it and all that."

"Don't knock it 'til you've tried it," he repeated, his brow wrinkling. God, he was so adorably *sexy.* "I'll try anything with you, Harper."

She groaned, taking his face in her hands and bringing his lips back to hers. He used his tongue to probe slowly inside her mouth, mimicking the same movement he was making with his hips, driving her crazy, driving her over—

"Ahem."

Harper let out a surprised gasp, sitting straight up, Jak jolting in front of her. She scooted quickly off the table, turning, straightening her shirt, and quickly smoothing her hair.

Jak's grandfather was standing in the doorway, staring at them with thin-lipped disapproval. "Sir," she said too quickly, too breathlessly. "Uh, hello, Mr. Fairbanks, sir, good to see you."

He gave her a cursory glance, his eyes doing a quick once-over of them both. She refused to look down at Jak, though she grimaced internally, knowing exactly what Jak looked like at the front of his previously pressed khakis.

Embarrassing didn't begin to cover it.

"Dinner's almost ready," his grandfather said. "The whole family's here. I wanted to make sure you joined us, Jak."

Harper didn't miss the way he pointedly said Jak's name but left her out. "Oh, well, I should go—"

"Harper will stay," he said, not breaking eye contact with his grandfather. Jak took her hand. For a tense moment, they stared at each other. Was she missing something? She realized this was an awkward situation, but Jak's grandfather was only making it ten times worse. Jak leaned forward, sniffing the air. "What is that?" he asked, a strange tone to his voice.

Jak's grandfather brushed at the front of his shirt, looking suddenly chastised for some reason. "Er, cigar smoke. Bad habit. I promised Loni I'd quit." He looked at Harper, giving her a slight smile. "Forgive my rudeness. I was surprised to find Jak had company. Of course, you may join us for dinner."

"Oh. Um—" Jak squeezed her hand, and she gave him a quick glance, understanding that he was telling her he wanted her there, not to decline dinner. *Please,* his eyes seemed to say. "Thank you for the dinner invitation. I'd love to join you."

He smiled in a way that looked halfway genuine. "Good. I'll see you both in the dining room in five minutes." With that, he turned, exiting the room, and Harper sunk back to the table, putting her face in her hands. "Ugh," she said, lifting her gaze to Jak. "I just made an awful impression, didn't I?"

His face did that thoughtful thing it did for a moment as he worked out a word. *Impression,* she imagined, and then he shook his head slowly. "The...*my* grandfather..." He looked behind her, seeming to be choosing the right words. "I think he was a different person before...my father died. A better person."

"What makes you think that?"

"His smile in the pictures here...the ones before and the ones...after. It's different."

She studied him. Trusted his judgment. He was perceptive. It made her feel a form of...honor that he wanted her in his life. He'd chosen her. Then again, it wasn't as though he had an assortment of choices. *Stop it, Harper.* She had this habit of convincing herself people only chose her out of default. Maybe that particular hurt had come from very real circumstances, but at some point, she had to find her own value and believe in it. Might as well be now.

She took his hand. "Come on. Introduce me to your new family."

As they drew nearer to the dining room, she heard voices, glasses clinking, and a woman's laugh. There was a powder room to the right, and Harper, feeling a burst of nerves, stopped. "I'm just going to freshen up and I'll meet you in there. Go on without me." She tilted her head toward the room beyond.

"Okay," Jak said, bending forward and kissing her quickly on the lips. "Hurry," he mouthed, giving her a wide-eyed stare and tilting his head toward the room where the others waited. She put her hand over her mouth so as not to laugh out loud, and his lip twitched too before he turned and headed into the dining room.

She took a minute to freshen up and take a few deep breaths and then walked quietly in the direction of the dining room. As she approached, she heard Mr. Fairbanks's voice saying her name and came to a halt. He was directly on the other side of the doorway and was saying something about her as she noticed clinking ice dropping into a glass. "I know you're new to civilized life, Jak, but we don't rut like animals," he murmured, obviously trying to keep his voice low. Harper's heart sank. *Oh God.* It was as bad as she thought it was. Shame washed through her.

"I wasn't rutting" came Jak's voice, matter-of-factly. "I was making love."

Harper grimaced while simultaneously having the impulse to laugh out loud. *Gah. Jak.* She pressed her lips together, suppressing a groan. He was so sweet and so damned unknowingly inappropriate sometimes.

Mr. Fairbanks choked on what sounded like a sip of his beverage, a short laugh emerging before he cleared his throat. "Be that as it, er, may, you have more important things to be focusing on right now." He paused, and Harper thought it sounded like he took a drink, the ice clinking in his glass. "I saw the pile of books in the library. Planning on reading them?"

"I already did read them."

There was a beat of silence—*surprise?*—and then Mr. Fairbanks said, "Very impressive. Good." She heard what sounded like a shoulder pat. "We'll get you up to speed yet, son. You'll be one of us in no time."

Harper backed up very softly and then made sure her footsteps sounded on the marble floor as she entered the dining room, a bright smile on her face.

Jak came toward her immediately, clasping her hand and kissing her cheek. She smiled up at him. "Harper," Mr. Fairbanks said in greeting.

"Sir, thank you again for having me."

"You're welcome. May I offer you a drink?" He nodded over his shoulder to the bar cart that he had obviously been standing at when Harper overheard him.

"No, thank you. Just water with dinner is fine."

The people standing in the opposite corner of the room approached. An older woman with long blond hair and a yellow dress, as beautiful and coiffed a person as Harper had ever seen, was in the lead. Jak's grandfather's wife, Jak's step-grandmother, she guessed. The woman held out her perfectly manicured hand. "I'm Loni Fairbanks. You must be Harper."

"Yes, ma'am." She shook her hand. The woman had a grip like an injured bird. "It's so nice to meet you. Thank you for having me to dinner."

"Oh, of course. I think it's so nice that Jak has a little friend."

Little friend?

She glanced at Jak, and Jak was looking at her with an expression that seemed to be half hostility and half confusion. Jak obviously was leery of the "bird woman." As a matter of fact, she *looked* like a tropical bird. Colorful and sharp. Beautiful, but might peck your eyes out if given the chance.

A second woman approached. She was about Harper's age with blond hair to her shoulders and Loni's same delicately pointy features. She smiled tightly at Harper, her eyes doing a once-over that made Harper want to fidget and explain why she was dressed so casually. *I didn't expect to stay for dinner. I didn't dress for what is obviously a dressier occasion than at most people's homes.* She thought briefly of the warm welcome they'd both received from the Gallaghers, the immediate feeling of inclusion, and felt a pang within. *I wish we were there now. Not here, with these people who obviously see me as an unwelcome outsider.*

"I'm Gabi." She held out her hand and gave Harper the same limp shake her mother had, offering her a phony-looking smile that was simultaneously bored.

"Harper," she said. The young woman stepped away, her smile having disappeared as quickly as it'd come, her face settling into an expression of supreme apathy.

"Well, hi there." A young man stepped forward, holding out his hand to Harper. She took it. Finally, someone who didn't seem afraid to touch her. He gripped her hand tightly in his, smiling, his teeth large and bright white. "I'm Brett." His eyes did a slow appreciative sweep of her that made Harper want to squirm.

"Hi. I'm Harper Ward. It's nice to meet you."

"Brett and Gabi are Loni's children, and Brett works for me at Fairbanks Lumber," Mr. Fairbanks said. "You're all about the same age, I believe. I've been trying to enlist Brett and Gabi to teach Jak what he needs to know about technology. Lord knows I'm pitifully inadequate when it comes to any of these apps the kids are using." He smiled at Brett and Gabi, and Gabi crossed her arms and rolled her eyes dramatically. *Wow.* Was she really Harper's age? She seemed petty, more like a twelve-year-old. Then again, Harper had probably come across as the town floozy. Everyone deserved a second chance, right? "I'd be happy to teach Jak the basics. I'm not on a lot of social media, but I can show him how it works." She smiled at Jak, and he looked relieved, taking her hand in his again. "He...probably needs a cell phone though," she said, thinking as much of him as of herself and how she'd felt like a stalker, calling him repeatedly over the last few days with no answer.

"Of course." Mr. Fairbanks grimaced. "I can't believe I let that slip my mind. Jak, my secretary will set you up with a cell phone."

Harper squeezed his hand again, letting go.

A woman in a black-and-white uniform poked her head in the door, telling them dinner was ready.

"Oh good. I'm starved," Mrs. Fairbanks purred. But her eyes were on Jak, and she licked her lips. Had she...had she *meant* that the way it seemed? Harper gave herself an internal head shake. *Surely not.*

"Allow me," Brett said, taking Harper's arm before she could protest. He led her to the table, pulling out her chair and immediately taking the one next to her. The one to her right was the head of the table and she looked back over her shoulder, flustered. Jak's jaw was tight as he moved around the table, taking the seat across from her. She shot him a helpless smile.

Mr. Fairbanks took a seat at the head of the table, Mrs. Fairbanks next to Jak, and Gabi next to her mother.

The first course was brought out, and the chitchat centered around the food. Harper took a spoonful of the rich tomato bisque, letting out an appreciative moan as the creamy soup hit her tongue. "Oh my gosh, that's good."

Brett leaned toward her, whispering so only she could hear. "I like the way you sound when you moan."

Wait, what? Heat rushed to Harper's face as she tried to work out what he'd said. She had to have misheard him. She gave him a shocked glance, and he smirked at her, tilting his chin. She hadn't misheard him. Good lord, who *were* these people?

You'll be one of us in no time.

God, please no.

She looked across the table to see Jak glaring coldly at Brett. Her skin prickled. A low growl emitted from Jak's throat, and his fingernails scraped across the wood table next to his bowl.

"Did he just...growl?" Gabi asked loudly and incredulously, a small laugh bubbling from her mouth. "Oh my God, he *did*. He *growled*."

"He sure *did,* didn't he?" Mrs. Fairbanks purred, unmistakably appreciative.

Harper didn't know whether to laugh or cry. She'd never met people with such a lack of class. And she'd grown up in the social services system. These were *Fairbankses*, for heaven's sake. Was this all a joke? Would they all start laughing any minute?

Brett's eyes widened as he took in Jak's angry expression, and he scooted away from Harper, suddenly obsessed with his soup.

"I, uh…so…Mr. Fairbanks, that painting is beautiful," Harper said, nodding at the oil painting of a field of flowers hanging over the buffet. "The ones in the hallway are by the same artist, aren't they?"

"You have a good eye," he said, giving her an appraising look. "Yes, Jak's grandmother painted those. She was an amazing talent." True sadness passed over his expression, and Harper thought back to what Jak had said about him being a better man…before his loss. But even so, why bring a group of barracudas into your home, she wondered, glancing at Loni, Gabi, and Brett.

"She was," Jak said, looking back at the painting, apparently having moved on from Brett and his lecherous comments. Harper breathed an internal sigh of relief. "She got the flowers just right. The way the sunlight hits them that way right before it goes down for the night." He lowered his eyes, appearing shy, uncertain about his comment.

"Well, nature boy would know," Gabi muttered, taking a bored sip of her water.

Anger gripped Harper, her hand tightening around her napkin. "Yes. He *would* know. He knows things none of us could learn if we studied every textbook ever written. He's a nature *expert,* and his knowledge is something we should all revere. I know I do." She raised her water glass to Jak, his smile shy but happy, his eyes wide.

"Hear hear to that," Mr. Fairbanks said, raising his own glass, a look Harper swore was respect in his gaze as she met his eyes.

"So, Harper, what is it *you* do, exactly?" Mrs. Fairbanks asked, abandoning her spoon in her still-full soup bowl. Hadn't she said she was starving?

Harper set down the roll she'd been about to slather

with butter. "I started my own company several years ago. I do nature tours, take tourists out to camp or to hunt or sometimes just for the day."

"I...see," Mrs. Fairbanks said, looking as though Harper had just told her she cleaned porta-potties for a living.

"Started your own company, did you? And so young. Very enterprising," Mr. Fairbanks said, and he seemed genuinely impressed. "Do you enjoy it?"

She smiled. "I do. But I don't believe I want to do it forever. I plan to start classes in Missoula soon."

Mr. Fairbanks gave her another nod and then picked up his glass once more, smiling around the table. "Well, let me propose a toast. To new endeavors"—he turned his eyes to Harper and smiled—"and to having my grandson back." He appeared to get choked up for a moment but just as quickly recovered. "It's been too long since a Fairbanks son has sat at the family table."

Everyone raised their glasses, Brett scowling, Gabi rolling her eyes again, and Loni's gaze glued to Jak. Harper suddenly wished she'd asked for something stronger than water.

The rest of the dinner went by relatively quickly, everyone seeming eager to get away. At least the food was incredible, though Jak seemed suspicious of it all and Mrs. Fairbanks pushed hers around her plate.

Harper noticed Jak watching the food being cleared, and as the woman picking up the mostly full dishes passed by, he stopped her, asking softly, "What do you do with the food?"

She looked down. "The food, sir?"

Jak leaned back, speaking more quietly. "The food we don't eat."

"We..." The woman glanced around helplessly, but no

one but Harper was paying attention to the exchange. "We throw it away, sir."

"Oh." Jak turned, the expression on his face embarrassed and dejected. He swallowed, and Harper's heart ached. She felt ashamed for every extra bite of food she herself had thrown in the garbage. How often had he starved? How often had he sat somewhere in the forest, hungry and alone? To see the excess here—the thoughtless waste—must be so incredibly distressing.

Finally, Mr. Fairbanks stood. "Thank you for a lovely meal, everyone. I have some work to get back to, but, Harper, it was nice to have you join us."

"Thank you, Mr. Fairbanks," she said as he left the table.

Jak came around and took her hand, shooting a threatening look at Brett, who had already stood and was moving away. She took Jak's hand eagerly and let him lead her from the dinner table.

They both seemed to breathe a mutual sigh of relief as they walked quickly down the hall and into the foyer. Nigel appeared as if out of nowhere, and they both startled, covering their mouths with their hands as he let them out the door. They both withheld their laughter until the door closed behind them, and then their laughter exploded, both fast-walking away from the house as they tried in vain to keep their hilarity muffled.

Jak swung her under the garage door awning on the other side of the house, and they gave in to their laughter. Harper had needed the release and felt a hundred times more relaxed once her giggles had subsided. It had all been so *ridiculous*.

They were awful. With maybe the exception of Jak's grandfather. But even he was obviously judgmental, only not where it counted. Why hadn't he turned that sharp-eyed judgment on Loni and her bratty, insufferable children? Still…they were Jak's family. He needed them if he was going to thrive in his new life. At the very least, he needed what they could provide for him. The Fairbanks name would open any number of doors that would never open for mere mortals—like her.

"What do you think of them?" Jak asked once their bout of laughter had completely faded away. "Do you…enjoy their company?"

She smiled. "They're not the Gallaghers." She reached up, moving a lock of hair off his forehead. "But they're your family. Your grandfather cares about your well-being, I can tell. He wants to help you adapt. To learn. To find success. I think you should let him."

"You do?"

She nodded.

"Okay." He laced his fingers with hers. "When can I be alone with you?" he whispered close to her ear, and she shivered. "I want it to be now."

She groaned. "I know. Me too. But, I don't want to be a point of contention between you and your grandfather." His brows did that up-and-down movement that meant he was figuring out a word, and she smiled with affection, standing on her tiptoes and kissing him. "I'll pick you up tomorrow and show you a little more of Missoula. We'll go to my place for a while afterward." She smiled at him suggestively.

"It won't be enough. I want the whole night."

She laughed. "Okay, greedy. But we'll make do with what we have for now. You can't be spending every waking hour with me. You still have about ten thousand books to get through." She winked, and he smiled, but looked disappointed. *This separation is hard for me too, Jak.*

He sighed. "Okay. Someday I'm going to have a house of my own, and you're going to live there with me and never spend another night alone."

"Oh, Jak," she said, before kissing him, breathing him in. His innocent simplicity. He wanted that so much right now. But she wondered again how his changing, his merging and blending with society at large would alter who he was and what he wanted. And she knew it wasn't fair of her not to let him go if, ultimately, him changing meant leaving her behind.

CHAPTER FORTY-ONE

The snow had melted, the earth soft and spongy beneath her feet. In the distance, she heard the occasional yap of a dog as she and Agent Gallagher made their way through the wooded area.

She'd been surprised when he'd called her that morning, asking for a ride to Isaac Driscoll's place, even though the roads were markedly better than they'd been the week before. Harper had assumed her less-than-prestigious police consultant career had officially come to an end. But Agent Gallagher had told her he not only needed a ride but he could also use her help "poking around in the woods," as he put it.

Harper had suggested that Jak come along and help too—or even instead of her. After all, no one knew those particular woods better than he did. But Agent Gallagher had said no, and she thought he'd acted cagey about it, and so there she was, stepping over a decayed log as she studied the piece of paper Isaac Driscoll had drawn and apparently kept in his bedside drawer.

"Boss?" came a voice from behind them.

"Yes," Agent Gallagher called, moving past her to the edge of the woods where the other man stood. She recognized him as one of the men who'd been holding a dog when they'd arrived half an hour before.

Harper looked away, studying the map again. Agent Gallagher had told her the word at the bottom—*obedient*—had something to do with the Spartans. Apparently, Driscoll was obsessed with them. Harper released a frustrated breath. Without any specific starting point, she had no idea what to look for. There was nothing that looked like anything she'd seen on a traditional map before.

"Two bodies, sir," the man's voice carried to her. She froze, her eyes widening. *Two bodies?*

She heard Agent Gallagher blow out a slow breath. "Children?" he asked, and there was something in his voice that made her think he already knew the answer.

"Appears so, yes. One very young, the other older. The lab will tell us more."

"Okay. Thank you, David. Did the dogs hit on anything else?"

"Not yet. We're going to widen the search, come back tomorrow if necessary."

"Thank you. Let me know right away if you find anything else."

"Will do."

Harper heard the man named David walking away, heard Agent Gallagher approach her from behind, and turned slowly to meet his eyes. He must have seen by her face that she'd overheard their conversation because he blew out a breath and said, almost to himself, "I hoped I wasn't right."

"Two children?" Harper whispered, the horror of that

coursing through her. There were two *children* buried out there. *Whose* children?

Agent Gallagher nodded solemnly.

"They found two," Harper said. "Do you...do you think this third marker is another one?" And if he did, why did he have *her* out there? The dogs seemed to be up to the task.

"I don't know. I hope not. There are two red ones and one black." If the red ones are the location of the two bodies, then the black one might be something different. "This wavy line here that looks like a stream or a river. Think we can find it now that some of the snow is gone?"

She swallowed, gathering her strength, feeling a... responsibility to those children. If there was something out there that would provide a clue how to get them back home to those they belonged to, then she would do anything she could to help.

She was supposed to pick Jak up in a little while, and as far as she knew, he didn't yet have a phone, nor would she necessarily get service out there anyway, but...he would understand. When she told him what she'd been doing, he would understand her delay.

"Can we go back out and see the location of the graves?" she asked. She hated even contemplating the word *graves*, but what else could she say?

Agent Gallagher nodded, and they exited the heavily wooded area, walking to the back of Driscoll's house. The dog handlers had moved farther away, letting the dogs lead the way apparently, and from where she and Mark stood, she could see the locations of the two areas that had been dug up, men and women in white suits and masks bent over both spots. A wash of sadness moved through Harper, and she did her best to ignore it. For now. She knew the value—the relief—of finally having answers, and two families were going to get those now. She would focus on that while she was out there. She could cry for those children later.

No wonder Jak had hated Driscoll, gotten a bad feeling from him. The things he'd been doing and why...she shivered. It was unthinkable. *Monstrous.*

And for the first time, she wondered if Jak wasn't telling the whole truth about his relationship with Driscoll, wondered if he'd left some of the story out. Wondered if he'd not only been lied to but *used* in some more heinous way he was too ashamed to talk about.

Oh, Jak.

She held up the map, lining up the two graves. They did seem to be positioned in the same way the two red boxes were drawn on the map. Her gaze moved to the place beyond, the place where the dogs were now searching.

"There's a river in that direction and a few small streams as well," she told Agent Gallagher. *If* the wavy line in fact indicated water. She thought about it for a minute. "I could take you to each of them, but they're miles away. Whatever Driscoll marked could be anywhere. Although"—she studied the map again for a second—"the marker is drawn right on the edge of the wavy line." Not that anything was to scale. Harper blew out a breath. This felt like hunting for a needle in a haystack.

"I know," he said. "It's frustrating. But we might have a couple of starting points now, and it's more than we had. I'll tell the searchers we're taking the truck to drive closer to those rivers."

She nodded. They couldn't drive straight to any of those bodies of water. But they could get closer and then walk. A few times she'd taken fishermen to one of those streams that had an excellent fishing hole. "I'll wait here."

He walked away, stepping carefully over the soggy ground. Harper looked at the map again, wondering why she was even bothering. It was so simply drawn, with four shapes and a word. She already had it memorized.

Agent Gallagher was talking to one of the men now, and she looked briefly up at the blue sky, filled with fluffy white clouds, soaking in the peace of the place. Terrible things had happened there, but those terrible things had all been done by humans. She wished it would be left to the animals—and only the animals—once more.

As she turned in the direction of Jak's old cabin, the one she'd barged into not once but twice, a small smile curved her lips. She recalled sitting at his table, their heads bent close together, reading with him, kissing him... The memory brought a twinge of melancholy. That wonderful simplicity would never be fully recaptured.

As she began turning back in the direction of the graves and Agent Gallagher, her gaze snagged on the mountains, low-lying clouds softening their peaks, making them look more like a wavy line in the sky than sharp spikes. She turned back. *What if...* She held up the map. The graves—the two markers—were behind her now, but what if the wavy lines indicated the mountains instead of any number of various water sources in the opposite direction?

The same problem remained though. The mountains were far off in the distance—miles—the third marker could be anywhere between the graves and the base.

Unless... Her eyes moved from the exact wave of the lines to the mostly cloud-obscured peaks. They matched in a *very* simplistic way. Because it was the most simplistically drawn map possible. So, with that in mind, what if the square drawn underneath the mountain simply indicated a visual sense of where the mountains touched the earth from exactly where she was standing?

Agent Gallagher was still talking with the other men, so she walked around Driscoll's house, heading toward the copse of trees in front of her, focused on that dark area. A good hiding spot for…anything really. But what? If the two red markers had indicated the bodies of dead children, what other horrors might be lurking out there? She decided to turn back. She'd wait for Agent Gallagher.

Just as she began to turn, the sun hit the side of the forest, and she spotted a large grouping of rocks beyond a couple of sparse trees. She walked toward it, entering the trees, her eyes adjusting to the dim light. She'd seen other areas like this, other…*yes*. It was an old mine shaft, a door set in the side of the rock. Her heart started hammering. Was *this* what Isaac Driscoll had marked? And why?

She pulled on the door, expecting it to be locked, but with a rusty squeak, it opened, light flooding the space. She leaned inside, the air colder in there, the smell metallic and dank. Her heart rate increasing, she turned on her phone's flashlight and shone it into the room.

She sucked in a breath. The small room, an entrance to a deeper portion of the mine at the far side blocked off, had a table and a monitor and pictures tacked up to every portion of the walls.

Jak.

In *all of them*.

Oh God.

What is this?

Harper swallowed, cold dread seeping through her.

Several kerosene lanterns hung from rafters, and she

stepped slowly toward the closest one, switching it on, brightening the space. She felt like she was in a dream, a nightmare, as she looked from one photo to another, her throat closing.

One was of Jak—for it had to be him, all of them seemed to be—as a small child, tears streaked down his dirty face, sitting on the snowy riverbank, his arms wrapped around his skinny legs. He was shivering. She could *tell* just by looking at it, and her heart cried out. She couldn't save him. He'd already saved himself. Had no choice even though a man had sat photographing his misery, not lifting a hand. The evil nearly brought her to her knees. *What sort of person could do this? How?*

There were other photos, hundreds, pictures of Jak biting into a bloody, fur-covered rabbit, his face gaunt, no more than ten. She cringed, looking away. How hungry, how *desperate,* had he been to bite into a fur-covered animal?

On the back wall were a series of pictures, and she stopped in front of them. Hot tears were streaking down her cheeks. Her heart leapt with horror when she saw that Jak wasn't alone in this series of photos. He was fighting a blond boy, who was skinny and obviously starving, sickly, and... deranged looking. There was a dead deer in the middle of them, and she wondered if that's why they had battled. Each photo was worse than the one before it, each scene like a movie she wanted to look away from but could not. And the end...she sobbed when she looked upon the photo of Jak, a wolf—*was it his beloved Pup?*—over his shoulder, the deer being dragged behind him, the dead boy lying in a pool of blood in the snow. The expression on Jak's face...utter devastation.

Oh God. It was too awful to bear. Had Jak killed the two children in those graves? Another sob came up her throat, and now she was outright crying.

She turned away, in a fog, spotting a bow and arrows leaning against the wall in the corner, one arrow clearly missing from its spot. She shook her head. *Too much, too much.* This was Driscoll's secret place. Those were *Driscoll's* bow and arrows. Had Driscoll killed the woman? Jak's mother? Her mind spun.

There was a laptop on the desk, but, of course, the battery was dead. She wondered what horrors were contained on that small device and shuddered. A recorder lay next to the laptop, and she pressed the button, expecting that to be dead too, and startled when a man's voice began speaking.

"The possum is out today, crying in the snow, snot all over his face, eating clumps of grass and then throwing them up." Her chest tightened with sorrow. She pressed fast-forward, in a daze, a horror-filled daze. "The young buck seems to have made an appearance, gaining confidence yet still wary. He was wearing a new coat today. He's learning. Adapting. Although I still see the possum far more than I'd like."

Her finger pressed fast-forward again.

"That's it. There's the wolf," the man's voice said excitedly, and Harper could only imagine what he was watching. She clenched her eyes shut. "There's the Spartan. The soldier. The beast of all beasts." He whooped softly, and she could *hear* the pride contained in that sound. It disgusted her.

She pressed stop on the recorder, unable to hear anymore. Her heart was shattered. How had Jak *survived* this? How was he so gentle and warm and loving...despite this? He was no "savage." Far from it. *He* was the one who had been savaged by cruelty and evil.

When Agent Gallagher stepped inside, his eyes darting around, his face etched in shock, she was sobbing.

CHAPTER FORTY-TWO

Jak stepped onto Driscoll's porch, his heart beating quickly like the flutter-fast wings of a hummingbird. He swung his bow and arrows higher up on his shoulder. *I'm going to kill him.* His knock echoed, ringing into the snowy air, wind snatching it up and tossing it away. But Driscoll's car was there, and there were footprints going up his steps. He tried the doorknob, and it turned in his gloved hand. Surprise made him pause.

Yes, he was going to kill Driscoll. But first, he needed answers. He needed to know why Driscoll had lied to him about the war. Why he'd given him a house and kept him out there in the faraway wilderness, alone for all his life.

Why he'd killed Pup. Taken his only friend from him. His throat felt tight. He pulled in a quick breath.

If Driscoll wasn't home, he'd wait for him. The door creaked as it opened, and the whispers hummed inside him. He took off his flat shoes and left them by the door. His hair stood up, and he knew something was wrong...different.

He sniffed the air and smelled...*blood. Fear. Coming death.* And below that, the scent of a strange campfire, something Driscoll had burned using wood Jak had never smelled before. *Strong. Ashy.*

His ears pricked up, and he listened for a minute before stepping forward, into the almost-dark room.

The smell of blood grew stronger, and he pressed himself against the wall, following it, crouching, going up on his toes, light-footed.

He heard a groan from the bedroom and moved toward it. Slow. Slow. *Silent.* The way he did when he moved through the forest, a deer in his sight, the arrow drawn back in his hand. He peeked around the corner, his heart slamming between his ribs, his eyes trying to understand what he saw.

Driscoll was pressed to the wall, an arrow through his chest, a lake of blood at his feet. Jak stepped into the doorway, and Driscoll's head lifted. "Jak," he croaked. "Help me."

He took another step inside the room, looking around for an enemy. "Who did this?"

"I don't know. I didn't know him...tall...man." His breath made a high groaning sound, and his face screwed up.

"You lied to me," Jak said. "You betrayed me."

Driscoll ignored him. "Please. Help me. You can't move me from this wall...will make it...worse for me. Just...my phone." Jak looked at the dresser, where he saw the small black thing Driscoll wanted him to hand to him. *Why should I help this man?* He looked back at Driscoll, who was watching him. Anger came into his eyes, and they bugged from his head like a green slimy frog. "If you don't help me, they'll lock you in a cell! In a cage like an animal! You *killed*, Jak. They won't understand. And if you let me die, it will be even worse for you."

378

Jak's head pounded, hatred for the man flaming like fire. He should walk out. He should let him die. He had planned to kill him himself. He was a liar and a cheat. *He* was one of the enemies. He'd killed Pup, and Jak wanted *vengeance*.

Driscoll's shoulders drooped. He made a strange jerky move, and blood came from his mouth "Please…my phone. I'm sorry you suffered just…hand me my phone."

Jak paused for another minute, the whispers growing loud within him, drowning out his hate even though he tried to hold it tight. The woman's voice rose up, above the whispers. *Let it go*. He knew her…her words…the things she would say to him. He heard her in his mind. *Let it go*.

On legs that didn't feel like his own, he walked to the dresser, picking up the object and moving slowly toward Driscoll, stepping around the puddle of blood and holding the phone out to him. He took it, pressing on it for a second. Jak stepped back, and Driscoll looked up, their eyes meeting for a moment. More blood came from Driscoll's mouth. His eyes grew soft. "To see you," he whispered, "a wolf over your shoulder and…dragging a deer behind you, the body of your enemy lying dead in the snow." More blood. A gurgle as if a river flowed in his chest, moving, bubbling. "It was a *marvel*. And only twelve years old." He laughed, and blood splattered. Red rained on his shirt. "I knew…then. *That* moment…you were a *warrior* of another era, worthy… of the Spartans. You…surpassed…all…" He straightened his neck, seeming to use the last of his strength. He brought his hand to his forehead and made a salute to Jak. Then a whistle sound came from his mouth, and his breath halted as his head dropped, the phone in his other hand splashing into the blood on the floor.

Jak stood there for a minute, the whispers quieting,

drifting away. Jak was alone. He turned, walking from the room, closing the front door behind him.

It was snowing. Soft, fluffy flakes. He put on his flat shoes and walked toward the trees on the other side of Driscoll's house. More footsteps in the snow, ones that went to the side window and disappeared. Jak's heart beat quickly. The snow was already filling them in. Soon they'd be gone. Jak raised his head and sniffed the air. The snow would stop soon, though there was more, high in the sky. But sometime in the near faraway, deep beneath the frozen earth, spring would begin to stir.

CHAPTER FORTY-THREE

Where is she? Jak's heart thumped nervously as he looked out the window for the hundredth time, hoping to see her truck pulling through the gate, but the gate was still closed.

He walked down the stairs and into the foyer where Nigel appeared as Jak had hoped he would, though he still couldn't figure out how he *did* that. Jak would say he was like a wolf and could smell people as they got near, but the man didn't have the feel of a wolf. He definitely had the feel of something slinkier. "Did I miss any calls?"

He cleared his throat. "No, sir. Not in the last twenty minutes."

He narrowed his eyes, sensing the man was using...sarcasm. He'd learned that word today from one of his books, learned the meaning. But his books hadn't said that some people used sarcasm to make people feel bad about themselves. *Slinky.*

He leaned closer, wrinkling his nose. He *smelled* slinky too. Oily. "How do you see people before they come into a room?"

Nigel lifted his nose like he was smelling something but didn't inhale. "The cameras, sir."

Cameras. Jak's heart dropped to his feet. "Cameras?"

"Yes, sir. There are cameras in the rooms, so the staff knows where the family may need service."

A buzzing had started in Jak's ears, like the cicadas—he'd learned the name of those insects that buzzed and sang in the trees, filling the forest with their noise, but only every seventeen years. They'd only come out once, but Jak remembered them—the whole forest had vibrated from their mating.

Jak turned from Nigel, walking toward the library, glancing up now and again, trying to spot the cameras.

He was being watched. Again.

He closed the large door behind him, standing against it for a minute as he fought to catch his breath. He felt...he didn't know the word. There were still so many words he didn't know. He walked to the table, picking up the dictionary and leafing through it like he might stumble upon the right word to tell him how he was feeling.

The door clicked. He smelled her before he saw her. The bird woman. She smiled at him and closed the door behind her.

"Jak," she purred. She was always purring, like a cat. But cats hated birds. Maybe that's why she liked to hear them cry. She came toward him, and he wanted to back away but held his ground, that slight cicada buzzing growing louder in his ears again.

She ran her bird talons down his chest, licking her lips and looking up at him. "Oh, the things I could teach you, Jak." She unbuttoned the top button of her shirt, then the second.

He understood what she wanted. She was going to get

382

naked like the redheaded woman and offer her body to Jak, though he'd done nothing to try to earn it. He stepped away, and her hand dropped from his chest. "I have a woman."

She laughed, but it wasn't like a laugh. More like the sound a coyote made right before it attacked something. Her tongue clicked, and she moved closer again. "Big man like you?" She looked down, her eyes stopping between his legs and then raising to his face. "One woman can't be enough."

"You're wrong."

"So sweet," she purred. "But I wouldn't stop you like she did. I'd let you do whatever you wanted. Would you like that? Hmm?" She reached down, rubbing her hand over his manhood, grasping him. He hissed with surprise.

I wouldn't stop you like she did.

She'd *watched* them? Him and Harper. Right there. He looked up, searching for the camera and spotting it in the far corner of the ceiling. His blood boiled, and a groan came up his throat. He'd felt *safe* there.

"Oh yess," she purred, rubbing him harder.

He took her by her arms and pushed her away. She stumbled backward, catching herself. "Don't ever touch me again," he growled.

Her eyes filled with anger, her cheeks getting red. She stepped toward him, her mouth opening to speak when a knock came at the door.

"Come in," Jak called, trying to cool the hot anger in his blood, the feeling of...*betrayal*. He took a deep breath, letting it flow through his body.

The door opened, and Nigel entered. "Agent Gallagher is here to see you, sir."

Jak didn't look at the cat-pretend-bird lady as he said, "Tell him I'm in here."

Out of the corner of his eye, he saw her lift her shoulders, and then her back was to him as she walked out. The room still held her smell. It made him feel…disgust.

Agent Gallagher entered and Jak sunk onto the edge of the table, letting it hold his weight for a moment. "Jak," he said, a strange look on his face. A mixture of sadness and…something else.

He straightened up, offering the agent his hand. They shook.

"Can we sit down?" the agent asked. Jak nodded, his heart beating faster.

"Is Harper okay?"

"Harper's fine. She was with me this morning. I just dropped her at home. This isn't about her."

Jak frowned. Why had she gone with the agent instead of picking him up like she said she would? Something was wrong.

They sat in two chairs near the stone fireplace, and Agent Gallagher leaned forward, his elbows on his knees. "We did another search of Isaac Driscoll's land, Jak."

"Okay," he said slowly.

"We found two bodies, both children, though of different ages."

Jak's blood turned icy. He didn't move.

The agent sat back, letting out a deep sigh. "We also found an old mine shaft that Isaac Driscoll used to store his…work."

The buzzing again. Louder. In his head. Under his skin. Everywhere.

"We found the pictures, Jak. And video recordings…of you. They begin when you're very young and continue until Driscoll was killed."

Jak's stomach knotted. He couldn't speak.

"We also found the bow that we believe was used to kill your mother. We found pictures of her from town and her purse too with her ID. It looks like he was following her."

Driscoll. Driscoll had killed his mother. It should make him angry, full of…rage. But he couldn't feel anything. *Why?*

"We believe Driscoll found out somehow that she'd interfered with what he was doing, that she planned to tell you the truth, or maybe she told him of her plans herself, confronted him, and he went to her room at the bed-and-breakfast and killed her."

Silence. Jak took in the words. He'd go over them later, try to *feel* something about them.

"I need you to tell me about the other kids, Jak," Agent Gallagher said, and there was only sadness in his face. And… disappointment. Deep shame rolled through Jak. Cold sickness.

"Did Harper see?" he finally choked out. *Does Harper know what I did? What I am?*

Agent Gallagher studied him for a second, his expression still sad. "Yes. Harper saw the pictures. She found the mine shaft."

Jak let out a sound that was like a dying animal.

"Jak," Agent Gallagher sat forward. "I need to know what happened. What really happened."

Numbness swept through Jak, and he sagged back in the chair, squeezing his eyes shut for a second. When he opened them, he said, "It happened the way I said, only there were three boys with me. One died in the fall. I pushed another one to a ledge, but he probably died too. I killed the third one. But that was later. We fought over food. I tried—"

"I saw the video, Jak."

Jak's eyes moved slowly to the agent's face. He couldn't tell what was there, but he could imagine what the man was thinking. *Beast. Animal. Killer.*

Video. Video was moving pictures. There was video of Jak stabbing that boy and leaving his body in the snow. Sickness moved up his throat, and with effort, he swallowed it down.

"Do you have any idea who those boys were?"

Jak shook his head but slowly. "No. I don't know anything about them."

Silence for a minute and then Agent Gallagher said, "We think the boy you...fought...lived under Isaac Driscoll's porch for a while. There were notes about a rat living under his porch and stealing his food, his knife. He talked about setting up a test. We think he set up that fight between you both to see what you'd do."

Numbness. Buzzing. Sickness. *Swallow it down, swallow it down.*

"Jak—"

"Why did he do it? Take me. Watch me..." It was the same question he'd battled with since he saw the photos from Driscoll's cabin. *Why? Why me?* Jak was filled with anger, and he didn't know what words to use.

Agent Gallagher's jaw tightened. "We think he was doing observational experiments. At first, they were mostly about survival, strength, fortitude. We believe he meant the house you lived in to house all of you, but you were the only one who survived. His notes indicate he was planning on more specific studies on you using contrived situations, actors..."

"I don't understand all those words," he admitted, his head swimming. He didn't like to say that, but he *needed* to understand.

"I'm sorry, Jak. I think Driscoll was going to use people to pretend they were someone they were not and watch how you reacted."

"The redheaded woman," Jak said. His voice sounded as dead as he felt.

Agent Gallagher nodded. "Yes," he said and his voice broke just a little. Was he sad? Disgusted? *Both,* Jak thought. "We saw the notes on that, the video…"

Jak hung his head. He wanted to cry. To howl until his voice broke and his lungs stopped working. He wanted to find a den and burrow there alone so no one would ever find him.

"Jak…did you kill Isaac Driscoll?"

He met Agent Gallagher's eyes. "No. When I got to his cabin, he was already dying."

There was silence for several minutes. "Jak, we need you to come down to the station and make a statement, but I wanted…I wanted to let you know all of this first. I can pick you up in the morning. How's that?"

Agent Gallagher was being nice to him, giving him time, he knew that. He didn't know why. Was it because he felt sorry for Jak and wanted to give him one last night of a soft bed and hot water before they locked him up? "Okay. Thank you."

"I'm sure once you process all of this, you'll have questions for me too. I'll answer anything I can."

Jak thought he might have nodded, but he was having trouble feeling his body. "Okay."

"Okay." Pause. "Jak, just one final question and then we'll talk tomorrow. Is there anything about Harper's parents that you didn't tell me?"

Jak met his eyes. "No. I told you everything I know about that."

The agent studied his face for a second and then nodded. "Okay. If you need me tonight, you call, all right?" He reached into his pocket and took out a small white card, handing it to Jak. "My number is on here. If you want to call me and your grandfather hasn't gotten you a phone yet, just ask someone around here to show you how to dial the number on the landline, all right?"

Landline. He had no idea what that was. He was lost. He'd always be lost. "Okay."

The agent stood, and so did Jak. The agent had a worried look on his face. Did he think Jak might hurt him too? Jak looked up at the corner of the ceiling. "There are cameras in here," Jak said. If he hurt anyone, that would be on *video* too. Just another thing to lock him up for. Also, he realized, what the agent had just told him had been recorded as well. But who cared? To know things and to see things was very different. Very different.

Harper.

His stomach knotted again.

The agent gave him a confused look but nodded. "All right. I'll show myself out. Then I'll be back in the morning. Nine o'clock, okay?"

"Okay." Jak watched as Agent Gallagher left the room, heard him say something to slinky Nigel in the hallway, and then the sound of his footsteps was gone.

Jak left the library, the place where he'd felt safe and... happy. For a time. Now, now there was nowhere he felt safe.

Brett stepped out of a doorway, opening his *stupid* big-toothed mouth to say something, and Jak growled, pushing him out of his way. He stopped, hoping Brett would want to fight him, but he stumbled back, letting out a high-pitched sound like a girl chipmunk. It would be no fun to fight a female squirrel. He'd crush him. "Jesus, you're an animal," Brett said to his back as Jak walked on. Brett was right. Jak couldn't hide it. He'd thought he could, but he was wrong.

The sound of the crying birds drew him. He entered the aviary, stopping and looking around at the beautiful sad creatures. The cat-pretend-bird lady was there, and she moved toward him. "I knew you'd come around."

Jak stepped by her, moving toward the cages. He flung one of the doors open and then moved to the other two, the birds quieting, hesitating. He reached in and took one of the bright-yellow creatures in his hand and threw it into the air, the bird whooping and fluttering her wings, flying free. "What are you *doing*?" Loni screeched.

He flung the third birdcage door open, and a few birds flew out. He began tossing more of them into the air, their wings flapping with happiness, and after a moment more followed.

Jak ran to the wall of windows, unlocking them and flinging them outward as Loni screeched some more, trying to get the doors of the cages closed. But she was taken over in a massive fluttering of wings, the bird cries turning to laughter that rang through the room, growing louder, more joyous. They rushed toward the window, following one another to freedom.

"You *beast*! You uncivilized *savage*!" she screeched. "You'll kill them! They'll all die out there!"

He walked past her, heading for the door. Yes, he knew that. Creatures couldn't live where they didn't belong. But at least they'd die laughing.

CHAPTER FORTY-FOUR

He'd disappeared. Apparently during a riotous bird jailbreak. Now no one knew where he'd gone. Harper's heart twisted as she paced her apartment. *Jak, Jak, Jak.*

She could only imagine the torment he'd felt when Agent Gallagher told him about what they'd found. He'd not only survived those unthinkable moments, but they'd been orchestrated, saved on film. Critiqued. Twenty-four hours later, she could hardly fathom the evil. Could hardly think about it without tears springing to her eyes.

"Where are you?" she murmured. The only place he knew was the forest. Would he go back there now that he didn't have a house to live in?

She had a feeling he would. She had a feeling he was hunkered down somewhere alone. A cave or a cropping of trees. Somewhere he felt safe. *Did you not come to me because you didn't know how? Because you felt so lost in this world?* Was it because she hadn't gone to him? She'd wanted to, only Agent Gallagher had thought it best that he deliver the news, get the answers he needed. And truth be told, she'd needed some time to get herself together after what she'd seen. God, her heart hurt.

She couldn't simply sit around waiting for news, and the sheriff's office wasn't mounting a search. He wasn't a criminal. Well, if you didn't count the whole bird-freeing thing (but his grandfather had apparently talked his step-grandmother into not pressing charges for that). Nor was he a missing person. He was a victim. And he'd walked away from Thornland Estate without a backward glance.

Harper threw on her coat and pulled on her boots, grabbed her purse, and locked her door behind her. Twenty minutes later, she was pulling off the highway onto the back road that led to the closed-off logging trail.

The walk to what had been Jak's house was easier now that some of the snow had melted. Despite her worry and fear that she wouldn't find him, Harper was able to appreciate the beauty of the forest. The air so clean and fresh, the birdsong all around her, the sense of being part of everything in some indefinable way. Jak had walked through this forest all of his life, thinking his own thoughts, dreaming his own dreams, learning, growing...*not a single person to share any of it with*. The loneliness he must have felt... She couldn't even fathom how he'd survived *any* of it, but mostly the loneliness. Mostly that.

She came to the house he'd lived in. Everything was still...hushed. She walked to the door and knocked but received no answer. At the back of the house, she put her hands around her mouth so her voice would carry. "Jak?" she called into the forest, stepping closer. She *felt* him; she swore she did.

"Jak?" she called again, louder. "Please come out. Please.

I'm alone, and I'm...afraid." It was true, but she knew she was using manipulation. If he could hear her, he would come. He wouldn't resist her plea for help. She *knew* him, and she used his goodness. *Because I love him,* she told herself. *Because I haven't even said it to him yet and he needs to know. He needs to know he's loved.*

She heard a rustling. Footsteps. And he appeared, stepping between two trees, his head lowered. He looked so different now than the first time she'd seen him standing amid the forest. His coat was store-bought, his boots clean and new, his jaw only showing the bare bit of scruff. When he looked up, the expression on his face was wary, afraid, filled with...grief. Shame.

"Jak," she said softly, using her arm to gesture to the forest around them. "You...you don't belong here anymore." *You belong with me. Come home with me.*

He looked down, shaking his head. "I know, Harper. But...I don't belong there either. I don't belong anywhere."

She rushed to him, wrapping her arms around his waist, pressing her face to his chest, breathing him in. "I know it feels like that, but it's not true," she said, holding him tighter. He'd gone still when she'd wrapped him in her arms, and now he let out a tortured sigh, his arms coming around her, running over her hair, her back, a groaning sound emanating from his chest.

She tipped her head, looking up at him. "Jak, I was so worried."

Confusion skated over his face before he let go of her, stepping away, turning again. "You saw," he said, his voice a broken whisper. "You don't have to pretend. I know you saw all of it. You saw. What I did. You...saw."

Oh God. He's...ashamed. So wrong. Although he had to be

more upset by the revelations she knew Agent Gallagher had shared with him, by the news of the terrible crime committed against him. She took him in, his shoulders hunched, head hanging low. He looked like a wounded animal. Lost. Her heart twisted, cracked.

She took a deep breath. "Yes," she confirmed. "I saw." She moved closer, putting her hand on his arm, though he still didn't turn toward her. "I saw pictures of you surviving in ways that will never be erased from my soul. *Not* because they disgusted me, but because my heart bled *for* you and rejoiced *with* you and found awe in your courage. Your will to live. The pictures I saw broke my heart, Jak, but more than that, they made me proud and deeply humbled by your strength. They...made me love you even more than I already did," she finished, her voice filled with the heartfelt passion that lived in her heart for the man in front of her, feeling shame for things he was not responsible for.

He turned then, though slowly, his face filled with wary surprise, a glimmer of hope. But as quickly as she saw it, it disappeared. "He described me as a possum sometimes, other times a deer." He stepped back, away from her. "He also called me the wolf." He let out a deep tortured breath. "And...I'm all of them, Harper." He said it as though his heart broke to admit it, such sadness in his eyes that she almost couldn't bear it. "I'm each one. I tried not to be, but I am." He shook his head. "I haven't been the possum for a long time. He was the scared boy. But the other two...they're who I grew to be, and I can't leave either one behind." He took a shuddery breath. "Do you want the buck who will shake hands and use *table manners* or the wolf who might tear you apart? And what happens if I can't promise you the wolf won't come out when you least expect it? I can't be just one or the other. I'm both." His voice broke on the last word, fading away.

She stood straighter, his words bolstering her. Yes, she'd known that, hadn't she? She'd sensed him holding back, for *her,* felt him trying to suppress that part of him—the wolf. She'd been glad for it because that side of him was an unknown and it scared her, but beyond her fear, there had been the spark of…disappointment, hadn't there? Disappointment at his restraint. And she understood what he was telling her. She couldn't have him in pieces. He'd spent his life surviving because of that wild, beastly part of him. To reject it would be to reject the very core of who he was.

"I want the wolf," she said softly. "I want you. I don't need you to hold back." It was the truest thing she'd ever said, she realized. She was willing to cast away any fear because she trusted him. There was no part of him she didn't want. Each piece of him had been hard won. Hard fought for, and she'd take them all.

He studied her, his eyes narrowing, watching. "Before I lived in that house, I lived in caves, Harper, or sometimes holes animals dug in the ground."

She raised her chin. "Good," she said. "Those places kept you warm."

He turned his head slightly, still studying her with such intensity, she began to shake. He took a step nearer, and she held her ground.

"Sometimes I was so starving I ate *bugs*. One after the other. I searched the ground for them, crawling on my hands and knees."

He watched, waited to see the disgust come into her eyes, she knew. Testing her. She swallowed, the picture in her mind—the knowledge of his excruciating desperation—hurting so much she wanted to fall to her own knees. She took in a breath, the vast respect—the immense love—she had for him filling every part of her soul. "Good," she whispered. "It kept you alive so when I walked into the sheriff's office that day, you were there. You were there."

He was silent for so long, she wondered if he'd speak again, wondered if he'd bring up one more horrifying element of his survival to try to determine if she really wanted what she was saying she wanted.

"The wolf is not like anything you know. He's wild, Harper. He's the very worst of me."

"Good," she said one more time, the intensity she felt wavering in her voice. "I *want* wild. I want you. All of you. The best and the worst and everything in between."

His eyes narrowed, and the air changed very suddenly, her awareness spiking, breath stalling. He was going to strike. Going to test the truthfulness of her words with action. *Do it,* she whispered in her mind, and his nose moved, very slightly as though he'd caught the scent of her acquiescence. Her need. They stared at each other, and she was trembling now, her entire body charged, her heart pumping blood through her veins, faster, faster. "I want wild," she repeated. She wasn't afraid. She would willingly surrender to him because she had *faith* in his goodness.

With a low growl, he stalked toward her, slowly, slowly. When they finally stood toe to toe, he moved quickly, grabbing her. She sucked in a breath. His mouth came down on hers, hot, demanding. He was holding nothing back, and a thrill spiraled within her, ending between her legs with a burst of wet pleasure.

He scooped her up in his arms and carried her to the front of the empty house that wasn't his anymore, opening the unlocked door and kicking it closed behind him. The blanket he'd slept with for most of his life was still folded on the bed, and he threw it on the floor, pushing her gently so she was on her knees.

Her breath hitched, arousal hot and heavy in her veins as his body came over hers from behind, so much bigger, harder. He could hurt her if he wanted. No fear moved within her. Only breathless anticipation. He leaned over, his mouth close to her ear. "Do you want *this*?" he asked, his voice gravelly in her ear.

"Yes," she moaned. It was the only word she could manage.

He tore at her clothes, the grunts and animal sounds coming from him making her lust spiral higher and higher. When he ran a finger through her wet folds, she thought she might come right then and there. She was panting, she realized, like an animal, like a woman being taken by the man she loved. This was mating. Elemental, ungoverned by any civilized laws or strictures. It was ordained by nature, by miracles, by the tides and the moon and the blood pumping in unison through their veins. Their bodies sang to each other, the same tune, melody and harmony, the notes pulsing, suspended around them.

He sniffed at her, licked her, his face probing between her thighs from behind as she gasped and moaned and clawed at the floor. *Yes, yes, yes.* She might have said it out loud. He was controlling this, she knew, and yet she'd never felt so powerful, so *free*. She let go, gave in to him completely. He was devouring her body, her soul, yes, *tearing her apart*, piece by piece by piece until she melted into him and they were one. This was how it should be, she knew it in her bones, in the echoing pleasure of women through the ages who had been loved and worshipped by their men.

She felt his hot naked skin at her back and, dazedly, glanced over her shoulder. His face was a mask of wild lust. *The wolf.* He had given in to the wolf, and she gloried in the knowledge that he trusted her enough to take him. *To love him. To keep him.*

His hands rubbed her breasts, fondling them, growling with reverence. Then his palms were moving over her rib cage, and his tongue found the spot that made her scream, licking, probing. She undulated her hips, rubbing herself on his face, begging for more. So close, so close. When he pulled away, a whimper escaped, a cry of frustration.

But as quick as that, his hardness was probing at her entrance, and the whimper melted into a deep groan of ecstasy.

He impaled her in one quick thrust, grunting his male pleasure loudly, the sound sending her over the edge before he'd even begun to move. To thrust. To take what was freely being given. And when he did, she came again, the pulsing bliss making her knees give out, her sobs mingling with his growls.

He grasped her around the waist to hold her steady, one hand gripping a handful of her hair to keep her from falling, pounding into her again and again as aftershocks of rapture shimmered through her. His fingers raked at her scalp, his arm clutched tightly around her, his hardness plunging into her mercilessly, his tight belly slamming against her backside. She was dying, dying a slow death of pleasure overload. The bliss. The euphoria. *Him.*

Their rhythm increased, his grunts growing louder, closer together until he howled with pleasure, gripping her hips, slamming into her, then slowing, slowing until it was only their mingled pants, the heat of their sweat-slicked skin.

The sky and the earth and the ground beneath them, still moving, rocking, pulsing in the same gentle undulations as their bodies.

The world returned slowly, dreamily as though they had been awake and only now were falling back to sleep.

He turned her, his eyes probing hers, moving over her face, looking for...what, she didn't know. But whatever he found made his lips turn up, made his gaze gentle as he pulled her to him, nuzzling her neck, her hair, kissing her lips, licking the tears from her cheeks that she hadn't realized were there. "You're crying," he said, but he didn't sound upset.

"Yes."

"Female wolves cry when they find their forever mate," he said, smoothing her hair back.

She laughed softly. She was undeniably human—all *too* human most of the time—but maybe there was a thread of uninhibited wildness in her too. An instinctive recognition of her life mate.

He spent long minutes soothing her, loving her, kissing away her tears, nuzzling, nipping softly at her skin so that she laughed.

"I love you," she said, nuzzling him back. "All of you. Maybe the wolf most of all because he was the one who ensured you lived so you could love me when I arrived."

The look on his face was filled with joy; Harper laughed with happiness. "I love you too," he said. But then he went serious, his face falling. "They're going to lock me up, Harper. I have to...I have to pay for what I did to one of the other boys who was left out here."

"Oh, Jak, no," she whispered. "No one blames you for that. They saw the pictures, Jak. Agent Gallagher saw the video. They know what happened, that you were only defending yourself. No one's going to lock you up."

His eyes moved over her face for a moment as though he was having trouble believing her. "I'm not in trouble?"

"Of course you're not. You're the victim. The lone survivor." She smiled. "People will write books about you someday, and you'll be the hero."

He looked at her in wonder, the relief in his expression so stark that tears sprung to her eyes again. *He'd thought they would lock him in a cage?* He had been prepared to pay for killing the other boy. What immense guilt he must carry with him. Guilt that only belonged at the doorstep of one man: Isaac Driscoll. Whoever had killed him, she was *glad* he was dead. She would have been tempted to kill him herself if he wasn't.

She rolled in Jak's arms, wrapping the blanket more tightly around them. They were on the hardwood floor, his sticky release drying on her thighs, and she'd never been more comfortable and content in her life.

They nuzzled some more, kissed. She languished in the feel of his rough, scarred male skin against hers, the heat of him in the cold cabin, the delectable earthy masculine smell. After a minute, she looked into his eyes, the worry she'd had nudging her, needing to be voiced. There was only honesty now, only truth. What they'd experienced together left no room for anything else. "I worry that as you learn and grow and change...as you become the man you're meant to be, you'll...leave me behind." She lowered her eyes.

But he stroked her hair from her forehead and kissed her there, causing her to lift her chin and meet his gaze. "You think everyone you love will leave you behind."

"I..." She looked away again but then raised her eyes, unable to look away for long.

"I understand," he whispered. "People have left me too. Lied to me, betrayed me. I know I have a lot to learn about the world. But, Harper, I'm not a child. I'm a man, and I know who belongs to me and who I belong to." He looked straight into her eyes, her soul. "Did you know the trees speak to each other?"

"No," she breathed.

"They do. They tell secrets in their roots, those deep, dark places that can't be seen. I think we're like that too. We know things deep, deep down, secret things, *ancient* things, that whisper through us, one to the other. You whispered to me. And I whispered back. You heard, didn't you?"

Her heart beat with love for him, at the sweetness of what he'd said. "Yes, I heard."

He used his thumb to swipe at her cheek, bringing the happy tear to his lips and tasting it. She smiled, snuggling into him, drifting for a moment. She could fall asleep here, if she knew they didn't need to get back. If she knew they weren't essentially breaking and entering. "Mm," she hummed, pushing the real world aside for a moment, fantasizing about being able to stay there indefinitely just like that. They'd fall asleep for a while, wake and make love—the wild wolf or the gentle young buck, she didn't care. She wondered if she could call to the wolf inside him with a look, a movement, a touch. Beckon him. Make him mindless. A delicious shiver of anticipation trembled through her. *Soon,* she told herself. *Always.* But not today. Still, they had a few minutes, and she let herself relish it, snuggling in deeper to the warmth of his chest. "What you just said, about the trees, it made me think of something."

"Hmm," he hummed against her hair.

"When I woke up in the hospital as a child, I didn't

remember much of anything. Just a couple of things. A few flashes of memory. I'd been angry with my parents, my mother specifically, because I'd gotten gum in my hair at school and she'd made me get it cut. It made me look like a boy." She laughed softly but then sighed. "The last thing I remember saying to her was that I'd never forgive her for it. I like to think she knew I was just being a bratty kid, but…" She took a shaky breath. "Anyway, the other thing I kept hearing in my head was this voice telling me to live. It was like a shout, a demand almost." She paused. "My father's voice maybe. Perhaps an angel, even God. I don't know." She tilted her head, looking up at him. He had stilled as he listened with rapt attention. "But it felt so…*real*. And that one word, it came to me again and again over the years when I wanted to give up. *That demand.* That…yes, that *whisper*. Deep down. It made me keep going, helped me hold on, helped me survive." Why was he looking at her like that? Like he'd just seen a ghost? "Jak? What's wrong?"

He removed the blanket from his shoulder, standing and walking naked to where he'd discarded his coat. She sat up, bringing the blanket to her chest, watching him, confused. He walked back to her and knelt down, holding out his hand. She looked as he opened his palm. A pocketknife. Old and… She picked it up, a feeling of deep gravity filling her chest…so worn it was practically coming apart. She knew this pocketknife, and she held it tightly, knowing what she would see on the back before she'd turned it over. Mother of pearl. "My father carried this in his pocket. Was it in the car? Is that where you got it?"

Jak shook his head, his eyes moving over her face like he'd just seen her for the first time. "Jak? What is it?"

401

"You gave this to me," he said softly, incredulously. "You put it in my hand."

"I…what? I don't understand."

"It was you. You went over that cliff with me."

CHAPTER FORTY-FIVE

The look on Harper's face was still…glazed. He related. He couldn't believe it either. Couldn't believe she was…the dark-haired boy on the cliff. It made him want to *laugh*. It filled him with joy. And yet, in some strange way he couldn't explain—not because he didn't have words, he'd gathered so *many* over the past few weeks—it made sense. He was *mystified* yet unsurprised. He'd *known* her, not only because of the whispers that flowed through him—through everyone if they knew to listen—but because she'd *been* there on the most life-changing night of his life. She'd *saved* him. If not for that pocketknife, he never would have survived. And he'd saved her. In that split-second decision…he'd saved the love of his life.

They'd both lived because of each other, survived alone yet together all these years so they could return to one another when the time was right.

They pulled up in front of the sheriff's office and both sat staring at the building for a moment. Harper had called

Agent Gallagher when they'd reached the highway, and he was meeting Jak there. Harper reached over, squeezing his hand. "You sure you don't want me to come inside with you? Or wait for you out here?"

He leaned over and kissed her quickly. "No. I can do this alone." *I need to do this alone. I need to be a man.* "But I can't wait to see you at your apartment. I'll ask Agent Gallagher to drive me when we're done."

She smiled, nodded. "I'll be waiting."

The three best words he'd ever heard from the woman he loved. *I'll be waiting.* He had someone waiting for him. And he'd never leave her waiting long. He grinned, kissing her quickly and getting out of the truck.

The sheriff's office looked different to him, but then again, he'd had different eyes the last time he'd been there.

"I'm here to see Agent Gallagher," he said to the woman at the front desk. Her eyes got big, and she dropped her pen, standing quickly.

"Oh, yes. Lucas, right?" Her forehead wrinkled. "No, Jak! I overheard Agent Gallagher... Well, in any case, I met you before, or saw you, anyway." She laughed, and it sounded high like the bay-breasted warbler. But he had to stop thinking of everything in terms of the wilderness, had to *enlarge* his...frame of something. There was a saying, but he couldn't think of it right then. But it meant that he finally had names for things he never had before, and he needed to start using them. He smiled, proud of the knowing he had already collected. "Right this way," she said, looking over her shoulder and blushing for reasons unknown to him. Some things were still a mystery. He followed her, walking to a room with a table in the middle where Agent Gallagher sat, a notebook in front of him.

He stood when Jak walked in, shaking his hand. "I'm glad Harper found you."

Jak looked down, feeling bad that he'd run away and still uneasy that this man knew so much about him, personal things he didn't think he'd ever share with another living soul. "I know you need to get me...on record, but Harper and I figured out something new too."

"What is that?"

"Harper was one of the children on the cliff that night. I thought she was a boy because of her hair. And...maybe I just thought we were all boys. But it was her."

The agent sat back slowly. "How do you know?"

Jak told him about the pocketknife, about pushing Harper up on the ledge, about her memory of him telling her to live.

Agent Gallagher was silent for several moments before he gave his head a slight shake. "Wow. Okay..." He was quiet again. "So Driscoll caused Harper's parents' car crash somehow or...lured them off the road maybe, and then Harper ended up with you on that cliff. She was going to be part of his study too."

A chill went down Jak's spine. "I don't know."

Agent Gallagher nodded, his eyes unfocused for a moment. "All right. I'm going to look at some different angles." He thinned his lips, his eyes focusing on Jak again. "For now, let's get your statement, and then I have someone I've asked to join us here."

Jak frowned, but the agent didn't look worried, and Jak trusted him. "I'm ready."

Agent Gallagher turned on a recorder and asked Jak every question he'd believed he would. Jak told him everything he knew, answering honestly and fully, and when it was done, when Agent Gallagher pushed stop on the small recorder, Jak felt like a boulder had been taken off his back.

The path before him had been cleared, and a sense of… *victory* swept over him. His life was his. It stretched out before him. And Harper was waiting to begin it with him.

There was a soft knock on the door, and Agent Gallagher stood, opening it and letting someone in. Jak looked more closely, standing, his mouth falling open.

It was the redheaded woman who'd told him about the cameras. She came forward, blushing when she saw Jak, lowering her eyes.

He took her hand and shook it, hardly believing she was there, in the real world. Not a part of that old world where war was being fought and enemies were all around. No, she had been a lie too. He was glad to know it.

It hurt to know it.

"Hi, Jak," she murmured.

"Hi…"

"Brielle," she said. "I told the truth about that." She blushed again and looked down.

"Brielle is here to give a statement," Agent Gallagher said. "Her name is unusual, and when you told me, I began searching in some of the programs Driscoll had volunteered for. I found your mother's name from a program she was in twenty-two years ago. And I found two Brielles from more recent programs. Only one had red hair."

Jak took in the information about his mother. That's how Driscoll had found her then. Pregnant with him. He pushed that aside, looking at Brielle. "Driscoll sent you to me," Jak said, already knowing the answer.

"Yes. He told me his son had lived his life in the wilderness. He was going to bring you back to civilization, but he was concerned your base instincts were too strong, worried you'd hurt someone, especially a woman. He wanted to place you in a real-life situation where you could turn toward those instincts or turn away." She paused. "I had been prostituting." Her face went pink. "For drugs. I guess he figured…it didn't matter what you did to me. Maybe I thought so too. I took the money. I took the job."

"Oh," Jak said, not knowing how to feel. He felt stupid and used, but he also felt sad for Brielle.

"But I saw the camera at the river." She made a sound that was sort of like a laugh, only not. "Maybe the old guy forgot it's second nature for junkies to make sure they're not being watched. Habit." She cleared her throat. "Anyway, I knew something wasn't right. Then I met you, and, well, I knew something was very wrong." She swallowed. "I want you to know, that after I met you, after I saw who you really were, it"—she shook her head—"I don't know. I'd tried so hard to get clean for so long. For me, even for my son, and I'd always failed. But after that…after you, I got clean. And I know it hasn't been long, but I've stayed clean. You inspired me. And now I'm trying to reunify with my boy, to get better…" A tear slipped down her cheek, and she swiped at it. "I'm so sorry for what I did, Jak. And thank you for what you were to me."

He nodded, and she stepped forward, wrapping her arms around him quickly and then letting go, turning. Agent Gallagher ushered her out of the room and closed the door. He walked back to Jak. He took Jak's shoulder in his hand, squeezing it. "I imagine you're ready to get home."

Home. Harper. Yes. But…he frowned, thinking. First, he needed to talk to his grandfather. "Yes. I do want to go home. But first, I need to go to Thornland."

"I'll drop you there and come back in an hour. I need to stop by my office anyway. Will that work?"

"Yes. Thank you."

Agent Gallagher smiled. "Let's go."

———————

Jak watched Agent Gallagher's car pull away, turning toward the grand estate that he'd once called a castle. Now he knew it was only a big house where lots of unhappy people lived. He took a deep breath, not looking forward to seeing his step-grandmother. He was sure she was inside sharpening her talons, ready to scratch his eyes out.

The door opened, and Nigel stood there, as slinky as ever. "Nigel," his mouth said. *Slinky,* his mind said.

"Sir," Nigel answered in that way that made Jak think he was about to sneeze. Jak felt his brow raise, waiting. No sneeze came. "Welcome home, sir." Nigel opened the door wider.

"Thank you. I need to talk to my grandfather."

"Mr. Fairbanks is upstairs. Should I call him for you?"

Jak nodded, stepping inside. "Yes. Thank you."

He wasn't sure he was welcomed there anymore, not as family anyway, so he walked to the big room near the door where he'd first met his grandfather, practicing what he wanted to say to him. *Thank you for giving me a name, but I don't need a home anymore.* There it was. Simple words.

As he waited, the quiet of the house seemed to close in on him. He walked to the desk, picking up the picture of his father and staring at the man's face. He *did* look like him; he could see that now. He wondered if he'd looked like him when he was a little boy too. The only pictures he'd seen of himself as a child were the ones he'd found in Driscoll's house. The ones that made him sick.

He opened the drawer of the desk, removing a big, thick book and opening it. It was the book of pictures—*the photo album*—his grandfather had told him about when he'd first met him.

He set it on the desk, turning the pages, seeing pictures of his grandfather, a brown-haired woman who must be his real grandmother, and the little boy who had been his father. Christmases. Parties with balloons and presents, lakes and boats and things Jak couldn't name. And in all of them, smiles. Everyone had been smiling.

His eyes stopped on one of the pictures, surprise making him pause as he brought the picture closer. His grandfather and his father, a teenager then, standing together with a trophy. Jak's eyes moved to the background, where there were round targets. Jak squinted, looking more closely at the trophy. The words on the front said "First Place Archery" and his father's name.

Jak swallowed. His father was good—*no, great*—with a bow and arrows.

His father was dead though. He couldn't have killed Driscoll. He stared back at the picture, the look of *pride* on his grandfather's face. Like he'd practiced with a bow and arrows right along with his son. Like they'd practiced together.

The whispers inside him—his *intuition*—spiked. He'd already known it, hadn't he? He'd *smelled* him there, the lingering scent of what he'd thought was a campfire but had really been the smell of his grandfather's cigar. He'd been at Driscoll's right before him. The footprints leading to the window had been his.

"Jak," his grandfather said from the doorway. Jak looked up. His grandfather frowned at whatever was on Jak's face.

"Archery," he said, tapping the photo album. "Driscoll. It was you. Why?"

His grandfather looked at the photo album, his face draining of color, and then away. He opened his mouth once and then closed it, a look of defeat coming over his face as his shoulders hunched. He let out a shuddery breath. "He took you, and then he made you into an animal."

His grandfather's words hurt him. He didn't want them to, but they did. "I'm not an animal."

"I *know*, son. I know. I see that *now*. But at the time." He walked farther into the room and leaned against a chair near where Jak was standing. "At the time, all I could see was my own regret. My own shame and rage. I gave you away, but he made it so I could never get you back. Never make things *right*. He ruined my last chance for happiness. And I *despised* him. He took the last piece of my heart, and so I took his." *He'd shot the arrow straight into Driscoll's heart. He'd gotten his vengeance using the same kind of weapon Jak's father had been so good with. He'd killed him with the love and pride he'd had in his son.*

His grandfather massaged his chest as though it pained him there, his face scrunching. "I thought he'd turned you into a...beast. Only"—he let out a laugh that sounded like someone was strangling him from the inside—"I'm the beast. *We're* the animals." He raised his arm and waved it around the house. "And I surrounded myself with *them,* casting off my own blood. You deserved...a life. Better than what...I only wish. Oh God, I wish—"

He clutched his chest again, and a loud moan came up his throat. His face went white and screwed up as he pitched forward. "Get help...Jak."

Jak caught him, going down to the floor, holding his

grandfather in his arms. His grandfather looked up at him, his face a grimace. But a pained smile turned up the corners of his lips as he reached up and ran his hand down Jak's cheek before his arm fell to the floor. "You're the best of us..." he whispered, his voice fading away as his eyes closed.

Jak laid his grandfather down gently and went for help.

CHAPTER FORTY-SIX

Harper smiled as the door swung open, laughing when Rylee pulled her inside. "Get in here immediately." She practically pulled Harper into the living room, pushing her down on the love seat. "Stay there," she demanded as she fast-walked out of the room. Harper took off her jacket, laying it on the edge of the couch and setting the bag with Rylee's belated Christmas gift down next to her, as Rylee came back in, a wine bottle in one hand, two glasses in the other.

Harper chuckled. "Isn't it a little too early to drink?"

"Um, no. Not when I haven't seen my friend in weeks and every time I hear from her, with a two-line text, mind you, her life has exploded again."

Exploded.

Not an exaggeration. Harper still felt shell-shocked.

"I'm sorry, Ry. You're right. So much has been happening, I've just been trying to keep up." And she'd been singularly focused on Jak and falling head over heels in love with him, she could admit that too.

She gave Rylee an apologetic look. "And I'm not going to be able to stay too long. Jak is with Agent Gallagher, but I told him I'd be waiting when he gets back."

"That's okay. I'll take what I can get." Rylee winked at her and poured them each a glass of wine and handed one to Harper. Harper took it, taking a sip and then letting out a deep breath.

Rylee had taken a sip of her own wine and now was looking at Harper over the rim of her glass. "You're in love."

She smiled, sitting back. "I am. Ridiculously in love, Ry." And despite the recent upheaval, she felt at peace inside, for the first time in what felt like forever.

Rylee smiled, looking like she might be about to cry. "I'm so happy," she whispered. "And I want to meet him immediately."

Harper grinned. "You will. He's coming to live with me." She held up a hand when Rylee opened her mouth to ask if she thought that was a good idea, Harper could tell. "I know it's sudden. But...it's right. Jak needs to figure out his own life, and he knows that. But we're going to do it together. It feels right."

Rylee watched her for a second and then smiled. "It must because I've never seen such peace in your eyes."

Harper grinned, taking another sip of wine. "There are still some loose ends as far as what exactly happened to Jak," she said. "But those questions will be answered eventually, or they won't. Either way, he's good. He's the strongest man I've ever known."

Live! The words he'd said to her on the side of that cliff a lifetime ago rang through her head as they'd done before— down deep in her subconscious and floating to the surface now and again, the rallying cry not to give up. And she *hadn't*. Because of him.

Then she told her friend what Agent Gallagher had discovered, what she and *Jak* had discovered after he'd disappeared into the woods, back to the one place that still felt like home to him, though she vowed she would change that. *She* would be his home. From that day forward. And he would be hers.

Rylee sat, mouth gaping. "Do the police think Driscoll killed your parents too? So that he could kidnap you and make you part of his study?"

Harper frowned. "They don't know. And I might never know. But yes, it's the best theory as of now."

"Good lord," Rylee said. "I can't believe something that demented was going on right here in Helena Springs."

"I know. I'm still trying to wrap my head around it all." And that would likely take a while. But she was a survivor. She always would be. Was there any reason to know the why and how about her parents? About why she had been chosen? Not really. It wouldn't bring them back. It wouldn't change the outcome of their lives. *I lived.*

And Jak was the greatest survivor of all time as far as she was concerned. Her hero. Her love. Her forever mate.

"So what happens from here?"

"Agent Gallagher is still working the case, trying to figure out who killed Driscoll. And he's trying to identify the bodies found on Driscoll's property." A shiver went through her—how close she'd come to being nothing but remains on Driscoll's land. A red X on his hand-drawn map. She took a deep breath. "But while that unfolds, I'm going to be taking some psychology courses in Missoula. I want to understand why people do the things they do." She wanted to work in the criminal justice field someday, helping agents like Mark Gallagher out on cases. Everything that had unfolded had been terrible and tragic and mind-boggling, but seeing the case being worked from up close had *inspired* her to do the same type of work. And she knew she'd have an advocate in Agent Gallagher.

In the meantime, she and Jak would run her guide business. To say he'd be a natural was an understatement. Who knew the wilderness better than he did?

Harper and Rylee talked for another half hour, exchanging Christmas gifts, laughing, and reminiscing, and when Harper got up to hug her goodbye, she felt even fuller. Being in love was a wonderful miracle, but having a community surrounding her and Jak would enrich life for both of them.

Harper smiled to herself as she walked down Rylee's steps, turning into the covered parking area, eager to get home and wait for Jak's arrival. Just as she was removing her key from her purse, she sensed movement behind her, turning halfway as someone grabbed her from behind. She opened her mouth to scream, inhaling a big breath of something sweet and noxious as a hand went over her mouth. Terror spiked through her. She tried to lift her arm, to hit, to flail, but her body was too heavy. The world wavered, faded. Blinked out.

She couldn't see. She could barely hear. Her head roared, and it was several minutes before she realized it wasn't coming from inside her own mind, but rather, it was outside, somewhere beyond the darkness. She listened, her brain clearing, memory returning piece by piece. *Water. It's water.*

She'd been leaving Rylee's house. Someone had come

415

up behind her. Taken her. Her heart raced, the brain fog clearing.

Whatever had been covering her head was removed suddenly, and she let out a short yelp, the sudden light blinding her. She opened her eyes, the smell of nature meeting her nose—trees and dirt and rushing water.

I've *been* here before.

She was standing on a cliff, a river flowing next to her, spilling into what she immediately recognized as Amity Falls.

"Beautiful up here, isn't it?"

She whirled around so quickly, she almost stumbled over her own feet.

A large, tall man with graying streaks in his mostly black hair stood in front of her, smiling casually. Next to him was an equally tall young man with bronzed skin and dark eyes, his expression blank. "My favorite place in all of this godforsaken wilderness." The older man smiled. "I'm Dr. Swift, by the way." He walked toward her but not too close. She gaped at him, her mind searching frantically to put this into context. *What is happening?*

"This whole thing started out with a ceremony, albeit an interrupted ceremony, and…it'll end with one." He smiled. "Of sorts. Though not in the same location, exactly. Isaac picked the first one. But he's not here anymore to choose anything, is he?"

"Isaac?" she murmured. Isaac Driscoll chose the first location. The first *ceremony*? The first time she'd stood on a cliff like this. With Jak. And two other unnamed boys.

Hazy pictures filled her mind, things she'd always thought were dreams or nightmares or bits and pieces of her fighting her way through the wilderness…the voices of the hikers who found her maybe…her fear, the cold. It'd all swirled together in her child's mind, creating confusion and too much that was unknown or out of context for the adult Harper to begin to understand.

His voice though. She remembered his voice. It drummed through her, triggering her brain to connect bits of memory, creating context.

"You," she said. "It was *you*. That night." He'd taken her...shot her parents? "Why?" she asked. "Why me? Why my family? What did you do to them?"

He let out a long-suffering sigh as though the whole ordeal was so terribly taxing. For the first time since Harper had opened her eyes, anger raced through her, mixing with the dread. *This* man. Right in front of her. He had killed her parents. Taken them from her.

"Because, Harper, your father, the sheriff, was looking into some missing kids—*our* missing kids—and getting far too close for comfort. We had to eliminate him."

Eliminate him? He said it like it was *nothing*. Like it had been as easy as swatting a bothersome fly.

"What happened to them?" she choked.

"Oh, don't worry, they didn't even know what was coming. One of my men shot your parents while they were driving, causing the car to crash. We didn't expect you to be there, but there you were, unconscious in the back. You'd survived. We put chloroform over your mouth so you'd keep sleeping and decided you would join the others. We knew they wouldn't search where we were taking you." He waved his hand around. "A million acres of wild land. A better hiding place doesn't exist."

They'd pushed the car into the canyon, hidden it so it'd never be found. *And it wouldn't have been, if not for Jak.* Her mind whirled. *But how did I get the pocketknife?* Had her dying father slipped it into her pocket somehow? At the thought, her chest ached because it was really the only explanation. The way her father's remains had been turned. Toward the back seat. Toward *her*. Her father's dying thought was to protect her.

Dr. Swift turned for a moment, and Harper considered trying to run at him and take him down, but he was too far away to be taken by surprise, twice her size, and she didn't have a weapon. Not to mention the younger man, who hadn't been introduced was there too, presumably Dr. Swift's security protection. Dr. Swift turned back toward her.

"Against all odds, you got out of the wilderness that night." He looked almost amazed for a moment. "We watched you closely for a while, but you didn't remember anything. Lucky for you. After that…we knew it was far too risky to attempt to take you again. By that time," he sighed, "there was only Jak. Our experiment had gone terribly awry." He smiled, looking beyond her, out to the falls. "But Jak… ah, Jak. If only we had a thousand just like him. Driscoll had begun to find out how he'd react to being introduced back into society. He was doing so well. Mentally strong and impressively…civilized. We were so *close* to being able to debrief him, enter him into more specialized training. Weaponry, hand-to-hand combat fighting…it would only have been a matter of a year, maybe less, before he could be put up for bid. I can just *imagine* the offers that would have come in for him. A shame. A *waste*." Deep sadness passed over his face before he inhaled a long, slow breath. "But it wasn't meant to be."

Her head spun with what had been done to Jak. *Debrief* him. Meaning, tell him his life had all been a terrible lie? Put up for *bid*? Horror clawed at the inside of her chest. If only *we* had a thousand just like him? Who was we? He and Driscoll? Or were there more? The twisted magnitude of what she was hearing made her feel lightheaded.

"You have no idea of the significance of what we're doing, Harper. No idea. I'm sorry I'm going to have to hurt you. But we simply *cannot* have loose ends at this stage, nor can we risk the others. There's far too much at stake. We should have taken care of that—of you—years ago, but now we can only learn from our mistakes, only be more... efficient in the future."

She shook her head, bewildered. Horrified. "What do you mean by *others*?"

"I mean we have programs set up all over. We have others like Jak who have already been such great successes. My protector, Daire, is a perfect example. My prodigy. Only nineteen years old." He looked back at the young man still standing stoically behind him. "Isn't that right, Daire?" Daire's eyes moved to him, and he nodded, his expression unchanging. "And," Dr. Swift went on, "there are even more who show much promise. I'm not the only one who supports the copious benefits of our overall program. There are many benefactors and bidders who understand that the unwanted children of addicts and thieves only bring forth a society's downfall. It's already happening. Look at our inner cities. How the government is addressing the problem is not working. It's only making things worse. *We* strive to improve society. Unfortunately, our first study failed for all intents and purposes. But we learned, adapted, and now, *now* such exciting things are happening. Survival stories like you'd never believe, skills of all sorts being exhibited from *throw-aways.*" He laughed, a joyful sound that even the wind didn't want. It rang out around them, loud and spine-chilling.

Harper swallowed. *Our first study failed for all intents and purposes. Our first study.* Her. Jak. The other two boys. *They* had been the subjects of the first study. And it had failed. So now this man was going to tie up loose ends. Two of the boys were already dead, so that meant *her.*

And Jak? Another wave of horror washed through her, and she groaned, but it was snatched by the roar of the falling water.

CHAPTER FORTY-SEVEN

Jak crept through the forest, the sound of the rushing water drowning out the other sounds around him. *Meet me,* the note had said, *at the top of Amity Falls. They know you're guilty, Jak. They know you killed Driscoll. I can't let them put you away. Let's disappear together, back into the forest.*

At first his heart had dropped. She thought he was guilty? Of killing Driscoll? She knew that wasn't true. He'd told her...everything. What they had shared...the plans they'd made... *Let's disappear together.* It didn't make sense. He'd gotten a ride from one of the police officers who had come to Thornland when his grandfather was taken to the hospital. He'd rushed to her door, wanting to tell her everything that had happened. But she was gone, missing from her apartment where she told him she'd wait.

Something was wrong.

He turned his face into the gentle wind, tilting his head to catch...*there.* He smelled her. Even over the fresh mineral scent of the rolling water, even over the scent of…another human. A male. No, two.

He moved forward, crouching, silent. He came to the edge of the trees, moving in the shadows, using the light and dark to draw closer.

"I know you're here, Jak," one of the men called out, making Jak freeze, a growl coming up his throat that he swallowed down. *That voice.* He *knew* that voice. "Cameras. They give the advantage despite your stealth." The man looked at Harper, who was standing closer to the falls, and smiled. Another man, a younger one, was standing behind the man who'd spoken, his eyes focused on the dark trees where Jak hid. "We can't have them everywhere, of course. But I get the numerous feeds on my phone. Riveting TV. A true reality show if ever there was one."

This man had been watching Jak too? The monster who'd been at the top of the cliff that awful night?

Anger moved within Jak, anger and *grief*, as he suddenly saw his life—all his suffering—in a different and even more terrible light. But on the top of both of those emotions was fear. His skin prickled. Chest burned. The fear of Harper standing in front of a man who Jak knew meant to harm her.

The man nodded back to the young man behind him. "Daire."

Daire pulled a gun from his coat pocket, making Jak's blood freeze.

"Come on out, Jak," the older man said, the one with white stripes in his dark hair like a skunk. "It's pointless to hide in the woods."

Jak paused for only a moment and then stepped from the shadows.

The man smiled, an expression that looked truly…

affectionate. "Hi, Jak. My, you're even bigger in person. It's…truly wonderful to see you."

"Jak," Harper said, her eyes darting to the gun in the other man's hand, her smile breaking. Jak moved toward her, pulled, but neither man stopped him.

When Jak had made it almost all the way to where Harper stood, the older man said, "That's good. Stay right there." He sighed. "I'm going to explain to you our mission. Why, you might ask, am I telling you? Because you *deserve* to know. You *deserve* to understand that your sacrifice will not be in vain. Quite the opposite. You are both part of something so much bigger than the two of you. Despite what must happen here today, I *revere* you. My pride in you and admiration for you both know no bounds."

Despite what must happen here today. Jak's brain spun, trying to understand. This man, he had been there the night it started. He was working with Driscoll. He'd watched the cameras. He'd seen everything. His thoughts tumbled, brain buzzed.

"I understand why you killed Driscoll, Jak. I truly do. It all went so wrong. If we had had a chance to debrief you, you would have understood your purpose, found *pride* in the suffering you'd endured." He looked very disappointed for a moment but then smiled. "Ah, well. What's done is done." The man thought Jak had killed Driscoll. *He* had left the note in Harper's apartment.

Jak's eyes met Harper's, hers wide with fear, searching. *Trusting.* She knew it wasn't true. Knew he didn't kill Driscoll. She'd trusted him that night too, he realized. She'd put the pocketknife in his hand because she'd trusted him to *do* something. He glanced at the man with the gun, too far away to rush before he could shoot them both.

423

In front of him was the gun; behind him were the deadly falls. Trapped. They were trapped.

"Dr. Swift, wha…what did Driscoll and his Spartans have to do with any of this?" Harper asked, her voice shaking. Trying to keep him talking. Giving Jak time so he could figure out what to do.

Dr. Swift sighed. "Driscoll was obsessed with history, with the Spartans." He waved his hand as if that didn't matter. "We like to give our camp leaders room for creativity." He turned toward the man behind him. "Daire knows all about that, don't you?" Daire didn't answer, but Jak saw something flicker in his eyes. But with a blink it was gone. Dr. Swift turned back toward Harper and Jak. "But, see, the Spartans brought up one very important fact. Driscoll was *right:* there's much to be learned. See, they started with the *children.* It's where our idea was first conceived. We try to alter adults, change people who cannot be changed. Study them, put them through useless programs that show dismal results. Nothing changes, do you see? It's all backward. And so the cycle continues. Your own mother was proof of that, Jak. Born to a junkie herself, raised in the system. What does she do? Becomes a teenage mother, hooked on drugs, willing to sell her child to feed her habit. And the cycle continues." He made a disgusted sound in his throat.

"What do you think would have become of you, Jak, if she had kept you? The same thing, that's what. You'd have eventually been placed into a group home, ended up either a menace or an inmate—either way, a complete drain on society, only to go on and create more just like you. You think it isn't true? Read the studies. Society has set up a system that incentivizes the *breeding* of degenerates, criminals, and predators."

424

Dr. Swift looked off into the distance for a moment before speaking again. "Isaac was right on another front. Jak was taken from his mother and raised by a singular caregiver in the vein of the Spartans. It seems to show the best success. But, of course, they knew their stuff, didn't they? You're understanding all this, aren't you, Jak?"

Yes, Jak understood. At least enough to feel sickness turning in his stomach.

"Just so you know, Jak, I tried to convince Isaac he should teach you how to make fire at the very least. But he said no. He liked discovering what you would come up with to trade for matches."

Make fire? The world spun. His heart dropped to his stomach. He looked at Harper and her expression…it looked like Dr. Swift's words made her want to cry.

"It's a sort of irony, isn't it, Harper, that you entered the foster care system, the one we deem a useless failure, because of us." He smiled, but his smile only made Jak feel sicker. "But because of it, you should understand better than anyone that the system doesn't work. Would it have been worse, Harper? To live out here? *Free?* Not listening for every bump in the night?" He looked at her, stared, like he knew what had happened to her as he swept his arm around. Harper looked down, her face almost as pale as the melting snow. Jak took a step closer, two.

Free? he thought. There was no *freedom* in being set up, watched, used, and lied to.

"So what are the applications for these programs we've set up, you might ask?" Dr. Swift went on as he paced one way then turned. Jak took the moment to meet Harper's eyes. *It'll be okay,* he wanted to say, if only to comfort her.

The river to the left, woods far off to the right. No way

to run to either before Dr. Swift's gunman shot them down, and then what? Buried their bodies out here somewhere they'd never be found?

"So many exciting applications," the doctor was saying. "These people, these *survivors*, later trained in weaponry of all kinds, will have proven their worth, their will to fight, again and again and again, under the most arduous of circumstances. Circumstances that would take down the strongest of men. And women. They're already being used by wealthy men and governments all over the *world*. Elite security. The guarding of assets. Even assassins when it's for the greater good." He smiled like a proud father. "They're soldiers—the best of the very best. Observed since birth. Revered. Their lives, their skill sets, their proven *grit* of great intrinsic value."

"And the ones who don't survive your...training?" Jak asked, his heart constricting as he remembered the faces of the other two boys as they'd looked on the cliff that night. The face of the boy he'd killed.

He shrugged. "Even if they die, they'll die heroes. A better fate than what would have been. We're trading one program for another, yes. But ours actually makes a *difference*." For the first time since Jak had arrived, he saw anger in Dr. Swift's face. He took a deep breath, seeming to get hold of himself. "If even a portion of these unwanted children enter our program, think of how the crime rates will lower. Think of the *benefits* to society. Just *think* of it."

"These are people," Harper said, her voice still shaking. "What makes you think they won't expose you?"

"Unfortunately, that's what all this is about." He waved his hand to the two of them, nodded to the gun Daire held. "As for the others, the ones who accept who they're meant to be, the ones who complete our camps and then the

426

debriefing, will go on to live exciting careers and be *heroes,* when otherwise they'd be losers and castoffs. The very dregs of humanity. We'll establish even *more* training camps, fill them to capacity. Instead of putting these children into social services, they'll enter *our* programs. They'll come in as victims and exit victors. The entire country will benefit, society will benefit, these *children* will benefit. *Eventually the world will benefit.*"

The people buying *the adult children will benefit,* Jak thought as the full understanding of what his life had been for swept over him in one sickening wave of red. All of it, every moment, had all been for *this.*

And if he didn't figure out a way to get Harper and him out of there, if he didn't figure out a way to *live,* then hundreds of other kids would go through the same suffering as he did, would be *watched* like he was, used, murdered, or left to die.

He listened to the thundering waterfalls behind him, fearing the only way out was down. Again.

427

CHAPTER FORTY-EIGHT

"Hello, Harper?" Laurie pushed the door open, the door that had already been slightly ajar when she'd arrived at Harper's apartment. She entered slowly, tentatively, worry skating down her spine. "Harper?" she called again. "It's Laurie Gallagher."

The little studio apartment was neat and tidy, the bed made, shoes lined up by the door. Despite the concern Laurie felt at finding the door open and no one home, she smiled at the obvious effort Harper had put into making her small apartment a home. It was sweet and lovely, understated, just like the girl Laurie had felt such an immediate connection to.

She entered the tiny kitchen, putting the bag of groceries on the counter along with the homemade banana bread. *Who has time to shop or to cook,* she'd thought, when they were dealing with something as life-altering as Jak was. And, as an extension, Harper too. She knew Harper loved him and that his struggles would be hers. Jak would be at the station for a couple of hours, so she'd picked up a few things at the grocery store for them and come over to drop them off. When she'd heard about the mine shaft, about the unthinkable things found there...she'd needed to *do* something. Mostly, she wanted them to know they weren't alone.

She unpacked the bag, her concern increasing when she didn't hear Harper coming in, having just popped over to a neighbor's maybe? Left somewhere close and hadn't bothered to make sure her door was properly locked? "You're being a busybody, Laurie," she admonished herself. Maybe it was just that motherly part of her who had loved and lost that would always jump to the worst conclusions when it came to people she cared about.

There was a pad of paper on the edge of the counter, and she stepped over to it, intending on leaving a note about the food. But there was already a typed note sitting on top. She read the first line, her concern growing as she picked it up, reading quickly.

She folded the note slowly, putting it in her pocket before rushing out of Harper's apartment.

Forty-five minutes later, she was pulling into her own driveway, and twenty seconds after that, she was rushing into the house. "Mark?" she called, tossing her purse and keys on the console table in the foyer.

"Mark?"

"Hey," he said, appearing from the kitchen. "What's wrong?"

"I've been calling you," she said, as he met her in the foyer.

"Sorry. I came from the hospital. Halston Fairbanks had a heart attack. Damn, I must not have turned my phone back on."

429

Laurie stopped, her eyes widening. "Halston Fairbanks had a heart attack? Oh my God." She shook her head in disbelief. That could wait for a minute. She brought the note from her pocket and thrust it out to Mark. "This was in Harper's apartment. She left it for Jak. It...doesn't make sense, does it?"

Mark read it quickly. "Killed Driscoll? Amity Falls? They're...running away together?"

"You talked to Jak earlier at length. Does it make any sense?" Her heart beat quickly. Was it only that she didn't *want* it to make sense? Was it only her own delicate emotions that were trying to insist two people who had suddenly attached themselves to her heart wouldn't possibly just pick up and leave?

Mark shook his head. "No. I took his full statement about Driscoll's death earlier." His brow wrinkled as though he was considering whether Jak had lied in some way. It smoothed out. "No. But Harper's not answering her phone, so I haven't been able to get hold of him. He could feel...I don't know, responsible somehow for his grandfather's heart attack? Apparently he found him and alerted the family. But this?" He held up the note. "No. And, what? Did he flag down a ride to the falls?" He looked to the side, pressing his lips together. "Hell, that man could have run there if he was inclined to do it."

Laurie stared at him for a moment. "I have a bad feeling, Mark."

They both stood there for a moment, so many things flowing between them. The memory of the moment Laurie had mentioned her concern over the bruises Abbi kept getting—bruises that were explainable by the sports she was involved in but that her motherly instincts told her were

430

worth a doctor's appointment. The diagnosis. The fight. The ultimate loss. The unthinkable grief. Their drifting apart...

He'd always listened to her intuition though. He'd never made her feel silly or irrational. "You need to go there. To the falls. They need you," she said.

He looked at her closely for another moment, nodding. "I'll get my coat."

She grabbed his keys for him as he put on his coat and boots. "They're fighters," she said, more to soothe herself, to *convince* herself they were okay.

Mark opened the door, pausing. He turned back, taking the few steps to her, his hands wrapping around her upper arms, holding on. "Our girl was a fighter, just like you, Laurie. She fought until the very end. She'd want us to fight too. We've stopped *fighting*. For *us*. We need to start again. I will not lose you." His voice was full of so much emotion, a lump filled Laurie's chest, so full she couldn't breathe. Joy sparked within her. A rekindling of their *life*.

Laurie nodded her head, tears slipping down her cheeks. "Come back to me," she choked. "And bring those kids with you."

CHAPTER FORTY-NINE

Society will benefit. The children will benefit. Eventually the world *will benefit.*

My God. He's a psychopath. Did he really think anyone in their right mind would accept this? And yet a cold spear of dread moved through Harper, the knowledge that already, others had subscribed to this madness. Not only subscribed to but put into practice. Who else out there was suffering? Trying to survive any number of unknown terrors and hardships right that very moment? She shuddered.

"You really think people are going to accept this?" she asked, not so much for the answer but to keep him talking, to come up with a plan. Something. No matter how small.

"You're right. I see the way you two are looking at me," Dr. Swift said, barely penetrating the careening thoughts in her mind. "It may be...unpalatable to some. They won't understand the scope, the benefits." He rocked on his heels. "But there are plenty who do, and they're the ones who matter. They know big change requires bold action. They understand it's the *results* that matter. And the results speak for themselves. Isn't that right, Daire?"

For the first time, the man named Daire spoke. "Yes, sir," he said, giving Dr. Swift a small bow of his head. *Oh God.* They *had* convinced at least some of the survivors that this was okay. The sickness was unthinkable.

The man had convinced himself he was improving society, and yet he was *profiting* off people's misery.

Next to her, Jak's mind was definitely whirling. She glanced at him and saw it, and even through her fear, her heart calmed. She'd trusted him fifteen years ago, and she trusted him now. Not to survive this, she realized. But to fight, to *try*. To go down swinging. She'd seen it in his nature, even then, she realized suddenly. *He'd curled his fists.* It came to her in a flash, the rush of the water filling her head, her mind's eye conjuring that dreamlike moment. He'd curled his fists. He'd trembled like the rest of them, but he'd curled his fists…and she had *known*.

She met his gaze, and time stilled. Deep intensity filled his expression before he glanced backward quickly and then away.

Backward. The falls.

It's our only way out.

Her stomach dropped. Fear spiked. The water roared, the man in front of them still talking, pacing, evil spilling from his lips. She couldn't hear him anymore, not over the rush of the falls, the buzzing in her head. Jak took a step closer, two. Harper met his eyes, and a strange calm descended.

The man in front of them was not going to let them walk away from this. Not before, and especially not now that he'd shared everything with them. They'd been a loose end before; now they were an extreme liability. He was going to shoot them, and whoever else might be working with him—some vast network or so it seemed—would help him dispose of their bodies somewhere in this immense wilderness. They'd never be found, or even if they were, there'd be no evidence about who killed them or why. And if they were never found? Would others believe they'd run away together? Even if they didn't, how could it be proven? They'd say Jak was a wild card, unpredictable, uncivilized, and that Harper was unfocused and emotionally unstable—scarred from the trauma of losing her parents and then growing up without a true home. Who could truly say *what* they'd done or why? They'd look for a while, and then…that would be that.

The man in front of them knew it too.

But he'd never expect them to jump.

Yes, their only way out was down. Just like the first time. They'd survived once, against all odds, but how likely was it that they could survive something with such meager odds again? Unlikely. Hopeless perhaps. The fall was one thing, the rapids just beyond were another. Treacherous. Deadly. Full of boulders and undercurrents that had taken several lives that she knew of. So why did she feel so *hopeful*?

Because they'd survive or they wouldn't—*together*.

Harper curled her fists. Jak's eyes moved downward. He'd seen. He knew.

Let's do this. Together. Again.

She was ready, she realized, incredulous at the calm, the *peace*, she felt. There, standing at the top of a precipice with Jak, about to risk it all, she saw so *clearly* how incredibly lucky she'd been, when she'd never deemed herself lucky before. So many things had aligned perfectly so she made it out of the wilderness that night. *Was* it luck, though, or more? Fate? A divine hand? Her parents' loving guidance?

She didn't know. She did know she was intensely *thankful* because, like Jak, she had survived, so she would be there when he arrived in her life for the second time.

Jak. Her Jak. He'd sacrificed his own life to give her hers, and she would not dishonor that by regretting a single moment of it. He had *saved* her, and she was grateful for every second she'd had because of it. Even the moments when she'd struggled and hurt and felt like a victim. She hadn't been a victim. *She* was the victor Dr. Swift had mentioned. Not because she'd been put through a program. *She'd* picked herself up, over and over, again and again. It had made her stronger, better, made her appreciate the good moments and respect her own ability to survive.

It was as if, for a fleeting moment, a cloud had moved away from the sun. And in that brief speck of time, she saw the bright, miraculous, sometimes searing, often blinding light of what her life had been. And she was grateful for it all. *All* of it. Every moment. Because it was *hers.* And she saw that she could not claim the joy without also claiming the pain. So she did. She took it inside and loved it all equally. That moment. Right there. She *loved* her life. And because of such great, unequaled love—the sudden and deep understanding of the many gifts she'd received—she was willing to take any risk to keep it. For herself. For him. *With* him.

Dr. Swift paced one more time. His words, she couldn't put them together. He was preparing himself though, ready to have them shot where they stood. Harper took a step back, and so did Jak. Daire saw what they were doing and raised the gun, and in that instant, they both turned, Jak's hand grabbing hers, gripping. She heard a blast, and something flew by her cheek. Jak pulled her so they wove, crouching as they moved. She heard Dr. Swift's yell coming closer, the same as that night, only this time it was accompanied by the whizz of bullets as they flew by her head.

The earth fell out from under them, and then there was only falling, only the thunder of the falls all around. The needle-sharp pain of the icy water as it hit her skin. Harper's scream was snatched up in the wild roar. Jak's hand gripped tighter. He wouldn't let her go. She knew he wouldn't. He'd already proven it once before.

Hold on, she heard through the rush of water.

Hold on.

That whisper inside, deep down, and yet filling her head, her heart, her soul. She was only sensation now, only instinct and the will to live, and she *heard* it so *clearly.* She knew the voice. That whisper. It had belonged to her mother.

She couldn't hold her breath any longer. Her lungs were burning, her body being battered, flailing as the thunderous fall went on and on and on.

Then the jarring impact of hitting the surface, her lungs screaming, hand gripping, gripping. He was gripping back. They were together, plunging down, down, and then back up, up, his powerful legs kicking mightily, pulling them both toward the light above, as her lungs caught fire and she tried to *hold on, hold on,* head bursting, lights blinking until—

She opened her mouth and took a gasping breath just as they broke the surface, air rushing in and filling her screaming lungs.

Then back under, the current pulling them as they tumbled, their arms stretching.

Hold on. Hold on.

The deadly rapids were ahead. Harper tried desperately to grab at something. Anything that would hold them steady, keep them from entering that rocky portion of water that would drag them under, keep them there.

"Grab this," a deep voice yelled. Harper gasped, not able to see who had said it with the spray of water, but spotting the large, heavy branch just in front of them.

She tried to swim toward it, but the current pulled her away. Jak's grip increased, and with a yell, he pulled them both closer, swimming against the current, both of them working together to make it close enough to the branch to grab hold.

Jak let out a mighty yell, moving them closer, and Harper reached out and grabbed the end of it, barely. She slipped, grabbed again, held on until Jak could come from behind her and grab hold of it too, both of them gasping for breath, anchored to that small piece of wood in a roaring cauldron of bubbling, circling water.

"Keep holding on. Don't let go." *Agent Gallagher?* It was Agent Gallagher, somehow, impossibly, *there.* He pulled the branch, towing them in against the tide, grunting with the effort, slipping—*oh, God*—but regaining balance, pulling, pulling. They met the shore, and he reached out his hand pulling her up the bank, Jak behind her. They both collapsed on the muddy riverbank, gasping for air, soaking wet, shaking.

Their hands still clasped.

Together.

CHAPTER FIFTY

Jak pulled Harper closer, though there really wasn't any way to get much closer than they currently were. Unless he took her to bed, which he wanted to—desperately. He wanted to roll around with her, sniffing her everywhere, taking, grunting, and howling with the thankfulness of life—

No. Those are wolf thoughts, he reminded himself. But she liked the wolf in him, he knew that too. He nuzzled her neck, pulling the hospital blanket more tightly around her to make sure she was warm. Now, if only they would let them out of this hospital with all the intense, unknown smells that were tickling his nose and fogging his brain.

Although he knew he'd come back the next day. His grandfather was on another floor, in what they called a coma. Jak's heart tightened. He was surprised at the sadness that filled him when he thought about his grandfather not getting better.

But he had Harper, and he had his own life, and that's what he focused on.

Agent Gallagher—*Mark,* though he still had a hard time thinking of him that way—had pulled Jak and Harper, soaking wet, freezing cold, and half-drowned, out of the water just a few...feet, yes, he knew that measurement now...just a few feet from the start of the swirling, rocky rapids.

Mrs. Gallagher—*Laurie*—had found the note in Harper's apartment and sent Mark to find them, but there had been a downed tree across the road that led to the top of the falls, so he'd ended up at the bottom instead. *Thank God.* If Dr. Swift had arranged the road being blocked, it had worked out perfectly for Jak and Harper. Turned out, Mark was right where they'd needed him to be.

Dr. Swift had disappeared. There was a hunt to capture him.

Harper turned her head, kissing his fingers where they lay at her shoulder and then lacing her hand with his. She looked back at him. "During the fall...I heard my mother." She looked down, her lashes making shadows on her cheeks. "She was with us both, Jak. I think...all this time." She looked up at him again, those big brown eyes that had stared at him at the edge of a snowy cliff in the long ago—no, fifteen *years* ago—and then today at the top of a waterfall and *trusted* him with her life. His chest expanded. He thought it might burst.

He let out a breath, thinking about the way her mother's notes had given him the will to live, to go on, when he'd given up on life, when the loneliness had taken and taken and taken until he had nothing left to give. She'd filled him again, with her voice, with the hopefulness of her thoughts, with questions to fill his head and his heart, and with words to remind him he was human. "Yes," he said. "She was."

"My father too," Harper said. "I believe it. I cherish all of it. It was for *something,* and it led us here. Jak, do you think you can find a way to believe that too?"

He looked away for a second. He knew what she was asking. She was asking if he could let go of the hurt and the anger and the…bitterness over what had been done to him. If he could believe that greater forces…operated and that those forces had guided him and loved him. He remembered how he'd felt her mother there with him—heard her whispers—when he'd found Driscoll dying in his cabin. *Let it go,* he'd heard deep inside, and he had, for that moment anyway, handing the man his phone when he'd asked for it. He knew now that Driscoll had called for help…bringing the deputy…who then brought Jak to the sheriff's office… to…Harper. If he had followed his need for vengeance instead, ignored those whispers, leaving Driscoll to rot as he walked away, returned to his lonely life…but he didn't want to think about that. He exhaled a slow breath. "I think so," he said. And he meant it.

He had seen what bitterness did to his grandfather. *Vengeance.* He would not become him.

Let it go.

Although now was the time for anger too. Not for himself, maybe, but for the other survivors out there who were living the same way he had, maybe worse. Killing, freezing, starving, loneliness shriveling their souls.

What would happen to those people when they were found? Nobodies with nothing. Throwaways like he had been.

The door opened, and Laurie Gallagher rushed in, looking…hmm, he didn't yet know the word for how Laurie looked in that moment. Worried, but beyond that. Harper stood, and so did he. Laurie made a crying sound in the back of her throat and rushed to Harper first, hugging her and then letting go, running her hands down her hair, touching her bandages and making clucking sounds, and looking at her face like she was trying to make sure she was really alive. Then she moved to Jak, making the same clucking sounds as she hugged him tightly and then stepped back, looking at them both.

"I was so distraught when I heard. Oh my goodness, well, sit down. You must be traumatized."

Distraught. That was the word. *Worried* only in a way that made your hair fly around your head, your eyes get big and round, and your hands flap everywhere.

Harper sat and so did Jak as Laurie pulled up a chair and they told her what had happened on the edge of the waterfall. Tears slipped down her cheeks as she listened, blotting at them with a tissue and shaking her head. "Thank God he was there. I knew, I just knew something was wrong." She grabbed Jak's hand, squeezing. "I'm just so thankful you're okay. Oh dear, and your grandfather. How is he, Jak?"

"He's in a coma," Jak said. He didn't remember the rest of the words the doctor had said because his step-grandmother had come in the room and Jak had left as quickly as possible after that.

Laurie's eyes were soft. "Whatever you need, Mark and I are here." She looked up suddenly, letting go of his hand. "Oh, the press conference," she said pointing at the TV, the show they'd been waiting to come on. Harper pressed the thing with buttons that made the sound on the television go up. He kept forgetting words because there were so many new ones running through his mind, and some were more important to him than others.

Mark stepped in front of a microphone, looking very serious. "Today the Montana Department of Justice has been made aware of an unknown number of illegal and highly

441

disturbing programs. These programs are being operated around the country using children who have been removed from the foster care system under false pretenses and/or babies who are bought from mothers who are members of social programs, most especially drug or alcohol. We're in the midst of specifically identifying who these children might be. These programs have been operating for many years. Some of the victims may currently be adults who have grown up in these programs." He looked straight into the camera. "If you have any information regarding this crime or if you are a person who was in a state-run program and asked to give up your child in exchange for money or play a *role* for money, please contact us." He paused, and the crowd grew quiet. "If you are one of these children, please contact authorities immediately. You have been wronged, and we want you to help us put those who abused you behind bars." He held up a photograph of Dr. Swift. "This man is a prime suspect and wanted for murder among a vast list of other crimes. If you see him or know of his whereabouts, please call the number on the screen. Do not approach him. He is armed and dangerous."

And angry, Jak thought. But…more angry. *Enraged.* Yes. He'd bet Dr. Swift was enraged. Just like Driscoll had been when he'd found out his mother had interfered with his study. Just like his grandfather had been…*enraged* enough to kill. But he hadn't said a word about that.

The crowd started yelling, and Mark pointed to a woman in front. "Agent Gallagher, for what purpose are these children being taken? What is this program exactly?"

"They're being placed and studied in harsh environments to determine survival skills. Perhaps trained. Each camp, for lack of a better word, may be different. But they're most likely being set up in remote areas miles from civilization. Then they're being sold to those who wish to use their talents."

"Agent Gallagher," a man near the back yelled. "How did you find out about this? What tipped you off?"

"I'm not able to discuss that at this time." He looked to the right and nodded at someone in a uniform, turning back to the still-yelling crowd. "Those are all the questions I can take right now. We'll update as we get more information."

Mark stepped off the small stage, and then the picture switched to two people sitting at a desk.

"Wow, Marcia, this is quite a story. Unwanted kids being trained in underground camps to be…what? Elite soldiers?"

The woman named Marcia shook her head. "I don't know, Gary. It all just turns my stomach."

Gary nodded. "Although you have to admit, the idea, if executed properly, would have huge societal benefits."

Marcia's mouth fell open. "You must be kidding. To achieve improvements in society, we turn to *The Hunger Games*? Is that it? Maybe eventually we could all get the abuse of these children in a feed straight to our mobile devices. Sounds *riveting*. A modern-day Roman coliseum."

Gary looked momentarily interested in the idea but then laughed, holding his hands up. "Whoa, whoa. I'm just voicing what others are thinking too. Now, I'm not saying the moral ramifications of the idea aren't too extreme to actually put into practice, I'm just saying, you have to understand your enemy to *fight* them. Or, in this case, even find them."

"Going by *your* comments, I'm worried more people will want to *become* them rather than fight them."

Then the two people named Marcia and Gary, who

443

must be very important for people to want to hear all their opinions, started talking about societies who fell to ruin and other things Jak tuned out because he was too busy sniffing Harper's hair. She still smelled like his Harper but also like the river. He attempted to pull her closer again, and she came halfway up his lap. She looked back at him, and he gave her a bashful smile. She laughed softly, running her hand over his jaw.

Laurie switched off the TV. "Well, that's probably enough of that. When do you two get out of here?"

"Hopefully any minute," Harper said.

"I'm sure you're tired and want to sleep. But if you're hungry, I could make dinner... Oh, I'm sure you want to be alone."

Between them, Harper squeezed his hand.

"Dinner with you and Mark would be good," Jak said, meaning it.

Laurie smiled like she'd just caught the biggest fish in the river. *No, no, like...like she was happy they wanted to be with her.* "Wonderful."

The door flung open, and someone else rushed inside their room. "Rylee," Harper said, standing up and hugging her friend.

"Oh my God, I couldn't believe it when I heard. Are you okay?" She stood back, looking at her the same way Laurie had.

Two men came in the room. "Hi, Jeff. Mr. Adams," Harper said.

"Harper." They both hugged her too and then turned to Jak and Laurie. Harper told them they were her friend Rylee and Rylee's husband Jeff and her father, Mr. Adams. Then she pointed at Jak and said his name, and Laurie as

444

well and everyone's head moved back and forth, and they smiled. *Introductions,* he remembered the word for that from his grandfather. *Good manners.* Now they were *acquainted.*

Jak saw Rylee look at Harper and mouth *oh my God* before she glanced at Jak and away. He wasn't sure what that meant, but he didn't think it was *good manners.*

"I'd love to have you all for dinner too if you're available," Laurie said, and Rylee took Harper's hand in hers.

"We'd love that."

Then everyone started talking at once, the way the birds did in the morning, happy to be alive for another sunrise and chitter-chattering to tell the whole forest about it. Or like… well, that was good enough for now. He couldn't second-guess every thought in his head. Civilized thoughts would come naturally to him someday…probably.

Harper met Jak's eyes, and they gentled. She smiled, and his brain went empty the way it did each time she looked at him that way. *I love you,* she mouthed. He mouthed it back. He loved her. He worshipped her. He cherished her. He would forever. And that was all.

That was all.

EPILOGUE

The fire crackled, shadows dancing on the library walls. Jak smiled, brought from his daze, as the scent of the woman he loved met his nose. "Hello, wife."

Harper laughed softly, coming around the chair and taking a seat on his lap. "Will I ever be able to sneak up on you?" she asked, wrapping her arms around his neck and rubbing her cheek against his stubbly jaw.

He smiled on an exhaled breath, nuzzling into her touch. "Maybe." He expected that his sense of smell would become…less once he'd been living in civilization for long enough and now that he didn't depend on his senses for his survival.

"Hmm," she hummed, kissing him softly. He ran his hand over the small swell of her stomach, their child cradled within the safety of her body. For the next five months anyway. Then it would be his job to protect them both. To make sure they were fed and warm and that their hearts were full. He never took that third part for granted after a lifetime of only being able to address physical needs. And often not even those. A shiver of gratitude moved through him. *My family.* The two words still made his breath catch with happiness.

Awe.

He and Harper married six months after they'd survived their jump from Amity Falls. No one had been able to convince him there was any reason to wait, though Agent—*Mark*—Gallagher had sat him down and given him a "man-to-man" talk about the "prudence of patience" and the "wisdom of waiting." He respected Mark, but he wanted a ring on Harper's finger. *His* ring, and that was all. He wanted everyone to know that she was his and he was hers. As soon as he'd learned that's what people did when they were in love and wanted the world to know, he'd asked Harper immediately. And she'd said yes. He was overjoyed that *she* didn't agree that it was prudent or wise to wait. They were married in the Gallaghers' backyard under a summer sunset, surrounded by their new and old friends. Jak thought of them as their pack, and he didn't deny himself the thought. The feeling. The way it made him feel connected. Maybe his senses would grow less, maybe not, but a part of him would always be wild—the boy who'd grown up alongside a wolf who he'd loved like a brother—and to deny that would be to deny Pup. To deny all that had brought him to the life he now lived. The life he loved with all his heart.

The baby had been unexpected, but since they'd both become used to the idea, they couldn't stop smiling about it. They'd lie in bed at night just talking for hours about what he or she was going to be like, the things they wanted to teach their son or their daughter, the miracle of the life they'd created after they'd both cheated death more than once. And that tiny miracle made Jak want to learn everything he could about how to be a good father. *A good pack leader.* Mark and Laurie would help them. Jak and Harper had already asked if they would act as grandparents to their baby, and Laurie had cried, and Mark had pretended that he had something in his eye.

Jak had reached out to Almina Kavazović—whom he couldn't help still thinking of as Baka—just a few months earlier, and though Jak wasn't sure what the future held as far as their relationship, he had needed to tell her he forgave her and that she had been with him during so many times of struggle and loneliness. She had been his strength and the reminder of his own. He had felt Harper's mother—his priest, his Abbé Busoni—smiling down on him as he told her so.

Jak stared into the fire as Harper snuggled. The fireplace where he'd burned the bow-and-arrow set that he'd found in a corner of the attic after his grandfather had passed away, never recovering from his heart attack. The bow-and-arrow set that had been missing one arrow—the one used to kill Isaac Driscoll. But only he and Harper knew that.

His grandfather had given Jak a name. In return, he'd made sure his grandfather would keep his good one. If he hadn't killed Driscoll, the program would have. With that assumption, the police had closed the case.

His grandfather had left almost everything to Jak in his will, providing a small settlement to his step-grandmother, who had flown into a rage in the lawyer's office, screeching like one of her caged birds.

Jak had had those cages taken apart and moved out of Thornland the same day he'd had all the cameras removed. He'd kept Nigel on. He was still oily, but Jak had come to appreciate him much more since he could sneak up on him and make him jump and squeak. Since Jak had inherited Thornland and Loni, Gabi, and Brett had moved out, he'd even caught Nigel *almost* smiling a time or two. Even oily creatures had their good points.

Mark had helped Jak hire an acting CEO for Fairbanks Lumber. Jak trusted the older man's instincts about people, and the company was doing great under the new management. Jak was taking his time learning the business and found it surprisingly interesting. Maybe someday he'd participate more actively in running it. Someday when there weren't so many other things to learn as well.

He and Harper had remained at the family estate that was close to Harper's school, though they'd also bought a few acres of wilderness of their own and built a small cabin. They planned to spend summers there when Harper wasn't taking classes and as many weekends as possible. Summers… when the rivers were bursting with fish, the berries were ripe and sweet, and the sun opened the flowers and warmed the earth. But…Jak had a feeling they'd also need the massive estate to offer sanctuary, if necessary, to those lost children, many who were now adults, whom the police were still searching for.

That dark feeling rose up inside when he thought of Dr. Swift and what might be happening in some godforsaken wilderness somewhere. He moved his hand slowly over the swell of his wife's stomach, his breath evening, calm descending. *Life. Miracles. Hope.*

Harper stretched her arm, picking up the book on the table next to them. "Again?" she asked, her voice filled with gentle amusement.

Jak smiled as she placed his beloved copy of *The Count*

of Monte Cristo back down. He'd just finished it for the sixth time. It was dog-eared and wrinkled. Cherished. Well loved. "Each time I read it, I find something new inside. Some different lesson." And a new favorite word or three.

She smiled, resting her head on his shoulder, stifling a yawn. "What lesson did you learn this time?"

He thought of one of the quotes in the book that had spoken to him the loudest during this reading. *All human wisdom is contained in these two words—wait and hope.*

"That if we can hang on—survive—through the hard times in life, there is something better waiting for us. There's a purpose we can't always see. There's an...order." He'd felt it—that whisper, that unseen something that flowed through him, into and around all living things and back again. There were no words he'd found that fully captured it. God, maybe. Fate? Miracles? The souls who had passed before them? All he knew was that it was loving and good and it sought to make things *right. Just.*

Those were new thoughts. Things he'd realized, taken in, *applied.* He felt proud. Changed. *Better.* "Yes," she murmured, kissing his jaw, lacing her fingers with his own. *"Yes."* She yawned again.

He brought her hand to his lips and kissed her knuckle. "Go up to bed. I'll be there in a minute."

She nodded, standing and giving him a small, sleepy smile before turning and heading upstairs. After a minute Jak stood too, leaving the library and making his way to the massive stone patio that ran the length of the house and overlooked the woods beyond.

The trees swayed, dancing to the sound of the wind, speaking an ancient language beneath the earth. He looked into the darkness, his mind picturing places far beyond what his eyes could see. Somewhere out there, the rest of his pack—his family connected by shared experiences few others would ever understand—lived and breathed, fought and struggled. He felt the whispers pick up inside. A song of unity and brotherhood. "Wait and hope," he whispered to those unknown souls. "Wait and hope."

Acknowledgments

Like Jak, my heart is full of gratitude—*awe*—for my pack. Thank you for guiding me, encouraging me, and helping me tell this story to the best of my ability.

To my editing team, Angela Smith, Marion Archer, and Karen Lawson—this story had an abundance of moving parts...the mystery, the romance, Jak's language, an unusual setting where every item the characters used had to be considered, and you three worked each and every angle, along with checking my grammar and keeping my characters' sighs to a minimum. My appreciation knows no bounds.

So much thankfulness for my amazing team of beta readers, Stephanie Hockersmith, Cat Bracht, and Elena Eckmeyer, who read this story first and told me where I needed to apply the sandpaper. Thank you for your honesty, your sensitivity, and your deep love of reading.

To my book club members and beta readers, JoAnna Koller, Ashley Brinkman, Denise Coy, Rachel Morgenthal, and Shauna Waldleitner Rogers. Thank you for making time to read this book and offer comments and suggestions that were insightful, smart, and funny and made me realize why I love talking *all* things books with you all so much.

Thank you to Sharon Broom for giving this book a final read-through. Your time and generosity mean so much to me.

Thank you to Kimberly Brower for doing all the things for all your people, at all times of the day and night. I'm so lucky to be one of them!

To you, the reader, thank you for coming along on this journey. It is my true belief that stories can save us in a myriad of ways, big and small. I am so honored that you chose one of mine, and I hope you close this book with a full heart and perhaps a new perspective or two.

Thank you to Mia's Mafia for your constant love and enthusiasm for my books.

To all the book bloggers and Instagrammers who make it their job to spread book love, your work brings beauty and happiness to the world, and I am so very appreciative to each and every one of you.

An updated thank you to Bloom Books for introducing this story to the wider world.

And to my husband: This sweet life I am so grateful for is because you whispered to me and I whispered back.

About the Author

Mia Sheridan is a *New York Times*, *USA Today*, and *Wall Street Journal* bestselling author. Her passion is weaving true love stories about people destined to be together. Mia lives in Cincinnati, Ohio, with her husband. They have four children here on earth and one in heaven.

Mia can be found online at:

MiaSheridan.com

Instagram: @MiaSheridanAuthor

Facebook: MiaSheridanAuthor